Tributes to James Cloud's
Brandenburg II: The Ninth Circle of Hell

"A Vital History Lesson. For those of you who, like me, are too lazy to read The Rise and Fall of the Third Reich, this is an attractive, readable alternative—and a damn good story to boot. An outstanding epic novel loaded with historical inserts that should serve as important teaching points for those of us who are concerned with the increasing polarization of our politics and the threats to our fragile democracy. Read and learn."
—**Ronald J. Adams**

"Brandenburg II: The Ninth Circle of Hell by James Cloud is a penetrating and well-researched story about Nazi Germany as told from the German perspective. While Hitler is the focal point, the struggles of those under the Third Reich keep the wheels of the storyline turning. As chaos reigns and the worldwide Depression has greatly impacted Germany, Adolf Hitler rises to power. With his impassioned speeches that draw many to support his cause, Germans are optimistic that this new Chancellor will get the country back on its feet. Hitler is more than willing to use misinformation to achieve his goals, a propagandistic reason for starting a war, regardless of whether it is believable or not. Over the course of Hitler's reign, the German people will undergo the difficulties and travails that go with the Nazi propaganda.

Brandenburg II is an interesting piece of historical fiction, an epic story that stays true to its historical material. Most of us are already familiar with Hitler's rise to power, but James Cloud gives this story a strong element of humanity by depicting the political, economic, and social conditions of those living under the Nazi ideology, and illustrates that not all Germans were sympathetic to Hitler. It is an exhaustively well-researched story that promotes a timely awareness, considering that we are continuously witnessing international tensions and crises. There is probably plenty of historical fiction that you would like to read, but James Cloud's Brandenburg II is one that you must read, as it ticks all the boxes when it comes to what history-based fiction should be."
—**Vincent Dublado for Readers' Favorite**

"Excellent! This gives us a different viewpoint of WW II. Excellent description of significant events within Germany. Look forward to future books."
—**Dennis W. Yarman**

"I have read a lot about WWII but I have not read any books that were written from the German perspective. I learned so much!"
—**Sharon Richardson**

"I really had to read the second historical novel to see what happened to the characters. I was not disappointed. You know you're reading something special when you care about fictional characters. And to see a different viewpoint of WWII really interested me. Fictional or not, it brought that period to life better than just something historical. Great job!"
—**Amazon Customer**

"Insightful and enjoyable. Brandenburg II is an insightful book dealing with the personal problems of the people living in Berlin during the rise of Hitler. It shows the economic and political situations of the time in a narrative form making it not just a history book, but an enjoyable read."
—**Amazon Customer**

Brandenburg II

THE NINTH CIRCLE OF HELL

Copyright ©2021 by James Zeno Cloud, jr
All Rights Reserved. No part of this novel can be reproduced in any format without the express written permission of the author.

www.JamesCloudBooks.com
The Ninth Circle of Hell: From Dante Alighieri – The Divine Comedy c. 1320

Map © "Berlin administrative divisions districts and boroughs" Licensed under Creative Commons Attribution-Share-A-like-3.0. https://creativecommons.org/licenses/by-sa/3.0/deed.en

Map ©2011-2014 "Berlin Germany - Baedeker 1914"
x-digital Old International Maps
www.mapsofthepast.com

Map ©1923 "Germany after the Peace Treaty of 1919"
Illustration from page 572 of The outline of history; being a plain history of life and mankind, the definitive edition revised and rearranged by the author, by H.G. Wells, illustrated by J. F. Horrabin. This work is in the public domain in the United States because it was published (or registered with the U.S. Copyright Office) before January 1, 1925

Map © "The Growth of Nazi Germany" Facing History and Ourselves
https://www.facinghistory.org

Maps © "GERMAN INVASION OF WESTERN EUROPE, 1940"
"INVASION OF THE SOVIET UNION, 1941-1942"
United States Holocaust Memorial Museum
https://www.ushmm.org
(The United States Holocaust Memorial Museum does not endorse James Cloud, Brandenburg II: The Ninth Circle of Hell, any third party or product, services, or opinions related to the author or this book.)

Map © "WORLD WAR II: GERMAN ADVANCES, 1939-1941"
https://asecondworldwar.weebly.com/hitlers-lightning-war.html

ISBN: 9798514181452

Cover design by Mary Ann Cherry
www.maryanncherry.com
www.maryanncherry.net
First Paperback Edition

DISCLAIMER
This novel is a work of fiction. Names, characters, businesses, places, events, locales, and incidents are either the products of the author's imagination or are actual locations and historical happenings used in a fictitious manner. Certain long-standing institutions, agencies, public figures, and historical events are mentioned, but the characters involved with them are wholly imaginary. Any resemblance to actual persons, living or dead is purely coincidental.

Man's inhumanity to man
belongs to no race
and
carries no passport.

James Cloud

DEDICATION

Dedicated to the citizens of Berlin.

IN APPRECIATION

My thanks to Mary Ann Cherry, Steven Huffaker, Tom Briggs, and Sabina Briggs, without whose support and encouragement this book would never have been completed.

Contents

Prologue   i - ix

Part I   **The Pied Piper**

                Chapters 1 – 21

Part II   **The Virus Spreads**

                Chapters 22 – 41

Part III   **Eruption**

                Chapters 42 – 54

Part IV   **Boomerang**

                Chapters 55 – 67

Part V   **Arrogance Will be Punished**

                Chapters 68 – 88

Part VI   **The River of Fire**

                Chapters 89 – 103

Epilogue

The First Round of the Ninth Circle is called Caina, named after Cain, who murdered his own brother, Abel.

The Second Round of the Ninth Circle is called Antenora, named after Antenor. He was the soldier from Troy who cheated on his own city to the Greeks. Here, the souls of people who betrayed their country are punished.

The Third Round of the Ninth Circle is called Ptolomaea, named after Ptolemy. He called his father-in-law, along with his sons, for a treat and killed them. Here, traitors who betrayed their guests are punished.

The Fourth Round of the Ninth Circle is called Judecca, named after Judas Iscariot, who betrayed Christ.

After crossing Judecca comes the Center of Hell. People who committed the absolute sin of treachery against God are punished here.

The Ninth Circle of Hell is where Satan resides.

Dante Alighieri
– The Divine Comedy

Berlin Administrative Districts

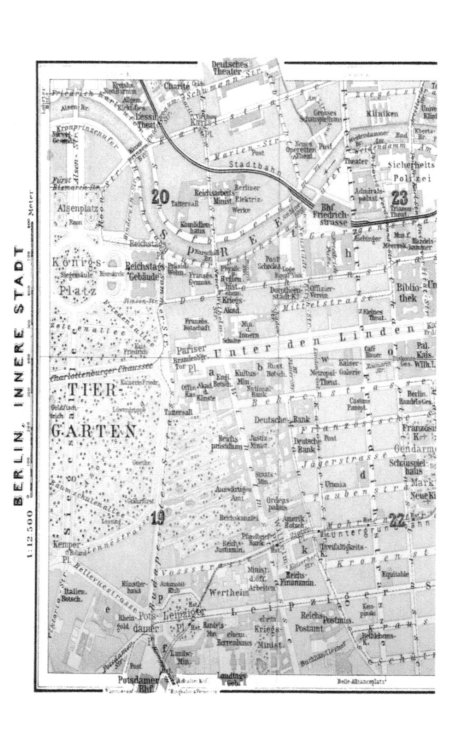

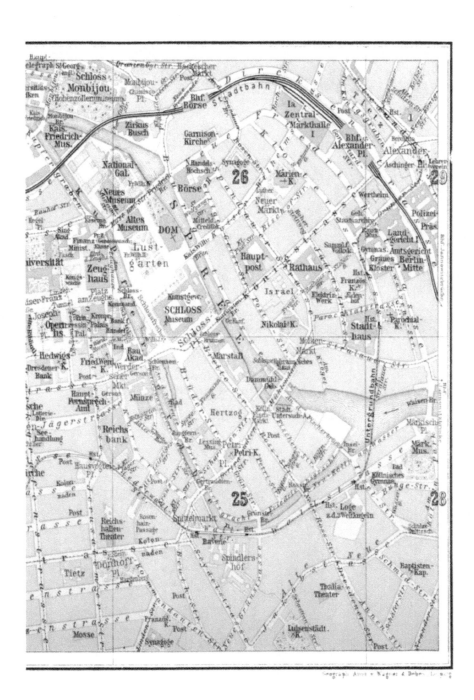

Prologue

Mein Kampf

An 18-year old young man born April 20, 1889, in Braunau am Inn, a small town near the German border in Austria, then part of the Austro-Hungarian Empire, was alone and dejected in Vienna on a day in 1903. He had seen himself as an artist and had even managed to sell sketches and postcards on the streets of the city, but his application for admission to the Vienna Academy of Arts and the School of Architecture was rejected. He had failed his school exams at age 15 and had not completed a formal education. So, he only managed to eke out a hand-to-mouth existence in the Austrian capital for the next several years. His name was Adolf Hitler.

It is believed that at this time he first became interested in politics and observed how the masses could be made to respond to certain themes. He was especially impressed by the anti-Semitic nationalist Christian-Socialist Party. He was Austrian, but had long been fascinated with Austria's vigorous, dynamic neighbor, Germany. In 1914, when World War I broke out, he volunteered to fight for the German Army, and gained respect as a corporal and a dispatch-runner. His several awards for bravery included the Iron Cross First Class. He was blinded by mustard gas in October of 1918 and was in the hospital when Germany surrendered. He was devastated by Germany's defeat, and fell into a state of deep depression, facing an uncertain future.

Small political groups had begun to form in the last years of the war. In March 1918, Anton Drexler formed one of these small groups. Drexler was a local locksmith and was bitterly opposed to the armistice of November 1918 and the revolutionary upheavals that followed. Drexler followed the views of militant nationalists, such as opposing the Treaty of Versailles. He held anti-Semitic, anti-monarchist and anti-Marxist views and also believed in the superiority of Germans, claiming to be part of an Aryan "master race". He accused international capitalism of being a Jewish-dominated movement and denounced capitalists for war profiteering. Drexler blamed the political violence and instability in Germany on the Weimar Republic for being out-of-touch with the masses, especially the lower classes. His small political party was called the *Deutsche Arbeiterpartei* (German Workers' Party), or DAP.

Following recovery from his war wounds, Hitler gained employment as a spy for the German Army and was ordered to attend a meeting of the DAP in September, 1919. Upon attending, he found he agreed with Drexler on his nationalistic, anti-Semitic views, but disagreed with how the party was organized. When the lectures concluded, Hitler got involved in a heated political argument with another visitor. In vehemently attacking the man's opinions, Hitler caught the attention of other party members in attendance. Impressed with his oratory skills, Drexler approached Hitler and encouraged him to join the DAP. On the orders of his army superiors, Hitler applied to join the party.

Once accepted, he quickly gained a reputation as a powerful orator, with his passion about the injustices forced on Germany by the Treaty of Versailles. Soon people were joining the party to see Hitler, and hear his rousing speeches, which seemed to stir audiences to near hysteria and be willing to do whatever he suggested.

Ernst Röhm was a former military officer who had distinguished himself during the war. Seriously wounded in the Battle of Verdun in 1916, he had spent the remainder of the war as a staff officer. He became interested in politics and joined the DAP in 1919. It was soon thereafter that he met Hitler and they became close friends.

One year later, the party changed its name to the *National Sozialistische Deutsche Arbeiter Partei,* or NSDAP. The name was abbreviated to Nazi. Hitler designed the party banner himself, placing a black swastika in a white circle on a red background. His bitter speeches against the Treaty of Versailles, other politicians, Communists and Jews, soon brought him widespread recognition, and in 1921, Hitler became the chairman of the NSDAP, replacing Anton Drexler.

Crowds were flocking to beer halls to hear Hitler's impassioned speeches. In order to protect gatherings of the Nazi Party from disruptions from Social Democrats (SPD) and Communists (KPD), and later to disrupt meetings of the other political parties, the small Nazi party began to organize and formalize groups of ex-soldiers and beer-hall brawlers. Many of the members were disgruntled war veterans like Hitler himself, and some even had prison records for being convicted of violent crimes. Röhm became the head of this newly-formed group. As the vanguard of Hitler's security forces, they quickly built a reputation as "thugs" who were given to violence with little provocation. By September 1921, the name *Sturmabteilung* (SA) (Storm Trooper) was being used informally for the group. The name was originally based upon the specialized assault troops during the war who used infiltration tactics and had been organized into small squads of a few soldiers each.

Brown was the original color of the uniforms for troops posted to Germany's former African colonies. After the war, with the loss of these colonies, the military surplus items became cheaply available and were distributed to the members of the SA. The SA then came to be known as *Braunhemden* (Brownshirts), and was dubbed *die braune Bewegung,* or the brown movement. The SA became the guardians of Hitler and his meetings, but they were soon disrupting the meetings of opposing parties, fighting against their paramilitary units, and intimidating anyone they disagreed with, but especially Jews.

In 1922, the Nazi Party youth organization, called *Jugendbund der NSDAP* (Youth Organization of the NSDAP), was established. Its purpose was to recruit future members of the (SA). Numerous youth movements existed across Germany prior to and especially after the war. The prominent ones were formed as political groups, which included the *Jugendbund.*

On November 8, 1923, Hitler made his first attempt at seizing power. Gustav Kahr, the Prime Minister of the state of Bavaria, was to be the keynote speaker at one of Munich's largest beer halls, the *Bürgerbräukeller.* After the meeting had been in progress for some time, Röhm and 2,000 SA brownshirts stormed into the hall allowing Hitler to take the stand and proclaim that the national revolution against the Weimar Republic had begun and to announce the formation of a new government. A riot ensued. The Brownshirts stormed the War Ministry, and held it for sixteen hours. This led to several deaths, but the coup ultimately failed.

The failed attempt to overthrow the Weimar Government came to be known as the "Beer Hall Putsch." Hitler, Röhm, and eight others were arrested and tried for high treason and sentenced to fifteen years in prison in Landsberg, which was one of the most lenient institutions in the German prison system. Hitler only served nine months of his fifteen-year sentence, during which time he dictated most of his volume of *Mein Kampf*, (My Struggle) to Rudolf Hess and Emil Maurice. This propaganda work, comprised of falsehoods and anti-Semitic invective, clearly laid out his plan for transforming German society based on racial superiority.

Political Confrontation

As the nation recovered from the post war hyperinflation of the early 1920s, and the roaring 20s took off, there was a darkness developing behind all the bright lights and fun, which all the good times couldn't prevent. In spite of the successes of the Weimar Republic, it nevertheless was not popular with many people. Partly because of the attitude of cooperation with the Allies, and effort made to accommodate the demands of the Versailles Treaty, the Weimar government was seen as feckless by some, especially among leaders in the military. They felt the government allowed Germany to be humiliated before the world. But on a practical level, the Weimar leaders were trying to walk a fine line and use moderation within the limited latitude they had at hand.

Berlin was seen as leftist and was dubbed by the rising Nazis as the "reddest city in Europe after Moscow", the Communists having won 52 percent of the vote in the 1925 municipal elections.

Joseph Goebbels, a journalist and holder of a PhD from Heidelberg University, came to Hitler's attention during what he called his "quiet years" between 1926 and 1929. Goebbels enjoyed a quick rise in the developing Nazi hierarchy, due to his huge talent for speech-making and developing propaganda. As a highly educated man, he was a rarity among the early Nazis. But as a little man who walked with a limp resulting from infantile paralysis, and who wore a built-up shoe on his right foot, he became the butt of cruel jokes.

For example:
Q. What does Goebbels carry in that box of a foot?
A. Batteries for his loudspeaker of a mouth.

Hitler named Goebbels his "Gauleiter in Berlin" (District Leader), and in October 1926, he was sent to the capital. At once, Goebbels undertook the formidable task of reorganizing and creating publicity for the previously ignored Nazi Party. He gained recognition for the Party through his organization of meetings and speeches. He later published a newspaper in 1927, *Der Angriff* (The Attack), plastered posters all over the city, and instigated confrontations with the Communists.

He had been in Berlin barely a week when he organized a march through a Communist stronghold, Neukölln, which developed into a street riot. His efforts began to bear fruit, as the Party membership grew. His storm troopers, however, once went too far when they beat up an old pastor, who had heckled Goebbels during a Party rally.

Police then declared the Nazi party illegal and forbade any Nazi speech-making in Berlin and the entire state of Prussia. The restriction was soon lifted in the spring of 1927, when Hitler came to Berlin and gave a speech to a crowd of approximately 5,000 supporters in the *Sportpalast* (Sport Palace – built in 1910 and demolished in 1973).

Soon, the SA brownshirts began to appear all over the city. Their role, in Goebbels' view, was the "conquest of the street." This was meant to reconcile the two conflicting worldviews: nationalism and "true socialism" free of Marxism.

Weimar's Last Days

The Great Depression hit America hard, and the effects on American society during those years has been well documented. But the impact on Germany was even worse.

The "prosperous" last five years of the Weimar economy in the late 1920s had been propped up mainly by American loans, more so than by industrial production and exports. Several German and Austrian banks failed due to loss of consumer confidence in addition to the decrease of demand for German products. The United States, which had been the largest purchaser of German exports, raised tariff barriers to protect its own manufacturers.

The Weimar government responded dismally to the situation. Rather than trying to stimulate the economy with the creation of job programs, such as were developed during the Roosevelt administration in the United States (WPA, CCC, etc.), the administration under the leadership of Chancellor Heinrich Brüning increased taxes, ostensibly to reduce the budget deficit, and then went on to implement wage cuts and spending reductions to lower prices.

Even though these policies were rejected by the legislative body, the Reichstag, President Hindenburg supported Brüning as he declared them to be "emergency decrees" in 1930. Understandably, these measures failed, and instead increased unemployment and public misery rather than alleviating it. They also brought about more government instability and division among the political parties.

The result was that by 1932, German industrial production dropped to 58% of the 1928 levels, which in turn brought about massive unemployment. By late 1929, 1.5 million Germans were unemployed. One year later, there were more than 3 million.

Packing-crate encampments of the homeless had sprung up in suburbs and parks. Young men could be seen all over the city trying to eke out an existence any way they could by begging, trying to sell shoe-laces, shining shoes, opening car doors, lining up at the Labor Exchange seeking casual day employment, hanging around public toilets and bars offering to prostitute themselves, stealing, picking up cigarettes butts off the street, etc.

The great beneficiary of all this was Adolf Hitler, who later declared the period had brought him unprecedented contentment. As public confidence in the Weimar government decreased, Nazi Party membership increased to record levels.

In the presidential election of March 13, 1932, no candidate for president won an absolute majority of votes. Therefore, it became necessary to hold a second round on April 10. The incumbent president, Paul von Hindenburg, ran as an independent, and competed with Adolf Hitler, who represented the Nazis. Erik Thälmann was the candidate for the Communist Party. Hindenburg came in first with 53%, Hitler was second with 36%, and Thälmann placed third with 10%. Although the Nazis failed to win the presidency, their gain in the second round represented garnering over more than two million additional votes between March 13 and April 10, 1932.

There was an air of relief that the elected president did not represent either of the two radical ideologies. This was mixed with apprehension and concern that a power vacuum would develop if something happened to Hindenburg. These were desperate times, and the people of Germany were ready to undertake desperate measures to prevent the return of starvation and sickness of the recent past.

By the end of May 1932, Hindenburg was swayed to dismiss Brüning as chancellor and replace him with Franz von Papen. Papen's cabinet had almost no support from the Reichstag and there was a vote of no confidence, led by the Communists. Only three days after his appointment, Brüning had Hindenburg dissolve the Reichstag and call for new elections for July 31. Therefore, the Reichstag could not dismiss him immediately.

Following the dissolution of the Reichstag, in the federal election held in July 1932, the Nazis became the largest party in Germany, having won 37% of the popular vote. Together with the Communists, the next largest party, the two groups made up over half of the Reichstag. Energized by the success in the election, Hitler asked to be made chancellor.

President Hindenburg was intimidated by Hitler's growing popularity and the thuggish nature of the Nazi SA Stormtroopers. Not a fan of Nazi brutality, he initially refused Hitler's request. Since no party received a majority in the last two free elections, Hindenburg, decided to require a run-off election, held in November 1932. The pro-Nazi vote actually declined, while the Communists gained an additional 4%.

Right-wing forces in Germany became even more determined to get Hitler into power. In a series of complicated negotiations, Hindenburg was convinced that to appease the Nazis, he should appoint Hitler as chancellor, with the understanding that non-Nazis in key government positions would contain Hitler. Hindenburg, seeing the election results as a weakening of the Nazi popularity and thinking that Hitler could be more controllable, reluctantly appointed him Chancellor of Germany.

§§§

Since 1914, the senseless killing fields of Ypres, Passchendaele, the Somme and the Spanish Influenza pandemic had combined to destroy an entire generation. The allied naval blockade brought starvation and deprivation upon the women and children left behind to fend for themselves. Following their bitter defeat in World War I, Germany was held totally responsible. The subsequent humiliation imposed by the Versailles Treaty required Germany to make reparation payments in gold, resulting in the incredible hyperinflation of the early 1920's and the complete collapse of the nation's currency. Following a brief recovery, the worldwide Depression in 1929 caused massive unemployment, and by the end of 1932, 6 million, or 26% of Germans were without work.

This unleashed chaos, with a rise in street fighting and terror brought about by the conflicting ideologies of the National Socialists and Communists. The nation was on the brink of civil war, and the German people were desperate for a leader to take control of the calamitous situation and restore order and stability. Adolf Hitler promised to be that leader.

Part I

The Pied Piper

Chapter One

In Flammen
Up in Flames

Monday, February 27, 1933 - 9:00 p.m.

"The Reichstag is burning!"

Deutsche Luft Hansa Flight Captain Rudi Bellon was approaching Berlin on his flight from Munich and watching the glow of a huge fire in the center of the city. Not yet having access to two-way radio communication to enquire what was burning, Rudi banked the Junker trimotor in a wide arc over the city center as he prepared his landing approach at Tempelhof Airport in southwest Berlin.

"It's the Reichstag!" he exclaimed to his crew and passengers whose noses were pressed to their windows.

"I can't believe it!"

"Look at that!"

Easing the three throttles back, Rudi descended for a low altitude steep turn over the glowing fire.

In the hospital below, nurse Meira Lenz, had been continuously assisting in emergency surgery since the beginning of her morning shift. She had just removed her shoes to ease her burning feet and aching back and was relaxing with a cup of tea in the canteen of the Surgical Clinic at Charité Hospital. She heard the roar of an airplane flying low overhead, followed by a young doctor shouting in the hallway that the Reichstag was ablaze. The building served as the seat of parliament of the German Empire. She thrust her shoes onto her sore feet and joined the throng of doctors and nurses hurrying to the third-floor windows, which faced south toward the burning Reichstag across the Spree River. The flames lit up the night sky and were reflected in the water. The frozen faces stared aghast at the spectacle.

"Da geht unsere Demokratie in Flammen auf!" (There goes our democracy up in flames), murmured a voice in Meira's ear. She turned and looked into the face of her father-in-law, Dr. Hans Joachim Lenz, chief surgeon at Charité Hospital. His face was marred by a saddened expression as he placed a hand upon her shoulder. Looking at those around her, Meira saw several faces wet with tears.

"Enough about democracy!" blurted young surgeon Helmut Köhler, understudy to Dr. Lenz.

"That's how I feel," added Gerhard Ziegler, assistant anesthesiologist. "What has democracy gotten us? Those democratic weaklings in the government have been nothing better than ass-kissers for the Allies, especially Britain and France."

"Exactly!" responded Dr. Köhler. "Hitler shows strength as a leader. We've been pushed around long enough. I'm optimistic that the new Chancellor will get this country back on its feet. I think he'll clean house." He did not elaborate on just how Hitler would accomplish that, but listeners agreed with nodding heads.

Sensing that any further comments were unadvisable, Dr. Lenz put his arm around Meira's shoulders as they moved away from the window and walked down the hall to the elevators. He shook his head and in a low voice confided, "I am seriously worried about the future of this country. I can understand the frustration of people like those young hotheads back there, but I can't believe that empowering a man like Hitler will do anything but make the situation worse – much worse."

Listening to her father-in-law, whom she loved and respected, Meira turned his words over in her mind. "I agree with you," she replied. "Hitler and his followers are rowdies and bullies. They have given evidence they have it in for anyone who opposes them or doesn't measure up to their standards of what it takes to be a 'good German'. Look at what happened to my father. He loves this country and always considered himself to be a patriotic German. His parents walked here from Russia with nothing. They were able to raise themselves up because of the opportunities available in a civilized dynamic country.

The beating he got from those Nazis last year shattered him." She stifled a sob. "I don't think he'll ever recover."

Hans Joachim Lenz listened with bowed head and after a moment responded, "I am as ashamed of my people as I have ever been. This is not typical of Germans. But when we look around at the things that have taken place here in the last few years, I'm beginning to have doubts. And now the parliament building is being destroyed as we speak – a symbolic end of the first real democratic experiment that has ever taken place in our country's history."

Placing her hand on his arm, she gave it a gentle squeeze. "Oh, Papa, if only everyone was as compassionate and good as you and my husband. I am so proud to be a part of your family."

In the western suburb of Spandau, Eckhardt Meinert, his wife Ursula and her mother Christina Bellon were listening to the *"Zwei Augen"* (Two Eyes) tango with the Paul Godwin *Tanz Orchester* on the radio at home. The broadcast was interrupted by the emergency announcement the Reichstag was on fire. Hurrying out to their backyard, they could see the glow over the central part of the city.

"How awful!" exclaimed Ursula.

"How could that happen?" cried Christina.

Wide-eyed, Eckhardt gazed at the spectacle with a blank stare. "Eckhardt, what's wrong?" asked Ursula, shaking his arm. Receiving no answer, she shook him again. As his eyes began to focus, he turned to her and said, "I have an ominous feeling. It reminds me of the flames I saw from the trenches."

The bitter February air blasted their faces as Karlheinz Lenz and his new lover, SA Lieutenant Lutz Steinhauer, raced northwest on the Avus speedway through the Grunewald forest. Lutz was driving his open black Mercedes SSK roadster. The *Sicherheits Abteilung* (SA) were Hitler's security division, known as "storm troopers" or "brownshirts". Dressed in their black leather coats and leather racing helmets, they were enroute to a party in the diplomatic quarter of Tiergarten. The radio blared. Karlheinz mimicked the dusky voice of Zarah Leander, a recently arrived singer from Sweden, doing a rendition of *"Das gibt's nur einmal"* (That Happens Only Once). An announcer interrupted the music with the newsflash that the Reichstag was burning.

"Good riddance!" blurted Lutz.

Looking at his friend with surprise, Karlheinz retorted, "What?"

Lutz continued, "It's just a rat's nest for diddling old men who didn't get anything done for Germany! Thank God for Hitler!"

Karlheinz, being a passive individual, did not respond and looked at his friend, startled at the vehement outburst. They raced toward the city center on Charlottenburger Chausee through the Tiergarten to Brandenburg Gate to see the inferno.

It had been just four weeks since the new chancellor had been sworn in.

Chapter Two

Reichstagsbrandverordnung
Reichstag Fire Decree

> **VERORDNUNG ZUM SCHUTZ VON VOLK UND STAAT**
>
> Decree for Protection of the People and The State

The newspaper headlines blared to the German public that certain civil liberties were suspended until further notice. Among these were freedom of expression, rights of assembly, and privacy rights of postal, telegraphic, and telephonic communication. The new law, passed the day after the fire, also allowed detention without trial.

Hitler was a man with an agenda. Hitler's Second in Command, Hermann Göring, Minister of the Interior, had been one of the first to arrive on the scene of the Reichstag fire. Marinus van der Lubbe – a Communist radical – was arrested and claimed sole responsibility for the fire. Göring immediately called for a crackdown on Communists. He ordered a raid on Communist headquarters two days later, after which the Nazis claimed that they had found material indicating the Communists were planning to attack other public buildings. Under the guise of national security, the Nazi's reacted by proposing the "Enabling Act", which would vest full powers in Hitler.

Arrests of known members of the Communist Party and those who had made public statements of opposition to the National Socialist movement began within a few days of the Reichstag fire. These events were viewed with alarm and great interest, not only by people within Germany but around the world.

On March 23, 1933, the Reichstag assembly, which had been moved to the Kroll Opera House, met to discuss the proposed Enabling Act. Paramilitary Nazi SA and SS troops were sent by Hitler to act as security, but instead they surrounded the non-Nazi political party members in an open display of intimidation. In fear of retaliation, the other party members voted with the Nazi's, and the Reichstag passed the Enabling Act. This law allowed the German Cabinet under Hitler to enact laws without the consent of the parliament and to ignore the constraints of the Weimar Constitution.

In keeping with Hitler's rhetoric, on April 1, Julius Streicher, one of the founding members of the Nazi Party, a member of the Reichstag, and publisher of the malicious anti-Semitic newspaper *Der Stürmer*, led a nationwide boycott of all Jewish-owned businesses in Germany. A few days later, the passage of the "Law for the Restoration of the Professional Civil Service" forced all "non-Aryans" to retire from civil service and the legal profession. At the end of April, the *Geheime Staatspolizei* (Secret State Police, or Gestapo), was established, and within four months, all opposing political parties had been shut down by Nazi pressure, and Germany became a one-party state.

During the months since the Reichstag fire, 24-year-old Dutch brick layer Marinus Van Der Lubbe, along with the head of the German Communist Party and three Bulgarian members of the Communist International, were indicted on charges of arson. Their upcoming trial was to be held in Leipzig starting in September and riveted the attention of the German public.

"You know, Van Der Lubbe admitted setting the fire on the night he was arrested," Herbert Lenz stated to those seated around the dining table in the Dahlem villa of his father, Dr. Hans Joachim Lenz. "He claimed to have set the Reichstag building on fire in an attempt to rally German workers against fascist rule."

Herbert and his wife, Meira, had joined their friends, Eckhardt and Ursula Meinert, for dinner on a summer evening at his father's home. They were a close-knit group who had shared a great many trials and joys over a period of twenty years. Because of the tempestuous events, they drew even closer together since the appointment of Adolf Hitler as Chancellor at the beginning of the year.

"Van der Lubbe was either a completely fanatic Communist or a fool," responded Eckhardt.

Meira then voiced what had been on so many minds, "That poor kid was railroaded. I've heard he's mentally retarded, and I find it incredible that he acted alone as we are now led to believe."

Ursula nodded, "What could he possibly have expected to

accomplish?"

"He said he was making a protest statement on behalf of German workers and Communists. But that only brought down the wrath of the government on the Communists," explained Hans Joachim.

"They're not the only ones who got a lot more unwanted attention," murmured Meira, as tears glistened in her eyes. All understood her inference, which reminded everyone of the beating her father, Benjamin Friedlander, had suffered the previous year.

"How has the boycott affected your father's store, Meira?" Ursula asked, referring to Friedlander's, the prestigious clothing store on Kurfürstendamm.

"The same Stormtroopers that beat him up last year came and stood outside the store passing out leaflets warning people not to patronize Jews. Then they posted a notice on the show windows which said: *'Deutsche, wehret Euch. Kauft nicht bei Juden!'* (Germans, protect yourselves. Do not buy from Jews). They harassed some customers leaving and shouted, *'Dieses Schwein kauft bei Juden Ein'* (This swine buys from Jews). They threatened Father when his bodyguard, Kurt Wollner, tried to chase them away.

A dark mood settled over the group.

"I'm sure we all understand that such discussions as this must henceforth not be spoken outside this group," declared Hans Joachim. Everyone nodded in agreement.

Hans Joachim rose from his seat and walked to the French doors leading to the garden. He stood with hands clasped behind him staring through the glass into the darkness. Turning, and in a soft voice he continued, "I turn it over and over in my mind, but I still try to understand how we have gotten ourselves into this situation and what this portends for our people. I understand the frustrations of the postwar years and the unfairness of Germany being forced to acknowledge before the whole world that we were solely responsible for the war. Like everyone else, I was furious and outraged by the terms of the Versailles Treaty imposed upon us by the victors. God, the humiliation!"

The others in the room watched as with lowered head he returned to the table. Tears glistened in his eyes as he slumped into his chair. Waiting for him to continue, no one else spoke.

"Then we have this Austrian Corporal who emerges out of

nowhere and seizes the opportunity to take advantage of the instability and fear that prevailed in those days to infect us with his diseased philosophy. Like flies drawn to a wounded animal, those that now surround him, jostling and competing with one another for power, moved in and rose with him through the chaos that has taken over Germany!

And Goebbels! He with his organ of his Propaganda Ministry, is one of the worst. He has manipulated and played upon the fears and pride of the German people like a master musician. He knows just which notes will resonate with them and can compose the music they will respond to.

Yes, Doctor Goebbels is the best educated and probably the most intelligent and most dangerous one of them all. He is Hitler's man of the hour and has become the voice of National Socialism, even beyond that of Hitler himself." Shaking his head, he fingered the edge of his napkin. "And I fear the worst has only just begun."

§§§

JANUARY 10, 1934

MARINUS VAN DER LUBBE HEUTE HINGERICHTET

Marinus Van Der Lubbe Executed Today

"Marinus Van Der Lubbe executed today," shouted the headlines of German newspapers in January, 1934. At the trial, only Van Der Lubbe was found guilty and sentenced to death for the Reichstag fire. He was executed by guillotine in a Leipzig prison yard on January 10th, 1934, three days before his 25th birthday. He was buried in an unmarked grave on the *Südfriedhof* (South Cemetery) in Leipzig. The four other defendants were acquitted.

Chapter Three

Kultur Angegriffen
Culture attacked

Einladung zum Verbrennungsakt am Opernplatz Am Mittwoch, den 10 Mai, 1933, Nachts 23.00 Uhr.

(Invitation to book burning in the Opernplatz Wednesday, 10 May, 1933, at 11:00 p.m.)

As he read the threatening posters on the *Litfaß Säule* (concrete announcement column) on Unter den Linden, Herbert's anger rose in indignation. He had already been accosted by university students on his way to work at the hospital, where he was in his last years of his surgical residency. They identified themselves as members of the National Socialist German Students' Association. Ablaze with enthusiasm about the new Government, they were in complete agreement with Propaganda Minister Joseph Goebbels' decree that books classified as "un-German" should be destroyed. They and the Hitler Youth had taken up the call to distribute handbills announcing the upcoming rally and to gather undesirable books and bring them to designated places throughout Germany to be consigned to huge bonfires. More than once, Herbert had to be forceful and brush aside impassioned students as they attempted to thrust the unwanted propaganda into his hands.

He turned away from the offensive notices, his mind turning to his beloved Meira and the ever-increasing attacks on her people. He reflected on how her devotion to him had been unwavering from the beginning of their relationship. In the face of opposition to her traditional Jewish father, she had entered the army nursing corps at the outset of the war in 1914. She wanted to accept duty in hospitals near the front where he had gone missing after being injured. Even though the likelihood for finding him had dwindled over many months, Meira had never given up hope and had been relentless in her quest. And now this!

It had already been made known the targeted books included Jewish writers and works from many other world-renowned authors.

Joseph Goebbels was one of Adolf Hitler's closest and most devoted associates. He had obtained a Doctorate of Philology, the study of linguistics and language in oral and written history, and was known not only for his skills in public speaking, but also for his deeply virulent antisemitism, which was evident in his publicly stated opinions.

Goebbels became the head of the new Ministry of Public Enlightenment and Propaganda, formed on March 14th, 1933. The role of the ministry was to centralize Nazi control of all aspects of German cultural and intellectual life. It supervised and regulated the mass media of Nazi Germany. An unstated goal was to present to other nations the impression that the Nazi party had the full and enthusiastic backing of the entire population.

Censorship was vital to the Nazi's retention of political control in Germany. The ministry quickly exerted control over the German news media, literature, visual arts, filmmaking, theater, music, and broadcasting throughout Germany. Goebbels was particularly adept at using the relatively new media of radio and film for propaganda purposes.

At the book burning, Dr. Helmut Köhler and his colleague, Gerhard Ziegler, joined in with the crowd singing, *Brüder, Vorwärts!* (Brothers, Forward!). Köhler, a surgeon at Charité Hospital, had spoken out in defiance against democracy on the night of the Reichstag fire. Ziegler, an anesthesiologist also at Charité, had supported him. Because of their newly awakened awareness of one another and their shared opinions, the two had met on several occasions outside of work and began to develop a friendship.

Together they watched the mounting conflagration as thousands of volumes were consumed. More than 40,000 people had gathered in the Opernplatz. Right-wing university students, Hitler Youth, and members of the SA and SS were feverishly throwing truckloads of books into the flames. At the outer edges of the pile, names of some of the world's greatest literary figures could be seen on still unburned covers: Thomas Mann and his brother, Heinrich Mann, Erich Maria Remarque, the author of the famous anti-war novel, *Im Westen Nichts Neues (*All Quiet on the Western Front)*,* Jack London, Ernest Hemingway, Helen Keller, Theodore Dreiser, Erich Kästner, Stefan Zweig, and many, many others.

As the fire died down and the crowd dispersed, the two friends strolled down Unter den Linden toward Brandenburg Gate.

"What did you think of that?" queried Köhler.

"*Herr* Goebbels should be happy."

The mood of the throng moving down the boulevard was boisterous and loud. Voices burst into the *Horst Wessel Lied,* the Nazi party anthem. The lyrics, which began with the rousing words, *"Die Fahne Hoch,"* (Raise the flag) had been composed by Horst Wessel, a young Nazi who had been shot in 1930 by two Communists and became a Nazi martyr.

"Look at these people!" continued Köhler. "If I were a Jew, I wouldn't want to be out tonight."

"For sure!" agreed his friend. "Nor if I were one of those democrats, like Hans Joachim Lenz, either."

"How about his son? Do you know Herbert Lenz?"

"I've seen him around. One of my friends tried to give him a flyer about tonight's gathering, and Lenz just shoved him away."

"Did you know he is married to that Jew nurse, Meira?" growled Köhler.

§§§

At the edge of the burning pile, a copy of the 1821 play by Heinrich Heine, "Almansor", lay open. The flames began to lick the corner of the page with the words, *"Dort, wo man Bücher verbrennt, verbrennt man am Ende auch Menschen."* (There, where they burn books, in the end they will also burn people.)

Chapter Four

Karlheinz und Lutz

"Hey, Karlheinz, wake up!"

Lutz Steinhauer shouted as he burst into the room they shared in the Steinhauer villa in Nikolassee. Magda Steinhauer, the widow of wealthy furniture manufacturer, Jorg Steinhauer, and a woman of elevated social background, was less than delighted with the friends her son had attached himself to in the past few years. She failed to understand why her son was attracted to the Nazi movement and especially his decision to join the SA, an organization she viewed as made up of hoodlums and barroom brawlers. So, when he had brought home Karlheinz Lenz, son of the prominent surgeon, she was relieved that Lutz was at last associating with a young man of a social status she deemed acceptable. When her son announced that his guest would be staying in their home for an indefinite period, she was somewhat taken aback.

When Lutz interrupted his sleep, Karlheinz, with headache and effects of the previous night's heavy drinking muttered, "Why are you up so early, and what's so important?"

"I just got word I'm to attend the SA conference in Bad Wiessee next weekend."

"What's that all about?"

"*Sturmabteilungleiter* Ernst Röhm has selected a small group of SA comrades to meet and spend the weekend as his guests at the Hotel Hanselbauer. I was invited by the secretary of Edmund Heines, Röhm's deputy. I know Röhm appreciates handsome young men, so I asked if I might bring you along," Lutz smirked. "The secretary cleared it with Heines, so we can leave on Friday and drive down to Munich. We can hit the bars in Munich and spend the night, then drive on to Bad Wiessee the next day. What do you say?"

At this news, Karlheinz shook himself out of his lethargy and his eyes widened with surprise. "Great! I can't wait! I've never been to Munich."

Magda Steinhauer's other child, Lutz's younger sister of sixteen,

Emilia, at first was smitten with the new arrival. But after her efforts to flirt with Karlheinz were met with indifference, she withdrew into sullen resentment and was determined to get even.

"Where do you get such ideas?" Magda Steinhauer had flung at her daughter. "Do you realize what you're saying about your brother?"

"But Mama, it's true. I know they're sleeping together, because I can hear the doors opening and closing late at night from my room. I've listened through the door of Lutz's room, and I can hear them laughing and talking – and doing other things."

"What do you mean 'other things'?"

Emilia blushed and looked away from her mother's penetrating stare. After a moment's hesitation, she replied in almost a whisper, "Nasty things."

"That's enough!" her mother snapped. "I don't want to hear anymore! You keep to your room and mind your own business. And don't you dare discuss this with anyone. Do you understand me?"

"Yes, Mama." As she walked away, Emilia had mumbled to herself, "But I'm telling the truth."

Magda Steinhauer let herself believe her daughter's accusations stemmed from Karlheinz's rebuff and resulting wounded teenage pride. Emilia, bitter and offended, had decided to let her mother discover the truth.

§§§

The two met with their circle of friends that evening at the Eldorado Club, a notorious gay bar in Berlin, and danced and cavorted into the late hours. Karlheinz couldn't resist bragging that he was invited to the SA conference the following weekend. This precipitated a round of ribald joking and teasing intimating that the "conference" would probably turn into a homosexual orgy, for which Röhm and his inner circle had become notorious.

"You'd better keep your back to the wall at Röhm's 'conference', " jibed one fellow.

"And stay vertical, or you'll end up *on* your back," added another.

This brought a renewed round of laughter.

"And you, Karlheinz. You're a newcomer, and you'd better watch out for Röhm. He's always on the prowl for fresh meat! If he makes up his mind you're his target, he'll be relentless and back you into a corner until he gets what he wants."

"Don't listen to these guys," Lutz assured him. "I'll make sure everyone knows you're with me."

"Hmmph!" snorted the agitator. "That won't even slow Röhm down."

By this time, Karlheinz, insecure by nature, wished he hadn't mentioned the upcoming weekend. He felt embarrassed and uncomfortable and whispered to Lutz, "Let's go."

For the next few days, excited but also somewhat apprehensive wondering what he might be getting into, Karlheinz could think of little else. Thursday morning, he awoke feeling as if he had an enormous hangover, even though he and Lutz had spent the previous evening playing chess. As he tried to rouse himself, he became aware of increasing nausea and body aches and pains. Deciding he wasn't interested in breakfast, he lay back down and fell into a fitful sleep.

He was awakened from a terrible nightmare wherein he saw his mother falling from the gallery in his parents' home, except there was no floor, and she just continued to fall with arms outstretched crying, "Help me, Karlheinz! Help me!"

Bathed in sweat and shaking, he made his way to the bathroom in the hall where he vomited until he was reduced to dry heaving. He heard Lutz, who had been washing his car in the backyard, coming up the stairs. Alarmed to find Karlheinz collapsed on the bathroom floor with his head resting on the edge of the toilet, Lutz lifted him to his feet and helped him to the sink and commenced to wash his face with a cool washcloth.

"My God! What's wrong with you? You're burning up and soaked with sweat."

"I don't know man. I think I've caught something – maybe it was something I ate."

"Couldn't be anything you ate, because we've been eating together, and I'm fine. Well, unless you make a miracle recovery by tomorrow, you won't be going anywhere. I think I'd better take you home. You can't stay here with me gone."

"I've told you, Lutz. I can't go back home. My father and brother and I had a big fight last time I was there."

"What else do you suggest then?"

With his head spinning and at a loss for another reply, Karlheinz mumbled, "Maybe I should call my father. But he might not talk to me. Could you do it?"

Returning home from the clinic, Dr. Lenz saw a black Mercedes roadster parked at the curb in front of his house. After parking his own car in the driveway alongside his villa, he walked to the front entrance where he met Lutz Steinhauer dressed in his brown SA uniform assisting his son to the door. He frowned with disapproval at the sight of a Stormtrooper preparing to enter his house, but without comment, opened the door and motioned the two young men to enter.

"Thank you for bringing my son home."

"This is *Lieutenant* Lutz Steinhauer, father."

Unimpressed, Hans Joachim reiterated, "Thank you again, *Mr.* Steinhauer."

Annoyed and red faced at the pointed omission of his rank, Lutz responded icily, "Of course."

Turning to Karlheinz, "And you, son, will be taken care of here until you are well. But let me reiterate what I told your friend on the phone: you are here on condition. Herbert and Meira are often here and regard this as a home where they are welcome anytime. I will not tolerate any of the rudeness you have been so free in displaying to them in the past, or to anyone else I see fit to welcome into my home. Because if you do, I will not hesitate put you in a hospital or a care facility. Do you understand me?"

Angry and humiliated by the dressing down in front of Lutz, he nodded his head and mumbled in agreement.

"What did you say?" pressed his father.

Raising his head and with a defiant glare, Karlheinz raised his voice, "Yes, *sir*!"

"Are you going to take that tone with me already?"

Seeing that he was being embroiled in a family dispute, Lutz excused himself and opening the door made his escape and promised, "I'll call you when I get to Munich, Karlheinz."

After having received the promised phone call from Lutz when he arrived in Munich on Friday evening, Karlheinz heard no more from his friend over the weekend of June 30 and July 1, 1934. Pacing the floor, he fretted, *Maybe, he's met someone he likes better*. But then he corrected himself. *No, Lutz has never been the fickle type. He's always been attentive and I have no doubt he loves me.*

By the middle of the following week, he knew something terrible must have happened and finally called the Steinhauer residence. Emilia answered the phone.

"Steinhauer."

"Emilia? This is Karlheinz Lenz. Is Lutz there?"

"No."

"He was supposed the get back Monday. Has he returned?"

"No."

"Have you heard from him?"

"No."

At a loss for what to say next, Karlheinz asked, "Is your mother there?"

"She is but can't be disturbed."

"Why? Is she ill?"

There was a long silence, broken by the sound of the girl weeping.

"Emilia, what's going on?"

He waited for a response.

"Mother called the SA on Monday afternoon, but the phone was answered by someone who said they were taking no calls. Then we drove to the Lützowstrasse headquarters and found the building locked with a notice posted on the door that the offices were closed."

Emilia's voice wavered and Karlheinz waited for her to compose herself.

"Please go on Emilia."

"We came back home and she tried to phone again. The message was repeated. They were taking no calls, with the warning added that no one should call again. Mother was told she would be advised as to the whereabouts of her son in due time. She broke down and has been in her room since, refusing to eat or talk to anyone."

As he heard this, Karlheinz was overcome by a sense of dread and panic.

"Thank you, Emilia. Please call me as soon as you hear anything."

"Yes, Mr. Lenz."

The phone went dead.

Chapter Five

Nacht der langen Messer
(Night of the Long Knives)

Ernst Julius Günther Röhm was the commander of the SA Nazi militia. During all the years from 1924 until 1933, Hitler and Röhm remained close friends. Hitler used the German language familiar *du* form for "you" with very few persons over his lifetime, but Röhm was one of those. He also addressed Hitler as "Adi" instead of the obligatory *"mein Führer"*. Röhm was himself a brawler and an open homosexual for most of his adult life, of which Hitler was aware from the beginning of their friendship. Nevertheless, they remained close friends and associates throughout the years of the Nazi rise to power.

The SA were the spearhead troops in all the conflicts with Communists and other opposition parties in the post-World War I years. But gradually their reputation for street brawls, heavy drinking and the homosexuality of Röhm, his deputy Edmund Heines and other SA leaders began to bring disrepute upon the Nazi movement. Still, after Hitler's appointment as Chancellor in January 1933, the SA were appointed auxiliary police and directed to eradicate "all enemies of the state". Consequently, local government offices' authority was superseded by the Nazis. The SA considered themselves to be the irreplaceable watchdogs of the "National Socialist Revolution" and expected power and rewards for their support of Hitler. In reality, Hitler no longer needed their strong-arm enforcement. Röhm and the SA had become an embarrassment for the new Germany.

However, the SA had become a force of over 3,000,000 men while the German army was limited to 100,000 men by the Treaty of Versailles. At a cabinet meeting in February 1934, Röhm demanded that the SA and the army be merged into a "people's army" under his command. The army officer corps regarded the SA as nothing more than a mob of morally corrupt street brawlers and thugs, but with a huge cache of weapons. The officer corps opposed Röhm's proposal and a deep power struggle developed. This involved the officer corps and those close to Hitler, including Prussian Premier Hermann Göring, Propaganda Minister Joseph Goebbels and *Reichsführer-SS* Heinrich Himmler, who also wanted to position the *Schutzstaffel)* (Security Staff - SS) to replace the SA.

Nazi intimidation continued to escalate, but Ernst Röhm and the SA had begun to operate on their own. Röhm's homosexuality had never been an issue between him and Hitler before, but now, Hitler declared that such perversion could no longer be tolerated. The die was cast: Röhm had to go!

On June 30, 1934, Hitler and a large contingent of SS and regular police flew to Munich and drove to Bad Wiessee arriving at the Hanselbauer Hotel about 6:30 am. They found Röhm, his adjutant Edmund Heines and other SA leaders in bed with young men. Hitler ordered Heines and his young companion taken outside and shot, while Röhm and other SA leaders were removed to Stadelheim Prison in Munich. There in the prison courtyard, several of the captives were executed. Those not executed were brought back to Berlin and confined in the Leibstandarte barracks in Lichterfelde, given one-minute "trials", then executed by a firing squad. This purge of the SA between June 30 and July 2 resulted in over 1,000 arrests and an estimated 150 to 200 men executed.

Hitler couldn't bring himself to immediately order the execution of his old friend, but eventually did so. He ordered that Röhm should be given the option of suicide. On July 1, *SS-Brigadeführer* Theodor Eicke and *SS-Obersturmbahnführer* Michael Lippert visited Röhm in his cell and gave him a Browning pistol loaded with one bullet telling him he had ten minutes to decide, or they would do it for him.

Röhm responded, "If I am to be killed, let Adolf do it himself." After the allotted time had elapsed, Eicke and Lippert returned and found Röhm standing with his chest bared in gesture of defiance. They summarily shot him.

On July 2, Propaganda Minister Joseph Goebbels declared in a radio announcement that Hitler had prevented Ernst Röhm and former Chancellor Kurt von Schleicher from overthrowing the government. Details were not provided and the German public was left in the dark.

Then on July 13, in a nationally broadcast speech to the Reichstag meeting in the Kroll Opera House, Hitler stated the challenge:

> *"If anyone reproaches me and asks why I did not resort to the regular courts of justice, then all I can say is this. In this hour, I was responsible for the fate of the German people. I gave the order to shoot the ringleaders in this treason, and I further gave the order to cauterize down to the raw flesh the ulcers of this poisoning of the wells in our domestic life. Let the nation know that its existence – which depends on its internal order and security – cannot be threatened with impunity by anyone! And let it be known for all time to come that if anyone raises his hand to strike the State, then certain death is his lot."*

This was the turning point for the German government, nation and people. Power was then solidified behind Hitler, Göring, Goebbels and Himmler. On August 2, President Hindenburg died of lung cancer. The army and other reactionary forces then urged the consolidation of the presidency and the chancellorship. Wasting no time in taking advantage of the crisis, a plebiscite election was held on August 19. With all opposition virtually eliminated, Hitler gained a 90 percent majority. Thus, he became the dictator of Germany.

§§§

Karlheinz had a sense of fear and foreboding at the end of his conversation with Emilia Steinhauer. *I barely missed being caught up in a deadly calamity! Oh, Lutz, what happened to you?*

As the days went by, this mood of apprehension began to settle over the whole population.

Chapter Six

Triumph des Willens
(Triumph of the Will)

"Alright. We'll meet you at *Kranzler's* for coffee about 5:30 and then we can drive to the theater in our car for the premiere," offered Herbert.

"I don't know about trying to drive there, Herbert," warned his friend. "We won't be able to park anywhere near *Gloria Palast* on *Ku'damm,* because it'll be blocked off to normal traffic."

"Except for the Big Shots!" Herbert interrupted.

"We'd probably better leave our cars parked on *Unter den Linden* at *Kranzler's* and take a taxi. Let's hope they'll let our taxi drop us off in front."

"You're right. I should have thought of that. Anyway, thanks for inviting us. I'm looking forward to it. It's supposed to be quite a production. Leni Riefenstahl has really made a name for herself as a movie producer. I hear her cinematography is magnificent. I can't wait to see it. I hope I can sell Meira on the idea. Thanks again. We'll be in touch."

"Who was that on the phone?" questioned Meira, wiping her hands on a dish towel as her husband returned to the dinner table.

"Eckhardt. Siemens gave tickets to their managers for the premier of Leni Riefenstahl's film, *Triumph des Willens* at the *Gloria Palast* on the 23rd, and he and Ursula have invited us to go with them. We need to wear evening clothes. It's supposed to be quite an event."

"*Triumph des Willens!* That's that Nazi propaganda film about the Nazi Congress in Nuremberg. Why would you think I would want to see that?"

"Yes, but Riefenstahl is an up and coming film producer who has developed some revolutionary cinematography, and I would really like to see it."

"Well, then *you* go!" She threw the dish towel onto the counter as she continued, "But I wouldn't go anywhere *near* it! And to be surrounded by all those Nazis? No doubt the whole gang will be there, from Hitler and Goebbels right on down. The whole idea makes me want to throw up!"

After a few moments, Herbert agreed, "You're right. I told Eckhardt you might not be keen on the idea."

"*Keen* on the idea! Do you know me at *all*? After the way the Nazis have been treating my family? I'm really surprised you would even consider suggesting such a thing to me!"

"I'm sorry, sweetheart. I'm being selfish. I'll call Eckhardt right back and explain that we can't go."

Leni Riefenstahl was a Berlin-born movie actress whose career began in 1925 and who starred in five successful motion pictures. In 1932, she directed her own film, *Das blaue Licht*. She then turned her efforts to directing Nazi propaganda films. In 1933, she produced *Der Sieg des Glaubens* (The Victory of Faith). Because Hitler and Ernst Röhm were shown together in the film, the party attempted to destroy all copies after the Night of the Long Knives.

Much of Goebbels propaganda work focused on Hitler himself, and was reflected in Riefenstahl's big success, *Triumph des Willens*, featuring him as a heroic and infallible leader. The film portrayed the 1934 Nazi Party Congress in Nuremberg attended by over 700,000 spectators.

The film utilized innovative techniques, including Albert Speer's "Cathedral of Light" where 152 vertical searchlight beams were projected into the night sky, and the revolutionary use of music was introduced.

The film contains excerpts of speeches by Nazi leaders, including Hitler, Rudolf Hess and Julius Streicher. However, because of the purge of the *SA* during the Night of the Long Knives, many prominent *SA* members were conspicuously absent. The overriding theme of the film was the resurgence of Germany as a great power, with Hitler as the leader who would exemplify the renewed determination and willpower of the German people in bringing glory to the nation.

The movie premiered at the *Gloria Palast* on March 28, 1935. Riefenstahl won several awards, not only in Germany, but also in the United States, France, and Sweden. It won the Gold Medal at the 1935 Venice Film Festival.

Chapter Seven

Der "kleine" Eckhardt
("little" Eckhardt")

Eleven-year old Eckhardt Meinert and some of his friends laughed and chattered as they got off the bus bringing them home on a beautiful Saturday morning in July, 1935. They were returning from the two-week Boy Scout Jamboree in the Eifel region near the borders of Belgium and Luxembourg. Eckhardt and Ursula, who had come to meet their son, smiled at the enthusiasm and high spirits he and the other boys exhibited.

"Look how tan and healthy they all are," exclaimed Eckhardt.

"Yes, and I was also thinking how handsome your son is – just like his father," Ursula teased.

"I can always count on you to build up my ego."

They looked at each other with unconcealed love.

Seeing him waving, Ursula cried, *"Da ist mein Augapfel"* (There is the apple of my eye). He rushed over to them smiling and babbling about his grand adventure.

"Mama, Papa! I'm so glad to see you. Where's Grandma?"

"She stayed home to take care of your little brother, Detlev. He wanted to come with us, but he's been sick with a summer cold," explained Ursula.

"Well, how was it?" queried his father, as he picked up his son's bag.

"It was great! I'm glad to be home, but I wish we'd stayed longer. I got two merit badges. One for swimming and one for woodcarving."

"I wish I'd had such opportunities as a kid," Eckhardt murmured.

"Why didn't you, Papa?"

"We were too poor. And what little money we had went for my dad's booze."

"Why did he do that, Papa?"

"Sssh, Eckhardt. He doesn't need to hear about that," admonished Ursula.

Looking at his father, his curiosity unsatisfied, young Eckhardt wanted to pursue the matter further, but realized he had better not. He had not heard his father mention his own childhood very often and was surprised at the trace of bitterness in his remark. He grew up seeing his father as a mild-mannered kind man who rarely criticized others, and who indeed had always shown a generous non-judgmental attitude toward his fellow man.

As they drove home in the small 1.2 litre Opel sedan his father had purchased a year earlier, young Eckhardt talked about some new friends from camp and spoke with admiration about a boy who was a year older than himself.

"My tentmate was Jürgen Lauterbacher. He's tall and has lots of muscles and is really smart. We went hiking a lot together. His uncle is Hartmann Lauterbacher who works for *Reichsjugendführer* (Nazi Youth Leader) Baldur von Schirach. He talks a lot about the German Youth and says his uncle wants him to drop out of Boy Scouts and join them. He says his dad and mom aren't keen on the idea, but his uncle says the DJ go on really great trips – even outside Germany, and he asked me if I'd join if he did."

At this, Eckhardt and Ursula exchanged startled glances.

"What do you think, Papa?"

After a long pause, Eckhardt replied, "I don't know about that. I think you're doing just fine where you are. You've been really happy in Boy Scouts and you've just been telling us what a great time you've had. Why would you want to leave?"

"Yeah, but the Boy Scouts don't have all the great activities the DJ does. And what about those trips I just told you about? Besides, I get along great with Jürgen, and we have such a good time together."

A long silence followed. Finally, Ursula spoke up, "Just let us think about it."

§§§

The Nazi youth organizations, *Deutsche Jugend* or *DJ*, (German Youth) for boys 8 through 14, and *Hitlerjugend* or *HJ* (Hitler Youth) for boys 14 through 18, were organized in 1922. The aim was to recruit young boys into these youth organizations and later to become members of the SA. As a result, a generation of German youth was indoctrinated to become ardent Nazis.

In 1931, Baldur von Schirach was appointed *Reichsjugendführer* by Hitler. He was born in Berlin in 1907. He was a descendant through his American mother of two signatories of the United States Constitution and three of his four grandparents were Americans from Pennsylvania.

After the Nazi rise to power, the growth of this organization was meteoric. In January 1933, when Hitler was appointed Chancellor, the Hitler Youth had a membership of 50,000 members. By the end of that year, there were more than 2,000,000 members. Other youth groups, especially the international Boy Scouts, came under attack. The Hitler Youth took over many of its activities and traditions. Camping trips, crafts, hiking and summer camps were things that made the Nazi youth movement popular and attractive. The boys wore uniforms, sang and gathered around campfires. Of course, Jewish boys were barred from membership.

The female counterpart to the Hitler Youth was the *Bund Deutscher Mädel* or *BDM* (Band of German Maidens) which like the *HJ was* established in the 1920s, and in 1930 became the girls' auxiliary of the Hitler Youth and was at first voluntary.

Chapter Eight

Die Nürnberger Gesetze
(The Nuremberg Laws)

"That's outrageous!" fumed Hans Joachim Lenz. "How can they revoke a person's citizenship. Especially someone like you. You served honorably as a medical officer near the front in the war. You have your Iron Cross First Class for bravery for continuing to operate when your hospital came under fire."

"Nevertheless, I am no longer a German citizen under the law," replied his long-time colleague and friend, Julius Ehrenfeld on a crisp Fall day in October 1935. They sat on a park bench in the Tiergarten as children played on the grass nearby. "But I was foolish. I shouldn't have been surprised when I received the notice I was to surrender my passport. My wife also. She took it really hard, because we have always looked forward to our holidays with her family in Provence in the south of France, and now that is out of the question."

When Hans Joachim had learned of the Nuremberg Laws passed at a special session of the Reichstag convened at the Nazi Party Rally in that city, he was furious. But when it affected someone he knew personally, he was numb. He looked at his friend with a feeling of helplessness. *What is happening to us?* he wondered. *Good people who have contributed and sacrificed for Germany like this man.*

"I know it sounds trite, Julius, but I will be ready to help you in any way I can."

"Thank you, Hans Joachim. You have been a good friend all these years. This is no reflection on you or other good Germans."

"Isn't it? Why are we allowing *him* to dehumanize us?"

§§§

Hitler had never been secretive about his hatred of the Jewish people. He had put forth his anti-Semitic agenda in *Mein Kampf* and had vilified them at every subsequent opportunity. After his rise to power in 1933, racism and antisemitism had become the official ideology of Nazism. This was codified in the first piece of legislation on April 7, 1933. The "Law for the Restoration of the Professional Civil Service", which as the title suggests barred Jews and other non-Aryans from membership in various organizations and professions in the civil service.

Then on September 15, 1935, Hitler announced the Nuremberg Laws at the annual Nazi Party Rally. These encompassed two laws: The Reich Citizenship Law and the Law for the Protection of German Blood and Honor.

Under the first component, one's nationality was to be determined by the Reich nationality laws. The second explained how citizenship would be determined: a person must be of German blood or be of Germanic origin. For example, northwest Europeans (English, Scandinavian, Dutch). Citizenship was conferred only with an official certificate of Reich citizenship. Only Reich citizens could enjoy full political rights.

§§§

"Es ist jetzt Zeit, wir sollen endlich diese kommunistischen Rattenneste hier in Wedding ausrotten!" (It's now time we should finally clean out these Communist rats' nests here in Wedding).

Ursula's mother, Christina Bellon, was seated behind two men in the black uniforms of the SS on the Seestraße subway. She couldn't help but overhear their conversation. She clenched her fists and her pulse began to race.

It was a bitter November day in 1935. Since the Röhm purge during the previous summer, brown shirted SA men were seen less often on the streets of Berlin. Instead, black uniformed SS men with death heads insignias on their caps had replaced them.

Returning from a visit in Wedding to look up old friends and neighbors, Christina had been saddened to learn that many from former days had passed on or moved away. Most disturbing was the discovery that acquaintances she had known among the Communists were not to be found. In the early 1920s, Christina and many like her from working class districts in Berlin such as Wedding, Friedrichshain, Kreuzberg and Prenzlauerberg were attracted to the ideas put forth by the Communists.

In the aftermath of the Reichstag fire and the trial of Marinus van der Lubbe, attention had been focused on anyone affiliated with the Communists. The block leader and other leaders of the cell in her old neighborhood in Wedding had been arrested, but their fate had never been revealed. The district of Wedding, long known as "Red Wedding", was targeted as a Communist stronghold.

What if my name was mentioned in an interrogation by someone under arrest? Christina panicked. In her rational mind, she knew a plainly dressed old woman like herself would probably not be noticed by cocky young SS men. Nevertheless, she wished she'd never gone back to Wedding. If only she had stayed home in the snug little house in Spandau where she lived with Ursula and Eckhardt Meinert and their two boys.

She thought back over the past twenty years. Those years had included the hardship and sorrow of war, food shortages, the flu pandemic that had taken her husband and two children, hyperinflation, the stock market crash, and the world's perception that the Germans had brought much of this on themselves. In spite of all that, she would rather have any of it back than the pervading sense of pure dread that was now invading her country.

She began to reflect on the resilience and toughness her fellow Berliners always had displayed in hard times, the present being no exception. She recalled with amusement and some pride the situations where Berliners had indicated their true feelings about the new regime and its members.

A few weeks earlier she had been standing at a bus stop on Unter den Linden and overheard two middle aged men chuckling and exchanging subtle comments about current events.

The German verb *wählen* (sounds like "vaylen") means "to choose or to vote", but can also mean "to dial" as on a rotary dial telephone.

Christina heard the one fellow ask the other: "Did you hear about the guy who dialed the wrong number right after the last election?" This referred to the last free election of March 5, 1932.

"No, I guess I missed that one."

"This guy dialed the wrong number and then apologized. *Entschuldigung. Ich habe falsch gewählt"* (Excuse me. I dialed wrong). He heard the reply, *"Ja, das haben wir alle."* (Yes, we all did vote wrong).

Chapter Nine

Das rosa Dreieck
(The Pink Triangle)

The gloss of wet pavement reflected the headlights of traffic on Charlottenburger Chausse, the great east-west boulevard, near the roundabout of *Grosser Stern,* overseen by the gilded victory goddess atop the *Siegessäule* (Victory Column). Three kilometers to the east, the Brandenburg Gate stood in floodlit bathed glory, four huge swastika flags hanging in each of the side portals as traffic flowed through the main center portal. Karlheinz Lenz sat in his Mercedes roadster parked facing eastward under a streetlamp a few meters west of the roundabout and watched the few pedestrians, mostly men, strolling slowly along the sidewalk. The recent rain had ceased, but left a chilled dampness in the autumn evening air. Some of the men, dressed for the most part in raincoats and hats, paused and regarded each other with intense interest. Occasionally, Karlheinz observed a man approaching another ostensibly to request a light for a cigarette, or to huddle in conversation. Some would continue to walk on side by side, and from time to time a pair of men would disappear into the forest of the nearby Tiergarten.

Then a well-built young man dressed in a black raincoat and fedora paused on the sidewalk and gazed at Karlheinz through his windshield, signaled him with a slight nod of his head, and slowly continued on his way. Gathering his courage, Karlheinz stepped out of his vehicle, locked it and proceeded to follow, noting the man looking over his shoulder before turning into a pathway into the depths of the Tiergarten. After some distance, the man waited for Karlheinz in the darkness of a grove. The two met and after a pause, grasped one another in a wordless embrace.

At the conclusion of their erotic frenzy, trembling with spent emotion and fear, Karlheinz returned to his car. As he seated himself behind the steering wheel, he was startled to see his erstwhile partner tapping on the window. His first impulse was to drive away as fast as possible, but then he rolled down the window anyway.

"What do you want?"
"Why are you running away so fast? I wanted to talk to you."
"I'm sorry. I really have to go."
"Could you give me a lift?"
Karlheinz turned this over in his mind before asking, "Where to?"
"Wherever you want."
After a moment of nervous hesitation, he reached across and unlocked the passenger side door.

Gray morning light filtered through the drawn blinds of the windows in a large bedroom. As he recalled how he came to be in bed with the sleeping man from the night before, Karlheinz turned the circumstances of their meeting over in his mind. As his eyes wandered around the dimly lit room, he bolted upright into full awakening as he recognized the sinister death heads insignia of the SS on a black uniform cap resting on the bureau across the room. *Whose is that? What have I gotten myself into?* raced through his mind. Breaking into a sweat, he slid out of bed trembling as he slipped into his clothes.

After the bloody purge of Ernst Röhm and many of his SA men in July of 1934, the Nazi regime had come down mercilessly on the homosexual community of Berlin and across Germany. The few remaining gay bars had been shut down and thousands of gay men had been arrested and deported to concentration camps. In the camps, they were issued prison garb with an inverted pink triangle sewn on the right breast. They were then subjected to further harassment and brutality by the guards and other prisoners. As a consequence, Karlheinz and others like him had been forced to curtail their activities and live in constant fear of arrest.

"Good morning, handsome. Why are you up so early?"
Startled, Karlheinz turned to face his smiling bedmate. "Sorry. Didn't mean to wake you. I have to get going."
"What's wrong with you? You're white as a ghost!"
Inadvertently, Karlheinz glanced once again at the menacing uniform cap. Following his gaze, Dieter chuckled and said, "Does that make you nervous?"
"Whose is it?"
"It's mine."
"Are you in the SS?"

"Yes. Surprised?" After allowing this to sink in for a moment, he continued, "Welcome to the bed of *Sturmbahnführer* Dieter Lehmann."

Unable to control the terrified look on his face, Karheinz stammered, "B-b-but I thought you people hated gay men!"

Noting the effect, he was having on his "guest", Dieter teased, "You're right! Should I arrest you?"

Thoroughly unnerved, Karlheinz began to tremble and begged, "Oh, God! Please let me go!"

Like a cat tormenting a mouse, the SS man retorted, "Well, I don't know. The *Führer* has entrusted us with the duty of restoring morality to this country, and I can't make up my mind what to do with you."

"But you approached me and asked me to come home with you. Why would you do that, if you only wanted to trap me?" wailed his now tearful victim.

After not responding for a long moment, Dieter then smiled and said, "Of course I'm not going to arrest you. You're too pretty. And they'd have you for breakfast, lunch and dinner in one of our new special camps. Come here and get back in bed. But let this be a lesson to you, you bad boy. Don't do anything so foolish again."

Shaking with relief, Karlheinz did as he was told.

A very conflicted Karlheinz Lenz pulled his car away from the curb in front of the elegant Wilhelmine apartment building on Lützowplatz.

Why do I feel so scared around Dieter? He wondered.

Dieter Lehmann was the prototypical Aryan superman. Almost 2 meters tall, blond and blue-eyed with an athletic build, he could have easily served as a model for Josef Thorak, one of the most admired sculptors of the Third Reich. Karlheinz was dazzled by the man, but like one of Thorak's statues, his handsome chiseled face had a menacing quality about it.

"You must promise me that you won't do something stupid again like you did last night, Karlheinz. I wouldn't want to have to punish you," Dieter had threatened as they lay together. "You're my *Mäuschen* (little mouse) now. Understand?" he said, giving Karlheinz a hard pinch on the buttocks with a chuckle.

"Will you make me the same promise?"

"Never mind about that," came the reply. "You just mind what I say and there'll be no problem."

Was he just joking?

A sudden blast of a horn startled him out of his musing, as he cut off another car at the intersection of Schillerstraße. Shaking and bathed in sweat, he pulled his car over to the curb, stopped and bent over the steering wheel.

Like many in Germany, Karlheinz admired the SS men in their stunning black uniforms. But now he had slept with one. The thought excited him and at the same time stirred a feeling of foreboding in him. After his close call two years previously at the time of the massacre of SA men, including his lover, Lutz Steinhauer, he had promised himself to steer clear of uniforms. And yet, here he was: involved with a member of the most dangerous military organization of the Third Reich.

§§§

Paragraph 175 was a provision of the German Criminal Code which existed from 1871 to 1994 and prohibited sexual acts between men. But as long as there were no outrageous public displays of homosexuality, the police and legal authorities looked the other way. After the purge of the SA and execution of Röhm in 1934 however, the full weight of the law was brought into force, and in the fall of 1935, the Nazis introduced a more severe version of this law. This made it possible to be prosecuted if there was any suspicion whatsoever that a man might be homosexual. If any action were construed to be a "flirtation", if a suspicious look were to pass between two persons, or if an innuendo were overheard, one could be arrested and sent to a concentration camp.

Chapter Ten

Christina's Question

Hearty laughter echoed around the table. Herbert and Meira had joined their friends Eckhardt and Ursula and her mother, Christina, for dinner at their house in Spandau.

"Do you think they're really sorry Hitler is in power?" Christina had just related the joke she had overheard at the bus stop.

"It's hard to know," responded Herbert. "There are a lot of mixed opinions about Hitler these days. I think most people are disgusted and frightened by the brutality of the Nazis, but are in a quandary what to do about it. When they tell little jokes like that, they're testing the water. I'm surprised you overheard it at a bus stop with people standing around. How did other people react?"

"There weren't that many people there, and they seemed to be middle-aged working-class folks like me. But most of them chuckled, or at least smiled. One older man spoke up and warned the two guys to watch out what they say. It got pretty quiet after that."

"You're right, Herbert," interjected Eckhardt. "Germans are hard to read. We don't like the way Nazis treat certain people, but you have to admit that Hitler promised to end the Depression in this country, and he has made remarkable progress *doing* that! Look at the economic policy for his public works. We have built railroads, airports, canals and the Autobahn, and the results are stunning!"

In his excitement, Eckhardt flipped a piece of steak off his plate. He turned crimson with embarrassment, muttering an apology. Herbert smiled and the girls giggled.

He composed himself and continued, "Besides, the German people needed someone to come in and restore order, and Hitler has done it. He also promised to end the Depression in Germany in four years, and he has almost done that. Three years ago, there were about six million unemployed. Now there are less than two million. Look at all the public works programs underway that have provided jobs – the Autobahn, for example. And many companies have more than doubled their workforce. At Siemens, I see a lot of new faces in the cafeteria every day. People are saying that Hitler has saved Germany!"

"My father would disagree with you about that!" Meira declared.

After a moment of nervous glances, Ursula reached across the table and placed her hand on her friend's arm. "Of course, he would, Meira," she said with an admonishing look at her husband. "And all of us here are horrified at what your family has endured. But once bad people like the brown shirts are weeded out, things will get better. We have to appreciate the good things that the *Führer* has brought us. Our little Eckhardt is eager to join the Hitler Youth. They do all the things the Boy Scouts do and more. They even take the kids on excursions everywhere for free."

"I'm sorry, Meira," continued Eckhardt. "I'm an idiot, and I didn't think about your father when I said what I did. It's just that we were at the end of our tether after all that happened in Germany after the war. The government was out of control, and people were scared. Hitler has put millions back to work and families are no longer starving. It goes without saying that what bad Nazis have been doing to your people is barbaric and must stop. But I think once the *Führer* is really aware of what some of those thugs are doing, he'll deal with them. Just like he did with Röhm and those perverts last year."

"Are you listening to yourselves?" Meira retorted. "How come those monsters that beat up my father and are desecrating his store windows aren't arrested? Papa's bodyguard, Kurt Wollner, says the police are almost taken over by the Nazis and they can't be relied on to do anything about these outrages."

"I understand where you're coming from, Eckhardt, when you talk about the impressive things Hitler has done to put Germany back on track economically. But when comparing Hitler and Roosevelt and their efforts to end the Depression, we have to keep in mind that each leader worked through an entirely different process. Both leaders came to power within two months of each other. Both nations put forth maximum effort, but the results are quite different. Hitler has totalitarian power, and he is able to demand and receive support needed to implement his programs without question, whereas Roosevelt has to work through the legislative process," rebutted Herbert. "But there's no question that Hitler's tolerance of injustices is disgraceful. There's also the question of how much he not only tolerates but outright condones."

"Do you really believe that, Herbert?" Ursula spoke up.

"I believe it!" interrupted Christina who had been listening with interest. "Back in the days when I was still living in Wedding, some of the leaders at the Communist meetings I used to go to said that Hitler would be unstoppable in eliminating any opposition if he ever got in power. And look where we are."

"Well, Communists, of all people, have no room to talk," countered Eckhardt. "Look at how they have enslaved Russia! Look at the beastly way they deal with opposition there! Look at the inhumane way they murdered the Czar and his whole family!"

Meira opened her mouth to speak, but Herbert, putting his arm around her shoulder, said gently, "I think we need to stop this. Look at what's happening to us. These are turbulent times, and we need to remember how our friendship has pulled us through some terrible times in the past. We're going to need each other in the days ahead – perhaps more than ever." Heads nodded, and Eckhardt arose, came around the table and embracing Meira said, "He's right. Let's not let these things break us up. You know, Meira, Ursula and I consider you and Herbert part of our family. Let's keep it that way."

Christina sat nearby immersed in anxious thought. During the past year, more of her former associates and friends in Wedding had been arrested because of their past Communist affiliations. Some had returned to their homes, gaunt, undernourished, withdrawn, and refused to discuss their experiences during detention. Many had never returned, and their families had no knowledge of their whereabouts. Christina, herself, lived in terror, expecting a knock at the door anytime.

When will they come for me?

Chapter Eleven

Winterhilfswerk des deutschen Volkes
(Winter Relief of the German People)

The wipers of Benjamin Friedlander's big Horch sedan whispered as they pushed the light rain and snow from the windshield. Enroute to "Friedlanders", Benjamin's prestigious clothing store on Kurfürstendamm near the intersection of Joachimstalerstraße, Benjamin and his bodyguard and driver, Kurt Wollner, rode eastward on the big boulevard. Crowds huddled under umbrellas as they hurried to their destinations on this day, the so-called Day of National Solidarity in late December, 1935.

As they drew nearer, Benjamin noted with increasing apprehension swastika flags displayed in great number around the Kaiser Wilhelm Memorial Church on Auguste-Viktoria-Platz, (today Breitscheidplatz).

"Look at that crowd!" Kurt Wollner remarked.

"Of course," muttered Benjamin. "I forgot. Today is the day when all the Nazi bigshots turn out to do their bit for the *Winterhilfswerk*. Goebbels, Goering, Himmler and the others will be making a big show of getting donations with their speeches and bands blaring. The Brownshirts and the *HJ* and *BDM* will be out there rattling their cans. Hitler himself will probably make a showing. I wish I had remembered," he groaned.

"So, what shall we do, Mr. Friedlander?"

"Let's pull into the alley behind the store and let me think about it."

Easing the big car into its parking space, Wollner let the engine idle while waiting for his employer's decision.

"Well, let's open up as usual," Benjamin said. It's important to be there for my customers, if I'll have any."

His employees began to arrive soon after, although their mood was subdued, and their greetings to one another were spoken in lowered voices.

A few longtime customers entered the store and began to make purchases. As one customer left, she was accosted by two young boys strutting around in their brown Hitler Youth uniforms and sporting swastika armbands.

"Hey, lady! Don't you know that's a Jew store?"

Ducking her head and trying to blend in with the crowd, she hurried toward the subway entrance. The youths pursued her shouting, "You should be ashamed of yourself, you stupid cow!" Most of the other customers remaining in the store took note of what had happened and quickly laid their selections aside and tried to slip unnoticed out the door.

However, a middle-aged gentleman, a regular customer, brought the underwear and socks he had selected to the counter and with a determined voice stated to Benjamin, "What a disgrace! To think I fought in the war for this country and see such things as this. I'm sorry, Mr. Friedlander. My family has been served by your family as far back as I can remember. I shudder to think what my father would say to those criminals if he were alive. And now, they're poisoning the kids!"

"Thank you, Mr. Bergstrasser. I appreciate your support, but you must not confront those people. They're capable of anything. Two of them nearly killed me last year, and I spent weeks in the hospital with a fractured skull."

"Yes, I heard about that. To think! When a person isn't safe in a civilized country like Germany! Surely these people can't last."

Kurt Wollner, standing in the background, spoke up, "I wish I could be certain you're right, but I have been appalled to see how the Nazis have won over many of my former colleagues with the Berlin Police. I'm ashamed to admit that the Germans are like the children of Hamlin following the piper. This Hitler and his followers are something out of the Dark Ages, and he has played upon the fears and anger of the German people – a master musician playing a giant organ. It's mind boggling and horrifying."

Benjamin Friedlander, his customer, and his employees listened as the words of the former policeman sunk in. Finally, Benjamin suggested, "You should leave through the rear entrance, Mr. Bergstrasser." But the proud veteran, with head held high, declared, "No thank you, Mr. Friedlander. I survived the Somme and Passchendaele, and I'll be damned if I'll let an Austrian corporal and his gangsters turn me into a coward."

Resolutely, with his parcel tucked under his arm, he marched out the front door, and no one accosted him as he walked away.

"I think I might as well close for the rest of today," Benjamin sighed. "All of you are dismissed, and I thank you for coming. We'll open again tomorrow and hope to have a better day. Any of you who wish to, may leave by the back entrance. Thank you again," he said, and he began to remove money from the cash register.

His employees put on their wraps, said their goodbyes, and except for two young male clerks, all left through the front entrance.

"Well, that's that, Wollner. We may as well go, too, and see who shows up tomorrow."

§§§

The German relief organization, which came to be known as the *Winterhilfswerk* (Winter Relief), had been established under the Weimar Republic in 1931, with Heinrich Brüning as Chancellor. Adolf Hitler claimed it to be a program developed under Nazi leadership. After the Nazi takeover of the German government in 1933, it ran annual donation drives from October to March. The youth organizations, the Hitler Youth and Band of German Maidens were heavily involved in collecting donations.

Carrying their red painted collection cans, the *"Kann Klappern"* (can rattlers) were seen on the streets and in public venues throughout the Third Reich. They were tireless in their pursuit of donations from German citizens, and those who did not donate were harassed in public. Neighbors, acquaintances and family members were encouraged to report shirkers to their block leaders so they might be "persuaded" to contribute. It even came to pass that employees were discharged for not donating to *Winterhilfe*. On the other hand, one could be relieved from commitment to join the Nazi Party by making large donations. After 1933, the *Winterhilfswerk* scheduled the *Eintopfsonntag* (One-Pot Sunday) whereby food consumption was reduced and the money saved was to be donated. Restaurants were forced to offer an *Eintopf* meal as well.

Chapter Twelve

Celebration?

Kislev 25 – Hanukkah (Day 1)
December 21, 1935

Taking her husband's hand, Meira approached her parent's front door. They each touched the *Mezuzah* to the right of the door. The *Mezuzah* contains a handwritten text from the Torah which proclaims that there is only one God and commands that those words be written on the doorpost of the home.

"*Hanukkah Sameach!*" Benjamin Friedlander greeted his daughter and Herbert, as he embraced and kissed her. He grasped his son-in-law's hand in both of his as he exclaimed, "Welcome, Herbert."

Golda stepped forward, embraced Herbert and kissed him on both cheeks. Edna followed suit, first with her sister and then with her brother-in-law. Although they had married just after the war in April 1919, sixteen years earlier, this was the first time Herbert had been invited to celebrate *Hanukkah* at the Friedlander home since the falling out Meira had had with her father, who had been outraged at his daughter marrying a Gentile.

A nine-branched *menorah* was placed on a side table in the front hall. In former times, the *menorah* was proudly displayed in the front window, but because of the ever-present danger of harassment by Nazi's, the *menorah* had been hidden in the hallway out of public sight.

"What does the *menorah* signify?" asked Herbert.

"The *menorah* was used as the Eternal source of Light in the ancient Temple in Jerusalem. *Hanukkah* is known as 'The Festival of Lights'. A tyrant king from Syria ruled over the Jews and forced them to worship the Greek gods. A small group of Maccabee rebels fought the army of Antiochus IV Epiphanes and liberated Jerusalem. To rededicate the temple, they needed oil to light the *menorah*," explained Benjamin. "They could only find enough to keep the flames burning for one night. Here's the miracle that we celebrate: The *menorah* burned miraculously for eight days!"

"Hanukkah must be an important holiday for you," responded Herbert.

"Yes, but it is a very different type of holiday than Christmas. Our celebration follows the Jewish calendar and lasts for eight days. Because it is lunar-based, the days it falls on each year vary in the secular calendar. It's just coincidence that it falls around Christmas." Benjamin continued, "This taller candle in the middle is the Shamash, which means 'helper'. It is lit first, and then you use that to light the others. On each subsequent day, we add another candle, adding from right to left and lighting from left to right, until all are burning on the eighth and final day."

"Very interesting," commented Herbert. "You certainly have lots of tradition to celebrate there."

"Yes, we do observe many traditions throughout the year," responded Benjamin. "Are you familiar with the *Passover?*"

"Yes. I've heard the word, but I don't really understand what it's about."

"That's enough, Papa," Meira laughed and interrupted. "Let's not overwhelm him."

"It's okay. I'm interested in traditions."

"Well, that's enough for tonight," stated Golda. "Dinner is already on the table."

After they seated themselves around the beautifully laid table, the women covered their heads with shawls and Golda offered the *Amidah* prayer. Herbert could feel the warmth and affection in this family. Benjamin radiated a glow of satisfaction for having his family reunited once again, and his acceptance of Herbert was unexpectedly cordial.

Golda's wine-braised beef brisket was succulent, done to perfection and accompanied by *Latkes* (fried potato fritters) with applesauce, and *tzimmes* (a mixture of carrots, sweet potatoes, parsnips, prunes and cinnamon). A beautiful golden loaf of *challah* (braided bread) graced the center of the table. Benjamin praised his wife for the splendid meal and compliments were added by everyone. Golda, basking in the glow of satisfaction of being surrounded by those she most loved, wondered to herself if the next Hanukkah season would see them all gathered around her table again. After the remnants of the main course were cleared away, Edna proudly brought forth her contribution to the feast – sweet *kugel* (noodle pudding) with dried cherries."

As Golda and her daughters carried dishes to the kitchen, Benjamin and Herbert moved to the drawing room. Settling himself in his favorite leather upholstered chair, Benjamin asked, "Well, Herbert, what do you think about the changes in our country these days?"

Gazing at a portrait on the wall behind Benjamin's chair, he paused before answering, "I think Hitler has surprised everyone."

With raised eyebrows, Benjamin responded, "And how do you mean that?"

"The way he has attacked unemployment and brought hope back to many people has been astounding. His public works programs have changed the whole atmosphere. Everything seems to be more efficient and modern."

"But that hasn't benefitted everyone. Indeed, there are those who feel left out of all the gaiety and excitement – and even feel increasingly threatened," Benjamin countered.

"That's true. And I was coming to that. What you have had to endure is criminal and is not worthy of a civilized country. So-called 'civilized'. My father is outraged. You can't even mention Hitler's name in his presence. It just gets him started on a rant. We have to caution him constantly to keep his comments to himself outside his home."

Smiling, Benjamin replied, "That doesn't surprise me – not at all. Your father's reputation as a just, fair-minded man is well known. But what about your brother?"

"Ah, yes. My brother," Herbert sighed. "He was such a quiet withdrawn kid growing up, and my mother coddled him from the start. I'm not blaming her for Karlheinz's stupid behavior, but he seems bent on rejecting everything he was brought up with. He and my father have become almost bitter enemies since mother died. Karlheinz is fascinated by Hitler and justifies everything the Nazis do. He is not a deep thinker."

Benjamin turned this over in his mind, but decided to not comment further. Changing the subject, he concluded, "Although I was opposed to Meira marrying outside our faith, I have now come to appreciate some Germans like you and your father. In times like these, we need to not allow ourselves to paint an entire people with one brush. I only wish more people felt the same way when dealing with us."

Chapter Thirteen

The Christmas Ornament

Weihnachstmarkt 1935

"Hey, Papa! Look at this." Little Eckhardt dangled a hand-carved Christmas tree ornament before his father's eyes.

Eckhardt and Ursula had brought their sons, little Eckhardt and Detlev, to the *Weihnachstsmarkt* (Christmas market) in Spandau two days before Christmas.

Eckhardt's brow furrowed as he focused on the figure dangling from the string held by his son.

Then his eyes widened in recognition as he demanded, "Where did you get that?"

Pointing to a man behind the counter of a booth decorated with small swastika flags several yards away, little Eckhardt declared, "He sold it to me. It only cost 50 *Pfennig.*"

"You throw that thing away!" commanded Ursula. "That's horrible!"

The ornament was a carved wooden figure of a man with a prominent nose wearing a flat-brimmed hat and a long coat suspended by the string around its neck.

"I think it's funny. It looks like a Jew, and I want to show it to Jürgen. His father thinks we ought to hang all the Jews anyway," retorted little Eckhardt

Eckhardt looked at Ursula, then he said softly, "Well, we don't agree with everything *Herr* Lauterbacher says. Have you ever seen a Jew who looks like that?"

The boy looked down as he considered this.

"Meira is a Jew, and you like her, don't you?" interjected Ursula.

"Sure, I do. But she's different. Anyway, she's married to Herbert, so that's not the same thing."

"So, does that tell you anything?" Eckhardt threw back at him.

"What do you mean?"

"You see Meira in a different light because she is someone you have known all your life. But that doesn't make her any less a Jew. You have to decide if her Jewishness makes her any less a person you care about or not."

Perplexed by the challenge placed before him, little Eckhardt stammered, "I don't think so."

"Well then you have to realize that just because you don't know other people who are Jews, doesn't mean you should dislike them for it" admonished Ursula.

Little Detlev taking this all in, spoke up, "What's wrong with Jews, Mama?"

"From the mouths of babes!" muttered Eckhardt, shaking his head.

Ursula frowned as she studied her husband's face. "We need to talk when we get home, Eckhardt."

§§§

Heiligabend in Dahlem
(Christmas Eve in Dahlem)

"Frohe Weihnachten, Papa," Meira greeted her father-in-law as she embraced him. Herbert stepped forward shook his father's hand, and patted him on the back. After removing their wraps, Herbert and Meira accompanied Hans Joachim into the drawing room where they seated themselves before a fire burning brightly in the large tile-faced fireplace. Karlheinz then entered the room, nodded in the direction of his brother, said curtly, *"Guten Abend,"* and sat in a large upholstered chair opposite.

"Guten Abend, Karlheinz," said Meira.

Looking directly at her for the first time, he replied, *"Guten Abend, Frau Lenz."*

The group sat for a few moments as if numbed by the chilly atmosphere. Finally, Dr. Lenz offered, "Would anyone like a drink before dinner? Meira?"

"A glass of sherry, please."

Herbert responded, "Yes, Papa. Do you have Scotch?"

"Of course. How would you like it?"

"Just a dash plain, please."

Turning to his youngest son, Hans Joachim queried, "Karlheinz?"

"Not now, Papa."

"If you change your mind, help yourself."

After going to the liquor cabinet and serving the drinks to the others and himself, Hans Joachim continued, "And how are things going for the two of you?"

"Nothing really new, Papa. Just the usual," said Herbert. I've been thinking about buying another car. The old *Laubfrosch* (Tree Frog – 1924 Opel roadster, so-named because of the green color) is getting pretty tired. I'd like to try out the new autobahn from here to Frankfurt when it's completed, but not in my little old car." He laughed and added, "Those big Mercedes and Maybachs would eat me up!"

"That's for sure!" interrupted Karlheinz. "Get a real car."

"Whose beautiful black roadster is that in the drive?" asked Meira. Staring at her before answering, Karlheinz retorted, "It's mine!"

"When did you get that?" queried Herbert.

"I bought it from Lutz Steinhauer's mother after he died."

At the mention of that name, Hans Joachim's face darkened. A sardonic comment about the friendship between his son and Steinhauer was on the tip of his tongue, but he caught himself. This was the first family reunion in three years, since shortly after his wife's death. At that time, there had been a major altercation between his sons after Karlheinz uttered anti-Semitic remarks about Meira to her face. Karlheinz's behavior had become so unacceptable that Hans Joachim had to virtually banish him from the home.

Just then the newly-hired butler, Anton Fiedler, a tall silver-haired Austrian, announced, "Dinner is served."

Rising, Hans Joachim offered his arm to Meira and enquired, "May I escort you into dinner, my dear?" Herbert and Karklheinz followed them into the candlelit dining room, which was permeated by the aroma of fried carp.

"I see you're still maintaining the old traditions, Papa," commented Herbert.

"Yes, I try to do things for family holidays as your mother would have done."

"I miss mother," said Karlheinz.

Herbert looked at his brother, startled by the unexpected remark. Karlheinz had not shown any tenderness since Frederika's death. After she had fallen from the upper gallery onto the front hall floor, the unresolved question of whether or not it had been a suicide had hovered like an albatross over the Lenz family.

A soup made with carp was served, followed by fried carp filets with potato salad accompanied by a highly acidic Riesling wine.

"Tell me again, Papa, why Christians in Germany always have the same foods on the holidays?" asked Meira.

"Carp is the traditional food for Christmas Eve in many areas of Central Europe," answered Hans Joachim.

"In fact, that's why many people don't get to take baths for several days before Christmas because of that," interjected Herbert.

Meira laughed. "So that explains why I have to hold my nose when people lift their arms on the street cars a few days before Christmas. You have the carp swim in your bathtubs until Christmas Eve so they can clean out, isn't that right?"

"That's true," answered her husband.

"Fortunately, we have the deep sinks in the laundry room where the kitchen staff prepare the fish. You don't have to worry about sitting next to us. We took baths today," joked Hans Joachim.

Laughter went around the table. Karlheinz even showed a hint of a smile.

Finally, the butler placed small bowls of cherry *Rote Grütze* (red berry pudding and cream) in a silver creamer on the table. He served each person their portion as the cream was passed around. This was followed by a large steaming silver coffeepot of coffee and was poured into cups at each place setting.

As the mood mellowed and a relaxed atmosphere developed, conversation turned to events in the nation.

"I can't wait for the Olympics next Summer," began Meira.

"I know. Berlin will be a showplace for the government," commented Hans Joachim. "Let's hope that the presence of so many foreign visitors will influence radical elements here to modify their behavior and develop a better image for Germany."

"That would be wonderful," said Meira. "But I hope such changes would go deeper than just a desire to provide window dressing for foreigners. It shouldn't take any kind of influence from outside to make us realize there are things happening in this country that should make the German people cringe with shame."

At this, Karlheinz looked at her and seemed about to speak, but decided to refrain from comment.

Herbert, aware of his brother's reaction, readied himself to defend his wife against an attack that never came.

Chapter Fourteen

Julius Ehrenfeld

"Good morning, Julius. Leaving early?" Hans Joachim greeted his friend and colleague the day after Christmas as they met in the corridor of the surgical unit.

"Yes. For Good!"

"Stopping in his tracks he grasped his friend's arm. "What do you mean?"

"I've been dismissed."

"You've been what?"

"Yes. The enactment of the last part of the Nuremberg Laws took effect before the holidays. I've been on eggshells waiting for the other shoe to drop. So, I wasn't surprised this morning when I found a message on my desk that the director wanted to see me. I could tell he was sorry to have to break the news to me."

"He can't do that!" retorted Hans Joachim. "I'm gonna' go talk to him right now."

"No, please don't do that. There's nothing you or he can do about it. It's the law."

"The law!" snorted Hans Joachim. "Where is the law of common decency?"

Julius smiled sadly. "*Ich fürchte, da jener Zug in Deutschland abgefahren ist.*" (I'm afraid that train has departed in Germany.)

The two faced each other with tears in their eyes. Then, very out of character for German men of that period, they embraced. Holding him at arm's length, Hans Joachim said in a choked voice, "I'll be in touch, Julius. As I told you before, I'm going to do what I can for you. We need to talk."

"You need to be careful, Hans. Being seen in a social situation with a Jew is risky – for both of us."

"Don't forget, I have a Jewish daughter in law. I'm seen in 'social situations' with her regularly, as well as here. Oh, my God! I just realized. This probably affects her, too."

"Yes. You have your hands full taking care of your own family.

Don't put yourself at further risk on my account."

"We're surgeons, Julius. We work with risk factors every day. This is just different."

"God bless you, Hans. I always knew you were one of the best people I have had the privilege of knowing. I'll be in touch," he reiterated as he watched his friend and one of Germany's most skilled surgeons walk away.

"Where's Meira?" he asked Inge Sohl, the head nurse at the nurse's station.

"Oh, Dr. Lenz. I was just going to find you. She hasn't come in yet. Your son called to say she wouldn't be in. Have you heard what they're doing to all our Jewish staff?"

"Yes. I just saw Dr. Ehrenfeld on his way out."

Out of the corner of his eye, he saw Helmut Köhler approaching further down the hall just as Inge blurted, "What an outrage. I'd like to ...."

Hans Joachim shushed her and whispered, "Be careful," as Köhler drew near. After he had passed, he murmured, "You have to watch yourself around that one."

"I know what you mean. He has made no secret of his politics. I remember his little rant the night of the Reichstag fire."

Squeezing his arm, she said softly, "Meira's a great nurse and an even better person. Let her know she has a friend in me."

"I will, Miss Sohl. Thank you."

Chapter Fifteen

Das "Wirtschaftswunder" Hitlers
(Hitler's Economic "Miracle")

"Look at him in his uniform with his four captain's stripes. Isn't he beautiful?" said Erika Bellon beaming at her husband with pride. Erika, as a former stewardess, and Rudi as a pilot for Luft Hansa, had become best friends before falling in love and marrying a few years earlier.

Rudi was crimson with embarrassment. *What does she see in me? She says things like that all the time, and with her beauty she could have had any one of a dozen guys.*

Eckhardt grinned and commented, "And I thought I was the only one whose wife constantly propped him up and helped him maintain his self-esteem."

Everyone laughed, gathered around the table in Eckhardt and Ursula's house on a February evening.

"I'm glad 1936 has started so well for you, little brother," chided Ursula.

"Yes, and we're proud of you, too, Captain Bellon," added Meira.

Still blushing, Rudi responded, "Thanks. But with the Depression practically ended, air passenger traffic has almost doubled since Hitler came to power, and Luft Hansa has expanded and needs more new pilots. That's created opportunities for more senior pilots to move up. Hitler has kept his promise to slash unemployment and people are talking about his economic miracle. You have to admit: the man has turned things around for Germany."

Noticing Meira's withering look, he murmured, "But of course, it's been rough on some people, and you're right. I do have to admit I'm disappointed about that."

Herbert, observing the expression on his wife's face, intervened, "I'm more than disappointed! I'm outraged. And my father is, too. Some of us at Charité are ready to walk out since people like Meira and Dr. Ehrenfeld have been terminated – Jews, of course!"

Christina, still fearing that the attention of the Gestapo might be focused on her at any time because of her former Communist connections in Wedding, spoke up, "I know how they must feel. Some of my friends and neighbors have been arrested just because they had family members who fell out of favor with the Nazis."

"About Hitler's so-called 'economic miracle'," continued Herbert, "my brother, Karlheinz, has tried to harp on that theme to my father. And Papa, who's no Hitler fan, pointed out that there's another side to the big claims Hitler makes about his building projects and recovery plans.

For example, many jobs have been vacated by such things as I just described with Meira and Dr. Ehrenfeld. Since the Nuremberg laws have been put in place, employers all over Germany are letting their Jewish employees go. Also, women, who had steadily entered the labor market during the Weimar years, are being pressured to leave their jobs and go home. So, of course this leaves jobs vacant for others to occupy."

"That may all be true," interrupted Eckhardt. "But you can't deny that the unemployment figures, which were at about 30% when Hitler took office, have been slashed to almost 10%. And much of that is due to the creation of new jobs. I see it at Siemens. What about the new building projects? Take the autobahns, for example."

"Ah, yes. The autobahns," returned Herbert. "Hitler likes to take credit for the autobahns, as if they were his invention. The first stretch of autobahn was built in 1929 between Cologne and Bonn using unemployed labor under the Lord Mayor of Cologne, long before Hitler had any authority."

Remembering this information, Eckhardt countered, "Well, look at the new Olympic Stadium under construction for the Olympics next summer."

Herbert laughed, "Well, that's another theme my brother brought up. Papa says that the stadium built for the 1916 games here in Berlin was adequate. Of course, because of the war breaking out in 1914, the games were cancelled. But nothing is too grandiose for Hitler, so he has a stadium demolished which was just twenty years old to make way for this 100,000-capacity showpiece."

"But that, and other building projects all over this country, are providing work for people who otherwise have nothing," insisted Eckhardt.

"Yes. Tempelhof Airport is almost finished and is going to make Berlin an air hub," declared Rudi, enthusiastic at the prospect of landing there. "You should see it. It's beautiful and modern. They even designed it so the planes will be parked under a roof overhang to shelter passengers and baggage handlers in bad weather. I don't have to get wet anymore!"

"Anyway, my father and some of his friends feel that many of Hitler's projects are being financed with money that doesn't exist," responded Herbert with determination. "The German economy was propped up by foreign banks, mainly American, until the stock market crash. Now, we are running on credit, which may turn around and bite us."

"Even if all this were as wonderful as Goebbels and his Propaganda Ministry would lead us to believe," Meira spoke up, "there is still the matter of people losing their basic rights in this country – and now their citizenship. We have always learned in school that Germany is the land of poets and thinkers. What happens to a culture when barbarians take over? What kind of country are your sons going to grow up in, Eckhardt?"

Eckhardt and Ursula looked at one another. Then Ursula said in a troubled voice, "Remember the Christmas ornament!"

Chapter Sixteen

Das Rheinland wird wieder Deutsch
(The Rhineland Becomes German Again)

The fragrance of coffee greeted Ursula as she stepped into the warm atmosphere of Kranzler's on a rainy day in early March, 1936. She looked over the crowded room until she saw Meira waving to her from a corner table. Hurrying over to her friend, she exclaimed, "I'm so glad to see you, Meira," as she embraced her.

"Me too," responded Meira. "I've already had a coffee. I hope you don't mind. I was so chilled walking from the subway. But I'll have another with an eclair this time."

"Good idea," Ursula said as she seated herself. "As a matter of fact, let's get a half pot."

After their order was placed before them, they allowed the pungent aroma of coffee to surround them as they prepared to enjoy their refreshments and each other's company.

"How's everyone at your house?" began Meira.

"Health-wise everyone is fine, except Mama's arthritis is getting to her. Every year, the Berlin winter and lack of sunlight gets her down. When she starts getting nostalgic about the old neighborhood in Wedding, I remind her she should remember that cold water flat and having to lug briquettes and chamber pots up and down the stairs."

This elicited a chuckle from Meira and they enjoyed a moment of banter about the luxuries of central heating and flush toilets.

"The boys are strong and boisterous, for which we're grateful," continued Ursula.

"Little Eckhardt is deeply involved with the Hitler Youth and their activities, and now little Detlev is getting interested, too."

At this, a slight frown played across Meira's brow.

"Oh, I'm so sorry," Ursula said as she reached across the table to grasp her friend's arm. "I didn't mean to bring up anything to do with that." Lowering her voice, she said "I should remember what you and your family are going through here."

"It's alright. None of that is your fault. And how's Eckhardt?"

"Oh, he's doing great. He loves his work at Siemens and is doing very well there. He was surprised when they announced the remilitarization of the Rhineland and was enthusiastic at first, but he has had some second thoughts about it since then."

"He should talk to Herbert about that. And Herbert's father really has something to say on the subject," replied Meira.

"Oh, really? How do they feel about it?"

Meira looked down at her coffee.

After a few moments, Ursula prodded, "Meira, what do they say?"

In a soft voice, "I can't say anything here."

Deciding to drop the subject, they discussed the upcoming Olympics and how Berliners were looking forward to it.

Savoring their coffee, they giggled about "sinfulness" of eclairs, as they indulged themselves in the rich pastry.

"Enthusiastic, did she say?" Herbert grumbled in the darkness of their bedroom as Meira reported her conversation with Ursula to her husband lying next her.

"What's the matter with the man? What's the matter with many Germans nowadays? Mark my words: March 7, 1936, will be remembered as a turning point for Germany – maybe for the whole world. Nobody loves this country more than my father, nor me either, for that matter. I wish more people could see Hitler for what he is. He's bent on expanding his Reich, no matter what. This time it's the Rhineland and the Rhine! But my father is convinced it's only the first step. Of course, the propaganda machine plays on the legendary aspect of the Rhineland – a cultural German icon. But Papa says it's only a matter of time before he makes his next move."

"Darling, calm down. You'll ruin your sleep," soothed his wife. She kissed him and stroked his brow. "You know, I'm very sorry that you and Eckhardt are not as close as you used to be."

"I'm sorry, too," replied Herbert. "He's like a lot of Germans now – all dazzled by Hitler's accomplishments but not seeing the evil that he promotes. I wonder how many of them actually don't see, and how many just choose *not* to see."

Letting his words sink in, Meira murmured, "You have stood by me and my family since the Nazis began to attack Jews, and my parents love you for it. And I've loved you since long before any of this trouble started. I do really love you, sweetheart. What would my life be without you?"

Herbert turned and pulled his wife close. "I love you, too." *How many men can claim their beloved literally went to battle for them? She joined the nursing corps only to go to the front and search for me after I went missing.*

§§§

Under the stipulations put forth in the Treaty of Versailles in 1919, and later reiterated in the Treaty of Locarno in 1925, the Rhineland, an industrial region which produced much of Germany's coal and steel, was to remain permanently demilitarized. Subsequently, France completely occupied and controlled all important industrial areas after 1920. The French objective was to make it impossible for Germany to invade France, and the German military was banned from entering all territory west of the Rhine or within 50 km east of it.

The Treaty of Versailles was a *diktat* imposed on Germany by the victorious Allies of World War I, whereas the Treaty of Locarno, signed by Germany, France, Italy and Britain, was regarded as Germany's voluntary acceptance of demilitarization. Although Germany was to retain political control of the region, the German population felt it was one more humiliation blaming them for the war.

The Nazis took power in 1933, and Germany began to develop plans for the rearmament and the remilitarization of the Rhineland. Contrary to the Treaty of Versailles, Adolf Hitler sent 32,000 German troops into the Rhineland on March 7, 1936. As a result, Hitler's bold move was considered by many Germans to be a just reestablishment of national prestige, which caused joyous celebrations across the country. Afraid to risk war, the French and the British refrained from enforcing the treaties.

Germany had begun developing her military in 1933, but by 1936 was still not in a position to defend against a counter attack by either France or Britain.

"The forty-eight hours after the march into the Rhineland were the most nerve-racking in my life. If the French had then marched into the Rhineland we would have had to withdraw..."

Adolf Hitler

Chapter Seventeen

The Olympic Year

"I can't believe it!" Herbert sputtered in indignation. "Gretel Bergmann was taken off the Olympic team because she's Jewish, and she just set a new record of 1.60 meters in women's high jump."

Herbert and Meira Lenz were gathered with Hans Joachim at the dining table in his home in Dahlem. It was a Spring evening and the swish of sprinklers on the back lawn could be heard through the open French doors leading to the garden, the only sound in the room as each person contemplated what had just been spoken. Meira looked at her husband.

"What do you not understand about the Nazis' reason for doing that, son?" Hans Joachim Lenz looked searchingly at Herbert. "Why would you be surprised?" he pressed. "I would ask any German adult the same question, but I'm especially astonished by your reaction. The Nazis have reiterated their intentions in regard to Jews from the first days of their movement. Hitler stated them in *Mein Kampf.* But I wonder if many people have ever looked at that book. You, Herbert, of all people, shouldn't doubt the sincerity of their intentions toward the Jewish people.

Look at what happened to your father-in-law before Hitler even came to power. Look at what he has had to put up with since then. Just remember, the Nazis declared a one-day boycott of Jewish-owned businesses, and Jewish lawyers, judges and civil servants were forced into retirement in '33, just months after Hitler was made Chancellor. If I were a Jew, I would be making plans to get out of this country. What does your father say about that, Meira?" he asked, turning to his daughter-in-law.

Meira felt the calm and softness of the Spring twilight fill the room. The fragrance of the lawn and shrubbery had lulled her into a languid detachment from the bristling conversation going on around her.

"I'm sorry, Papa. What did you say?"

"I asked if your father has considered leaving the country as a result of what has happened to him here?"

Exhausted by the matters under discussion, she felt the peacefulness she had been savoring fade away and forced herself to respond to the question.

"You're right, Papa. My parents and Edna have the same conversation over and over. Of course, the question of emigration comes up all the time. My father has Kurt Wollner to guard and accompany him when he goes into the city, which has worked well until recently, because of the respect Mr. Wollner had with former colleagues in the Police. But now, even the police have been so infiltrated by the Nazis that they can't be relied on to back him in conflicts with them. As far as leaving, my parents have talked about it. But some of their friends who have tried to sell property had to practically give their homes and businesses away. Some have even had their bank accounts frozen or had to pay exorbitant fees to withdraw their own money."

"But I thought things were getting better this year. Don't you think it's possible the Nazis might change their policies?" interjected Herbert. "I've noticed that Brownshirts aren't out and about as much as they used to be."

"That's just window dressing, because other nations have threatened to boycott the Olympics," retorted Hans Joachim. "Yes, Goebbels and others on the radio have been toned down considerably this Spring. And that Nazi rag, the *Völkischer Beobachter* has stopped printing a lot of their radical articles against Jews, Communists, and everybody else they usually attack. But wait until the Olympics are over, and then you'll see."

"Your father is right, Herbert," said Meira. "Kurt Wollner told my father word has come down that harassment of Jews and minorities is to be curtailed *'vorübergehend'* (for the present time). Restrictions against Jews patronizing 'Aryan' restaurants and businesses disappeared overnight," she declared. "The police have been instructed to put their best foot forward for the foreign visitors. It's all so transparent. Wollner thinks it will come back with a vengeance after the Olympics are over and the tourists go home."

Eckhardt spoke up, "I have a friend at Siemens whose brother is an importer and works with companies in Holland and Switzerland. He travels a lot to Amsterdam and Zurich. He told me that when Hitler came to power, it was reported in Swiss newspapers that the

International Olympic Committee seriously considered changing the venue for the games back to Barcelona."

"Why Barcelona?"

Turning to his wife, who had raised the question, Herbert continued, "In 1931, the IOC met in Barcelona to vote on the location for the 1936 Games. Berlin was chosen over Barcelona. Since that time, Hitler is not held in high regard outside of Germany. It leads one to hope that he would take note of such reaction and might also be why all the Nazi noise has receded significantly."

Shaking his head, Dr. Lenz replied, "I wish I could share your optimism, but I still think you and a lot of other Germans had better be prepared for the Nazis' return to their old ways. And as I said before, I won't be surprised if they aren't worse than before."

Meira gazed through the open doors as the lawn sprinklers continued to whisper.

§§§

As the heat of summer continued to build in the German capital, people seemed to walk with a lighter step, and a holiday mood increased as the opening day of the Games, August 1, drew nearer. Red, white and black flags emblazoned with the swastika began to appear everywhere. Often, a cluster of flags of the competing nations would also appear, but they too would always include the Nazi flag.

But in all the color and jubilation, the ominous specter of antisemitism lurked in the background. When other nations threatened to boycott the Games, Hitler attempted to play down the hateful rhetoric of past years. His public comment on the event only served to demonstrate the hypocrisy of the Nazi movement.

> *"The sportive, knightly battle awakens the best human characteristics. It doesn't separate, but unites the combatants in understanding and respect. It also helps to connect the countries in the spirit of peace. That's why the Olympic Flame should never die."*
>
> Adolf Hitler's comment on the 1936 Berlin Olympic Games.

The Olympic Flame referred to had been reintroduced at the 1928 Games in Amsterdam, which were the first Games held after World War I. Relay runners bringing the flame from Olympus, Greece to the current venue was pioneered for the 1936 Berlin Games.

§§§

"We might see Jesse Owens there," exclaimed little Eckhardt at dinner. It was the Sunday evening before the last week of the Olympics. "Jürgen's uncle Hartman is gonna take a whole group of *HJ* to tour the Olympic village out in Wustermark. They'll meet *Reichsjugendführer* Baldur von Shirarch in the dining hall for lunch, and he'll introduce us boys to some of the athletes. I'm glad the *Führer* has disbanded the Boy Scouts and merged them with the Hitler Youth. We never did such things before.

Jürgen showed me the photos his uncle took of the opening day parade. Hitler's big Mercedes led all of cars through the Brandenburg Gate. His uncle took him and his family to the opening ceremonies at the Olympic Stadium. The athletes all marched past the *Führer's* box and saluted him and lowered their flags – all except the Americans! They were the only ones who didn't. What's the matter with them? Jürgen said the funniest thing that happened was when they released about 25,000 pigeons. They fired a cannon which scared the pigeons and falling pigeon poop sounded like rain."

Ursula exchanged glances with her husband.

At the conclusion of the Olympic Games, the host nation (Germany) was in first place, winning a total of 89 medals. The United States came in second with 56 medals. The Nazi intention had been to use the Games as an opportunity to demonstrate the ideals of racial superiority, but as history has recorded, athletes of various races participated and succeeded in winning medals for their respective countries. Not the least of these was the African American athlete, Jesse Owens, who won four gold medals in the track and field events, completely discrediting Nazi race ideology. His German competitor, Lutz Long, showed true sportsmanship by offering advice and support to Owens.

The Games were over. The tourists had left. The euphoria of the

Olympic summer was gone. Just as Dr. Lenz had predicted, any hopes Jews might have that life for them would return to normal, were soon dashed. As the summer days gave way to the chill of Autumn, life under the Nazi regime darkened their lives with renewed vengeance.

"How dare they do this to us!" Benjamin Friedlander exclaimed as he entered his store one morning in late October 1936.

"Juden raus! Deutsche! Wehrt Euch! Kauft nicht bei Juden!" ("Jews out! Germans! Protect yourselves! Do not buy from Jews!") These insults and crude Stars of David had been painted on the windows of Friedlanders before he and Kurt Wollner arrived shortly before opening time. Benjamin stood numb before the desecration as pedestrians moved around them, some pausing out of curiosity. Many hurried past with averted gaze, others with hardened expressions of contempt.

As opening time approached, only a few of his employees presented themselves for work. The others had turned away as soon as they registered what had taken place.

In the days that followed, customers ceased coming, and Benjamin soon realized that keeping the doors open was no longer feasible.

One morning in early December, Kurt Wollner and Benjamin turned into the parking lot behind the store to find the reserved parking space occupied. A large Maybach cabriolet with a low Berlin license number conveyed the sense that the owner was someone not to be trifled with.

"Look at that!" exclaimed Kurt Wollner, red-faced with indignation. "Let me see if I can find out who that bastard is."

A red flag of caution sprang up in Benjamin's mind. "No, that's alright. Let's just go home."

Looking at his employer in surprise, Wollner replied, "But this is why they do these things. By doing nothing, we empower them."

"Of course, you're right, Kurt. In principle, I couldn't agree with you more. But can't you see, I have already become a target. I wouldn't be surprised if this person is deliberately trying to provoke me, hoping I might start something. No, Kurt. This is a lost cause. I think I'm done here. Let's go."

Scenes such as this were being played out all over Germany. Harassment and intimidation of Jews or anyone out of favor with the regime became the order of the day.

Chapter Eighteen

Indoctrination of the Youth

"Is Meira a dirty kike, Mama?"

Stunned, Ursula looked at her son. "Where did you hear that?"

"In our *Rassenkunde* class at our meeting of DJ this afternoon, *Jugendleiter* Lippitz gave us an assignment to think of any Jews we know and turn in a list at our next meeting," explained little Eckhardt. *Rassenkunde* were the racial studies taught by the *Deutsche Jugend* – junior branch of Hitler Youth, for boys age 8 to 14.

Her brow furrowed in concern, Ursula considered how to answer her twelve-year old son. "You like Meira, don't you?"

"Of course. I love Meira – and 'Uncle' Herbert, too. But, I told *Herr* Lippitz about Meira, and he embarrassed me in front of everybody."

"What do you mean?"

"He said that was a good example of what he was talking about. That Germans have allowed Jews to sneak into our country and into our lives. That they have cheated and stole from us and gotten us into wars like the last one. He also said the *Führer* is trying to save us and our country, and we should help him throw the 'dirty kikes' out. So, is Meira a dirty kike?"

Without speaking, Ursula pulled the roasting chicken from the oven and basted it as she tried to think of what to say next.

"Well, Mama. What do you think?"

"I think we'd better talk about this some more when your father gets home. He'll be home soon. You go get little Detlev, and the two of you get washed up."

Turning to leave the kitchen, the boy muttered, "Why can't you just answer me? It's not a hard question."

Tempted to respond, Ursula kept her thought to herself. *Oh, yes, it is, son. Much harder than you realize.*

As Eckhardt escaped into the welcoming warmth of his house on a November evening, he was greeted by the succulent odors of his wife's cooking. After hanging his coat and hat on the hall tree, he went straight to the kitchen. Walking up behind Ursula, who was dishing up vegetables, he whispered in her ear, "Hello, *Schätzle* (little darling)." He liked to tease her with the dialect variation of the endearment from his native Swabian homeland.

"Wait 'til I get done here, and I'll pay you back for that," she countered.

"I'll be waiting," he retorted with a chuckle.

After giving her husband a long kiss, she placed her hands on his shoulders, gently urging him to take a seat.

"There's something I want to tell you before the boys and Mama come down to supper."

"Is something wrong?"

"Yes, but I want to see how you think we should handle it."

She then related the earlier conversation she'd had with their son.

Without answering immediately, Eckhardt studied the pattern of the tile floor.

"Well, what should we tell him?" urged Ursula.

Finally, raising his head, Eckhardt said softly, "That's a tough one. We can't come across as contradicting the leaders, or they could take our children from us. But at the same time, we can't betray our lifelong friends."

"Exactly my feeling. I didn't know what to say."

"I'm glad you told me in private. No matter what, we have to show our kids we are a team. With all that's going on right now, we have to reassure them that this family and our home is a safe place for them – always."

Ursula turned from the stove with a worried frown. "The Nazis are indoctrinating these kids in their most impressionable years. I've even heard of children being removed from parents who are opposed to the regime, and they even influence youngsters to denounce their parents or family members who openly disagree with the government."

Chapter Nineteen

Feliz Navidad 1936

"What does Rudi say about Spain?" Ursula asked her mother.

Christina Bellon had been reading the letter enclosed with the Spanish Christmas card sent by her son, Rudi. He had been conscripted as one of 20 Luft Hansa pilots after July 26, 1936, to transport Moroccan troops from Spanish Morocco to Spain, as requested by General Francisco Franco.

"Rudi says when the conflict broke out in July, it was between leftist Republicans and Nationalists led by Franco. The Republicans requested support from the Soviet Union, and the Nationalists turned to Germany and Italy. So, it came down to a war between Communists and Fascists. Rudi calls it the Spanish Civil War."

Christina sighed, "It's all beyond me. He says the country is in turmoil and he feels badly for the Spanish people, but our leaders assure us that it is necessary to stop the Bolsheviks from gaining ground in southern Europe."

Ursula looked closely at her mother for a change of expression and waited for further comment on Rudi's last statement, because Christina had never renounced her sympathies for Communism.

Christina continued, "He hopes that after this campaign is finished, he will be able to return to Berlin and be back with Erika before the baby is born."

They had informed the family of Erika's pregnancy just before Rudi was called away by the Air Ministry. Erika had suffered two miscarriages in the three years since their marriage, when she gave up her job with Luft Hansa as a stewardess. She then took up her role as a full-time housewife and looked forward to starting life as a mother. The families on both sides were severely saddened by Erika's misfortune and anxiously awaited, along with Rudi and Erika, the arrival of another "little" newcomer.

"Rudi is devastated not to be home for Christmas and asks that we make sure Erika is well looked after."

Ursula chuckled. "Of course! He knows that. We'll make sure to have her come out here over the holidays, when she isn't with her own parents."

Christina looked out at the bleak December day and looking up to the sky said softly, "I pray God will watch over my boy."

Ursula looked at her mother, at first somewhat surprised, but then thought to herself, *I never did think Mama really bought into the Communist atheist propaganda.*

§§§

The Spanish Civil War was fought from 1936 to 1939 at the cost of about 1 million lives. It has often been called "the dress rehearsal for World War II", where both sides used it as a testing ground for weapons and equipment that would later be deployed in that conflict. Many German and Soviet aircraft were designed and developed then and were considered to be "cutting edge".

A notable outcome of this conflict was to bring Hitler and Mussolini closer together through their cooperation in supporting Franco, who would later establish a pro-Nazi military dictatorship.

On April 26, 1937, at the behest of Franco's rebel Nationalist forces, German and Italian planes bombed and strafed the Basque town of Guernica resulting in over 1,600 civilian deaths, which is commemorated in the 1937 anti-war painting of the same name by Pablo Picasso.

Chapter Twenty

Wer ist Arisch?
(Who is Aryan)

"Mama!" wailed little Detlev.

"What's wrong, sweetheart?" asked Ursula as she turned to her youngest boy in tears running to her open arms.

"Eckhardt made me leave our room and is mad at me."

"Mad at you? What are you talking about?"

"I don't know. He just said he didn't want to look at me and told me to leave him alone," her boy sobbed.

"There, there, calm down. You know your brother loves you," she soothed, stroking his blond hair.

After rocking him in her arms for a few minutes, she spoke up brightly, "Aren't you lucky! I just baked a pan of apple strudel. Let's wash your face, and you can have some with a glass of milk. And I'll talk to Eckhardt."

After she had seated the boy at the small kitchen table with his treat, she went up the narrow stairway to the closed door of her sons' room. She knocked and said softly, "Eckhardt, would you open the door, please?"

Getting no reply, she waited a few moments and knocked again. Slowly the door opened, and she faced her son wearing a downcast expression. He turned without a word and returned to his desk in the corner of the room, sat down and put his head down on his folded arms.

Ursula followed and placing a hand on his shoulder, asked, "Eckhardt, what's the matter?"

After a moment, the boy in a choked voice stammered, "Why can't I be Aryan?"

Dumbfounded, his mother blurted, "Aryan?"

"Horst Weber said I'm not a true Aryan at school today."

Ursula stiffened. "What does he mean?"

"Today, *Herr* Buchholz, our German teacher, said the ideal Germans are Aryan, and that means people who are tall and blond. This stupid girl sitting in front of Horst raised her hand and said, 'Like Horst?' She has a crush on him and is always smiling at him and hanging around when we walk in the hall or sit in the lunchroom. Horst laughed and said, in front of the whole class, 'But not like Eckhardt, huh?'

After class, I left as quick as I could, but Horst ran to catch up with me and asked why I didn't wait for him. I told him because he probably wouldn't want to be seen with a non-Aryan like me. He said he was only kidding. And so we walked on together. But I thought a lot about what *Herr* Buchholz said. How come I have brown hair and brown eyes like you, and Detlev is blond and blue eyed like Papa?"

Stunned, Ursula struggled to come up with an answer to this offensive idea that had invaded her home. Finally, she said, "I don't know why *Herr* Buchholz would say such a thing to a room full of students, but I'm sure he didn't mean to say everyone who isn't blond are not good Germans. Listen, son, you are a handsome boy who is turning into a handsome young man. You and I show our French Huguenot blood, and we can be proud of that. Besides, you just told me your friend said he was joking. He should be more careful with what he says, but we all say stupid things without thinking sometimes. But anyway, you shouldn't take it out on your little brother. He worships you and is always eager to see you come home. Why were you mean to him? Because he's blond? You're doing the same thing to him that was done to you today. You're punishing him for the way he looks. Did you say anything to him about that?"

"No, I just told him I didn't want to look at him, but I didn't say why."

"Well, I'm certainly glad of that, and don't bring it up again. He would never understand."

"I'm sorry, Mama. I'll go down and apologize to him now."

"Good! And you can have some strudel, too."

With her arm around son's shoulder, they walked together to the door.

Chapter Twenty-one

The Fighter Pilot

Rudi walked along the row of new fighter planes parked along the airstrip at Staaken Airfield in the western district of Spandau. Against the wishes of Erika, his wife, he resigned his position of flight captain with Luft Hansa and had joined the Luftwaffe in the summer of 1937. He then entered flight training at Staaken, the airfield in the western suburb of Spandau. It was at this same airfield in the *Deutsche Verkehrsfliegerschule,* under the direction of Helmut Stock, he learned to fly and earned his pilot license shortly before Christmas of 1928.

Rudi had flown an airliner for years and had played a small part in flying transport aircraft in the Spanish Civil War. He was inducted into the Luftwaffe as a *Leutnant*. With nearly 10 years of flying experience with Luft Hansa, he found the primary military flight training to be easy and finished at the top of his class.

Given his choice of aircraft, without hesitation he chose the brand-new fighter, the Messerschmitt BF 109E. With his adeptness in mastering the Messerschmitt, he was promoted to *Oberleutnant* immediately.

As he walked to his plane, he reflected on his life and couldn't help but feel a rush of pride. As a poor boy from the tenements of Wedding, he had risen far beyond the limitations of his background. From the time he was a little boy, he had long admired the fighter aircraft he had seen from a distance. He enjoyed his career with Luft Hansa but had eventually become bored with the routine of commercial aviation.

Under the terms of the Treaty of Versailles, Germany was prohibited from having an air force, and the former German Empire's *Luftstreitkräfte* was disbanded in 1920. However, German pilots had secretly trained for military aviation, first in the Soviet Union during the late 1920s, and then in Germany in the early 1930s. In Germany, the training was done under the guise of the *Deutscher Luftsportverband,* the German Air Sports Association.

Following its May, 1933, establishment in secret, the creation of the German air force was openly announced in February, 1935, in blatant defiance of the Versailles Treaty. *Reichsmarschall* Hermann Göring was its Commander-in-Chief, and as Hitler's second in command used his political capital to allocate significant resources to the Luftwaffe, more so than even to the army or the navy.

During the Spanish Civil War, the Condor Legion, a Luftwaffe detachment, had provided the new air force with a valuable testing ground for the latest tactics and aircraft. As a result of this combat experience, the Luftwaffe had become one of the most sophisticated, technologically advanced, and battle-experienced air forces in Europe.

For Rudi, the formation of the new Luftwaffe had opened the door to a range of new experiences, and he relished the opportunity to be part of the most prestigious air force in the world. He was attached to Jagdgeschwader 25, which was based at his home airport, Staaken.

Rudi grinned as the liquid-cooled, inverted-V12 Daimler-Benz engine rumbled to life. *Throttle: 1,000 U/min, Oil Radiator: Voll Offen, Wasser Radiator: Auf, Flaps: 20°, Trim: 3, Oil Temperatur: 40°C, Wasser Temperatur: 40°C, Canopy: Geschlossen.* As he ran through his after engine start checklist, he couldn't have been prouder. The engineers and mechanics had produced the most aerodynamically and structurally advanced aircraft in the world. No other air force in the world could compete with the pilots of the German Luftwaffe. Advancing the throttle for takeoff, he felt a surge of power as he accelerated down the runway and lifted off the ground. This was his true calling, and the rush of adrenaline was like nothing he had ever experienced in all his years of flying a transport category aircraft.

Part II

The Virus Spreads

Chapter Twenty-two

Ausdehnung des Reichs I
(Expansion of the Reich I)

"*Ö*STERREICH KOMMT WIEDER HEIM INS REICH!"
(Austria returns home again into the Reich).
Josef Goebbels voice resounded over the loudspeakers in the cafeteria of Charité Hospital on the morning of March 13, 1938.

Herbert registered the news with a sigh. He had just finished lancing a boil on an elderly patient, his sixth menial procedure since before sunrise. His frustration deepened by what he was hearing. A rousing cheer by many staff members at breakfast went through the room. Upon completion of Goebbels's speech, several stood and began to sing *Deutschland über alles,* followed by arms raised in the Nazi salute and rousing *Sieg Heil!* Some, however, stared at their plates in silence, as did Herbert.

A hearty back slap startled him from his thoughts, and turning, he found himself looking into the smug face of his fellow surgical resident, Helmut Köhler.

"Well, Lenz, your father and I just finished performing open heart surgery. Have you had the chance to massage a still beating heart? It's quite an experience."

This is where we're at? An incompetent like Köhler is allowed to serve as understudy to my father while the same opportunity is withheld from someone like me who is married to a Jew and doesn't suck up to the Nazi elite!

"Have you heard about the new cutting-edge research in the field of human studies of less desirables? That will open up a whole new field of opportunities."

Herbert retorted sharply, "Less desirables? What do you mean when you say, 'Less desirables'?"

Deflecting the question, Köhler responded, "I've been saying all along, this country is on the move, and Hitler is going to lead us. We're making history here, man, and people like you and your Papa had better get on the right side, while you can. Our brothers in Austria are happy this day has come. I hear they're lining the streets and roads and cheering as the *Führer* drives along.

But Lenz, you need to get loose from that wife of yours and change your attitude. A good Aryan like you should be ashamed of himself," he concluded as Herbert got up from his chair.

Stepping within inches of his heckler, Herbert glared into his eyes and growled with barely controlled rage, "You don't say another word about my wife! And as for my father, I wouldn't push him, if I were you. Don't forget, he's been here a long time and has a lot of respect from a lot of people. He attended *Frau Goebbels* personally. So, all things considered, I don't think my father's good opinion – or the opinions of some of the people who respect him – is something you want to lose."

Scowling, Köhler retorted, "Well, there are also people here who have noticed your father also cultivates friendships with some pretty unsavory types, like that Jew, Ehrenfeld. You notice *he* got his walking papers, and with the changes taking place in this country, you can bet he won't be the last," sneered Köhler.

"Are you threatening me? Are you threatening my father?"

"Just friendly advice. *Heil Hitler!*" Köhler flung over his shoulder as he walked away.

Seething with rage and tempted to follow, Herbert forced himself instead to sit back down and finish his coffee.

Later that day, he related the incident to Meira. "Remember, dear, last year after Germany remilitarized the Rheinland, you predicted that would be just the first step for Hitler?"

"I take no pride in being right about that, and I truly believe he's now really determined to fulfill all his promises he made in *"Mein Kampf"*. I wish we had all paid more attention to him back then. But I'm afraid many Germans have convinced themselves that he holds the destiny of this country in his hands – for better or worse! I'm afraid for the worst."

§§§

Germany had until the 1870's existed as a collection of hundreds of separate principalities and free cities. Over the centuries various rulers had tried to unify the German states without success. Austria (then the Austro-Hungarian empire) had pushed for a *Großdeutsche Lösung* (greater Germany solution) which would have united all German states, including non-German regions of Austria. The issue eventually came to a head during the Austro-Prussian War of 1866, resulting in the defeat of Austria. German Chancellor Otto von Bismarck persuaded the various principalities in 1871 to unite for the first time into a single country, which became the German Empire. Austria was excluded.

The diversity of various ethnic groups within the Austro-Hungarian empire included Hungarians, Croats, Czechs, Italians, Poles, Romanians, Russians, Serbs, Slovaks, Slovenes and Ukranians – all ruled by a German minority. The ensuing tensions between all these groups resulted in loyalty of some of these to areas outside the empire. For example, many German Austrians were loyal to Bismarck and the newly formed Germany. Adolf Hitler was one such Austrian.

After the end of World War I in 1918, and the dissolution of the Austro-Hungarian Empire, an attempt was made to amalgamate German Austria with the new German Weimar Republic, – a pre-Hitler *"Anschluß"*. However, Britain and France feared a larger Germany and played a significant role in the prohibition of this as set forth in The Treaty of Versailles. The constitutions of both the Weimar Republic and the First Austrian Republic set forth the goal of unification and was supported by the democratic parties in both countries. Popular support for the union was overwhelming, although Hitler's rise to power made it less attractive.

In July 1934, Austrian and German Nazis together attempted a coup but were unsuccessful. An authoritarian right-wing government then took power in Austria. In February 1938, Hitler invited the Austrian chancellor Kurt von Schuschnigg to Germany and forced him to agree to give the Austrian Nazis virtual control of the state. Schuschnigg tried to resist by holding a plebiscite on the *Anschluß* question, but he was bullied into canceling the vote. He obediently resigned, ordering the Austrian Army not to resist the Germans. On March 12, Germany invaded, and the enthusiasm that followed gave Hitler the cover to annex Austria outright the next day. A Nazi controlled plebiscite of April 10 gave a 99.7 percent approval.

§§§

Meira and Herbert sat on the banks of the Havel on a beautiful fall evening. Meira listened intently to Herbert's agitation. "I'm disturbed by the people here who see this as an opportunity to encroach on another country. Using the *"Heim ins Reich"* argument as an excuse for the *Anschluß* because it involved another German speaking country, was one thing – although you and I both disagreed with it – but to raise the possibility of taking another country's territory because ethnic Germans live there, is quite something else. Hell, there are ethnic Germans living all over Europe: Switzerland, Liechtenstein, Russia, Romania, just to name a few. Of course, as we both know, the Sudetenland was part of the Austro-Hungarian Empire, and when that was dismantled after the war, ethnic Germans were left behind. But it's what it is, and people need to move on. If Germans want to emigrate into Germany, I guess they could. But the regime no doubt wouldn't want that. The Reich is already densely populated and one of Hitler's main arguments put forth in *Mein Kampf* was that Germans need more *Lebensraum* (living space). Losing territory to Poland after the war only added fuel to the fire. So, let's face it: after success in the Rhineland, and now in Austria, Hitler is on a land grab roll!"

Meira, gazing out at the Havel river, thought to herself, *Yes, and he's not just grabbing land. He's bent on stealing whatever he wants, both inside and outside the country. My father is losing everything he's worked for to the Nazis. I wonder how safe he and Mama will be in Holland.*

Chapter Twenty-three

Ausdehnung des Reichs II
(Expansion of the Reich II)

Hitler continued to make inflammatory speeches demanding that Germans in Czechoslovakia be reunited with their homeland. By May 1938, it was clear that Hitler and his generals were drawing up a plan for the occupation of Czechoslovakia. The military plan, named *Fall Grün*, was to build support among the officers of the army. With the exception of Ludwig Beck, Chief of the Army General Staff, and a few others, the majority of Hitler's senior officers were won over by his arguments. Consequently, *Fall Grün* laid out the strategy for an aggressive war against Czechoslovakia. Some of the plan's psychological warfare and use of paramilitary actions had already been carried out.

"The man has nerve," declared Hans Joachim to Herbert and Meira as they sat on the terrace near the Funkturm (radio tower) adjacent to the exhibition halls on a beautiful afternoon in late August.

"Ludwig Beck has resigned his position as Chief of the Army General Staff. He was a close friend of my wife's brother, Michael-Friedrich. As a matter of fact, I recall hearing he was a guest at the von Hohenberg estate before the Great War. I have wondered whether or not he might have had ideas about Frederika."

At this Meira smiled, and said, "I can easily believe that. She was a beautiful woman when I first met her, and as a young girl she must have been a stunning beauty."

Hans Joachim nodded and agreed. "She was. I never understood what she saw in me, but I can tell you, she was the love of my life, and she always said I was for her, too."

"Well, how did you hear about Beck's resignation, Papa?" asked Herbert.

"His personal physician is a friend of mine, and he said that Beck and Hitler had been at loggerheads for weeks, but Hitler would not be dissuaded from the idea that Czechoslovakia must be subdued, even at the risk of war. Beck apparently is convinced that all this talk about rescuing Germans living in the Sudetenland and pushing for control of that area, is just window dressing for Hitler's real intent: he intends to eventually take the whole country. If Hitler makes the move, Beck is convinced it will lead to an all-out European war. Therefore, he won't support it and in protest has resigned his position as Chief of the Army General Staff."

"Amazing!" declared Meira. "Those are the kind of Germans my father has always admired."

"Yes," added Herbert. "Too bad there aren't more of them."

§§§

Neither France nor Britain felt prepared to defend Czechoslovakia, however, and both were anxious to avoid a military confrontation with Germany at almost any cost. Both the French and British leadership believed that peace could be saved only by the transfer of the Sudeten German areas from Czechoslovakia.

In mid-September British Prime Minister, Neville Chamberlain, offered to go to Hitler's retreat at Berchtesgaden to discuss the situation personally with the *Führer*. Hitler agreed to take no military action without further discussion.

"I'm surprised at Chamberlain," grumbled Hans Joachim to Herbert and Meira as they strolled along the sandy path of the Havel peninsula, Schildhorn in the Grunewald, toward the Wirtshaus Schildhorn (restaurant) the day after the British Prime Minister had met with Hitler on September 15, in Berchtesgaden to discuss the Sudetenland issue.

He explained, "Konrad Henlein, the Sudetan German agitator in

Czechoslovakia, has persistently roused the German population in that area to support his movement to cede from the Czech state and join with the German Reich. He claims that Sudetan Germans are being abused by the Czech authorities. Encouraged by the easy success of the *Anschluß* of Austria, Hitler is seizing upon the opportunity to exaggerate those complaints and mount a campaign to 'liberate the German Czechs'."

The Munich Agreement of September 30, 1938, concluded by Germany, Great Britain, France, and Italy, permitted German annexation of the Sudetenland in Czechoslovakia.

§§§

"Do you remember Evka Horačková, Papa?" Meira asked Hans Joachim as she placed the goulash-filled tureen on the table one evening in the first week of October. Herbert and Meira were having him over frequently for meals, which he very much appreciated.

His brow furrowed in concentration, Hans Joachim replied, "I'm not sure. Where would I have seen her?"

"I remember her," volunteered Herbert. "She's that pretty little Czech girl who works in the pharmacy at Charité."

"Oh, the little blond girl with the cheerful personality and pretty smile?"

"That's the one," Meira assured her father-in-law. "Anyway, I saw her this afternoon at the bus stop on Pariser Platz, and she looked terrible. We sat together on the bus and she told me she's going home because her mother has had a stroke."

"Where was she from?" Hans Joachim asked.

"Český Těšín, on the northeast border with Poland. Except now it's Polish."

"What do you mean 'Polish'?" asked Herbert.

"Apparently, in the breakup of Czechoslovakia last month, Poland demanded to have the *Teschen* district in the Moravian-Silesian region returned to them. They claimed it was taken after the war in 1920.

Evka's family was notified by the Polish authorities they have to move off their farm, and the shock was too much for her mother, who has been in poor health for some time."

"Why did they have to move?" queried Hans Joachim.

"They were leasing the farm from a Polish owner, and he wanted to move some of his family onto the place, so Evka's family has to get out. She needs to go home to help with the move, but because of her mother's condition, she won't be back. It's a shame. She has a German boyfriend and really loves Berlin, but with the new Nazi laws about intermarriage of Germans with so-called 'inferior races', the relationship with her German wouldn't have had a future here, anyway."

Hans Joachim, his knuckles white with outrage grasping his cutlery, declared, "That poor country. They have been a jewel in the crown of Europe! What they accomplished in the twenty-plus years of their existence astonished the world. Tomas Masaryk was one of the most forward-looking statesmen of this century. As founder and first president of Czechoslovakia, he established a democratic, dynamic powerhouse in the heart of Europe. The Czech standard of living enjoyed by their citizens was the envy of all their neighbors, including Germany.

His American experience before the war at the University of Chicago and his American wife all had a lot to do with his thinking. He was a highly intelligent champion for the rights of oppressed people in Europe, and not just Czechs."

"He had an American wife?"

"Yes. She was Charlotte Garrigue from Brooklyn, New York." Shaking his head, he continued, "Now Hitler and his British and French buddies have torn the whole thing apart. It's good Masaryk died last year and didn't live to see what has happened to his life's work!"

Dismemberment of Czechoslovakia

May 1938

Hitler mobilizes the military to annex the Sudetenland - northern, southern, and western border districts in Bohemia, Moravia, and Czech Silesia

September 15, 1938

British Prime Minister Chamberlain meets with Hitler to discuss "peaceful solutions" to Sudetenland question

September 22, 1938

Chamberlain agrees to let Hitler annex Sudetenland - Czech military mobilizes

September 27, 1938

Poland demands Czechoslovakia surrender Tešín

September 29, 1938

Britain, France, Italy, and Germany sign Munich Agreement. Germany to "guarantee" Czech borders - after Poland gets Resin and Hungary gets some of Sub-Carpathian Ruthenia. Czechoslovakia not represented at the meeting. At the same time, Slovakian region demands independence. Czechoslovakia agrees to grant them more autonomy and hyphenate the country's name: Czecho-Slovakia.

March 1939

Hitler backs Slovak drive for independence. Slovakia wins independence. After 1940, Slovakia joins Axis powers.

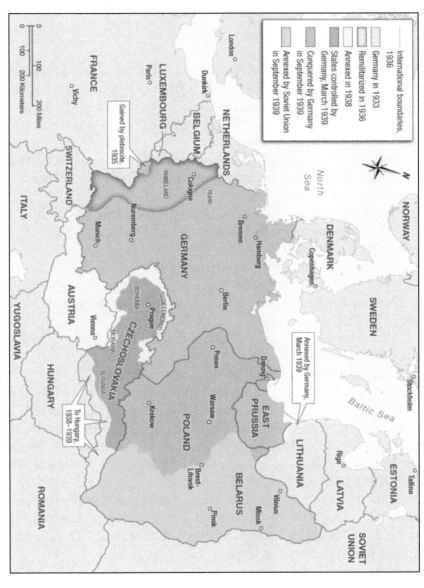

The Growth of Nazi Germany

Chapter Twenty-four

Ein arischer Mann
(An Aryan Man)

"What do you mean, he hit you?" Ursula asked her youngest son, Detlev, as she wiped the tears from his face with her apron.

Before he could answer, his older brother, Eckhardt, entered the kitchen and sneered at him, "There you are. I knew I'd find you here, *Muttersöhnchen* (Mama's boy)!"

"You stop that, and tell me what happened," demanded his mother.

"As a woman, you wouldn't understand," replied Eckhardt as he turned to go upstairs.

"What did you say?" she shouted as she walked toward him.

"I said, a woman wouldn't understand," which was immediately followed by a slap across his face.

"Don't you ever take that tone with me!"

Wide-eyed, he stared at her.

Hearing the altercation, Christina came downstairs and found her family glaring at each other.

"Nu, wat iss hier los?" (Now, what's going on here?) she asked in her Berlin dialect.

"Eckhardt punched me," volunteered little Detlev.

"It was an accident," responded the accused. "I was telling him all about the outing with the *HJ* in the *Grunewald* yesterday and about the training they're giving us. They drill us like soldiers and teach us self-defense and boxing. The runt here wanted me to show him some boxing moves. I showed him how to keep his guard up with his fists in front of his face and how to dance around. We were doing fine, until he hit me hard in the stomach. He got cocky and started calling me names like *Schwächling* (weakling). So, I swung at him and caught him with his guard down. I didn't hit him that hard," he related, with another scornful glance at the plaintiff.

"I've never been happy about him hanging around with those Nazis," declared his grandmother. "They're no good, and they're gonna take this country down. Just wait and see!"

"You'd better watch yourself, you old Commie!" shouted Eckhardt.

Another slap across the face!

"You're getting above yourself, young man. Wait until your father gets home! You apologize to your grandmother right now!

"Don't try to tell me what to do, you Jew lover!" Eckhardt stood before his mother, trembling with controlled rage.

Ursula stared back in disbelief at her son. Never in all the years since he was born had he ever turned on his family in such a manner. She looked at her mother, who stood ashen-faced at the foot of the stairs.

When he stepped in the door that evening, Eckhardt had sensed a heavy atmosphere in his home. Greeting his wife with a kiss, he enquired, "Is something wrong?"

After a pause, while she served up the components for the evening meal *(Abendbrot),* cold cuts of meat, *Quark* (similar to Greek yoghurt) and *Roggenbrot* (rye bread), she murmured, "We need to talk later."

The meal was eaten without conversation, until little Detlev spoke up, "Eckhardt hit me today, Papa."

"That's enough, Detlev. I'll explain it to your Papa later. Eat your supper," his mother declared.

"Yeah, but it was his own fault," the older boy chimed in.

"You were rude and disrespectful to me and your mother," interjected Christina.

The sharp slap of Ursula's hand on the table resounded through the room like a gunshot.

"I said, that's enough!" she shouted.

A curtain of silence fell. All eyes were focused on the wife and mother.

Eckhardt stared at his wife in total surprise. He was seeing a side of her he had never witnessed before. Everyone returned to their meal while Eckhardt continued to study Ursula's flushed countenance and her tear-filled eyes.

As soon as he closed their bedroom door, Ursula flung out her question.

"What do you think they're teaching those kids?" Ursula asked her husband.

"What do you mean?"

She then related the events of the early afternoon and added, "I've noticed a gradual change in Eckhardt, but I never expected anything like what happened here today. You know as well as I do that these theories of racial superiority have been the Nazi doctrine from the beginning. This is being stressed to the kids by their teachers and youth leaders to stifle compassion and empathy. They want to wipe out any tolerance for human differences – they want to develop a race with no compassion! They want these kids to obey without question. A stone can be worn away by water a drop at a time.

When I tried to talk to Eckhardt alone, and I pointed this out to him, he became more belligerent. He said Detlev needs to toughen up. That his *HJ* leader said it was the duty of every German boy to become a strong *arischer Mann*. That there was no room for sentimental, feminine softness in the new German man."

With furrowed brow, her husband said in a lowered voice, "Yes, we hear things like that in our political assemblies at Siemens. I haven't really taken it all too seriously, because political types are all the same. They love to stand up before a crowd and pontificate – like preachers. But I'm surprised they're indoctrinating the kids like that."

"You're too good natured and always look for the best in everybody, Eckhardt. I know when Herbert has tried to tell you about what this regime is trying to do, you have just brushed it off because he's married to Meira, and you think he has become a real sympathizer of the Jews."

His head bowed in thought, he replied, "I guess that's true. I had hoped that Hitler was going to fulfill his promises to make Germany a progressive modern nation that would regain the world's respect. What he accomplished the first few years in ending the Depression was phenomenal. Unemployment had virtually been wiped out, and work on the infrastructure went forward to a level that astonished the world. What foreigners saw here during the Olympics made me proud to be German."

"Are you proud of what I told you little Eckhardt is being taught in the Hitler Youth? Do you want Detlev to be introduced to the same thing? Do you want loving, respectful sons, or do you want them to be hard, insensitive 'Aryan Men'?"

Chapter Twenty-five

Friedlander Diaspora

Benjamin gazed through his tears at the crudely painted Stars of David smeared across the shop windows of his elegant store on Kurfürstendamm.

What a great day that was! Benjamin recalled the glorious day in 1886, as he and his father stood gazing proudly at the sign proclaiming *Friedlander und Sohn,* emblazoned in gold lettering. The original store on Leipzigerstraße near Spittelmarkt had just opened and was the culmination of many years of struggle by Gershom and Rahel Friedlander since their arrival in the German capital in 1859, the year of the pogrom in their village of Furmanivka in Russia, where Gershom had been a tailor.

As a youth, he strolled the elegant boulevard of Unter den Linden admiring the beautiful shops, cafes and restaurants along the way. In 1886, the steam tram service running from Zoologischer Garten to Hallensee was established and the construction of Kurfürstendamm quickly followed and became the upscale business district in the western part of the city. Benjamin promised himself he would one day own a store on the beautiful thoroughfare.

They had fled their home in the middle of the night and made the 1,000-mile trek to Berlin on foot, with Rahel giving birth to a stillborn child, a boy, by the side of the road near Krakow in Poland. After burying their baby in a nearby field, they continued on with Gershom carrying his wife on his back. They survived by begging and Gershom working sporadically for farmers in return for food. Upon arriving in Berlin after three months on the road, penniless and malnourished, they had been taken in by a Jewish family who had a small shop selling used clothing in the working-class district of Kreuzberg.

For the next several years, Gershom and Rahel worked with their hosts collecting, mending and cleaning used clothing for resale.

Gershom was able to acquire a sewing machine and gradually begin producing work clothing, which found a ready market in Kreuzberg. Then he turned his skills to producing men's suits and was able to demonstrate his ability by turning out goods of exceptional quality. His reputation was eventually established to the point he was able open the store on Leipzigerstraße.

During those years of struggle and great effort, the couple had to experience the trauma of another stillborn child, a little girl, in 1863. But finally, Rahel brought forth a healthy son, Chaim, in 1865, and another, Benjamin, in 1869.

Friedlander und Sohn prospered in the last years of the nineteenth century, and in 1905 the store was moved from the original location to a new building on bustling Kurfürstendamm. Unfortunately, Gershom Friedlander's health declined markedly in the years afterward, and he passed away in 1908, followed by his wife, Rahel, in 1912.

It's over, resolved Benjamin within himself. Turning to Kurt Wollner, he declared with grim determination, "Our time in Germany has ended."

They entered the building, and Benjamin surveyed the remains of the once-sought-after merchandise upon which he and his father had built their reputation.

"What's next?" queried his friend and protector.

"A representative of a group of so-called "Aryan" clothing manufacturers has been trying to negotiate with me for the sale of my store. Beginning in January, the new government policy of the "Aryanization" of the economy has forced many Jewish owners to sell their businesses. So, it's only a matter of time until I'll be contacted by the police – or even by the Gestapo, if I refuse to sell."

Kurt Wollner, though not surprised, heard the words of defeat from a man he respected with sadness and shame for what had become commonplace in his country.

"I'm sorry, Mr. Friedlander. As I've told you before, I'm ready to help you in any way I can.

After Albert Grsesinski was removed as police president, I've lost contact with many of my old comrades. Nowadays, it's hard to know what some people think of the regime, in spite of all the "hurrah" noise they make when they think someone is watching. But as far as the current man in charge is concerned, this von Helldorf person, I don't know him personally. Some of my old pals with the police think he's a decent chap, but again, how do you know for sure? So, expecting any backup from the police is too risky."

Putting his arm on his friend's shoulder, Benjamin replied, "That's alright, Wollner. You've done so much for me already. I don't want you to put yourself and your family in more danger. But I appreciate your concern."

Regarding each other with mutual respect, they turned and after locking the front doors, walked through the back entrance to the car waiting outside.

Upon returning home, Benjamin and Golda called a family conference at their Charlottenburg home for the following evening. Herbert and Meira were contacted, and all were present as planned. Benjamin laid out his plans for the sale of the store and their house. Golda was reduced to tears at the thought of leaving her beloved home but was comforted by her daughters, Edna and Meira. Herbert witnessed the wrenching tragedy brought on this family by fanatics among his own people, not the least of these being his own brother.

Finally, Benjamin concluded by saying, "We should count our blessings. We have assets with the sale of our property and the liquidation of our stocks. Fortunately, the Nazis are still allowing us to withdraw our savings and take most of our money out of the country if we emigrate to Palestine. Think about Jews all over Germany who don't have such resources to fall back on. I dread to think what they might be facing if this regime continues on its present course."

Herbert spoke up, "Be assured, Mr. Friedlander, my father will be ready to do what he can for you when he hears about this." Meira looked with love and admiration at her man.

"Thank you, Herbert for that. And please be assured, we won't involve him unless we absolutely have to."

"I know Papa Lenz," Meira interjected. "He'll want to be involved.

His compassion for others knows no bounds. He has defended Herbert and me whenever anyone hints that our marriage is unacceptable to them."

Benjamin felt the heat of shame upon hearing this. He had never forgiven himself for his own rejection of his daughter and son-in-law when he had learned of their relationship and subsequent marriage.

"Oh, Benji! You look exhausted," Golda cried as she helped him remove his coat and hat. "I've kept your dinner warm for you. I expected you much earlier." It was well past their normal dinner hour one evening in April 1938. Benjamin had spent a good part of the day awaiting a turn to speak to an official at the British Embassy.

"Thanks, dear. You wouldn't believe what I've heard today about leaving this country. It's going to be much, much harder than I thought."

"But didn't you say the government is encouraging Jews to emigrate to Palestine and will even allow us to take most of our money with us?"

"Yes. Dealing with the German authorities is the easy part, for a change. But it turns out the British are resisting Jewish emigration into their jurisdiction."

"Why?" asked Golda, her eyes wide with surprise.

"The man I spoke to was very courteous, as the English usually are. But his government is concerned that a large influx of Jews would cause conflict with the Arab population there. And listen to this: apparently some Jews already living there would also not welcome us because we would occupy their already limited living space. Can you believe that?"

Golda stared at her husband in disbelief.

Chapter Twenty-six

Christina's Lows and Highs

"*Guten Morgen, Frau Meinert!*" greeted Ursula's neighbor.

"*Guten Morgen,*" responded Ursula. It was a sunny spring morning in 1938.

"How have you been? Is everyone doing well at your house? I see those boys growing up. My, they are fine looking boys."

"Thank you. Yes, we're doing fine. And you?"

"Oh, can't complain. But at my age, what good would it do?" A chuckle.

"I'm glad you're doing well."

"How's your mother? I don't see her out in the garden like I used to."

With a slight frown, Ursula thought to herself, *some people may not be nosy, but they still have to know everything.*

"She's well." A pause. "She's just keeping to her room a lot."

"In weather like this? She used to spend so much time with her flowers. I've said before: your mother has always kept the finest flower garden on the whole street. And those roses! I see you haven't put any new ones in this year."

"No, I've always left that up to Mother. But she just hasn't shown any interest in it."

"How odd! You're sure she's alright?"

Ursula concentrated on a weed before bending over and pulling it up. *I might as well tell her. She won't let up until I do.*

"Actually, Mother has been in a downer, since my brother joined the Luftwaffe."

"The Luft Hansa pilot! My goodness. What prompted him to do that?"

"After he returned from the civil war in Spain, where he flew a bomber, he's been restless. And like a lot of the rest of us, he's afraid a war is coming. If it does, pilots like him will be conscripted, anyway. Then he's sure he'll be assigned to fly bombers after flying airliners for years. He was assured he would be able to choose fighters, if he volunteered now. He was right, and now he's in training on the new fighter, a Messerschmitt.

But my mother has taken it really hard. She lost my Dad in the last war, and another son and a daughter in the 1918 pandemic. So, Rudi and me are all she has left."

Shaking her head, *Frau* Lortz commiserated, "I can understand how she feels. I lost two brothers in the war. It nearly killed my mother."

Then she brightened and said, "I have just the thing for her. It will really bring her out of it."

"What's that?"

"It's a new antidepressant. You don't need a prescription. I have a cousin, a merchant sailor in Rostock, who was almost suicidal after he lost a foot in a shipboard accident. He's taking it now, and his wife says he's a different man. Hardly sleeps, but has boundless energy."

"Hmm. It sounds like mother could really use something like that. I'll get my mother to try it."

"Eckhardt. Wake up. What's that noise?"

Groggy, Eckhardt grumbled, "What noise? What time is it?"

Looking at the wall clock in the early morning light, Ursula declared, "It's only 5:15."

"So much for a nice Saturday sleep-in," complained her husband, rising from his bed. Ursula followed suit. Together, they went to the back door, opened it, and peered into the garden.

"Mama! What are you doing out there?"

Christina, furiously digging up earth in the rose garden, paused and answered, "Oh, good morning. Did I wake you? I'm sorry. I was getting a shovel out of the garden shed. I'm getting the ground ready for some new roses."

Ursula looked at her husband and smiled. "What in the world has she been given?"

Eckhardt, annoyed, grumbled, "She's probably on Pervitin."

"Pervitin?"

"Yeah. You can get it over the counter in any pharmacy, and it's really popular now."

Chapter Twenty-seven

Tulip festival

The front door slammed. Edna came out of the kitchen finding her father pale and shaking in the front hallway.

"Papa! What's the matter?"

"Those bastards!" exclaimed Benjamin white with fury. "I met with the representatives of that Aryan Clothing Manufacturers Association at the store today to close the sale. They had looked the property over months ago and we had agreed on a price. They're practically stealing the place anyway, but now they claim I had misrepresented the amount of goods that goes with the store. They actually accuse me of stealing merchandise and selling it. They want me to "replace" merchandise back to the inventory level of three years ago, when I was still in full operation. I told them out of the question, and one guy actually threatened to take the keys away from me and throw me out! Out of my own store! Lucky Wollner was there. He was able to smooth things over. They left and said I would hear from them in the near future. That could be bad – very bad. On the way home, Wollner urged me to get my affairs in order as quickly as possible and get out of here. But what can I do? Until this issue with the store is settled, I can't do anything."

By this time, Golda had come down from upstairs and upon hearing the last part of Benjamin's rant, grasped his arm and said with determination, "Benji, stop!"

"Yes, Papa. Come into the kitchen and sit down. I'll make tea and you can calm down."

"Calm down! Stop! Do you people hear yourselves? We hear of Jews all the time being arrested and disappearing. We could be next. There's nothing to stop these people from grabbing everything we have and taking us God knows where."

Both women looked at each other as if to get help from the other in dealing with their distraught husband and father.

After a few moments, Golda said softly, "Benji, there's really nothing new in all of this. We've known for a long time now that the Nazis are ruthless and dangerous. You mustn't provoke them. Of course, you can't afford to restock the merchandise you had three years ago, but you must find a way to get the store sold and then this house. Offer to lower the price, if they will take the store as is and we'll take what we can get and go."

"Mama's right, Papa. You're in no position to bargain with them. I talked to Meira on the phone yesterday, and now she's afraid Herbert will lose his position at Charité, and he's only been in practice for a little over a year. Even with his father's connections, they're concerned. People like him who are married to Jews are getting a lot of pressure now, too. Under the racial laws they have the audacity to call it *"Rassenschande."* (racial pollution)

"Imagine! *Rassenschande!* What are we? Dirt?" sputtered Benjamin.

"Of course. To them we are," rejoined Golda. "But your moral indignation is of no interest to them, so don't waste your time getting yourself worked up over that. It's what it is. We've got work to do."

The silence was broken by the rumble of distant thunder heralding an early spring rain.

"A trip to Holland?" retorted Golda in astonishment, as she helped Benjamin remove his coat and hat on a pleasant evening in April.

"Yes," responded Benjamin. "Remember the trip we took to Holland ten years ago to the Tulip Festival at the Keukenhof in Lisse? You always wanted to go back, but we just never got around to it."

"I don't know how you can think of a vacation at a time like this," responded Golda, still puzzled.

"I think a little break from all this going on here will do us good," affirmed Benjamin. "Fortunately, we both have current passports which we used over the years on buying trips outside Germany. Wollner will be driving us, so he will accompany me to the Dutch consulate in the morning to apply for tourist visas."

"You say 'both of us'! What about Edna?"

"I've discussed this with her, and it was her idea that you and I should go first. Wollner will return here and assist Edna with the final sale of the store to the 'Aryan' clothing manufacturers. We might as well resign ourselves to the fact that we're not getting much for it anyway. Wollner knows a family who will give us a better price for the house than we would probably get on the open market. It won't be anywhere near what it's really worth, but at least we can get it sold quickly."

"But to leave Edna here by herself!" cried Golda. "That's insanity! I won't consider it!"

Taking a deep breath, Benjamin responded with carefully chosen words, "As I just said, Edna suggested this, and it's a brilliant idea. We have very capable daughters who have demonstrated they have minds of their own. Herbert and Meira are in on this and have assured me that they and Dr. Lenz stand ready to jump in if anything goes amiss. Besides, it will look better if we have unsold property here, and also, all three of us aren't trying to leave together. I will withdraw only enough money from one of our bank accounts to appear as a reasonable amount for travel expenses for a week or so and present a statement to the Dutch consulate. That way it won't look like we intend to stay in Holland, which should make acquiring a tourist visa easier."

Still not convinced and smarting from the fact that she had been left out of the decision making, Golda, after some hesitation, replied in a bitter tone, "Well, it looks like you've thought of everything, and I can see that everyone has their minds made up. But why wasn't I consulted? Don't I have a say in these things, or are we back to Benjamin Friedlander wrapping himself again in the mantle of 'the Jewish patriarch'"?

Deciding to let the sarcastic remark pass, he said in a softened tone of voice, "I'm sorry you see me that way, Golda, but this is a very dangerous situation, and I expected that you as a mother would object, but I didn't plan this from the outset, and things just seemed to fall into place. Edna sees the situation for what it is, and I am grateful for her courage and selflessness. You should be proud of her."

Seeing that further protest was useless, Golda threw out as a parting shot, "Tourist visas? For Jews? To leave Germany in times like this! Do you think the Dutch are stupid? How many families do we know who have already fled to the neighboring countries - including Holland! Good luck with that one, Benji!"

Without further comment, Golda returned to the kitchen stating, "Dinner will be ready shortly."

The line at the Dutch consulate was comprised of hundreds of visa-seeking people, including families with children, many of whom had been represented in line for weeks by family members taking turns from early morning until late in the evening. They endured all kinds of weather, doggedly determined to keep a place in line, until Berlin police forced them to leave – or be arrested for loitering and vagrancy. Benjamin, upon seeing this as Kurt Wollner pulled the car over to the curb, quickly decided to try another approach

"Take me back home, Wollner. I need to change, and then we'll go to the Thomas Cook & Son travel agency on Unter den Linden."

Having made sure to dress as smartly as possible, Benjamin presented himself at the front desk of the prestigious office as a confident Berlin businessman wishing to take a spring holiday. A middle-aged distinguished-looking travel agent conducted him to a small cubicle and began to interview his client.

"Well, Mr. Friedlander, how can I be of assistance?"

"My wife and I were impressed with Holland when we visited there a number of years ago. We were especially struck by the beauty of the tulip Festival, and we would like to experience that again. Would you book us at a good hotel in Lisse for one or two nights? After that, we would like to take the sea air at Zandvoort and would also like you to book us at the beach hotel there for two or three nights."

"Will you be requiring transportation while you're there?"

"Not necessary. I have my own car and driver, who is a retired Berlin police officer."

Impressed, the agent enquired, "Have you secured your Dutch tourist visas?"

"I have little time, and I would appreciate it if you could take care of that along with the bookings."

"May I ask you for your passports, please?"

"Of course," replied Benjamin as he handed over the documents.

When he had first heard the name of "Friedlander", the agent suspected he might be dealing with the owner of the prominent store of the same name, who he also knew was Jewish. This was confirmed as he opened Benjamin's passport and saw the heavy black stamp of "**J**" for *"Jude"* (Jew). This was followed by a long silence, after which the man enquired with lowered voice, "I see you are Jewish, Mr. Friedlander. Do you intend to return to Germany?"

He had expected this question, and Benjamin placed his hands palms down on the desk and leaning forward confided, "That's correct. But rest assured, I do not intend to put you to any unnecessary inconvenience."

Removing his hands from the desk, a 1.76 ounce 24 karat gold bar was left lying on the green felt pad.

The agent's eyes widened with astonishment. "I'm sorry, Mr. Friedlander. I didn't understand the urgency of your plans," he stammered.

"Well, now you do. This will be yours, if you can accomplish what I'm asking of you," Benjamin said, again pocketing the gleaming treasure.

Chapter Twenty-eight

Die Bekanntmachung
(The announcement)

Karlheinz walked beside his father along the shoreline of the Grunewaldsee. The rustle of new spring leaves betrayed the mood of the conversation. They walked along the beach across from the former Kaiser's hunting lodge.

There was a sadness which Hans Joachim could not conceal as he thought of his youngest son. *How oblivious I was when you were so young and innocent. You wanted my attention more than I ever knew, and I wasn't always there to provide you the guidance that a boy like you needed. I see now that I depended too heavily on Frederika to see to your needs when you needed your father.*

He paused and gazed across the water with a twinge of guilt, reliving the words of his beloved wife, Frederika: *A boy needs his mother. A boy must have what he wants. Give the boy what he wants. Oh, my baby, come to mother.*

"Why did you ask me here, Karlheinz?"

"I asked you here today because I have an important announcement that I want to share with you, Papa. We used to come here together when was I was a boy, and it is one of my favorite childhood memories. I can't think of a better place to share this with you."

However, when he informed his father what he was planning, Karlheinz encountered cold opposition.

A dark scowl clouded Hans Joachim's face. "I'm sorry, Karlheinz. I try to understand how much this means to you, but I don't understand you at all. We're not that kind of people. Why have you been attracted to those...*people?* What do you think your mother would say, if she were here?"

Stung to be reminded of the person who had always been his support, Karlheinz blurted, "Why can't you be proud of me? It's not just now. You and Herbert have always treated me as someone you're both ashamed of. I never do anything right. Mama is the only person in this family who ever loved me. Why can't you be more like her?"

"I love you with all my heart, Karlheinz."

Karlheinz only shook his head and turned away. His father's response had seriously upset him. "But you don't see what an honor this is for me? The *Führer* has done so much for us, Papa! Before he came, we were a defeated people! People were starving and begging in the streets! Think of the humiliation when they took Grandfather's estate and gave it to a foreign nation! The *Führer* has told us to lift our heads high! Be proud to be German! He gave the starving bread and jobs and land and pride! My service to the *Führer* is a small sacrifice, but it is a dedication demanded of the Aryan race!"

He turned to walk away.

"Karlheinz, please come back here," pleaded Hans Joachim as he caught up to his son. He placed a hand on his boy's shoulder and shook his head at this sudden outburst of fanaticism.

"Of course, I love you, and your brother does, too. But think about the things you've said to him. You have offended his wife on more than one occasion, and you have chosen to associate with some of the most reprehensible and dangerous people of our society. Think of your friend, Lutz Steinhauer, and what happened to him! Doesn't that tell you anything? And this Lehmann fellow: Who is he? Where does he come from? Is he the one who talked you into this?"

"Leave Dieter out of it! I decided to join them on my own. It offers career opportunities to any good German male who can qualify."

"What career opportunities? A career of intimidation of others? Of persecution of the defenseless?"

"Somebody needs to stand up for the Aryan race, before the Jews and gypsies push us out! What kind of German are you, always befriending Jews and standing by while your son marries one?"

"Don't go there, Karlheinz! Meira has proven herself to be a person of real character and one who loves your brother devotedly. It's a rare woman who would put herself at such risk as she did, volunteering as an army nurse in order to search for her man at the front – and she did it in opposition to her own father! Countless German soldiers would have been dead if it weren't for her. Now her family has been broken up and her parents driven out of their own country by people like the ones you call your friends! How can you expect me to be happy about that?"

Breaking away from his father's grasp, he walked along the path, tears coursing down his face.

"You will always be my son, Karlheinz, but don't bring Dieter Lehmann or any others of that kind to my home."

§§§

"You look stunning!" exclaimed Dieter Lehmann as Karlheinz admired himself in the full-length mirror in their bedroom. His new SS uniform was a perfect fit. The black tunic, breeches, and polished boots set off the blond good looks of the wearer.

With Dieter's endorsement, Karlheinz had passed the induction requirements of the elite organization with flying colors. Now he could see himself as a true champion of the New Order.

Chapter Twenty-nine

An Empty House

After waiting anxiously for word from the travel agent at Thomas Cook for almost a week, Benjamin received the phone call from the man informing him that the visas and confirmation of the hotel reservations could be picked up. He related this to Golda, who had been busy for days sorting and deciding what to pack. Kurt Wollner, who was to drive them to Lisse, was notified.

"Golda would like you to come for dinner this evening, Wollner. Could we say about *neunzehn Uhr dreißig* (7:30 pm)? My daughter, Meira, and her husband will join us. In fact, why don't you bring your suitcase with you and you can sleep here tonight. Then we can leave directly from here in the morning."

"Thank you, Mr. Friedlander. I've had the car serviced and fueled, so it's ready."

"Excellent. We'll go by the travel agency, pick up the visas and leave straightaway."

After concluding the excellent meal, Benjamin looked at his family and friend, and with deep emotion began, "You are my dear ones. We are gathered around this table for the last time, and I want you all to know how much I regret, due to my stubbornness, we lost so much time when we could have enjoyed gatherings such as this."

Meira, mist-eyed, reached out and grasped his arm, "Don't Papa. That's over. We both could do things much better, if we were to do them again. I was defiant and determined to declare my independence. I should have been more direct and open when I realized I loved Herbert. Instead, I went behind your back and lied to you, saying I was staying overnight with a friend when Herbert and Eckhardt went to the front in the war."

"Now you're doing it, Meira," admonished her sister, Edna. "We should be looking forward, not back."

"You're right, Edna. I'm glad you're being practical. You're taking on a lot, my girl. Fortunately, you'll have Wollner here to help you."

"That's right, Mr. Friedlander. As soon as I get back, I'll get in touch with the people who are buying this house. And Edna, I'll be with you when you close the deal for the store with that 'Aryan' clothing manufacturer bunch."

Golda nodded, "Thank you, Mr. Wollner. It takes a load off my mind knowing a good person like you will be watching over my little girl."

"Mama, don't take on so. Edna is not a 'little girl'," corrected Meira. "We're talking about a woman picking up huge responsibilities for her family. And of course, Herbert and I will do whatever we can, too."

"That's very well, Meira. But you and Herbert are on thin ice, too, and you need to be making plans for your own future, which I doubt will be here much longer, the way things are going," counseled her father.

Kurt Wollner took this in and interjected, "I can't tell you people how ashamed I am of my own people. I would never have believed such things could happen in our country."

"Amen to that!" concluded Herbert.

Edna watched the car go around the corner and disappear. She then turned and entered the empty house, closed the massive front door, and made her way through the darkened hallway to the library. Sinking into her father's chair, she surrendered herself to the sense of fearful loneliness.

What have I done? I can't do this by myself. Why didn't I go with them? Forget the house! Forget the store! The thoughts battled each other in her mind. Shaking with gut-wrenching sobs, she put her face into her hands. *Will I ever see them again?*

The Maybach limousine rolled quietly along the new autobahn past Magdeburg heading west. Leaving his Horch behind for Edna's use, Benjamin had purchased the car in preparation for the trip from his banker and brother-in-law, Marcus Eisenstadt, at *Mendelssohn & Co.*

Golda's brother had been assigned to take over the London branch of the bank when the directors had decided to close the Berlin facility due to increasing antisemitism in Germany.

Gazing at the sandy plain of Brandenburg, Golda tried not to think of the home and daughters she was leaving.

Benjamin, on the other hand, contemplated the arrival of his grandparents in the German capital penniless, and how after years of struggle they worked their way up to establishing themselves in the clothing industry, and ultimately opened the first store of *Friedlander und Sohn.* Now all that was left behind, soon to be sold at a giveaway price. He had to force himself to brush away the image of the black cloud of danger that hung over his family like the albatross of Coleridge's poem, *The Rime of the Ancient Mariner.*

At the Dutch border crossing of Enschede, Benjamin, Golda, and Wollner surrendered their passports to the officer at the checkpoint, who looked at the well-dressed couple, their "chauffeur", and the big car. The large "J" stamped on Benjamin's and Golda's passports caught his eye and prompted him to ask, "How long do you plan to stay in Holland?"

"About two weeks. We're here to see the tulip festival at the *Keukenhof* and stay a couple of nights in Lisse, then spend some time at the seaside at Zandvoort."

Scrutinizing Benjamin very carefully, the officer finally stamped the passports and handed them back. As they rolled away from the border, Wollner looked in the rearview mirror and saw Benjamin tearfully embrace his wife, who was sobbing uncontrollably.

Chapter Thirty

Prelude to *Kristallnacht*

"The Graubarts have been deported," cried Meira to Herbert as he came home the evening of October 28th.

"Who's that, and what are you talking about?"

"They're old friends of my parents. They used to attend Saturday *Shabbat* (Sabbath services) together. I was talking to Edna this afternoon and she told me. The government expelled 'Polish' Jews over a week ago and sent them to Poland. Now the Nazis are arresting Jews of Polish origin, and other *Ostjuden* (eastern Jews). The Graubart family have been living in Germany longer than my family have, but their ancestors originally came from Poland. Edna is terrified, because maybe that makes our family 'Polish', too, even though my grandparents only came through Poland after leaving Russia."

"What craziness will the Nazis think of next? Edna should come here. It's not good that she's alone in that big house, anyway. Why don't you call her and tell her to drive over here? If she's afraid to come alone, I'll go over there on the bus and come back with her."

The hall phone shrilled in the darkness of the Friedlander home.

"She's not picking up!" wailed Meira. "Oh, I should have gone right over as soon as she called."

"No, you shouldn't have. I hope nothing has happened to her, but I'm glad you weren't there. You might have been picked up, too, if that's what has happened to her."

"What are we gonna do?' anguished Meira.

"I'm calling the police."

After a long wait, Herbert was able to speak to a police captain. "We have nothing to do with that, Dr. Lenz. That would be a Gestapo matter," and he abruptly hung up.

Staring at the phone receiver in his hand, Herbert was enraged. "Bastards! I'm driving down to Gestapo headquarters myself. They'd better have some answers!"

"You're not doing any such thing, Herbert. You're not going into that hornet's nest. Your temper will get the best of you, and we'll all be in trouble. And that won't help Edna, if they've arrested her."

"You're right. I'll call and do my best to be humble."

After being told he would need to come to the Gestapo building, Herbert called his father.

Upon hearing the shocking news, Hans Joachim directed, "You meet me at Prinz-Albrecht-Straße, Herbert, but leave Meira at home. I'll drive by the Friedlander house on the way and have a look."

When he relayed this to her, Meira objected in the strongest terms. "It's my sister we're looking for, and if she's there, I need to be the one to meet her."

"Think about what you're saying," retorted her husband. "If the Gestapo are looking for members of your family, they'll arrest you on the spot. It would save them the trouble of looking for you. They probably know by now your parents are out of reach and will be doubly eager to get their hands on you. Besides, I'm sure somebody there wants to take down the high and mighty Friedlander family. No, you stay here out of sight, and don't answer the doorbell. As soon as I know what's happening with Edna, I'll call you. I'll let the phone ring three times, then hang up, and immediately call again. When you answer, don't speak to anyone except me."

Subdued and tearful, she nodded her head slowly that she understood. As Herbert took his coat off the hall tree, the phone rang.

"Meira, answer that please. I need to go," and he went out the door. He had only descended a few steps when Meira rushed out and leaning over the railing, cried, "Herbert! Come back! Your father is on the line and needs to talk to you."

"Herbert, you need to get right over here! Don't bring Meira. She mustn't see this."

"What is it?"

"Just get here!"

As he pulled up to the curb, Herbert's attention was drawn to the small group of people gathered before the front gate of the Friedlander home, among them a couple of SA men, who were in an argument with Hans Joachim.

Front windows had been smashed, the entry door kicked in, crude stars of David smeared on the walls in white paint. The curious onlookers muttered among themselves, and Herbert overheard comments ranging from, "That's right, arrogant Jews!" to, "What a disgrace!" which led to little disputes among themselves.

"That Jew bitch brought this on herself, with her wise-ass mouth. People like her need to learn whose country this is and be put in their place!"

Red-faced, Herbert's father leaned in close to the husky young Nazi, with their faces a few inches apart. "I hope to God you don't think this country belongs to people like you. Bullying a woman living alone. Are you gonna' clean this mess up?"

The young SA man challenged, "Who are you, old man? You better get outta here, before you get hurt."

"Clearly you haven't been watching the latest productions from Minister Goebbels about me and my work. Next time I am asked to treat the *Führer*, perhaps I should mention your name and have you enlightened?"

Dr. Lenz watched the blood drain from his tormentor's face as the recognition of whom he was addressing came into the mind of the young SA man. The thought of a reprimand by such an important figure terrified him, and he was unable to move. Seeing their comrade lose control, two Nazis began to separate him from the enraged Dr. Lenz.

Grasping his father's arm and choking down his own anger, Herbert said softly, "Come on Papa. This accomplishes nothing."

Uttering a few more blistering comments, Hans Joachim allowed himself to be pulled away.

"Good Lord, what happened here?" began Herbert, as they entered the house and were greeted with the sight of ransacked rooms, drawers open which had been emptied with contents thrown on the floor, smashed mirrors, and furniture smashed and overturned.

"One of the neighbors said a group of teenage hooligans came by here earlier and stood outside the gate harassing Edna," reported his father. Apparently, she came outside and got into an argument with them. You know Edna. She and Meira are not girls to take much off anyone. But Edna should have picked another battle, given what's going on nowadays.

Anyway, things got pretty heated, and the kids started throwing rocks at her. She threatened to call the police and went back inside. The punks finally pulled up some paving bricks and threw them through the windows. They only dispersed when a big Mercedes pulled up, and four Gestapo guys got out. They apparently didn't wait for Edna to answer the door; they just kicked it in, hauled Edna out, put her in the car and drove away. The punks who had been watching around the corner or hidden across the street, came back, went inside and did all this – probably got some paint that Benjamin had and smeared all that graffiti on the walls."

Herbert looked around in dismay and shock. "That settles it! It's time for me to get Meira out of here. Can we come out to your house tonight?"

"Of course. You bring what you need – just what you can carry! You can go back to your apartment in a couple of days, and if nothing has been disturbed, you can pack more stuff. This might blow over for a little while, but I think you're right. These people will eventually go after all Jews, no matter where they are. And you can bet you're on their list, too, for being married to one. Yes, it's time for you to go.

As far as you going to the Gestapo with me, you better forget about that. I'll follow up on Edna. They won't touch me – at least not yet."

§§§

On October 16, 1938, the German government arrested 12,000 Jews, most of whom were holders of Polish passports, with the intent of deporting them to Poland. The Polish government, however, would only admit 4,000 into the country, leaving 8,000 stranded on the German-Polish border. Less than two weeks later on the 28th, the Nazis arrested 17,000 more Jews of Polish descent with the intent of forcing Poland to admit them. The Poles refused, leaving about 25,000 people in the no-man's land on the border between Germany and Poland. Finally, at the end of October, the Polish authorities allowed the homeless refugees to settle in Poland, which many did. Some managed to emigrate to other countries. But in the end, not only Poland, but other countries closed their borders to stem the flood of Jewish immigrants.

Chapter Thirty-one

Kristallnacht
(Night of Broken Glass)

Little Eckhardt looked around his father's shed at the tools hanging on the wall."

"Hurry up!" yelled Jürgen from the truck piled with rowdy teenagers as it sat idling at the side of the curb. "We're going to miss all the fun!"

Sprinting to the vehicle with his arms full, he threw his selected load into an open box of weapons. He jumped into the back, and before he could find a place to sit, the truck, driven by a man dressed in an SA uniform, lurched as it sped off.

The clock in the hallway chimed the hour of three early in the afternoon of October 9, 1938, as a clearly disturbed Ursula stepped out on the front porch. "Eckhardt, come quick! Something is happening out here! Eckhardt just snuck out with his friends from the Hitler Youth before I could stop him!"

Thick columns of smoke were seen rising from all directions of the city, and Ursula was in a panic. "There are fires everywhere, and listen to all those sirens! Oh, Eckhardt, this is really bad!"

Eckhardt, opening the front door and seeing the black smoke for himself, immediately pulled her into an embrace and tried to soothe his wife. "I wouldn't worry about it too much. It's just a reaction to Goebbels's speech. They're probably just heading to some demonstrations and are going to blow off a little steam. You know how teenagers can be."

"You should be ashamed of yourself, Eckhardt!" was Ursula's vehement reprimand.

"Well, I'm sorry you feel that way, but I still say those people bring some of these things on themselves," Eckhardt flung back his stubborn response.

"A crazy kid shoots a German, and the Nazis use that as a pretext for persecuting a whole community of people! And you agree with that?" countered his wife. "Think about our friend, Meira, and what her family is going through. Her parents are refugees and gone, and now her sister has disappeared. She and Herbert are leaving soon, too."

"I don't condone it, and you should know me better than that. But any Jew who attacks a German in times like these should think about how such a thing could backlash on his people."

"Are you avoiding Herbert? I don't hear about you two getting together anymore like you used to," queried his wife.

"I'm sorry about that, but every time we talk, he starts a rant about the leaders. He refuses to see another side of the story."

"And of course, you always point out the great things the Nazis have done."

"Well, facts are facts. Look at your brother. A slum kid like Rudi would never have had his success, except for the forward thinking of this government."

"I think Rudi should get most of the credit. He's smart and has worked hard to get where he's at. And now Nazis are running loose in the streets. It's like no one is trying to use judgement anymore. While we're on the subject, what do you think about the things we hear from our son? He's really changed since he's gotten involved with those people in *Hitler Jugend.* Where is he heading now? Probably out there running with them and acting like a wild animal."

With a thoughtful expression, Eckhardt concluded, "Well, I agree with you on that. I have to talk to him."

"Be careful with that. Kids nowadays talk to their youth leaders and teachers. I've heard of some parents being questioned by the Gestapo about things their kids have reported. We have seen several anti-Jewish outbreaks in Germany since Hitler came to power, but never anything as nauseating as what this appears to be."

With a worried expression, Eckhardt considered his wife's admonition.

After a 30-minute race through the streets of Berlin, the truck full of teenagers and young SA men approached the central district of Charlottenburg before coming to a stop in the middle of a crowded street, unable to proceed any further.

Jürgen immediately jumped out. An uneasy little Eckhardt followed, after some hesitation. Urged on by their rowdy and boastful travel companions, they proceeded to choose their selected tools. The city was loaded with hordes of hooligans indulged in an orgy of destruction.

"They have no rights!"

"The Jews are an occupying Power!"

"Get the Devils!"

The rallying cries from all around led Jürgen to pick up a rock and throw it through the front window of a business with a crude white Star of David painted on the brick facade. Urged on by the crowd and his friend, Eckhardt squeezed his hammer and became one with the masses as they surged into the Jewish businesses. The pace of the attacks on all things Jewish had accelerated into a frenzied riot. Racial hatred and hysteria seemed to have taken complete hold of an otherwise decent people. Fashionably dressed women were clapping their hands and screaming with glee, while other respectable middle-class mothers held up their babies to see the activities.

Leaving a desecrated shop, Eckhardt and Jürgen raced out the door onto the sidewalk. They ran across the street to the next target. This was a small watchmaker's shop, which had already been smeared with paint. As they neared the entrance, Jürgen shouted, "Look! There are a couple of old Kikes. Let's get 'em!"

Eckhardt's attention was drawn to an elderly couple clutching to one another and trembling with fear. He looked at the old woman's tear-stained face. Jürgen raced up to them and shoving them aside, smashed the window of the shop. He then turned and tore the old man away from his wife, began to beat him, and threw him on the sidewalk.

"Dirty Kike, Jew bastard!" followed by kicks to his unfortunate victim, now lying in the fetal position.

Eckhardt neared the old woman, who shrank back from him in terror, her hands clasped beneath her chin. Her eyes brimming with tears, she pleaded, "Why, why, why?"

The question penetrated his consciousness. *Why am I doing this?*

Jürgen, having satisfied his lust for vengeance, turned and asked, "What are you doing, Eckhardt? Hit her! What's the matter with you?"

Eckhardt turned and wordlessly walked away.

§§§

Although there had been many anti-Semitic attacks on the Jewish population, this was the first coordinated, nation-wide attack on Jewish citizens under the Nazi regime. On November 8, a 17-year-old German born Polish Jew, Herschel Grynszpan, had murdered the third secretary in the German Embassy in Paris, Ernst vom Rath. It was widely assumed that the assassination was politically motivated. Word of vom Rath's death reached Hitler, leading Propaganda Minister Joseph Goebbels to deliver a speech in which he said, "The *Führer* has decided that... demonstrations should not be prepared or organized by the party, but insofar as they erupt spontaneously, they are not to be hampered." The message was clear. Goebbels had commanded the party leaders to organize a pogrom.

The German civilian population, led by SA Stormtroopers, unleashed a two-day pogrom on the 9th and 10th of November against the Jewish people throughout Germany, Austria, and the Sudetenland. Synagogues and Jewish owned homes, hospitals, schools and businesses were burned by rioters. So many store windows were smashed with sledgehammers that the streets were littered with broken glass, leading to the euphemistic name, *Kristallnacht* (Crystal Night).

The damage done on that November night in 1938 went far beyond broken windows. Around the country, thousands of Jewish citizens were attacked. Hundreds were murdered, and 7,500 businesses were looted or destroyed. Cemeteries were desecrated with tombstones uprooted and graves violated. 267 synagogues, some of them hundreds of years old, were burned, and over 20,000 Jews were arrested and sent to concentration camps.

The real motive behind the murder of vom Rath is unclear. Both Grynszpan and vom Rath had been seen in Paris gay bars, and some sources indicate that they were homosexual lovers. One proposed motive for the murder was that vom Rath had reneged on a promise to secure a French residence permit for Grynzspan, who was without German citizenship, due to the Nuremberg laws, which denied citizenship to many German born Jews.

On November 12, the Jewish community in Germany was fined 1 billion Reichsmarks by the German government as a penalty for the death of Ernst vom Rath.

On December 6, French Foreign Minister Georges Bonnet allegedly informed German Foreign Minister Joachim von Ribbentrop in Paris, that the French government henceforth would recognize all of Eastern Europe as Germany's exclusive sphere of influence. This statement, which Bonnet denied having made, was ostensibly a major factor in the formation of German policy in 1939.

Chapter Thirty-two

Auf Wiedersehen Berlin

"We should go and get my father's car, before some Nazi 'confiscates' it," declared Meira, as they laid clothes out on their bed for sorting a few days after Edna's disappearance. "We can carry a lot more if we take the Horch instead of our little Opel."

"That's true," replied Herbert. "If we knew where Edna was, and when she might be coming back, we would leave it for her, as Benjamin would want. But we'll leave our car with Papa, and I'll sign it over to him. He can give it to Edna, or sell it, as he sees fit."

"I'm sorry to involve your father in all of my family's problems. I hope he won't get himself in trouble bothering the Gestapo for information about my sister."

"When are you going to look at our two families as one? And Papa will keep trying to get answers about Edna – you can depend on it."

"Thank you, sweetheart, for saying that. I must have done something really good in another life to get you as a husband, and I'm grateful for you."

"I'm the one who should be grateful. You have stood by me from the beginning, like no other wife would have. I tell people about you volunteering as an army nurse during the war, just so you could go to the front and look for me. Half of them probably think I'm making it up," he said with a grin, as he gave his wife a big bear hug.

"We were young and thought we could do anything in those days. Kids that age think they're bulletproof," she replied with a chuckle.

"Well, we're gonna' need some of that courage now. Everybody is. We see now where this regime is leading this country."

Shaking her head, Meira admonished, "Let's not think about it now. We've got to get out to Dahlem."

The farewell dinner in Hans Joachim's dining room had been partaken of by the three for the most part in deep introspection. As he surveyed the remnants of his family, his thoughts turned to times in the past when his dear Frederika presided over the table. He had to push away the memory of the night of her death, which seemed to have marked a turning point in his family. Although there had previously been strife which had played out around this table, the division between his two sons had become more pronounced after her demise. *Oh, Karlheinz, where are you, my boy?* The question plagued him.

"I'm really going to miss you, Papa," declared Meira in a choked voice, as she reached across and grasped her father-in-law's hand.

He returned her misty-eyed gaze. "And I'm going to miss you, my dear. I can never adequately express the gratitude I and my wife felt for your loyalty to Herbert during the war. I only wish I didn't have to send you two away from here, out into the wilderness of a Europe about to plunge itself into another war."

After a moment, he turned to Herbert and enquired, "So, have you gotten in touch with your contact in France to let them know you're coming?"

"No, not yet. I won't do that until after I cross the border. I don't want to do anything that might let anybody in Germany know where we're going."

Nodding his head, Hans Joachim agreed. "Of course. I should have thought of that. And in that connection, please rest assured I won't say a word to your friends Eckhardt and Ursula. With their son heavily involved in *Hitler Jugend*, the less they know at this time, the better. I hear horror stories all the time about parents being questioned by the Gestapo for things their kids have reported or inadvertently passed on to the authorities about them."

"And I hope you're not offended, Papa, when I say Karlheinz mustn't hear a word about this until we're long gone," inserted Meira.

"Of course I'm not offended, dear girl. I love both my sons, but the direction Karlheinz has taken his life, broke his mother's heart – and mine along with it."

"And I also hope you're not offended, if I don't tell you the route we're taking and where we'll cross the border," added Herbert. "The less you know the better in case you are questioned by the Gestapo. I will say this, though. I think I'll try to cross at some out-of-way border crossing."

"Oh, no I don't agree. You should choose a crossing point on one of the major roads with a lot of traffic, especially a lot of long distance trucks. The officers will be so busy, you'll have a better chance of blending in with the crowd. And anyway, if for some reason the Gestapo wants to track you down, they will issue an all-points bulletin to every crossing station."

"Why are they so intent on harassing Meiria's family, Papa? There are thousands of Jews they're arresting now for various reasons, but it seems they have especially targeted the Friedlanders. Arresting Edna was extreme."

After a long pause, Hans Joachim replied, "I didn't want to tell you this. You've got enough to worry about, but I had a call from Kurt Wollner yesterday."

"Kurt Wollner?" interrupted Meira. "I wonder if he's heard any more from my parents. He called last Spring and said everything went well at the Dutch border, but I haven't heard from him since."

"He didn't say anything about that. The reason he called was to say it's urgent that you leave as soon as possible. He already knew from somewhere about Edna and offered apologies that he didn't know anything more about her. But it turns out that he has a contact through one of his buddies in the police department, who has a source close to Reinhard Heydrich, head of the Gestapo. In turns out that Heydrich has a nephew in the SA. He had a run-in with Benjamin Friedlander years ago for passing out Nazi propaganda in front of his store. He was the leader of the gang of Brownshirts who beat up Benjamin. That guy, Jörg Clausen, has had it in for Benjamin ever since. He's been pushing his uncle Heydrich to go after everyone in Meira's family, including Meira."

Shaking his head, Herbert declared, "And all this time, we thought it was because of Benjamin's family background, or because he was a wealthy Jew with a prominent store on Ku'damm. Wow! Well, in that case, we'd better not try to leave in Benjamin's car. The Gestapo will have word out to look for that car and its number plates."

"I've already taken care of that, or at least Wollner has. He's gotten you another car – a small Mercedes 170 V sedan with other plates and auto documents. He's outside with a police buddy moving all your things into the other car as we speak."

Meira and Herbert stared at him. Finally, Herbert spoke up, "Is my father amazing, or what?"

Meira arose, came over and embraced Hans Joachim, with tears running down her face. She kissed him and exclaimed, "You are the kind of German who will save this country when this nightmare is over."

After having discussed it in the privacy of Herbert's old bedroom, the couple decided to leave that very night and drive straight through to the border crossing at Strasbourg. They changed into comfortable clothing, packed their few personal items and went downstairs. They went through the house to the back courtyard, where they found Hans Joachim in conversation with Kurt Wollner and his friend.

As they approached the men, Hans Joachim said, handing the swastika-emblazoned passports to Herbert, "Here are your passports, and the French tourist visas are already in them. Benjamin already had the *"Kraftfahrzeugbrief"* (automobile title and accompanying documents) for the Horch changed over to Edna. I just had it changed to Meira instead."

"How did you get these things done so fast, Papa?" inquired Herbert, knowing how complex dealing with government agencies could be.

"Last month I was notified that Goebbels was sending a film crew to the hospital to record my next surgery. He is using me as a glorified representative of 'National Socialist Germanic science'. They wheeled my operating table into the auditorium, and I had to perform surgery in front of an entire room full of government bureaucrats. We had a question and answer session right there in front of my poor patient, under anesthesia, and trying his best to survive under my scalpel. If Goebbels is going to use my name and reputation to promote the Reich, I have no reservations about using the Nazis for favors. When you've lived in this town and met as many people as I have, you get to know where favors can be gotten."

"I'm sure there are many in Berlin who are grateful to you for what you have done, too."

With a shrug, Hans Joachim brushed the comment off and concluded the discussion with, "Well, what goes around comes around."

"*Herr* Wollner, how can I ever thank you for the great support you have been to my family all these years," said Meira, embracing the startled man.

"The pleasure has been all mine, *Frau* Lentz. I'm glad your parents had the foresight to leave when they did, and I'm heartily sorry for what they and their children have had to endure. I regret I have no more news about your sister."

"I thought you and Meira had gone to bed, Herbert," interjected his father.

"We've decided to leave now, Papa. I wish it weren't necessary, but after what you said at the dinner table, we need to get out of Berlin – and Germany – as soon as possible."

"But don't you need to get a good night's sleep and start out fresh at daylight?" responded Hans Joachim.

"No, I agree with Herbert, Dr. Lenz," replied Kurt Wollner. "Given what happened to Meira's sister, I'm rather surprised the Gestapo haven't come after them already. No, they need to leave without further delay. I wish I had had time to get you different passports, but at least your car won't be so conspicuous. We'll hope they haven't put a bulletin out to the border control points, yet."

"Well, I'm sure you know what's best, *Herr* Wollner," conceded Hans Joachim. "Step over here for a moment, son." Handing him a leather packet, he explained in a lowered voice, "Here's 5,000 Marks in cash. Sorry I didn't have enough time to exchange it for you. You can exchange that for French currency as soon as you cross the border. That should be enough, until you get where you're going. After that, you can always access our account at the *Handelsbank* in Zürich. We have over 100,000 in Swiss Francs, plus bonds there."

After tearfully embracing his father, Herbert and Meira shook hands with Kurt Wollner and his friend, got into the Mercedes and started the engine. Driving down the long driveway, Herbert glanced into the rearview mirror at the three men standing together and wondered to himself, *Will we ever see my father again?*

Chapter Thirty-three

Nordischer Typ
(Nordic Type)

"Of course, the *Führer* likes me better than you," sneered Detlev, shoving his little olive complexioned classmate down on the sidewalk in front of their school

"Don't you still like me, Detlev?" responded the boy, tears streaming down his face.

"No, because you're dirty. You need to wash your face."

The small group of boys surrounding the two laughed and jeered. One shouted, "Go ahead and hit him, Detlev. He's probably a Jew. He looks like one."

"Yeah," added another boy. "And anyway, he talks funny."

"I'm not a Jew," wailed the victim. "My mother's Italian and my father is Austrian."

One observer, attempting to bring peace to the conflict, declared. "I have an aunt from Vienna, and she talks like that."

"She's probably a Jew, too," countered another heckler, which brought a renewed round of laughter.

Finally, being egged on by the bystanders, the pushing and shoving escalated to a pitch point, and Detlev landed a resounding smack on the victim's face, whose nose immediately began to bleed. The sight of blood seemed to unleash a frenzy among the group, and they piled on the terrified boy, delivering kicks and blows, until a teacher ran out the door shouting for them to stop.

"What do you think you're doing? Get off him!"

The group broke up, leaving the sobbing child lying curled up. The teacher, a middle age single lady who taught music, knelt and helped the disheveled boy to his feet.

"Who started this?" she demanded from the sullen group.

Receiving no answer, she turned to the boy, "Who hit you first, Franz?"

He did not meet her gaze, but instead kept his eyes down and would not answer.

Noticing that a few of the boys were trying to slink away, she shouted, "Dieter, Horst, Detlev, Karl! You get right back here!"

"Nobody's leaving until I know who started this."

After another long wait, one boy said, "Detlev was telling us how his brother said he was a true Nordic man because he's blond."

Another added, "And Franz said his mother said that was Nazi propaganda. Then Detlev told him to take that back, and Franz wouldn't do it."

Beginning to see where this was going and having extracted the information she wanted, the teacher held up her hand and directed, "That's enough. You boys go home. Franz, you come with me and we'll get you cleaned up. Detlev, you come, too. You will wait in my room until I take care of Franz."

"But my mother doesn't want me to come home late," he protested.

"That's too bad. You should have thought of that before you started this."

"But . . .," he argued.

"That's enough! I said you'll wait. And I'll be in touch with your parents and explain why you're late."

"Oh, please don't tell my mom."

"You have no say in this. Now go to my room."

Eckhardt had embraced and kissed his wife when he got home, as usual, but noticing her unresponsiveness, he enquired, "Is something wrong?"

Not looking at him, she replied, "After supper we need to talk."

Chilled by the icy response, his apprehension told him something really serious was afoot.

As the family sat at the table, little Eckhardt began to relate how his friend, Jürgen, had told the class about an uncle who had recently been accepted into the SS and had sent them his picture in his new uniform.

"The neatest part of the uniform is the deaths head insignia on the cap. Jürgen says the skull has a grin that looks like he's saying, 'Watch out Jews. I'm comin' to get you'. Isn't that funny?"

Christina stared at him, and the rest of the family continued to focus on their food. Only little Detlev started to snicker until his mother cut him off, "That's enough! You eat your supper, and you go to your room!"

"But Eckhardt is teaching me how to play chess."

"Not tonight. You do what I say. Now eat!"

Her husband frowned with a puzzled look. *What has her upset?* he wondered.

"We're not having that!" asserted Ursula, after describing her conversation with Detlev's music teacher and the episode of the afternoon.

"Eckhardt is becoming unmanageable, and now Detlev is starting. If it were up to me, I'd pull Eckhardt out of that *HJ* and I'd never let Detlev get involved. He'll be eight next year, and that's when they'll want him to start in *Deutsche Jugend*. Frankly, based on what we've seen with our oldest son, the whole thing makes me sick."

Taking this all in without comment, Eckhardt gently urged, "You need to calm down. And anyway, you can't talk like this around the boys. If word gets back to the youth leaders that you're criticizing them, they'll turn you in and next thing you'll be interrogated by the Gestapo. And you're fighting against the current, because ninety percent of German boys are *HJ* members. Aside from the political pressure, kids that age never want to be different."

"So, what do we do? Turn a blind eye and let them make brawlers out of our sons?"

Looking at the floor, Eckhardt murmured, "I know. I think about it, too. We lose so much time every week with those damned indoctrination meetings at Siemens. And it's often a rehash of the same thing over and over: Blame the Jews! Blame the Communists! Blame the Catholics!

I'm really so disappointed in Hitler. I had such high hopes that we'd get past this constant rant about who's to blame for all of Germany's problems and get on with the great programs he started out with.

And I'm with you about what to do with our kids. But I don't have an easy answer. All we can do is continue to show them we love them and not say anything that will put them – or us – in jeopardy."

Putting an arm around her husband's shoulder, she soothed, "I know, darling. I think about Herbert and Meira and her parents. I wonder how they're doing. Sometimes I wish we could leave all this behind, too."

Chapter Thirty-four

Bienvenue en France
(Welcome to France)

Driving through the city past many familiar landmarks, Herbert and Meira were already nostalgic about their hometown, their Berlin, which they loved. After leaving the Grunewald, they entered the access to the former six-mile long Avus racetrack recently connected to the *Reichsautobahn,* which would take them south via Stuttgart and on to the border at Strasbourg, a distance of 752 kilometers (467 miles). They settled in for the long journey away from their homeland and people dear to them.

After a long twelve-hour drive in rain and light snow, the exhausted couple joined the long queue of cars and trucks moving slowly through the border checkpoint at Strasbourg. Meira forced herself to keep her clenched white-knuckled fists still in her lap, and they finally crept up to the German border officer, who looked at them with a disgruntled stare. *"Ausweiß!"* (Identification documents), he barked. Wordlessly Herbert handed the documents to him. The man bent over and scrutinized them, glancing back and forth between the passport photos and their faces. After what seemed an eternity, he turned and handed them to the officer seated at the window of the small kiosk, who flipped through the pages of the passports checking the exit visas. After satisfying himself that all was in order, he rubber stamped them and handed them back to the waiting officer who in turn passed them back through the car window to Herbert. Border guards raised the barricade to allow them to cross the border, leaving Germany behind.

Putting the car in gear, Herbert slowly drove another 60 meters to the French checkpoint. After going through the same procedure, the French officer, waved them off with a cordial *"Bienvenue en France"* (Welcome to France).

Minutes after Herbert and Meira had passed through the border checkpoints of both countries and driven out of sight, the teletype machine in the German control point began to chatter. A border control officer picked up the waiting strip of tape and read, *"Haftbefehl für Herbert Lenz und Meira Lenz nee Friedlander – Jüdin"* (Arrest warrant for Herbert Lenz and Meira Lenz born Friedlander – Jewess).

"Well, how do you feel?" asked Herbert, as they drove through Strasbourg.

Her brow furrowed in thought, Meira responded, "I was just going to ask you the same thing. I'm relieved that we are leaving the Nazis behind, but I'm also sad we're leaving the people who mean the most to us."

"I know just what you mean. But we had no choice. Now we need to focus on the life ahead of us. I always wanted to come back to France and bring you with me, but I hadn't foreseen it would be under these circumstances."

As she leaned over to kiss him on the cheek, she whispered, "At least we're together – and we're safe."

"Amen to that!"

"What does that sign say?" enquired Herbert as he squinted through the rain and evening dusk.

"Amiens – 521 kilometers. What's there?" questioned Meira.

"We have to go in that direction to get to the farm, which is just outside the village of Bray sur Somme. I owe these people my life."

Looking at him for a long moment, Meira, with a tremor of voice, said, "Then I owe them, too. I'm anxious to meet them."

He patted her arm and added, "You'll like them.

"It's gonna be a long drive. Shall we stop overnight?" he suggested.

"I think we should, or let me drive for a while. You've driven straight through from Berlin, and in this rain and darkness, we could end up lost – or in a ditch."

"Okay. If you see a hotel, speak up."

Without further conversation, they peered intently down the tunnel of light from the headlights, the hum of the engine only punctuated by the swish of windshield wipers.

Finally, as they neared the village of *Königshoffen*, a few miles outside of Strasbourg, Meira pointed to a dimly lit building set somewhat back from the road with a few cars parked in front.

"That looks like an inn" she cried.

"Oh, yes. I can barely make out the words '*Hotel Krone*' on the wall."

"Why are the names in German? I thought we were in France." she asked.

"This is the Alsace region. It's gone back and forth every time there was a war or conflict between Germany and France. It used to be German, but was ceded to France after the last war."

"Hitler would probably like to change that!" quipped Meira.

"No doubt" agreed her husband.

After finding a parking space between a small Citroën and a sleek Delage sedan, they climbed the stone steps and entered a dingy hallway. The registry desk to the left of the entrance was unoccupied. To the right, was a small taproom, populated by a few locals engaged in muted conversation. The musty air was heavy with a mixed odor of stale tobacco smoke, beer and fried foods. Conversation ceased as the newcomers entered the room. Feeling all eyes upon them, Herbert and Meira made their way to the bar, behind which a large-bosomed middle-aged woman stood. Her unblinking stare scrutinized the Berliners, taking in their urbane dress and manner, which was evident in spite of their having spent long hours traveling.

"We would like to register in your hotel, but there is no one at the desk" began Herbert in German.

Continuing to stare wordlessly, the woman finally replied in heavily accented German, "I can do that. Where are you from?"

"Berlin," answered Herbert.

Another pause. "We only have two rooms available. Paid in advance. Bathroom down the hall. Breakfast at seven."

"That will do very well. Can we get something to eat?"

"Kitchen is closed. I can give you sausage and cheese."

"Fine. We'll have that and two beers, please."

After registering and paying for the room and food at an exorbitant exchange rate, they were served their repast, which they carried to a small table in a corner.

As they ate, the hum of conversation was resumed by the other patrons, who, from time to time, glanced surreptitiously in their direction.

Finally, the exhausted pair ascended the narrow stairway to a hallway, illuminated by a single lightbulb hanging from the ceiling.

The unheated room's décor was in harmony with the rest of the establishment. A faded floral wallpaper of pinks and greens declared it had been in place for many decades and begged for replacement. The wrought iron bedstead, which hailed from a long past nineteenth century period, supported a thin, sagging mattress bedecked with a frayed coverlet of uncertain blues and grays. A washstand in a corner supported a chipped porcelain washbasin and pitcher, long unused and coated with dust.

The weary travelers looked at one another with smiles of resignation, quickly undressed, slipped beneath the dingy down comforter to escape the icy chill of the room, and fell into an exhausted slumber.

Morning light released Herbert from a terrifying dream of being pursued by a pack of dogs as he struggled through a dark forest while carrying Meira, who lay dead in his arms. Bathed in sweat, he turned and looked at his wife sleeping beside him, her countenance peaceful with a slight smile on her lips. As he lay gathering his mental resources for the day ahead, his mind was turned to the actuality of where he was. He was lying next to the love of his life, safe from the terror of Berlin, but moving toward an unknown future in times fraught with uncertainty and danger.

"Good morning, sweetheart" Meira's soft words interrupted his reverie. "How long have you been awake?"

"Not long. Did you sleep well?
"Like the dead."

Her last word momentarily brought the dream to his recollection, causing a brief shudder to course through his body.

"Are you alright?" queried his wife. "You're shaking."

"I'm fine" he blustered. "It's this damned room. It's freezing. Let's get dressed and get out of here."

She agreed and joined him in slipping back into the clothes from the day before, not having brought any luggage from the car.

They entered the taproom, now empty except for two other couples who, like themselves, were quickly consuming the meager breakfast and making ready to resume their travels.

"*Guten Morgen, Madame,*" Herbert greeted the same dour woman form the night before. Nodding wordlessly, she seemed ready to challenge his assessment of the morning.

They were served breakfast at the bar, which consisted of a bit of cheese, two hard rolls, and tea. An open jar of marmalade was available to those who required it. Taking their food to the same table in the corner, they seated themselves and exchanged the traditional, *"Mahlzeit"* and *"Guten Appetit".*

"Before we leave, I should try to call the farm. They didn't have a phone when I was there before, so if not, we may have to just arrive unannounced. I wish I had had time to write her before we left."

"Perhaps you could send her a telegram," suggested Meira.

"That's an idea. But Bray sur Somme is such a small village of less than fifteen hundred people, they might not have telegraph service there. After breakfast, I'll ask the proprietress here where the nearest post office is. I also need to find a bank and exchange our Reichsmarks for Francs."

After being directed to the post office on the main square of the village, Herbert and Meira walked outside and were relieved to see that the rain had ceased and the overcast seemed to be clearing.

The small post office was staffed by two German-speaking employees, one male and one female. When Herbert explained his dilemma, the more cordial of the two, the lady, offered to check with information in Albert to determine whether or not the name was listed. After several minutes, she returned to state that unfortunately there was no listing, neither in Albert nor in Bray sur Somme. When he enquired whether he could send a telegram, the woman replied they could provide no telegraph service. She suggested that when they reach Albert, it being a larger town, they might enquire at the post office. Disappointed, but determined to continue on, Herbert asked after a bank which could exchange currency. The courteous woman advised that there was no bank in *Königshoffen* that could provide such service, and they should probably return to Strasbourg, where there would no doubt be several banks that could. Seeing that the travelers were not comfortable with that suggestion, she offered to exchange a small amount, say RM100, to provide them with enough to reach Albert, where they could be taken care of. This offer was gratefully received and the transaction was made.

After filling the tank with gasoline, which was considerably cheaper than in Germany, they continued on their journey. Their destination was in the heart of where the great battles had taken place in 1916.

Chapter Thirty-five

Return to the Somme

The drive to Albert was long and arduous. The day had promised to be slightly overcast but without precipitation. After they had progressed a little more than two hours westward, however, light snow began to fall, later turning to rain. In spite of the heavy coats they were wearing, they were not ever warm, and the less than adequate heater did little to dispel the chill. So, they struggled on, until late afternoon with dusk falling, when they finally managed to reach Albert.

With darkness coming on and it being past closing time for the bank and post office, and with less than half the money they had received from the kindly postal clerk, they were forced to look for another subpar hotel – somewhat below the level of the one in *Königshoffen*. Finally, in the neighborhood of the railroad station, Meira spotted a small dubious looking establishment with the word *"Hotel"* painted over the small entrance in weathered letters. After parking on a narrow side street around the corner, they walked back and stood contemplating their choice before entering. As they stepped inside, they were confronted with a beyond middle-age buxom blonde woman whose weathered face was adorned with heavy makeup. The lipstick was a shocking crimson and the mascara and false eyelashes contrasted with the neon blue of her eyes.

Ja, bitte schön? (Yes, may I help you?), she greeted the newcomers. Hesitating with some apprehension, Herbert enquired after the price of accommodation. The low amount quoted, startled him and Meira. Wondering what they might have gotten themselves into, they paid and after receiving the key, made their way up the stairway and down a long hallway and were astonished to discover that the dim light came from a gaslight mounted on the far wall. Their astonishment was reinforced when they entered the room and could find no light switch. The meager light through the open doorway revealed a box of matches on a small table just inside the door. Mounted on the wall directly above the table, was another gaslight fixture. After removing the frosted glass shade, Herbert lit a match, turned the valve, and the gas flame immediately appeared.

Turning to his wide-eyed wife, he laughed and exclaimed, "We've gone back in time to the last century!"

Nodding her head in agreement, she murmured, "It's actually kind of romantic."

They turned their attention to the bed and were greeted by a large brass bedstead supporting a mattress on which were two fat down-filled pillows and two very thick eiderdown comforters. Again, however, as in their room of the night before, there was no heat and they hastily undressed, extinguished the gaslight, and submerged themselves beneath the heavy bedding.

A bright sun crept between the heavy draperies, heralding the start of a new chapter of their lives. Through the slits of his half-open eyes, Herbert contemplated the beautiful mouth and the stunning face of his softly breathing wife. *Here we are almost back where we found each other all those years ago. How would our lives have turned out if we hadn't? This woman laid her heart at my feet and overcame a multitude of challenges to be with me. What can I do to be worthy of her?*

After another unspectacular breakfast, they continued in rain on to Bray sur Somme. The little town lay in a valley surrounded by hills to the east and west. As they neared their destination, the landscape began to reveal the scars of war. The earth was slashed with trenches and shell holes, which, although overgrown with shrubbery, stood out in stark contrast to nearby cultivated fields which had been spared the ravages of conflict. Herbert slowed the car, taking in the visual impact.

Suddenly, the scene of that terrible day played again in his mind. He found himself with Eckhardt cowering in a trench as a British tank crawled across the landscape as if hunting human prey. He could hear the roar of the engines and chatter of machine gun fire. He felt only helplessness as the tank slowly meandered along the precipice of his trench, firing a never-ending barrage of bullets into the terrified German soldiers below. As the bodies of his friends were torn to pieces, Herbert and Eckhardt searched in vain for an escape from the carnage. Herbert felt the impact of a bullet strike his left knee. Like lightning, pain shot up his leg and through his whole body.

Alarmed, Meira reached across and grasped his arm. "Darling, what's the matter?" Not receiving a reply, she shook him.

As if coming out of a trance, Herbert brought the car to a stop and sat shaking, bathed in sweat, his hands clenching the steering wheel. He looked at her uncomprehending.

"Herbert, do you hear me? You'd better let me drive." She then switched off the engine. "Here, move over," she urged, as she opened her door and proceeded to walk around the car. Upon opening the driver's door, she found Herbert still sitting rigid and wordless. "Move over. I can drive for a while."

As her words registered, he nodded in agreement and gradually took his place in the adjacent passenger seat. Herbert continued to shake as Meira seated herself behind the wheel. Recalling the soldiers in her field hospital, an understanding Meira slid across the seat and enfolded him in her arms. She placed his head on her shoulder as Herbert began to sob and convulse uncontrollably. The two refugees clung to each other, oblivious to the stares of passersby, whose curiosity was heightened by the sight of a Mercedes with Berlin number plates.

When it was all over and she finally felt the tension flow out of his body, Meira started the car and slowly drove down the narrow lane leading into the town.

After finding a parking space near the Gothic, Romanesque stone church in the center of town, which they later learned to be known as *Eglise Saint Nicolas*, she switched off the engine and turned to her husband. "Now, darling, tell me what happened back there."

Nodding his head, he explained in a muted voice, "I don't know what came over me, but when I saw all those trenches, I knew that was where I had been wounded. It was like I was back there again on that fateful day, and there was nothing I could do about it. Oh, Meira, you've rescued me again."

Smiling, she replied, "We rescued each other. The day I saw you standing on the back terrace of that hospital, I felt inexplicable joy and relief that all the time I spent out here searching for you had finally come to an end."

The rain had ceased and the sun made a timid appearance.

"Let's get out and walk a bit," suggested Meira.

As they strolled about the picturesque little village, the peacefulness seemed somehow to be mocked by the evidence of monumental tragedy that lay all about in the surrounding countryside. They returned to the church and Herbert turned to her and asked, "Would you mind if we went inside?"

"Of course not, darling."

The dim interior was typically chilly and musty with the imprint of centuries. The small votive candles near the altar flickered in an effort to dispel the gloom. A few older people knelt in prayer, some whispering to their rosaries. Herbert and Meira sat in a rearward pew and were soon lost in their reveries. Herbert removed one of the missals from the book rack on the back of the pew in front of them. As he leafed through the well-worn pages and scanned the Latin text, he wondered how people of a religion could go to war with others of the same faith.

Meira thought back to her childhood and the many years she had spent immersed in her own faith. Although not really familiar with Catholic churches, she looked around the vast space and mused that although a synagogue was different, the similarity of places of worship was very apparent. *We worship the same God, and yet can't seem to focus on what we have in common. Instead we let ourselves be separated by doctrines and traditions. Human beings are a contentious species.*

The chilly dampness prodded them to awareness, and in unspoken agreement they stood and walked through the massive doors. The brightness of the day encouraged them to continue on their way.

"Let's have lunch," Meira suggested.

They decided upon a small café across from the church where they were introduced to a limited menu. Using his newly-revived French, Herbert enquired after the house specialty, which was onion soup and a variety of beef stew, accompanied by a simple Merlot. Without hesitation, they ordered the food and wine and were delighted with the selection.

After sharing an éclair accompanied by good coffee, they concluded it was time to locate their hostess. The proprietress responded immediately when presented with this enquiry.

"*Madame? Mais Oui.* Her farm is only about 8 kilometers from here. You follow the road south to *La Neuville les Bray* and she lives only a short way past that."

Thanking her, and restating that the lunch was excellent, they returned to their car and proceeded in the direction they had been advised. A short way out of town, there was a marker beside the road at a German military cemetery.

"I need to stop here. There were countless fellows in our outfit who were killed here and are probably buried in this cemetery."

As they strolled among the crosses, Herbert's eyes began to fill as he encountered names of fallen comrades. Seeing this, Meira slipped her arm around his waist. Suddenly, they came upon a slab marker engraved with a Star of David. Herbert stared intently at the inscription:

Isidor Appel
Landsturmmann
Gef. 25.6.1918

(Isidor Appel, member of Prussian and Imperial German reserve forces, Fallen 25 June 1918)

"My father knew a family in Berlin named Appel" exclaimed Meira. "I wish I could ask him if he ever heard of this boy."

"I wonder if Hitler ever thinks about people like this who gave their all to the Fatherland, and now he persecutes their families and drives them from the country," Herbert growled through clenched teeth.

"It makes you wonder, doesn't it?" concluded Meira.

Passing through the hamlet of *Le Neuville les Bray,* Herbert was delighted to see familiar landmarks. He was especially excited to see the small chapel where a kindly old priest had hidden him for a week. After pointing that out to Meira, he declared, "I wonder if the old fellow is still alive. I'll ask about that."

Soon after, they rounded a bend and he instantly recognized the lane leading up to the house set back from the road in a grove of trees. As they turned in and approached the house, they saw a young man staring intently at them.

"Who's that?" enquired Meira.

"I don't know. He looks too young to be her brother."

They drew nearer and stopped. Getting out of the car, Herbert introduced Meira and himself. A smile broke across the young man's face and he exclaimed, "*Monsieur* Herbert Lenz? My wife has talked about you for years. I am Jacques Bouchard. Come in, come in!"

Stepping to the door, he opened it and shouted, "Mama, come out here."

Two women appeared, one older and frail, and a younger woman with a little boy and girl peering wide-eyed around her skirt.

Upon seeing Herbert, their faces lit up and they both exclaimed, "*Monsieur* Herbert!" He stepped forward and with an arm around each, embraced *Madame* Fournier and her daughter Celestine, his rescuers from all those years ago.

Chapter Thirty-six

Escape to Uruguay

"Golda, we're leaving!"

"When?"

"In two days. We sail on Wednesday from Rotterdam to Montevideo."

After spending a year in the Netherlands, from April 1938 to February 1939, Benjamin and Golda had all but given up hope for their daughter, Edna, joining them and leaving Europe together. After being taken into custody by the Gestapo shortly before Kristallnacht, Edna had vanished without a trace. Kurt Wollner had used every avenue of influence he knew on her behalf among former colleagues in the police department, in the government, and even among contacts in the Gestapo – to the point he was advised to cease, or risk putting his own family and himself in danger.

As a result of the vandalization of his store on Kurfürstendamm and his home, the final liquidation of Friedlanders' property was stuck in limbo. Benjamin had resigned himself to relying solely on the resources he had brought with him: his gold bars and his car.

"A wealthy Dutchman, an executive with Philips, the electro concern, has been after me to sell him the Maybach. We concluded the deal this afternoon. He paid me 6,000 Marks, and with what's left of our gold bars, we now have over 12,000 Marks (about $5,000 at that time)."

"Where is Montevideo?"

"It's in Uruguay, in South America. We can wait there for visas into the United States."

"But what about Edna? I'm not leaving Europe without her" declared Golda flatly. "If I have to, I'm going back to Berlin and get her out myself."

"Golda, don't talk nonsense. If Wollner can't do anything, what do you think you can accomplish, except get yourself arrested? You're not doing any such thing. I have managed to get a sponsorship in Uruguay through the JJDC (Jewish Joint Distribution Committee). When we get ourselves settled in Montevideo, we can continue to work for Edna from there and get the JJDC to help us. Meanwhile, I trust Wollner to use the money I left with him, and when he finds Edna, to send her to us."

"How did you manage to get their help? You tried to work with them before, but didn't have any luck."

"Well, actually, that was part of the price for the car. Money talks – even with them – if you know the right people inside the organization. The buyer of the car is Jewish, and he has a contact inside JJDC. It has to be kept quiet, but I had to give 3,000 Marks to his friend, who managed to get us passage and arrange things with our sponsor in Uruguay, who has gotten us visas there. We can pick them up from the consulate of Uruguay in *Den Haag* (The Hague) tomorrow."

"My head is spinning," she declared as she sat on the bed in their small room. "I still don't know if I can force myself to leave Europe without Edna."

Putting his arm around his wife's shoulder, Benjamin assured her, "Everything that can be done for her, is being done. And be glad that we got word from Dr. Lenz that Herbert and Meira have left Germany. He didn't say where, but Meira will let us know as soon as she can," he chided her with a grin.

To get her mind off her children, he exulted, "Look at the bright side, girl. Think about my grandparents walking from Russia. You get to take a tropical cruise on a luxury liner."

After picking up their visas from the Uruguayan consulate in *Den Haag*, they presented themselves at the dock in Rotterdam the next day with their luggage and tickets in hand. The "luxury liner" turned out to be a dirty tramp steamer, that had obviously seen many years of service. They were shown to their cabin, which was one flight below the main deck in the midsection of the ship. Two narrow bunks – one up and one down – a small closet, and a porthole. Washroom and toilets on the main deck to be shared with the other passengers. There were only seven other passenger cabins, the main purpose of the vessel being to carry cargo.

Looking sadly at the small dingy space allotted to them, which they would occupy for the better part of six weeks, Golda shook her head and could not resist a bit of sarcasm, "Well, where is the ballroom?"

Her thoughts were interrupted by the shrieks of children running in the passageway. Opening the door, she observed through the open door of the cabin across from them, that it was apparently occupied by a family of swarthy people. A heavily-built barefooted man in pants and undershirt filled the doorway, smoking a pipe as he smiled and displayed a collection of several gold-capped teeth in a large thick-lipped mouth.

He nodded and greeted her in an unfamiliar language, and smacked one of the children on the behind, who squeezed past him.

Giving a small nod of acknowledgement, Golda closed the door and turned to her husband with a wry grin, "Bon voyage, *Herr* Friedlander. Welcome to your tropical cruise."

§§§

"Feldmann, Esther"
"*Anwesend*" (present)
"Franck, Dora"
"*Anwesend*"
"Friedlander, Edna"
"*Anwesend*"
"Friedlander, you must report at Director Kögel's office, immediately!"

A bolt of fear shot through her brain. *What does this mean? What have I done wrong, now?*

It was 6 a.m. roll call on a sunny May morning in *Lichtenburg* concentration camp where Edna Friedlander had lived since her arrest in October 1938. As she walked to the office, she replayed her actions of the past several days and could find no incident which should have put her in disfavor with her Nazi keepers.

She entered the castle, which had been taken over as a camp, and climbed the stairs to the director's office. She presented herself at the reception desk and stated her name. The middle-aged woman behind the desk ignored her as she finished work on a file folder. Raising her head as if she had not heard the prisoner, enquired, "Yes! What do you want?"

"Edna Friedlander reporting to Director *Herr* Kögel as directed."

After a pause, the receptionist ordered, "Wait here," and turned and knocked on the office door behind her.

"*Herein!*" (Come in).

Opening the door and peering inside, she reported, "Prisoner Friedlander to see you."

"*Ja, sagen Sie ihr momentan.*" (Yes, tell her I'll see her momentarily).

After relaying the information, the woman returned to her work and left Edna standing for what seemed like an eternity. Finally, a buzzer went off and the receptionist sprang to her feet and opened the door, retrieved instructions and turned to Edna and with a sharp, "Go in now!"

Presenting herself, tingling with anxiety, Edna repeated, "Excuse me, *Herr* Director. I was ordered to see you."

"Ah, yes, Friedlander. You are to go to the registry office and collect your identification booklet and your release papers. You will then go the main gate where you will be met by your sponsor. That is all."

Sponsor? What is he talking about? she wondered to herself. *But don't ask questions. Just go!*

Hurrying to do as she was told, she soon found herself at the main gate, which, when opened, revealed the unexpected presence of Kurt Wollner.

"*Herr* Wollner!" she cried and rushed to embrace him. "How did you manage to get me released?"

"It's a long story. Your father asked me to look for you, and I had just about given up. Quite out of the blue, I was talking to an old retired colleague from the police like me, and he mentioned he knew this man Kögel, who had told him about you; that he had the daughter of Friedlander, big store owner, in his custody.

According to my colleague, he's not the most 'unreasonable' man. Anyway, let's just say, my man offered to persuade Kögel to look again at your case. Also, your father left me with some 'resources' to use for persuasion, if the opportunity should ever present itself. I had some of these 'resources' offered to Kögel, and he proved to be 'reasonable'." He turned to her with a smile, as he opened his car door.

"Where are we going?" she asked, as they turned northwest, instead of north-northeast toward Berlin. "Aren't we going home to Berlin?"

"You're not going back to Berlin. There's nothing there for you now, except more trouble."

She looked at him, with a look of consternation.

"We're going to Hamburg. You're leaving tomorrow on a ship bound for Havana."

Chapter Thirty-seven

Voyage of the *St. Louis*

"*Señor Friedlander?*"

"*Sí. Soy señor Friedlander.*" Benjamin was proud to use his Spanish, for which he had employed a young tutor.

"*Gracias,*" he said, then tipped the young man and took the proffered message.

"Golda, Golda! Come here!"

"What is it?" she asked, wrapping her housecoat around her, as she came out of the bedroom of the small apartment they had leased since their arrival in Montevideo two months earlier.

"Edna's coming to us!"

"Edna? Where is she? How do you know? When is she coming? Oh, thank God. My girl is alive – and she's coming!"

"Whoa! Slow down, girl. I just got a cable from Wollner. He has just put her on a ship to Havana," he said as he embraced her.

After weeping uncontrollably for several minutes, they finally regained their composure and Golda started with a new line of questions. "Havana? Where's that? Why Havana? How is she coming?"

"It's in Cuba, and he didn't go into detail about that, but we can find out about that later. She's coming on the *St. Louis*. I need to exchange a gold bar at the bank and get plane tickets to Havana."

"We're going to Havana? When?"

"Well, let's see. Today is May 13th, and the ship arrives in Havana on the 27th, so that means we'll have to leave at least two days early on the 25th – maybe earlier. I'll have to check the flight schedules. I have a lot to do," as he moved toward the door.

"Wait. I'm going with you. Let me get dressed."

At 8:00 p.m. on Saturday, May 13, 1939, the passengers cheered as engines of the *M.S. St. Louis* rumbled into life, and the ship began to slowly move through the harbor of Hamburg. They lined the railings and watched as they moved past the lights of the city and out of the harbor, into the Elbe toward Cuxhaven, and on to the open ocean of the North Atlantic.

Edna's thoughts were taken up with the frantic events that had occurred since she had been ordered to report to the director's office at *Lichtenburg* that morning. Everyone standing around her was relieved, but also apprehensive. They had their Cuban visas and landing permits, which had been secured with the help of TAJJDC (The American Jewish Joint Distribution Committee), and for which they had had to pay $500, plus an additional $500 for a bond to the Cuban government. However, the Cubans had already cancelled their landing permits due to anti-Semitic demonstrations in Havana five days before. But the Jews on board were desperate to get out of Germany, so they were hopeful that TAJJDC, which was working in their behalf, would be successful in persuading the Cuban authorities to allow them to land, nevertheless.

I'm not going to worry about all that now, she thought to herself. *I'm out of Lichtenburg, and that's a miracle. I just have to count on more miracles. Otherwise, I'll go mad.*

For many of the young passengers and their parents, the trepidation and anxiety soon faded as the *St. Louis* began its two-week transatlantic voyage. Captain Gustav Schröder, with over twenty years of service as an officer with *HAPAG (Hamburg-Amerikanische Paketfahrt-Aktiengesellschaft),* and secretly an anti-Nazi, looked down on his charges from the officer's bridge. He had directed his crew to treat the Jewish refugees with the same courtesy as they would any other passengers, in stark contrast to the open hostility Jewish families had become accustomed to under the Nazis. Due to his efforts, the voyage was made as pleasant for them as possible. On board, there was a dance band in the evenings and even a cinema. There were regular meals with a variety of food that the passengers rarely saw back home, and even though his ship flew the swastika flag, along with the *HAPAG* house flag, he made arrangements for the Jews to conduct their *Shabbat* services while en route and even removed the painting of Adolf Hitler from the main dining room.

Following their crossing, the Havana sun beat down on the loved ones and friends in the small boats and cruisers the Cubans had allowed to circle the *St. Louis* anchored in Havana harbor, after being denied permission to dock at the pier.

Benjamin and Golda, both in their seventies, were exhausted after their arduous journey from Montevideo to Havana. They had quickly learned that air service was almost non-existent in South America in 1939 when they had tried to book flights to Cuba. They were able to fly to Rio de Janeiro but from there had had to go by ship to Havana, which had taken more than two weeks on a small steamer with no air conditioning. They reached Havana on the afternoon of May 28, the day after the *St. Louis* had arrived.

Because they were able to produce tourist visas acquired through TAJDDC in Montevideo, round trip tickets, plus one intended for their daughter and permanent addresses in Uruguay, they were permitted to disembark in Cuba.

After clearing through Cuban customs and immigration, they immediately sought out one of the tents set up along the pier selling space in one of the boats taking family members out to the ship. After waiting in line for what seemed an interminable time, they eventually were able to get standing room on a small cruiser.

As they searched for a glimpse of Edna among the throng of shouting waving passengers lining the rail, Golda finally cried, "There she is!" and began to frantically wave her handkerchief. Benjamin joined her with his large white handkerchief.

"How thin she is," lamented Golda.

Eyes brimming with tears of outrage and sorrow, Benjamin muttered, "What have those bastards been doing to my little girl?" After what seemed like an eternity, Edna caught sight of her parents and began to wave in return. The armada of small boats circled the ship for more than an hour, with passengers lining the railings on both sides of the *St. Louis*.

Benjamin, and many others, pleaded with the pilot of their boat to draw closer to the ship so that they might be within shouting distance of their loved ones, but to no avail. Cuban Navy patrol boats prevented them and the other boats from moving any closer to the ship. After several turns around the ship, bullhorn announcements were heard from the patrol boats that visiting time was over, and all the civilian craft were to clear the harbor and return to the piers. It was announced that they might return the following day, if they wished. There were shouts of protest and anguished cries from those aboard the ship and in the boats, but the navy boats continued to edge them away from the ship. Watching Edna's face disappear and merge into the crowd of passengers, Golda then turned, broke down in heaving sobs, and buried her face in Benjamin's chest, as he, too, succumbed to grief.

The hapless Jewish passengers on board the *St. Louis,* unbeknownst to them, were caught in a power struggle resulting from political infighting within the Cuban government.

On the one hand, when it came to light that the Director-General of the Cuban Immigration Office, Manuel Benitez Gonzalez, had illegally profited from the sale of landing permits and had allegedly enriched himself for as much as $1,000,000, he was forced to resign. On the other hand, two prominent newspapers, *Diario de la Marina* and *Avance*, fueled by Nazi propaganda, claimed that the Jews on the St.Louis were Communists, which enraged many Cuban citizens, many of whom, like Americans at the time, were suffering from the Depression. This resulted in the largest anti-Semitic demonstration in Cuban history on May 8, five days before the *St. Louis* sailed from Hamburg.

The struggle to gain admission into Cuba for these victims of circumstances involved several advocates of differing backgrounds: The US-based TAJDDC, represented by the former president of the Cuban-American Chamber of Commerce, Lawrence Berenson, attorney, together with Captain Schröder, as well as relatives of passengers, struggled for weeks with Cuban officials, including Cuban President Federico Laredo Bru. During this time, one passenger, Max Lowe, attempted suicide by slashing his wrists and throwing himself overboard. He was subsequently rescued and admitted to a Cuban hospital. But all came to naught, and on June 2, President Bru ordered the *St. Louis* out of Cuban waters, and Captain Schröder began to sail slowly toward Miami.

Watching on the shore as the ship sailed out of the harbor, relatives were beside themselves with outrage and grief. Several became hysterical and had to be subdued by Cuban police and escorted away from the pier.

Benjamin and Golda watched through a mist of tears until the ship disappeared from view, at which point Golda collapsed. Benjamin knelt and embraced her. She murmured in an almost inaudible voice to herself. He asked, "What was that, dear?"

She turned her grief-stricken face to him and replied, "She's gone. We'll never see her again."

Chapter Thirty-eight

Last Summer of Peace

The tension in the Meinert household continued. Young Eckhardt maintained an icy distance from his parents – especially his mother. He never spoke to his grandmother, Christina, unless spoken to, and then only grudgingly. She, for her part, went out of her way to not antagonize her grandson, and lived with the gnawing fear that he might – intentionally or unintentionally – denounce her to his youth leaders or teachers for her past Communist affiliations. She had long ceased to have contact with any of her former associates in Wedding where she had been born, grown up, married, and had raised her children – and where she had become involved with Communists in the 1920s, but she still worried.

The youngest boy, Detlev, although more cautious with boasting about his "Aryan" appearance, had never made up with his classmate, Franz. In fact, he had gradually assumed the role of leader of a group of boys who set themselves apart as an elite group of "true Germans". Others, like Franz, thus became more and more marginalized and dominated.

The efforts of Nazi youth leaders and teachers began to bring about visible results in German youth in 1939, reflecting the separation and subdivision of German society being practiced by their elders.

"I think we should take the boys on more family outings, like we used to," suggested Eckhardt. "The weather has been fine this year and it would do us good to get away from everything going on," suggested Eckhardt one Saturday afternoon in June.

"Oh, I couldn't agree more," responded his wife. "The boys are really becoming a handful, and we need to bond with them again. What do you have in mind?"

"For starters, we could go out to Wannsee and go to the beach. Or we could take a cruise around the islands. We haven't been out to Pfaueninsel (Peacock Island) in years."

"That would be nice, but with the heat we've had this summer, don't you think *Wannsee* will be overcrowded? And what would the boys do on Pfaueninsel?"

"Well, how about the Zoo?"

"I don't know," Ursula hesitated. "Eckhardt is 15 and really involved with the *HJ*, and you know how kids are at that age: they aren't usually interested in going with their parents and a little brother to the zoo."

Throwing up his hands, Eckhardt retorted, "Well, then what do you suggest?"

Her brow furrowed in thought, she finally proposed, "Let's talk to the boys and see what ideas they might have."

Later that evening, when young Eckhardt returned home from a day playing *Fußball* (Soccer) with his friends, his mother looked up from the book she was reading aloud to Detlev in the living room.

"Hello, dear. How did your day go?"

"Fine," he replied noncommittally.

"Come sit down. Your father and I want to talk to you boys."

"Now, what have I done?" came the belligerent response.

"Nothing. Sit down. I'll call your father." She walked to the backdoor leading to the backyard where her husband was busy in the small garden.

"Eckhardt" she called. "The boys are ready for us."

Removing his gardening gloves as he walked to the house, he enquired, "Why is Eckhardt getting home so late?"

"Never mind that, now," she said softly. "Let's try to have a pleasant conversation with them."

After he left his muddy shoes on the back step, he entered and greeted his sons, "Hello, youngsters. How did the game go, son?"

Shrugging his shoulders without a response, he didn't meet his father's eye.

Determined to not let it get to him, Eckhardt glanced at his wife, whose face wore a pleading expression not to escalate the encounter.

Settling himself in his favorite upholstered chair opposite his family seated on the sofa, he began, "Your mother and I have been talking about a family outing, and we wanted to hear what you think about that?"

Young Detlev's face brightened and his eagerness was shown in his prompt reply, "A trip? Oh, boy! When? Where are we going?"

"Now hold on. I didn't say 'trip'. I just meant a day together. Maybe take a picnic out to Pfaueninsel, or to the beach at Wannsee or Müggelsee. Or how about the Zoo? Or perhaps we could go out to Potsdam and visit *Sanssouci* (Without Care)."

The look of disappointment on the little boy's face was reinforced by the contemptuous look of his brother, who followed with, "We've been to the Zoo with our classes. And we went to *Sanssouci* with the HJ last year. Don't you remember? And anyway, there's nothing to do there except walk around and look at old paintings and gardens. And I've been to the beach several times this summer with my friends."

Feeling somewhat deflated, he looked to his wife for support, and could detect a slight smile playing on her lips. She seemed somewhat amused by his frustration.

Now he can see what I have to contend with when he's not here.

"Why not a trip, Papa?" pressed Detlev. "Every year we do the same thing on your vacation. We go to things around here, and you work in the yard or on the house. We never go anywhere with you and Mama."

After a pause, he offered, "Well, I do have some more vacation time owed me. We've been so busy at Siemens setting up for new military contracts, that I've a hard time taking time off. But I'll see what I can do."

Looking at his sons, he was encouraged to see a look of real interest on his oldest son's face, and the enthusiasm of the younger boy was infectious. *Yes,* when he thought about it, *the idea of a trip with his family began to excite him.*

§§§

"Well, Lenz. I hear you finally got rid of that Jewish daughter-in-law" greeted Helmut Köhler, slapping Hans Joachim on the shoulder, as they changed out of their scrubs after surgery.

Peeling off the bloody rubber surgical gloves without comment or response, he focused intensely on the task, in order not to react to the barb.

"You'll find life a lot easier – and safer – now that you've got that off your back," continued the needling.

Why do I have to put up with this creature? Hans Joachim asked himself, as he turned to walk out the door.

"People like you are gonna see some great days ahead and wish they had made better choices sooner," Köhler flung at him.

As he continued walking, he turned the events of the past few months over in his mind and wished that he were out of it all – like his son and the just contemptuously referred to daughter-in-law. But then there was his other son. Even though he had no influence over Karlheinz, he ached for the boy – now an SS man, of all things. Frederika must be turning in her grave.

§§§

The summer of 1939 was a time of peace on the surface only, and a busy time for Hitler. Beginning in the early part of the year, he was busy preparing for war. In January, "Plan Z" was implemented for the expansion of the navy and in the Reichstag, he made a speech threatening "the annihilation of the Jewish race in Europe." German troops occupied the remaining parts of Czechoslovakia in March, and soon after he ordered the German military to start planning for the invasion of Poland.

> *"With minor exceptions German national unification has been achieved. Further successes cannot be achieved without bloodshed. Poland will always be on the side of our*

adversaries... Danzig is not the objective. It is a matter of expanding our living space in the east, of making our food supply secure, and solving the problem of the Baltic states. To provide sufficient food you must have sparsely settled areas. *There is therefore no question of sparing Poland, and the decision remains to attack Poland at the first opportunity. We cannot expect a repetition of Czechoslovakia. There will be fighting."*

Adolf Hitler, May 1939,
statement to his generals.

By July, the last Jewish firms and businesses were shut down by the Nazis. Finally, in August, Hitler and Stalin concluded the Molotov-Ribbentrop Pact, whereby they agreed to divide up Europe between themselves.

Chapter Thirty-nine

Return to Europe

The ship arrived offshore from Miami, so close that the passengers could see the lights of the city. Several passengers cabled President Roosevelt pleading for refuge, but Roosevelt never responded. Instead, a State Department telegram was sent to the ship declaring that under the quota system, the passengers must wait their turns on the immigration waiting list to obtain visas for admission into the United States.

Finally, in a last-ditch effort to save his passengers, Gustav Schröder cabled an appeal to Canadian Prime Minister MacKenzie King, who is reported to have remarked in a private conversation, he didn't care to have too many Jews in his neighborhood.

On June 6, almost a month after sailing from Hamburg, short of food and out of other options, Captain Schröder turned his ship back toward Europe.

As the last glimpse of North America at Nova Scotia disappeared from view, most passengers kept to their cabins and an air of despair and hopelessness enveloped the ship.

Edna, one of the few on deck watching the horizon vanish, leaned over the railing and gazed downward into the dark depths of the cold Atlantic. The furrow of water curling away from the side of the hull, seemed to mock, "Come in, come in."

Edna, and other passengers crowding the rail, looked at the busy port of Antwerp as the *St. Louis* prepared to dock on June 17, 1939, after more than a month at sea.

"At least they're not sending us back to Germany," remarked an elderly man standing next to her.

Nodding her head, "At least not that."

"Even though our stay in these countries is only temporary, I'm grateful there are still people who care what happens to us," continued the old gentlemen.

But do they really care? Edna wondered to herself.

Belgium, France, Great Britain, and the Netherlands granted the refugees temporary asylum under the assumption they would leave as soon as their names came up on the US quota lists, or as soon as they had another place to go. Government officials of these countries made it clear that the treatment of the *St. Louis* passengers was an exceptional case and not to be misinterpreted by others fleeing Germany who might expect the same leniency.

Edna and the others had completed questionnaires, issued before they were allowed to leave the ship, which asked for names of friends or relatives they might have in the host countries. This would determine which country they might enter. Those without such contacts were directed to their destinations as the immigration authorities saw fit.

Edna had named her sister Meira and husband Herbert, who were residing with *Madame* Fournier's family in France. She, and others bound for France, were directed to board a freighter which would dock in Boulogne sur Mer on June 20. From there, they were sent to several French towns for temporary housing.

Edna was taken to Laval, where she was able to send a telegram to the post office at La Neuville les Bray near *Madame* Fournier's farm. After an overnight stay in a refugee center, she was waiting in the reception center for a reply from Meira, when suddenly, Meira and Herbert appeared at the front counter.

"Edna!" shouted Meira as the two sisters ran toward each other and with tears of relief and joy, they fell upon each other's necks.

"How did you get here so fast?"

"It's less than two hours from here by car," responded Herbert as he embraced Edna.

"Oh, Herbert. You are amazing."

Laughing, he picked up Edna's two suitcases and followed the sisters as they walked arm in arm to the car.

As they pulled up before *Madame* Fournier's house, she emerged smiling from the house, followed by Celestine and her family.

"Miss Friedlander, at last you're here. You are so welcome. *Monsieur* Herbert and *Madame* Meira have been so worried about you. What an ordeal!"

"This is my daughter, Celestine, her husband Phillippe, and these little ones are Marcel and Angelique."

Smiling, Celestine and Philippe extended their hands.

Eight-year-old Marcel frowned at being introduced as "little," but his six-year-old sister just giggled as she observed his discomfort.

Putting her arm around Edna's shoulder, *Madame* Fournier announced, "Now you must be famished. Lunch is ready for you. I hope you like Bouillabaisse."

"That's a traditional country soup, and it's delicious," informed Meira.

Overcome with relief and gratitude, Edna walked misty-eyed with her hostess into the house.

Chapter Forty

Wir müssen von hier 'raus!
(We need to get out of here)

"Can you imagine such a film being shown in Germany?" Herbert and Meira walked out of the small cinema in Bray sur Somme on a warm evening in late July, 1939.

Herbert chuckled and shook his head. "I'd like to know how it got shown out here in the sticks. I've read that some of the big movie palaces in Paris wouldn't show it."

"Well, then you knew beforehand what it was going to be like, you rascal."

"Guilty as charged, *Madame.*" Another chuckle. "When I saw that *'La Règle du jeu'* was being shown here, of all places, my curiosity got the best of me. I thought if I told you too much about it, you wouldn't come."

"Why? You think I'm easily shocked? Don't forget, you're talking to a Berlin girl."

"Yes, but I thought you were a nice Jewish girl. What would your father think?"

"I thought we'd given up worrying about what my father thinks. Remember, I decided to spend our first night together in the same hotel!"

"Wow! Aren't you the racy thing! I'll deal with you later." He looked around before giving her a pat on the butt.

"You behave. Look at our car. What's happened to it?"

As they neared the Mercedes, they could make out the crudely painted graffiti on the windows and windshield.

Mort à tous les merdes Boche (Death to shitty Germans).

The hood and sides were smeared with dung.

As Meira started to walk toward the car, Herbert grasped her arm. "Don't go near it. If somebody is watching, they'll expect us to get in it."

"Herbert, you're scaring me. We can't just leave it. How are we going to get home?"

"We're going to have to leave it. I should have gotten rid of it right after we got here. A German car with Berlin plates! What was I thinking? I've noticed heads turning when we drive through these little towns. Anyway, it's only eight kilometers to *Madame* Fournier's farm. Can you walk that?"

"At night? In the dark? Herbert! We can't do that. And anyway, with your knee, you'd never make it."

He hated to be reminded of his war injury, which he had sustained all those years ago right in this vicinity. But he knew Meira was right. *But what to do?*

Then it occurred to him.

"Remember the first day we got here, we parked near that church?" as he pointed across the square. "I'm sure it's never locked. We can spend the night there, and in the morning, we can go to the post office and have a telegram sent to *Madame* Fournier. Her son-in-law, Phillipe, can come pick us up."

Meira frowned. "I don't know about that. One of those ladies at the post office might connect us to *Madame* Fournier and implicate her family. You can bet in this little village, they know everybody."

Nodding his head, Herbert agreed. "That's true. Well, let's go across to the church. We'll try to figure something out tomorrow."

The early light streaming through the stained-glass windows threw a kaleidoscope of colors on his wife's face, as she lay on the pew of the old church. Although not deeply religious, as Herbert studied her face, words of spiritual gratitude coursed unbidden through his brain. *Thank you, God, for this woman.*

He was enshrouded with a feeling of this time – this place. *The Somme! This is the place where I experienced the worst nightmares of my life and they have haunted me in all the years since! But this is also the place where the love of my life and I truly found one another!*

"Meira! Wake up, sweetheart. We need to get going."

Escaping from the embrace of sleep, she smiled and reached out her hand. He bent and kissed her.

"I was just reflecting on how our lives were changed forever by what we lived through here. I'm still amazed at your devotion and dedication to me in those days."

She embraced him. "It was hard and scary, but now I'm grateful for what we went through back then. It drove home that you are the love of my life. If I had it to do over, I wouldn't change a thing."

They stood and walked outside. They looked once more at their abandoned car, and turned and began to walk in the direction of the German military cemetery and on to *Madame* Fournier's farm.

"Herbert, you can't do this. That left leg won't let you."

"I know, I know – my knee! Well, we'll go as far as we can, and then we'll see where we are. Are you hungry?"

"Of course, and you are, too. But we need to put as much distance between ourselves and this town as we can."

As they reached the cemetery, they paused.

"Look! The same bastards that trashed our car have been out here, too. Look at some of the graffiti on the headstones. And see how some have been overturned. Let's go see if they did anything to that Jewish boy's grave."

"You mean Isidor Appel?"

"Yes."

As they neared the grave, it became obvious that it, too, had been vandalized, the headstone broken off at the base and lying on the ground. They stood mute before the desecration. A tear trickled down Meira's cheek.

"Now we see that bigotry and hatred is focused on both of us – you as a Jew and me as a German! I thought when we came through here the first time, people here were showing a generous spirit of hospitality and reconciliation. But now, our country has brought condemnation on itself by allowing Hitler and his gangsters to take us back to the Dark

Ages – all in the name of Germany! Here we see evidence of the resentment Germans are bringing upon themselves."

"You're right, Herbert. I'm afraid the Germans are dancing with the devil!"

"What's the matter, sweetheart?" She noticed his grimace of pain, as they continued on from the cemetery.

"It's nothing. Just a little twinge in my knee."

"Herbert, if that leg is bothering you, let's take a break."

"Maybe that's a good idea. Just for a few minutes. But I don't think I'd better sit on the ground. I might never get up." He chuckled. "Let's go back to the cemetery. We just left there, and we can sit on a bench."

"Here, lean on me," she offered.

"I'm too heavy."

"Nonsense! I had plenty of experience helping wounded men get around during the war."

"That's true. But just let me put my arm on your shoulder to steady myself."

After putting his left arm on her shoulder, they returned to the desecrated cemetery.

Grateful to be able to get the weight off the protesting leg, and seated on a cast iron bench in the refreshing shade of a large old tree, they sat leaning on one another. He grasped her hand.

"I always intended to bring you back to this country, where we both endured so much, and introduce you to these good friends, but I never expected it to be under these circumstances."

Affectionately squeezing his hand, she countered, "I know, but up until now, it's been a relief to get away from everything going on in Germany. And I've always looked forward to meeting *Madame Fournier*. You always talked about her and what she did for you."

"Maybe so, but now it's like the madness in Germany is spreading all over Europe – like a virus – and it's reaching out to catch us!"

After a lapse in the conversation, he said, "Well, we'd better get going. In case those hooligans come back, we don't want to get caught in here. By now, our car has got everybody in town wondering where we are," as Meira helped him to his feet. Once again, they ventured out on the road and resumed the trek to *Madame* Fournier's farm.

They had only been walking about fifteen minutes, when they heard a noisy vehicle approaching and were greeted by the sight of Phillippe's battered Model T pickup. As he spotted them, he gave a blast on the Oogah horn. Pulling up alongside them, he cried, "Where have you been? We've been worried sick. Edna is about to go out of her mind! I was going into town to look for you. Where's your car? Get in."

Meira, who had taken French, as well as English, in school, was surprised at how quickly her fluency had developed in the short time she and Herbert had been living with *Madame* Fournier's family. Herbert, who had become fluent during the years he had been under her care, now had a near-native command of the language.

They squeezed into the narrow seat, and Phillippe turned around and headed back toward the farm. Herbert began to explain what had happened. Phillippe, hearing about the car, shook his head and said, "I hate to say it, but I'm not surprised. Some people have asked me what we are going to do with 'our Germans'."

"I'm sorry we brought this on you and your family. We're leaving, just as soon as we can get ourselves and Edna packed up."

"We'll talk about that, later. Right now, we'll get you home, and Celestine and her Mama can get you fed and rested up."

"I won't argue with you about that," responded Meira. "I'm famished, and I can't wait to have a bath and wash my hair. I must look frightful."

Both men chuckled. "You look fine to me," assured Herbert. "When it comes to Berlin girls, I'll always say 'I got the pick of the litter'."

Meira blushed.

Chapter Forty-one

Bonjour à Paris

The next morning, after sharing their last breakfast with their amiable hosts, Herbert, Meira and Edna, with heavy hearts, prepared to leave the little family.

"Phillippe will drive you to the station," directed *Madame* Fournier. "I hate to see you leave, but I understand why you feel you must go. Come here, *Monsieur* Herbert." She embraced him and kissed him on both cheeks. Slipping a folded piece of paper into his hand, she explained, "When you get to Paris, contact this man if you have any problems. He is the husband of a cousin of mine. I don't know what he does exactly, but when my cousin came here to visit my mother before she died, she had several frocks and a coat that were obviously expensive. And she had money. I've listed his office and home address and telephone numbers."

Turning to Meira, "And you, my dear, I'm so happy to have gotten to know you. I'm sure that if we had more time together, we would become close friends. Years ago, when your husband was living here with us, he used to talk about you in a way that I knew you must be special. Now that I've met you, I understand why." She squeezed Meira and kissed her as well.

Turning to Edna, she continued, "I'm sorry you had to come to us under such terrible circumstances, but I'm happy you have been here too. I can see a strong resemblance between you and your sister. You both obviously were raised by people of good character, who can be proud of their daughters."

Then addressing the three of them, she declared, "You will remain important to me, no matter how time and space may separate us. God bless you. Take care of each other, and let's try to keep in contact."

Celestine stepped forward and hugged each one. Meira and Edna kissed each of the children, Marcel and Angelique, on their cheeks.

Herbert solemnly shook hands with Marcel, and Angelique insisted he bend down to receive a hug around the neck.

The two women crowded into the seat of the Model T, while Herbert joined the luggage outside in the bed of the little truck. Phillippe set the emergency brake, pushed the spark control to retard the spark, turned the gas valve on, and then walked around front and gave the crank a half turn. The little four-cylinder engine immediately sprang to life. He moved into the driver's seat and began to drive away. Waving to their friends, the travelers were on their way into a new but unknown phase of their lives. Herbert, with a lump in his throat and tear-filled eyes, waved to *Madame* Fournier and Celestine until the pickup turned onto the road to Bray sur Somme, and they were out of sight.

As they passed their abandoned Mercedes, Herbert gazed wistfully at the small crowd of onlookers gathered around the vehicle. Two young men turned at the sound of Philippe's truck. One nudged the other and pointed as Philippe drove past. Looking straight ahead, he admonished Herbert, "Don't stare!"

Quickly averting his eyes, Herbert apologized. "I'm sorry. Of course, you're right. What are you going to tell them, when they ask where we've gone?"

"We'll simply say we asked you to leave. Given the present situation in Germany, they'll agree we did the right thing."

"How did *Madame* Fournier ever explain my presence here during the war?"

"Except for her priest, who has since died, she never told anyone. And Celestine and I have kept her secret."

Meira commented, "How hard that must have been for her. I am so grateful to her for saving my man, and I am forever in her debt."

Although they could have afforded a first-class compartment, in order not to attract any more attention to themselves, the trio settled themselves into a second-class compartment which appeared to be empty. They were discussing their plans in German, when a middle-aged woman accompanied by two young boys occupied the seat facing them. Silence prevailed for a few minutes, until the train began to set in motion. Then the older of the boys, after staring uninhibitedly at Meira's hat and fashionable attire, blurted, "D'où êtes-vous?" (Where are you from?)

Caught by surprise, Meira looked helplessly at her husband, who quickly responded, *"Ma femme est Suisse"* (My wife is Swiss).

Frowning, the woman shook the boy by the arm and murmured something in his ear, ostensibly to tell him to leave others alone.

Scowling, the boy sank into his seat and remained silent for the rest of the 2½ hour journey, of 124 kilometers (77 miles). Traveling almost due south, they were interrupted only by the conductor collecting tickets.

After arriving at lunchtime at the station, Chatelet Les Halles, near the famous open-air market district of the same name, Herbert announced, "I'm starved, and I'm in the mood for a good steak."

They checked their luggage in the baggage room of the station and ventured forth. After walking for a few minutes through the district, which abounded with restaurants of all descriptions, they settled on a small old-fashioned looking meat joint, with the mouth-watering fragrance of roasting meat wafting from the open windows. They entered the dining room crowded with customers, many of whom were obviously workmen from nearby Les Halles.

As soon as they were seated at a table covered with a red checked tablecloth, Herbert ordered his steak, and the ladies opted for roast beef. When the food was served, Herbert displayed his earthy Berlin humor with the observation, *"Mensch, det iss ja so groß wie ein Klodeckel!"* (Man, that's as big as a toilet lid).

Both women giggled. A waiter walking past, however, scowled, not understanding the comment, but recognizing the language as German.

The beef was accompanied by large portions of fried onion rings, potato salad, and a hefty Bordeaux. After eating their fill, they paid the surprisingly modest check, walked outside into the bright sunshine, and began to explore the area, which was not far from the city center.

"Before we go any further, I need to find an international bank and arrange to have some funds transferred from our Swiss bank," announced Herbert.

"How are we doing on money?" enquired his wife.

"We're fine for a few days, but we'll need to find an apartment, which will require deposits and prepaid rent. But after that, let's get to know this fabulous city."

Smiling at Edna, Meira exulted, "To be free in Paris on a beautiful summer day! Life is good!"

Part III

Eruption

Chapter Forty-two

Fall Gleiwitz / Feldzug in Polen
(Gleiwitz Incident / Polish Campaign)

> *"ÜBERFALL AUF DEN SENDER GLEIWITZ!"*
>
> (Attack on the radio station at Gleiwitz)

The newspaper vendors shouted this on the main Berlin boulevards on Friday, September 1, 1939, claiming that the German radio station had been attacked by Polish troops.

The Gleiwitz incident was only one example of the deluge of propaganda and misinformation being fed to the German public, and the world, throughout 1939. Hitler ordered the SS leaders, Heinrich Himmler and Reinhard Heydrich, to fabricate such reports of offenses against Germany. The German media was directed by the Propaganda Ministry under the leadership of Joseph Goebbels to run headline stories of Polish atrocities against German minorities living in western Poland and in the Polish Corridor. Newsreels featured Germans fleeing these areas because of Polish violence. There were no doubt valid examples of such injustices perpetrated upon ethnic Germans, but the Nazi propaganda machine exaggerated them for the purpose of rousing German public support for an invasion of Poland.

As early as January, 1939, on the sixth anniversary of his ascension to power, Hitler delivered his "prophecy speech".

> *"If the international Jewish financiers in and outside Europe should succeed in plunging the nations once more into a world war, then the result will not be the Bolshevization of the earth, and the victory of Jewry, but the annihilation of the Jewish race in Europe."*
>
> Adolf Hitler

By the late summer, Hitler admitted to those close to him his willingness to use misinformation in achieving his goals. In August, he declared to the military leadership he would provide a, "propagandistic reason for starting the war, regardless of whether it is believable or not. The victor will not be asked afterwards if he spoke the truth or not."

The incident which was presented to the German public as the reason for the attack on Poland was referred to as the "Gleiwitz incident". (The background of this was described by an SS officer, Alfred Naujocks, after WW II in 1945, who declared he had organized it as ordered by Reinhard Heydrich and then chief of the Gestapo, Heinrich Müller.) It was carried out during the night of August 31, 1939, by a group of Abwehr and SS operatives dressed in Polish uniforms. In order to make the action look more convincing, an unmarried 43-year-old German farmer, Franciszek Honiok, who was known to be sympathetic to the Poles, was dressed as a saboteur, murdered, and left with gunshot wounds at the scene to appear as having been killed while attacking the radio station. In addition, several prisoners from Dachau concentration camp were dressed in Polish uniforms, shot dead and left at the site with their faces disfigured to make identification impossible.

"So eine Frechheit!" (Such effrontery), fumed young Eckhardt. "We'll deal with those Polish swine, wait and see," as he turned off the radio and returned to the table.

Eckhardt, Ursula, young Detlev, and Christina, gathered around the breakfast table, looked at him without immediate response.

After a few moments, Christina posed the question, "What reason do you think the Poles had for attacking a German radio station?"

"Yes, I wonder about that, too," added Ursula.

Young Detlev piped up, "Are Poles bad people?"

"Poles and Russians and all Slavs are filthy ignorant pigs who ought to be wiped out – just like that traitor Honiok. Imagine! A German helping those swine attack a German station! He got what he deserved and those bastards they found with him!" ranted his brother. "Killing was too good for them!"

"Eckhardt! That's enough! You don't use language like that in this house!" commanded Ursula.

Red-faced with outrage and embarrassment at being reprimanded in front of his little brother, he grabbed his fork and angrily stabbed at a slice of ham on his plate.

His father studied his son and wondered how such a loving, obedient boy could grow into such an angry, bigoted young man. But then he corrected himself. *Of course! It was the influence of his youth leaders and teachers who constantly expounded the virtues of the "New Order" – and the duty of Germany to avenge the injustices imposed upon her by the Allies after the last war.*

At that moment, Eckhardt made a vow to himself that he would put a stop to this negative influence, and he would not lose his sons to Nazi ideology, although by 1939, over 90 percent of German boys had become members of the Hitler Youth.

§§§

The morning after the Gleiwitz episode at 4:45 a.m., the German invasion of Poland began with a bombardment of the Polish garrison at Danzig. Poland had counted heavily on the promised support of England and France, but this was not to be forthcoming until after September 3rd, when the two allies declared war on Germany – and with only token support. The French stayed behind the Maginot Line, the border fortifications between France and Germany. They were involved in a few border skirmishes, while the British reacted by dropping leaflets on German cities.

Although the news was touted in the press and on the radio, the Berliners in general displayed no emotion and went about their business with no fanfare. The idea of a new war was not popular across Germany, with the memory of the war two decades earlier still uppermost in most adults' minds.

Hans Joachim Lenz compared the difference of the public reaction today to that of August 1, 1914. Then, the streets had been filled with crowds marching along with the parading bands and regiments, with young women throwing flowers at the troops and rushing up to kiss them. A holiday mood had prevailed, and the outcome of the war was expected to be decided by the following Christmas – in Germany's favor, of course.

"Hochmut wird bestraft," (Arrogance will be punished) said Hans Joachim to himself, as he maneuvered his car toward Charité and his day in surgery. The thought that at least Herbert and Meira were out of all this gave him a measure of comfort.

However, driving west on Unter den Linden heading toward the Brandenburg Gate, newly promoted *SS Hauptsturmführer* Dieter Lehmann and his adjutant *SS Untersturmführer* Karlheinz Lenz, were exuberant – their faces tanned and bursting with robust health. They were proud and confident in their well-tailored black uniforms and completely convinced of their Germanic superiority, which they felt was exemplified in the German engineering of Dieter's magnificent open Mercedes 540K roadster.

"I can't wait to get my hands on some of those Polish bastards!" shouted Dieter against the wind in his face.

Nodding his head in agreement, Karlheinz let his mind wander back to the ancestral home of his mother's family, *Schloß Hohenberg* in Pomerania. This aristocratic estate had been expropriated by the

Polish government in July 1919, in accordance with the edict of the Treaty of Versailles.

Dieter continued, "The *Führer* has said we must obtain the living space we need, and the object of the war is to physically destroy the enemy. The 'Death's Head' insignia we wear means it's *our* duty as SS men. That means the we must be prepared to kill without mercy all Polish men, women, and children!"

Karlheinz looked at him with a shocked expression. *Was Dieter serious, or was he just boasting?* His thoughts returned to his Grandfather's estate, the only place he had ever truly loved, and he promised himself, with relish, *Yes, we have some scores to settle*!

Polish inadequacy to resist the Nazi onslaught became quickly evident at the Battle of the Bzura, fought near Kutno, Poland. This began as a Polish counteroffensive, but the German forces outflanked the Poles and took all of western Poland.

After the battle, the German strategists focused their energies on Warsaw. The Wehrmacht divisions were supported heavily by the Luftwaffe, which utilized Stuka dive bombers to indiscriminately attack civilian as well as strategic military and industrial targets. The intent was to demoralize the civilian population as quickly as possible in order to bring about a swift capitulation of Polish resistance.

§§§

"I can't believe it! Nazis and Russians as allies! And for what? To divide Europe between themselves?"

Christina's astonishment at the news of the Soviet invasion of Poland from the east on September 16th was felt – if not openly expressed – by many throughout Germany.

As she turned off the small radio, Ursula reprimanded her mother. "You have got to keep your mouth shut, Mama. I'm glad we're here by ourselves. It's bad enough you say such reckless things here at home, but I worry about what you say out in public. Don't you know what's going on in this country now?"

"I'm sorry if you can't control your own children. The very idea you're afraid they might get you in trouble with the Gestapo! Outrageous! And I'm very disappointed in your husband. He can't see the Nazis for what they really are. He should back you up in teaching your boys right from wrong. He's still trying to have it both ways. He wants to get along with these gangsters, but at the same time he wants to come across as a decent human being."

"That's enough! You talk about right and wrong, but you still believe the Communists are morally upright. Now they've joined Hitler in invading a neighbor. They're no better than the Nazis. And you have no idea what kind of pressure Eckhardt is under at Siemens. He tells me that the place is riddled with spies watching everything that is said and done there.

And the boys? They're getting bombarded with propaganda daily by their teachers and youth leaders just when they are in their most impressionable years. The Nazis are destroying German families at the same time they prattle about the family being the foundation of the nation!

Look where this has all brought us. Now we're at war again with the British and French. And your Communists have declared themselves on the side of Hitler – after all the years of those two groups trying to kill each other. Devils joining forces! Don't lecture me about right and wrong."

Ursula sat down at the kitchen table and put her head down on her arms.

Christina looked at her daughter and wished she could decide what she really believed, in light of these events.

§§§

After the Polish campaign began in September 1939, Rudi was eager to be involved in combat operations, but Erika, for her part, was apprehensive. "My father is very concerned that the recent events point to a war in the near future. If that comes, you would be in the thick of it," she warned one night when they lay in bed. "You had a good career with Luft Hansa, and they were good to us. Why couldn't you be satisfied?"

"Afraid of war! That's silly. The *Führer* is only reclaiming what rightfully belongs to Germany. The Rhineland should never have been given over to control by the French, and anyone can see how natural it is that Austrians and Germans are the same people and belong together. The *Führer* has explained why we need to expand our territory. Besides, the Luftwaffe has already demonstrated its strength in the Spanish War. You should see our new Messerschmitt BF 109 aircraft that has been developed. Nothing on earth can compete with it, and anyone would be foolish to take us on. Wait until you see me in my new uniform. All the other guys say girls fall all over them when they go out in uniform."

"You're starting to sound like one of Goebbels' speeches. Boastful and arrogant! Are you gonna let 'girls fall all over *you*'?"

"I think we'd just better stop now, Erika. I thought you would be proud of me. Come on, give us a kiss," he whispered, reaching to embrace his wife.

Turning to bury her face in his chest, she murmured, "I can't face the thought of losing you."

§§§

In accordance with the Molotov-Ribbentrop Pact signed the previous week between Germany and the Soviet Union, the Soviets invaded Poland from the East on September 17th.

The Poles were completely overwhelmed and on October 6, after the Battle of Kock, the German and Soviet armies conquered the whole country, marking the end of the Second Polish Republic. No formal declaration of surrender was ever concluded.

No declaration of war was brought against the Soviet Union by either Britain or France. The entire Polish campaign lasted 35 days.

Chapter Forty-three

The Silent War

> ***"Britisches Schlachtschiff 'Royal Oak' von siegreichem deutschen U-Boot versenkt"***
>
> (British battleship "Royal Oak" sunk by victorious German U-Boat)

Eckhardt sighed, laid the newspaper of October 14, 1939, to one side and turned off the radio with the blaring martial music. He gazed out the window at his back garden as the autumn twilight enveloped the city. Ursula and Christina, with very little to say to each other since their afternoon dispute, worked side by side in the kitchen, washing and putting away dinner dishes.

Young Eckhardt and his brother, Detlev, were deep in studies in their upstairs room.

The little family, like others across Germany, although conflicted by varying degrees of patriotic fervor on the one hand, were also tormented by inner apprehension on the other. The nation was held in suspense as to what might be coming next.

§§§

After the wrap-up of the Polish campaign, Rudi, at age 35, felt his age was holding him back. Jagdgeschwader 25 was kept at Staaken on standby and saw no combat. But the younger Messerschmitt pilots also grumbled among themselves about not seeing any action. This bickering made its way up the chain of command, until finally in the late Autumn of that year, it came to the attention of *Reichsmarschall*

Hermann Göring, who decided to address the issue himself and assure the disgruntled pilots that they would not be overlooked when the need arose.

One afternoon in early November, 1939, the *Reichsmarschall* and his retinue appeared unexpectedly at Staaken. Among those accompanying Göring was Major Adolf Galland, a hero of the Spanish Civil War. Galland had gained recognition as a pilot in the Condor Legion. Then, during the Polish Campaign, he had flown with *Staffelgeschwader 2* supporting the German Tenth Army and on attack missions with the 1st *Panzer Division*. During this time, he had developed the strategy of providing close air support operations, which were so successful that it had gained him the attention of Hitler and Göring.

The young pilots were fascinated with Galland, but Rudi especially so, even though Galland was eight years younger. They were both alumni of the *Deutsche Vehrkehrsfliegerschule* (DVS), which had been heavily subsidized by Luft Hansa. They both had also been pilots with that airline, and even though they had never yet met, Rudi was well acquainted with his reputation.

After Göring had addressed the group, some of the pilots mingled with the visitors. Rudi seized the opportunity to approach Major Galland and introduce himself. When the Major learned that he and Rudi shared a similar background, his interest sharpened.

"So, your instructor was Helmut Stock, *Herr Oberleutnant*? I knew Stock. I'm sorry to hear that he had to take an early retirement."

"Yes, *Herr Major*, his health took a turn for the worse after his wife passed on but he already had a bad heart condition."

Shaking his head, Galland continued, "He was one of the best flight instructors I ever met. He was demanding, but those who could meet his standards have proven themselves to be excellent pilots. And you have had more years with Luft Hansa than I have, so I would expect you have earned your rank, even though you have no combat experience."

Rudi felt a rush of pride at being praised by an accomplished pilot such as Galland. He looked at the Major and, smiling, ventured a personal question. "I heard that when you flew with the Condor Legion in the Spanish Civil War, you used to fly your Heinkel in swimming trunks with a cigar in your mouth, and your plane had Mickey Mouse painted on the side. Is that all true?"

Galland's pleasant face burst into a grin, as he replied, "I like Mickey Mouse. I always have. And I like cigars, but I had to give them up after the Spanish war."

Then he returned a question, "You say your name is Bellon? That's a French Huguenot name, isn't it?"

"Yes, that's what my mother says."

"Interesting. My people also come from Huguenots."

The group was beginning to disperse, and Göring signaled that he was ready to return to Berlin.

"Well, Bellon, it's been a pleasure talking to you. Let's keep in touch," as he offered his hand to Rudi.

"Thank you, *Herr Major*. The pleasure has been all mine."

Chapter Forty-four

Return to *Schloß Hohenberg*

With the outbreak of war, Dieter and Karlheinz were assigned to the Waffen-SS, the military branch of the SS, and attached to *Kommandostab Reichsführer-SS* (Command Staff) directly under the leadership of Heinrich Himmler. After the cessation of hostilities on October 6, they were re-assigned to the SS Central Administration Office in Warsaw under the direction of Josef Albert Meisinger.

Because of heavy war damage to the rail facilities in Warsaw, they travelled on a night train from Berlin to Danzig, where they were given a *Kübelwagen* (WW II Volkswagen military vehicle) for their drive from Danzig to Warsaw. After a hearty breakfast in the restaurant in the station, now taken over to serve German military personnel only, they drove through the war damaged city of Danzig. Karlheinz felt a rush of nostalgia as they ventured south through the Pomeranian countryside. In spite of the lapse of years and the damage of war, he recognized some landmarks as they travelled.

When they had received their assignment at the end of August in Berlin, he had been overcome with boyish excitement and had impressed upon Dieter the urgency of returning to the scenes of his boyhood before going on to Warsaw. Dieter had become drawn into the excitement and anticipation of seeing the place Karlheinz had spoken of so passionately on many occasions. He had also agreed to support Karlheinz in exacting vengeance on the Polish occupants of the estate.

Finally, in early afternoon, they neared the site of his mother's ancestral home. As they turned into the wrought iron gateway and drove up the long gravel drive leading up to the manor house, Karlheinz was relieved to see that the house and grounds appeared to have been well-maintained. As he brought the vehicle to a stop and switched off the engine, he was struck by the silence. Since they had turned into the estate, they had not seen a person, and an air of abandonment pervaded the air.

When they approached the massive front door, Karlheinz's attention was drawn to an ornate brass nameplate engraved with an unfamiliar coat of arms above the monogram "B". This had replaced the ceramic nameplate of the Hohenberg family. A gorge of anger arose in his throat as he grasped the massive door handle and flung open the unlocked door.

Entering the tiled front hall, he was confronted by a stooped figure whose face was unfamiliar. "Who are you?" he demanded brusquely. The old man replied in stilted German that he was the butler.

"And where are the occupants of this house?"

This brought an answer in Polish with a shrug, which further agitated Karlheinz.

Pushing the old fellow to one side, he and his companion mounted the long staircase and began to fling open doors to unoccupied rooms as they searched up and down the long hallway. Finally, after satisfying themselves that there was no one upstairs, they went back downstairs and continued their search throughout the whole house, until they entered the kitchen and seeing that food preparation had been interrupted by their arrival. They looked into the pantry's china storage room. Seeing a china service in the glass fronted cabinets with an unknown crest, Karlheinz tore open the doors and began throwing plates and dishes on the tile floor.

The old butler, hearing the crash of china, rushed into the room and frantically began tugging on Karlheinz's sleeve, crying in Polish, *"O nie! Proze̜ przestac', prosze̜ pana!"* (Oh, no! Please stop! Please, sir). Throwing the old man against the open cabinet, more china rained down on the man's head, and he fell violently to the floor. Standing to one side with an amused smile, Dieter kicked the old fellow as he struggled to regain his feet.

"Karlheinz, do you want me to get rid of this trash?"

His face florid and glistening with sweat as he continued to vent his rage, Karlheinz retorted, "As you see fit."

Grasping the old man by his collar, Dieter dragged his victim out through the kitchen and through the hall to the back entrance. Throwing the quaking man out into the back courtyard, the SS man drew his Luger out of the holster and fired three shots into the body of the fetal positioned figure on the ground.

As he returned to the kitchen, he heard the whimpering of someone in the larder, which they had not yet investigated. Opening the door, he looked into the ashen faces of a buxom middle-aged woman and two younger girls cowering against the far wall of the room.

"Karlheinz! Komm' mal her!"

Joining his friend at the open larder door, he took in the scene before them.

"Ihr, Schweine! Raus, sofort!" (You, swine! Out at once!)

Wailing and sobbing the three terrified women walked past the two SS men, Dieter giving a kick to the ample posterior of the older woman.

"Wer hier spricht Deutsch?" (Who here speaks German?) he demanded.

After a hesitation, the older woman raised her hand, *"Ich, ein bisschen."* (I do, a little bit.)

Both men began to pepper the woman with questions as to the whereabouts of the family living in the house.

At first, she protested she knew nothing about it, but after Dieter pistol whipped her across the face, she, in a state of near hysteria, finally admitted that the owner's family had taken refuge in the nearby estate manager's cottage.

Herding their victims out to the back courtyard, the women upon seeing the bullet riddled corpse of the old butler, began a renewed round of shrieking. They, being Catholic, genuflected repeatedly and babbled prayers, invoking the protection of God.

Karlheinz watched, transfixed in horror, as Dieter forced the women to their knees and calmly shot each one in the back of the head.

He numbly followed as Dieter marched determinably toward the estate manager's cottage. Kicking the door open, they found a middle-aged couple of aristocratic bearing and two teenaged boys and an older couple, presumably the estate manager and his wife, standing facing them as they charged into the room.

"Wer sind Sie?" (Who are you?) demanded Dieter, addressing the distinguished-looking gentleman.

In fluent German, the man responded that he was *Baron Konstantin Malinowski Budwinski.*

"Ah, Budwinski! That explains the nameplate on my front door," said Karlheinz.

"You, 'Baron'," he said, with a sneer, "you and your family! – out of here! And you," he said addressing the estate manager and his wife, "you stay here. I'll deal with you later."

Nodding his head eagerly that he understood, the man was visibly relieved.

Karlheinz, Dieter and the Budwinski family filed out the door into the waning late afternoon light where they lined up as ordered by their captors.

"Where's Lewandoski?" demanded Karlheinz, referring to the estate manager, who had served under his grandparents.

"He was let go when we came," replied the Baron.

"Why?"

"We had our own staff from our other estate."

"Your other estate! Did you steal that one, too?" goaded Dieter.

This was met with silence.

"Where is he now?" continued Karlheinz.

"They moved away. I don't know where they went."

"Alright! Enough of this," declared Karlheinz. "Show us around the place, and you'd better have good explanations if everything is not looking good."

As they walked through the grounds, it was evident changes had been made, but that they had been carried out with thought and good planning.

"Apparently your manager knows his job."

"Yes, and he has a good assistant. He's one of the staff we kept on here from before."

"Who's that?"

"Wojcek Kowalczyk."

"Wojcek?" came the startled response. "That's the fellow who became good friends with the ghetto kid, Rudi Bellon, that I had to bring up here when my grandmother was alive! Where is he?"

"He was drafted into the military when the war started."

"Good thing he's not here," growled Karlheinz. "He encouraged that Bellon kid to get above himself."

As they walked toward the mausoleum, Karlheinz noticed Dieter studying the two young sons of the Baron. Karlheinz had been too preoccupied to give them much thought, but as he followed Dieter's gaze, he realized that the young men were well built and handsome.

We'll get back to them later, he mused to himself.

As they drew near the iron gates to the building, the names of his grandparents and some of their forebears were not to be seen. Instead, the bronze nameplates bore the names of the Budwinskis.

A sudden suspicion flared in his mind as he turned to the Baron and demanded, *"Wer ist da drin?"* (Who's in there?)

The Baron looked him straight in the eye.

"I said, where are my grandparents?" demanded Karlheinz, jabbing a finger into the Baron's chest.

"We had them reinterred in the village churchyard."

Karlheinz removed his Luger and pointed it at the Baron.

"On your knees, you bastard!"

The Baroness clutched her husband's arm, but like him, her face reflected generations of aristocratic bearing and dignity. Neither the couple, nor their sons, wavered.

Karlheinz repeated his command, but it did not convey the same confidence as before.

The two SS men and their victims faced one another in a frozen tableau.

Dieter drew his pistol and without comment shot the Baron and the Baroness between the eyes in sudden succession.

Turning to the two horror-stricken youths, he coldly informed them they would suffer the same fate if they did not give themselves over to himself and Karlheinz without resistance.

Too paralyzed to respond, the older boy nodded his assent while his younger brother became convulsed in grief.

"What's the matter with you?" Dieter flung at his trembling partner. "You've been bragging ever since I met you about what you were gonna' do when you got here and get your hands on these people. But now you leave me to do all your cleanup. And then you find out they've removed your grandparents from their mausoleum and put Polish pigs in their place. Where's your family pride? You haven't fired a shot!"

Turning on his heel he prodded the brothers with his pistol in the direction of the manager's cottage, followed by a numbed Karlheinz.

Finding the terrified couple huddled in their kitchen, Dieter commanded, "Lock these two in your cellar and get the mess cleaned up around here. Get rid of those bodies."

In halting German, the estate manager enquired what should be done with the corpses.

"Get somebody to help you and bury them in the woods, but get rid of them. Are the graves of Karlheinz's grandparents in the churchyard marked?"

The manager nodded in the affirmative.

"Then you get that garbage out of those crypts and throw them in with the rest in the woods. We're going to the churchyard to find the Hohenberg graves. We'll be back here later, and I don't want to see any of these pigs lying around. You get those crypts cleaned out, and tomorrow you get those bodies out of the churchyard and brought back here. Are we clear?"

"One more thing: get a cook to make dinner for us this evening, and it had better be good."

Seeing the questioning look on the man's face, Dieter continued, "The cook and her assistant are dead in the courtyard. They gave us too much trouble, so I shot 'em. Get rid of 'em and the butler, too."

Turning to Karlheinz, he jibed, "Come on, pussy. Let's go find your family."

Chapter Forty-five

Graf Spee

"*Herr* Friedlander?"

Benjamin turned and looked into the face of the German seaman he encountered on his walk through the small park in Montevideo.

He read the name band on the sailor's cap, *Panzerschiff Admiral Graf Spee*. Then it dawned on him he was facing a crewmember from the German pocket battleship, which had been trapped in the harbor of Montevideo during the past month on December 13th. Ice water coursed through his veins.

"Wh- wh- Who are you?" he stammered.

"You wouldn't remember me, if I told you. But I remember you. You're Benjamin Friedlander, owner of *Friedlander und Sohn*, the big store on *Kurfürstendamm*."

Battling his urge to run, Benjamin couldn't hide his astonished stare. A rage went through his mind as he stood transfixed, staring at the swastika on the young man's uniform.

"My name is Max Gördler, *Herr* Friedlander. I grew up in Birkenwerder where my family has a small hardware store."

The young sailor continued speaking, "Our warship Admiral Graf Spee was deployed to the South Atlantic in the weeks before the outbreak of the war, to be positioned in merchant sea lanes once war was declared. Between September and December, we sank nine vessels before being confronted by three British cruisers. We inflicted heavy damage on the British ships, but not before they hurt us."

Benjamin fought the urge to cut him off short. *I don't want hear this. I've traveled half way around the world to get away from them, and they've separated me from my children. I have no interest in listening to a Nazi expound on his military adventures. Germans always want to take over the conversation, and the Nazis want to take over the world.*

"I know where you're from. Birkenwerder is between Berlin Pankow and Oranienburg," Benjamin replied curtly. "Now they've built a KZ at Oranienburg," Benjamin muttered with a pinched mouth of suppressed rage. (KZ is the German abbreviation for *Konzentrationslager* – concentration camp)

"What do people from Birkenwerder know about the concentration camp at Oranienburg?" challenged Benjamin.

The image of Kurt Wollner's face flashed into his mind! *Except for that German, we would have never made it out of Germany.*

Not hearing an answer, Benjamin prodded, "Why were you in my store?"

Startled the young man dropped his eyes.

"It was near Christmas when I was five," he began. "My father brought me to your store. He wanted to get something special for my mother. He bought her a new coat, and we had just stepped outside, and I fell on a patch of ice and hit my face on the pavement. Your daughter came out and picked me up and took me back inside."

"That must have been Edna. She helped in the store around the holidays," said Benjamin, his chin trembling.

"She took me up to your office and cleaned my face and hugged me. You came in, and after you heard the story, you went to your desk and brought out a big chocolate bar and gave it to me."

His brow furrowed in memory, Benjamin nodded, "Yes, I remember that now. Your father was very grateful. I remember he came back with your mother later in the Spring, and she brought Edna some flowers. How are your parents?"

"My mother died several years ago, and my father has remarried. We don't communicate much anymore. His second wife has a son about my age. He's a real Nazi. We don't get along."

"I'm sorry about your mother. I remember she was a really pretty small woman."

The young man nodded.

"What are you doing now? Are you going back to Germany soon?"

His face darkened, and his jaw clenched. "No, I can't ever go back there as long as the Nazis are running it. If any of us go back to

Germany, we would be subject to an inquest by the Naval authorities and then no doubt taken in for questioning by the Gestapo."

Max continued his narration. "I was conscripted when I turned eighteen two years ago. I had a friend in Hamburg who persuaded me to join the Kriegsmarine with him, but he was killed in our battle with the Ajax last December. A few weeks ago, we received reports of a massive British naval force approaching our ship. We were convinced they were true, and our Kapitän zur See, Hans Langsdorff, wasn't willing to risk the lives of his crew further by venturing into the range of the British cruisers.

So, Captain Langsdorff sought refuge in port here in Montevideo. He saw to the removal of injured German seamen and captives taken from merchant vessels we had sunk. The injured were taken in by hospitals in Montevideo, and the captives were released into the custody of their various governments.

Langsdorff and a skeleton crew of forty men scuttled the ship. The harbor is too shallow, and that's why everyone can see the top of our ship in the port, still over there above the surface of the water.

I still can't believe it, but on December 20th, Langsdorff shot himself in a hotel room."

Max's steady gaze belied his grief. "We will be interned in Argentina until the war is over. I will stay there."

Why are you here, *Herr* Friedlander?"

Benjamin considered the question, and gesturing toward a nearby park bench, suggested, "Let's take a seat there." He then related the events from the time he and his wife had left Berlin and also the tragedy of Edna being sent back to Europe aboard the St. Louis.

"That nice girl I told you about?"

"Yes, that's right."

"Oh, *Herr* Friedlander. I am so sorry. I am ashamed of what some of my people have done to you."

With a slight smile, Benjamin replied, "Thank you for saying that, *Herr* Gördler. But you must know there are Germans like you who try to help my people." Then he told about his friend, Kurt Wollner and his help getting them out of Berlin. As an afterthought, he added, "By the way. I have a non-Jewish German son-in-law."

At this, Max's eyes widened with surprise. "Really? You must tell me about him."

Benjamin briefly recounted the tale of Herbert and Meira and their present location in France.

"Your son-in-law is Herbert Lenz, the son of the surgeon at Charite´? What a small world it is!"

Shaking his head, Max empathized, "You and your family have been through hell, *Herr* Friedlander."

"Yes, but fortunately, we are all still alive."

"Where is *Frau* Friedlander?"

"She is here, but I'm sorry to say, not well. The experience in Havana, when we had to watch our daughter sail out of sight on that ship, almost killed Golda. She had a breakdown and hasn't been able to get back on her feet. I would invite you to come home and meet her, but I'm afraid it would be too much for her."

"Of course. But let me have your address. I'll be in Buenos Aires, and I want to see you again and meet *Frau* Friedlander."

Reaching into his pocket, he produced a small tablet and pencil and handed them to Benjamin, who wrote out his address. Handing it back to the sailor, he added, "Yes, *Herr* Gördler. I certainly want to keep in touch with you."

The young man extended his left hand as he stood. Benjamin took the proffered hand. He was confused as to why the left hand had been extended instead of the customary right, until he noticed the man's right hand was heavily bandaged as well as the right side of his face.

Max concluded, "It means a lot to me to meet you. I want to hear more about your family and any news about Edna."

They shook hands, and the young sailor walked away with a wave and a smile.

The wreckage of the Graf Spee is still visible in Montevideo to this day.

Chapter Forty-six

Operation Weserübung
Invasion of Norway and Denmark

"*Schön guten Morgen, Herr Meinert.*"
"*Guten Morgen, Frau Lindemann.*"
"What would you like for your second breakfast?"
"Bring me a pot of tea with a breakfast roll with ham and cheese. Are you alright, *Frau* Lindemann? You don't look well."
With eyes averted, the middle-aged woman busied herself writing down the order.
"*Frau* Lindemann?"
She and Eckhardt had known each other for over fifteen years, ever since he had returned to his job at Siemens as a veteran after the last war.
With red-rimmed eyes glistening with tears held back, "I received a telegram this morning."
Seeing that she was trying to control herself, Eckhardt waited.
"My Klaus was among the missing presumed dead on the Blücher."
At a loss for what to say, Eckhardt could only murmur, "I am so sorry, *Frau* Lindemann." He reached out and squeezed her hand. She nodded and continued down the row of cubicles in the engineering office taking requests.
"What the hell are we doing in Norway, anyway?" blurted his colleague across the aisle. "I didn't believe the bullshit that we were invading Denmark and Norway to 'protect' them from a 'British invasion' when they sent the troops in last week. Over two thousand crew and troops were on board the Blücher, and over eight hundred drowned or were burnt alive in the flaming oil slick from the wreck, when the Norwegians sank it on Tuesday."

"Careful, Müller. Just because we've known each other all these years doesn't mean you shouldn't watch what you say," cautioned Eckhardt.

"Well, if I can't trust old comrades like you, Meinert, what more is there to say? You never comment on anything the Nazis do, no matter how outrageous."

"Of course, you can trust me. But nowadays even the walls have ears," Eckhardt responded, just as a recently-hired young engineer entered the room.

Nodding his head in the direction of the newcomer, as if to reinforce what he had just cautioned, Eckhardt then returned to his work.

The event being discussed was the German invasion of Denmark and Norway on April 9, 1940.

"Well, I'm sorry, Eckhardt," declared Ursula. "Müller is right. You always look for some justification for any outrage Hitler commits."

Coming around behind him, as he buried himself in his paper, she bent down and put her arms around his neck and kissed him on the back of his head.

"Look, darling. I know you mean well, and because you always think the best of everybody is one of the main reasons I fell in love with you. But can't you see what's happening here now? Look at our boys. They are being so manipulated in the HJ and in school. Look at Eckhardt. He's become surly and disrespectful – especially to my mother. He's called her an 'old Bolshevik' more than once. And Detlev! He's always been such a sweet loving little boy, but he worships his older brother and tries to be just like him. And he has been told so often by his friends he's 'a real Aryan' because of his blond blue-eyed looks, it's starting to go to his head."

Laying down his paper, he reached around to grasp his wife, who kissed his upturned face.

"Of course I see what's going on. I also have to pick and choose every word I say, not only at work, but also here at home in front of the boys. And you and Christina had better realize that, too. Just as I told Müller, 'the walls have ears'.

Müller was telling me that one of his neighbors was hauled away by the Gestapo late one evening a week ago because he was shooting his mouth off in front of his kids about the invasion of Denmark, and his wife is Danish. I guess they just held him overnight and roughed him up a little bit. But Müller says the man is thoroughly terrified, and he and his wife are keeping to themselves now and hardly speak to anyone outside the home. The oldest boy is bragging to other kids that he got a commendation from his HJ leader for being a 'true Aryan' – probably because he denounced his father.

So, these are the times we're living in now. And we thought life was tough in the Weimar days!"

Chapter Forty-seven

Jetzt geht's los!
(Now it begins)

"I'm afraid we're really in it for the long haul, now," grumbled Kurt Wollner to Hans Joachim Lenz, as they strolled along the shore of the Grünewaldsee on a beautiful May late afternoon. They had become friends after working together to help Herbert and Meira escape to France after *Kristallnacht* in 1938.

It was now a week after the German invasion of Holland, Belgium, Luxembourg, and France on May 10, 1940.

"What do you hear from Herbert and Meira?"

"So far, nothing." Hans Joachim stared at the ground.

"And from Karlheinz?"

The doctor shook his head. "This is where Karlheinz told me he was joining the SS."

Wollner looked at his friend with sadness. "I'm sorry, Dr. Lenz."

They paused and gazed at the former Kaiser's hunting lodge across the lake.

"I wonder where we'd be now if we hadn't forced the Kaiser to abdicate," muttered the former policeman.

"My wife, Frederika, thought the world had come to an end that day," mused Hans Joachim. "I'm glad she's not here to see what's become of us now."

"I know what you mean. This Nazi freak show cannot end well for Germany." Wollner's nostrils flared. "But up until the dissolution of Czechoslovakia in '38, the majority of Germans were enthusiastic about Hitler. Then that, plus the tragedy of Kristallnacht, started to sober some of them up. If only Hitler had stayed fifteen minutes longer in the Bürgerbräukeller in Munich last November, that Communist carpenter's bomb would have taken him out," groused the policeman.

"Carpenter? Which assassination attempt are you referring to? There must have been more than just this one."

Wollner chuckled, "You have no idea! I know from my old colleagues there have been at least three. There must be other's that we don't know about, but this one in particular was an elaborate plot. Except for bad luck, it would have succeeded.

Knowing that Hitler would speak in Munich on the anniversary of the Beer Hall Putsch, Georg Elser spent months building his bomb. He stole some explosives from his workplace in Württemberg and moved to Munich. He began sneaking into the *Bürgerbräukeller* every night to hollow out a cavity in a stone pillar behind the speaker's podium. After several weeks of painstaking clandestine labor, he successfully planted his bomb. He set the timer to explode roughly half way through Hitler's speech."

Wollner clenched his teeth in frustration.

"It was a perfect plan! But Hitler changed the start time of his speech to 8 p.m. so he could be back in Berlin to oversee the war effort. He finished his remarks early and left the building thirteen minutes before Elser's bomb went off."

Hans Joachim cursed under his breath, "Damnit!"

Wollner nodded in agreement. "The whole pillar exploded and sent the roof crashing down on the podium. Sixty-three people were injured, and I guess one died later at the hospital. Hitler would have been killed instantly. Think of that!"

"Well, if one man worked up the courage to try to kill him, others will, too," assured Hans Joachim.

"We can hope. Let's have faith these trees aren't listening," quipped his friend.

The doctor smiled and continued, "What's going on with your daughter's husband. Didn't you tell me he was stationed in Copenhagen?"

"That's right. He sent a letter home telling about the attitude of the Danes, and they really resent the Germans being there. You know the Danes. Not inclined to be outright rude, but they show their feelings in little subtle ways. Horst, my son-in-law, wrote about the king,

Christian X, who rides his horse alone through Copenhagen every day with no guards whatsoever. The Danes aren't flamboyant and outright rebellious, but they let the Germans know how they feel. He even heard a rumor that the Danish king wears a yellow Star of David when he's out in public!"

Hans Joachim slapped Wollner on the back and laughed. "How's that for a political statement on Hitler's Nuremburg race laws!"

They continued along the path with their thoughts punctuated by the birds singing in the trees.

"I wish I knew more about what that son of mine is up to in Poland. He did write and tell me that he has 'liberated' the old estate of my wife's family, *Schloß Hohenberg*," sighed Hans Joachim.

"What about the Poles living there?"

"He didn't say, but knowing my son's temper and his cockiness, since he can wear an SS uniform, I'm not sure I really want to know."

They continued on down the path leading around the lake.

§§§

After planting his bomb and setting the timer, Georg Elser had immediately left for the Swiss border. He was arrested at the border and sent to Sachsenhausen concentration camp and later transferred to Dachau, where he was executed two weeks before the camp was liberated in 1945.

Chapter Forty-eight

Jugendliche Begeisterung
(Youthful Enthusiasm)

"Jürgen's uncle, Hartmann Lauterbacher, will drive us to Berchtesgaden in his new Maybach. His former boss, Baldur von Schirach, has invited *Herr* Lauterbacher to join him at the Berghof (Hitler's home near Berchtesgaden) with the *Führer* for lunch, to congratulate *Herr* von Schirach for the fine work he has done with the Hitler Jugend. The other boys from our HJ troop will travel down by bus and come out later in the afternoon. Just think! I'll get to meet the *Führer* personally!" young Eckhardt informed his parents one evening at dinner in May 1940.

Ursula exchanged glances with Eckhardt. Christina studied her daughter's reaction, and asked, "How do you feel about that, Ursula?"

"What's to feel?" blurted young Eckhardt. "To meet the *Führer*? That's the highest honor any right-thinking German could receive!"

"Are you gonna tell him Grandma's a Communist?" Little Detlev shot back.

Ursula stared at her mother's startled expression, then commanded her son, "You're not going to say any such thing!"

"I might," retorted young Eckhardt. "And what do you think he would say if I tell him my mother also has a friend who's a Jew!"

"That's enough! What's the matter with all of you? This family does not turn against each other, is that clear?" declared his father.

The sixteen-year old pulled himself up erect in his chair. "You just don't get it! Every good German realizes that we owe everything to the *Führer* and to the Fatherland – even our very lives. Nothing comes before our obligation to him! Not even the family!"

With that, the young man stood up, flung his napkin on his chair, gave a Nazi salute, shouted "Heil Hitler," and marched upstairs.

Wide-eyed, his brother asked his father, "Are you gonna let him go?"

Eckhardt studied his plate. Christina left the table.

"Of course," answered Ursula. "But you both are not to harass my mother. I won't stand for it!"

"But she is a Communist, and my teacher says they are not to be trusted."

Again, the husband and wife looked at each other with resignation.

"Do you think we're losing our boys?" Eckhardt murmured in the darkness of their bedroom.

Ursula replied, "I can imagine many parents all over Germany are asking themselves the same question. But what are we to do? If we don't allow our son to accept such an invitation as this, we would immediately come under suspicion as being subversive and un-German. You heard what he said. To turn down an opportunity to meet the *Führer*? It would be viewed as unthinkable, and that – in addition to any investigation of my mother's political background – would place our whole family under the microscope of the Gestapo. And I don't want to even think about how Eckhardt would react. For a sixteen-year old to lose face with his friends – not to mention the other boys at school and in the HJ? Yes, unless we handle this situation with great care, we could very well lose him. Forever!"

Eckhardt listened, turned it all over in his mind, and then replied, "You're right, of course. And that doesn't even take into consideration Detlev's reaction. He worships his brother and is also influenced by his teachers and youth leaders to see Hitler as the greatest man who ever lived. He would never understand why we would deny Eckhardt the chance to meet the man. You're right. I'll speak to him in the morning and tell him he can go to Berchtesgaden."

Midmorning on the following Saturday, the next-door neighbor, *Frau* Lortz, was chatting over her front fence with the neighbor from across the street, *Frau* Bertelmann. Both women ceased their conversation as a large gleaming maroon and black Maybach glided to a stop in front of the Meinert residence. The women's eyes were drawn to the pennants on the front fenders, which signified that the owner of the vehicle was someone at the top level of the Hitler Youth.

"Well," declared *Frau* Bertelmann, "who do you suppose that is? We never see a car like that around here!"

The passenger side front door opened and young Jürgen Lauterbacher emerged, went to the front gate, and rang the buzzer. The release buzzer immediately responded and the visitor opened the gate and walked to the front door, which was opened by young Eckhardt.

"*Schön guten Morgen, Jürgen,*" he greeted his friend. They shook hands as Jürgen entered the house.

"Did you hear that, *Frau* Bertelmann? 'Jürgen'? That's Jürgen Lauterbacher, Hartmann Lauterbacher's nephew."

"Who's Hartmann Lauterbacher?"

"He's on Baldur von Schirach's staff, the leader of the Hitler Youth. My sister's daughter is a secretary in von Schirach's office," declared *Frau* Lortz. "She has talked about Lauterbacher and what a show off he is."

"Ah, yes. That would explain such a flashy car. But how does a kid from this neighborhood know people like that?"

"Well, I know the Meinert kids are heavily involved in the Hitler Youth, and one day I heard young Eckhardt and that Jürgen coming home singing at the tops of their voices, until *Frau* Meinert yelled at them from the front window to shut it down."

Both women chuckled.

"*Der Führer* is absolutely the greatest man of our time!" declared young Eckhardt the morning after his return from Berchtesgaden.

"He was very kind to us and made us feel completely at ease. When he shook my hand, he took my hand in both of his. He's so different from the way we see him in the newsreels. But he is very strong. You can feel his power when you talk to him face to face. And he loves the German youth. He says only Germany could produce such brilliant young people," he continued as he drank his breakfast tea.

Ursula listened quietly as she prepared the *Sauerbraten* (rump roast cooked with red wine vinegar and spices), which needed to marinate all day for the evening meal. Christina, who was peeling potatoes for potato dumplings, frowned and pursed her lips in an effort to keep silent.

"His house, the Berghof, is magnificent. There is a huge window in the living room that faces the Alps. It can be rolled down like a car window, and you can smell the fragrance of woods surrounding the house.

"We had lunch on the terrace, and we met his friend, Eva Braun. She is beautiful and told me I was handsome." A short laugh. "Imagine that! I told her she should see my little brother, Detlev. That he's blond and looks like the picture of the perfect Aryan boy. She giggled and said all Aryans are not blond. Look at the *Führer*. He has dark hair. It was a day I shall never forget. I'm so proud to be German!"

"I was afraid of that," commented Eckhardt that evening, when Ursula repeated to him what she had heard from her son that morning. They lay in their bed after everyone else had retired.

"I want the boys to be proud of being German, but I don't like to see them completely taken in by the Nazis." he grumbled.

"How can you talk about being proud as a German when you see what's happening here?" retorted Ursula. "'The greatest man of our time!' We haven't seen the last of his greatness, just you wait and see!"

Not replying immediately, Eckhardt finally said in a low voice, "I'm concerned, too, Ursula. But what are our options? We can't contradict a young man who has just had lunch and shaken hands with the leader of his country. And look at what our troops have accomplished in France. They've taken Paris in only four weeks, when we fought and died for four long years to reach the same goal. And we didn't even succeed at that! So, you can't really blame the boys for being proud!"

"Proud! Proud of what? Invading and taking another people's country? I don't know, Eckhardt. Sometimes, you talk out of both sides of your mouth."

Raising up to fluff her pillow, Ursula then lay down and turned on her side away from her husband.

"Good night, Eckhardt."

He lay silent in the dark, turning her words over in his mind. *I hope she and her mother don't let their mouths get ahead of them outside of our home. I understand her concern, but walking the fence is never easy. And it's going to get worse before it gets better.*

Chapter Forty-nine

Blitzkrieg

2:00 a.m., May 13, 1940

The shrill ringing of the phone penetrated the consciousness of General Maurice Gamelin, commander of the French Army. Rousing from an exhausted sleep on a cot set up in his office in the Army headquarters on the outskirts of Paris, he was shocked into full wakefulness by the voice on the other end.

"The Germans have broken through the Ardennes forest near Sedan. They are in France!"

"C'est incroyable! Il est impossible!"

Impossible! That echoed the opinions of several French military leaders on the eve of the German breakthrough.

During the 1930s, the French had built the Maginot Line, a series of concrete fortifications, as well as obstacles and weapon installations to deter invasion by Germany. It was designed to divert them into Belgium, which could then be met by the best divisions of the French Army. The war would take place outside French territory, thus avoiding the destruction of the First World War.

The eastern edge of the Ardennes begins in Germany, but is located primarily in Belgium and Luxembourg, continuing west into France. It is a western extension of the Eifel, a low mountain range in western Germany and eastern Belgium consisting of extensive forests, rough terrain, rolling hills and ridges.

French General, Charles Huntziger, refused to accept the idea that the Germans could attack through the Ardennes. General Gamelin himself regarded the Ardennes as "Europe's best tank obstacle". Marshall Philippe Petain was said to have called the Ardennes "impenetrable".

But the fact remains the Germans did penetrate it!

The world was astonished at the speed with which the Wehrmacht had slashed through Holland and Belgium, but no one could have anticipated the German breakthrough in the Ardennes. French strategists speculated that such a maneuver would take up to nine days, were it attempted. The Germans accomplished it in 2½ days and with such force that it reinforced the Nazi propaganda that the German soldier was indeed *ein Übermensch* (a superman).

§§§

> ### *Les Allemands sont en Sedan*
> (The Germans are in Sedan)

The Paris papers shrieked the headlines. Panic spread across the city. Parisians were shocked that the enemy had managed to cross their border so quickly and were now charging toward them. Refugee columns soon choked the roads out of the capital heading south.

"Les Allemands viennent à Paris!" (The Germans are coming to Paris!) shouted someone on the street below their open bedroom window.

"Herbert! Wake up!" urged Meira, shaking her husband. "We've got to leave!"

Fighting off his sleep, he sat up and looked at his wife, trying to put her words together in his groggy mind.

"Turn on the radio!" she cried.

He reached to the small radio on the shelf next to the bed. Turning the dial, he found a strong signal of the main Paris radio station. The agitated voice of the announcer filled the room with rapid fire news announcements and directives from the government. The awful statements coming over the air reiterated what had awakened Meira.

Just then a knock came at their bedroom door, followed by Edna entering without waiting for a response.

Before she could speak, Meira declared, "Yes, we know already. We've got to go!"

"Let's not lose our heads," directed Herbert. "First, let's get dressed and get something to eat."

The effect of his words took hold, and Edna nodded, "Yes, you're right. We must avoid panic."

After dressing without much care, the three went down in the elevator, which was already filled to near capacity. The tension in the air was electric, and the passengers were oddly silent – as if still trying to process the dreadful truth that lay before them.

Crossing the street, they headed toward the small bistro further down the block where they often took their morning and midday meals. But it was to no avail. The steel roll down shutter covering the face of the establishment was still closed and locked.

The business establishments up and down the street had followed suit. The usual morning crowds were not to be seen, except for some people hurrying in many directions, their faces tense with fear – some wide-eyed with panic.

"Let's go back to the apartment," advised Meira. "We still have some sausage, cheese and bread."

"Good idea," responded her sister. "Then we need to talk about what our priorities are."

"Our main priority is to get the hell out of here!" growled Herbert.

"Yes, but as you said yourself, no panic," chided Meira.

Herbert, in anticipation of just such an eventuality, had prudently been withdrawing moderate amounts of cash from the Swiss account throughout the weeks since early Spring. Expecting that French currency would be rapidly devalued under German occupation, he had converted much of his reserves into U.S. dollars and gold.

"We need French passports," declared Herbert, as they finished their breakfast coffee.

"Passports?" Meira blurted, in astonishment. "And just how are we going to get those? Even if you knew how to get them, we don't have enough time. Don't you understand? The Germans are *in France!*"

Herbert and Edna looked at her in surprise. It was not like Meira to respond to her husband in such a challenging manner.

"Sweetheart, please don't talk to me like that. I'm sorry, I should have explained that I've already thought of a way to get them. When we were leaving *Madame* Fournier's farm that morning, she gave me the address of her cousin's husband here in Paris and said I should get in touch with the man if I had any problems."

"I remember hearing her tell you that, and I saw her hand you a note," interjected Edna. "I wondered what she meant by that, but I didn't feel I should ask."

"Well, I wish you had, Edna. That one must have passed me by. Why haven't you said anything about it to me until now, Herbert?"

"I should have, but I had so much on my mind that morning, I just slipped it into my pocket and didn't think any more about it until right now."

Rising and coming around the table, he bent down and embraced his wife. "I apologize, *Schätzchen* (little sweetheart). I need to remember you are a very capable woman, and I'll try harder to include you in our plans."

Kissing him, she replied, "And I'm sorry, too. We've got to rely on each other – not bicker."

Watching bemused, Edna admired the two of them for their strength and dedication to one another. She was glad that her fate was in the hands of two such resourceful people.

Returning to his seat, Herbert continued, "I'll get in touch with him right away. I don't know exactly what kind of person he is, but I'm sure he must be someone of influence, or *Madame* Fournier would never have recommended him."

"I, for one, will be glad to be rid of that German passport," cried Edna. "Every time I look at it, that big *J* stamped on the first page gives me such a chill."

"You're absolutely right, Edna," responded her sister. "If the Germans ever got hold of the two of us, we'd be headed right back to Germany and straight into the hands of the Gestapo. And if they made the connection to our parents – who slipped out of the country – we'd really be in for it."

"Well, that's not going to happen," stated Herbert. "That's why I need to get going."

"Good! Meanwhile, Edna and I will start going through our things and decide what to take and what to leave."

"That's right," nodded Herbert. "We need to be ready to leave at a moment's notice."

"How are we going to travel?" queried Edna. "By train?"

"Well, I've thought of buying a car, but I think that would make us stand out too much. We should just try to blend in with all the other refugees. Maybe we should even dress a little shabbily?"

"I agree," added Meira. "The customs officers will hopefully be so overwhelmed with the crowds, they might not take much time with us, and we shouldn't make it any easier for them. But we have to remember, the bottom line is we are at their mercy."

"I've had considerable practice being at the mercy of others the past few months," Edna pointed out.

"Amen to that, sister!" concluded Meira.

§§§

The German strategy of pushing through forests, supported by the Luftwaffe, was met with unexpected success. It caught everyone by surprise – even the German commanders. France's defenses were pierced, and the Allies were unable to close the gap.

The German Generals, Walter von Brauchitsch, Gerd von Rundstedt and Fedor von Bock, among others, saw the way to Paris open to them. The Germans had crossed into France at Sedan on May 13, and entered Paris on June 14. By contrast, in World War I, it took four years of battle, and the loss of 1½ million men for the Germans, to reach the outskirts of Paris.

In 1940, they had covered virtually the same distance in only four weeks, with a loss of only 30,000 men.

Thus, the legend of *Blitzkrieg* (Lightning War) was born.

§§§

Military historians have sifted through many possibilities of how the Germans reached Paris so quickly: good intelligence and surveillance, well trained and well-equipped forces, superior military leadership, growing up with years of Nazi indoctrination, etc.

Pervitin!

Pervitin is a form of methamphetamine, or crystal meth. It was developed by the Berlin pharmaceutical company, Temmler, and introduced to the German public in 1938 as an over the counter antidepressant.

The drug was distributed to millions of German troops before the invasion of France. This helps explain how the soldiers could display such high energy and alertness and march for days and nights without rest.

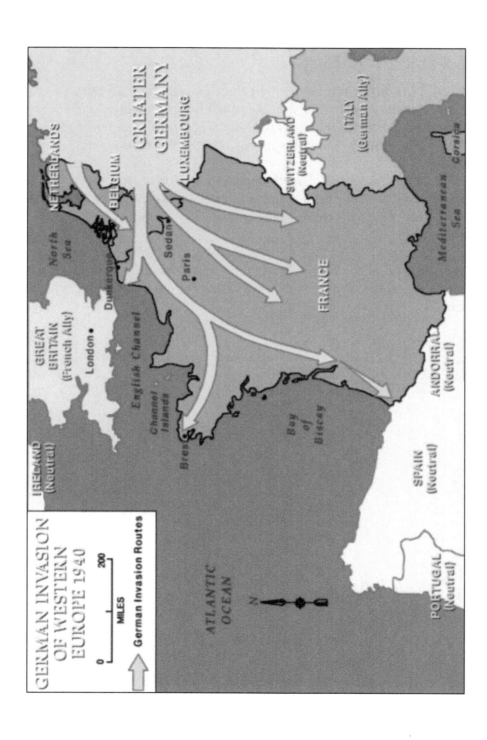

Chapter Fifty

A Guardian Angel

"Flaubert residence," said a masculine voice.
"*Monsieur* Flaubert?"
"No, I am his secretary. Who is calling, please?"
"My name is Herbert Lenz."
"One moment, please."
After a long pause: "Maurice Flaubert. What can I do for you, *Monsieur* Lenz?"
"I was given your number by your wife's cousin in Bray sur Somme."
"I know who you are, *Monsieur*. My wife has already heard from her cousin that you might be calling. I thought I might have heard from you before now."
Wondering what the man meant by that but not wanting to ask, Herbert continued, "I am sorry to disturb you, but I need to talk to you rather urgently."
"What do you need, *Monsieur*?"
Herbert paused, "I would prefer not to discuss it over the phone. Could you please permit me to meet you?"
"Of course. You can come to my house tomorrow at ten. I live in the 6th District in the Rue du Cherche-Midi."
"What's the address, please?"
"I will have someone meet you. Are you driving yourself? If so, please park your car at least a block away."
"No, I'll be coming by taxi. How will I find your home?"
"Call just before you leave, and tell me where you're coming from. My secretary will await you at the curb. He'll be wearing a dark green jacket. I'm sorry to be evasive. I look forward to seeing you tomorrow at ten. *Adieu.*" The line went dead.
Herbert hung up the phone wondering just what kind of person he would be dealing with.

As the taxi rolled at an almost imperceptible rate along the Rue du Cherche-Midi, Herbert searched the pedestrians for a man wearing a dark green jacket. Most were in short-sleeved summer clothing, with a few men in dark suits.

Then there he was! A short slightly built man waited motionless on the curb. He stood before an imposing gated entrance to a large yellow villa, set behind manicured hedges and shrubs.

"Stop here, please."

As the driver eased the taxi to the curb, *Monsieur* Flaubert's secretary walked to the door and opened it, as Herbert stepped out.

"*Monsieur* Lenz?"

"Yes. Good morning."

"Good morning. Follow me, please."

Expecting to be directed through the front gate, Herbert was surprised to be led through the driveway entrance, down a long drive, and to a back door of the building.

As they entered, they walked along a dark corridor past storage rooms, the kitchen, and into a butler's pantry.

"Wait here. *Monsieur* Flaubert will be with you shortly."

Left alone in a room of glass-fronted cabinets containing china and crystal, Herbert was perplexed by the strange behavior he had encountered so far. After studying the patterns on the several sets of china, all of which were obviously of high quality and costly manufacture, he wished Meira could see this.

The door opened, and a tall, silver-haired, mustached gentleman stepped into the room.

"*Monsieur* Lenz?" He extended a manicured hand wearing a large ruby signet ring. "I'm sorry to have kept you waiting in here, but in times like these, I have to be very circumspect whom I can admit through the front entrance." Without waiting for a response, he continued, "Let's get right to the matter. What is the reason you have contacted me?"

"I need French passports."

"Those can be obtained, of course, but will not come cheap." Herbert thought it odd he was not asked why he needed them.

"Obviously! But I need them right away – immediately, if possible!"

A slight smile played on the lips of his host.

"Then they will come even less cheaply."

Herbert explained that they needed to get out of France but could not with their German passports.

"I knew you were German. *Madame* Fournier had informed my wife as much. We are soon to be hosting your countrymen in Paris, and I am sad to say, there will be many like yourself who won't wish to be here to greet them."

Realizing that his interviewer no doubt already knew his female companions were Jewish, Herbert felt relieved that Flaubert did not press the matter any further but nevertheless volunteered the information.

"As I am sure you already know, my wife and her sister are Jewish. So, there is no question of 'greeting my countrymen', as you put it."

"I understand," followed by a slight smile.

"The passports will cost 1,000 dollars each. I hope that will not be a problem for you. All transactions such as this are being conducted everywhere in Europe nowadays in U.S. dollars. I can have them for you in a week."

"A week? Could they be ready any sooner?"

"I'm sorry. My resources are being pushed to the limit right now. As we have already mentioned, there are thousands, like you, who are anxious to leave Paris before the Germans get here. If you don't mind my asking, what is your ultimate destination?"

"We hope to get to Montevideo. My wife's parents are already there. And my sister-in-law has already had the experience of trying to enter the United States, so we know that option is closed."

"Your sister-in-law has tried to get a visa to the United States?"

"She was on the St. Louis."

Flaubert's eyebrows shot up.

"The St. Louis! What a tragedy! Those poor people. Your sister-in-law has endured enough already. If you wish, I can help you get passage on a ship to South America, but I would not advise trying to leave from a French port. The crush of people trying to leave is so great that passage on ships leaving from France has become almost impossible to obtain. I would suggest you try to get to Spain or Portugal and leave from there."

"Incredible!" declared Herbert. "The flood of refugees has built up that fast in twenty-four hours?"

"Actually, *Monsieur* Lenz, this has been going on for weeks – even months. Many have seen the handwriting on the wall with the Germans ransacking Europe. Begging your pardon."

With a wave of his hand, Herbert exclaimed, "You don't need to apologize, *Monsieur*. I am ashamed to admit that what is going on right now in Germany's name is barbaric. I know you might find it hard to believe, but there are many in my country who feel as I do. You just can't see them, because the terror that Hitler and the Nazis have unleashed has driven them underground and out of sight."

Shaking his head, Flaubert replied, "Then I will expend every effort to do what I can for you. *Madame* Fournier wrote quite highly of you to my wife. I can see why. I will look into booking you passage on a ship out of a Spanish or Portuguese port as quickly as I can. But I will need at least half of your money, in order to get my resource going on your passports. And I will need photos as soon as you can get them to me."

"No problem, *Monsieur* Flaubert. I can get fifteen hundred dollars to you this afternoon, and I have three recent photos of us with me."

"Excellent!" Extending his hand once more, he continued, "It's been a real pleasure meeting you, *Monsieur* Lenz."

Chapter Fifty-one

Adieu Paris!

"*Monsieur* Lenz, Maurice Flaubert here," came the welcome phone call four days later. "I have your passports, and I have found available space for you on a Portuguese ship sailing from Lisbon on August 9th, arriving in New York on August 19th."

"August? We wanted to be in Montevideo by then! The Nazis could be here any day. And New York! We don't have visas or landing permits for the United States. I already told you, my sister-in-law was on the St. Louis, and the Americans wouldn't allow any of them to land, either. And why so late? August?"

"I'm sorry, *Monsieur* Lenz. These are not normal times. You are three of tens of thousands desperate to get out of Europe now. I had a terrible time finding you available passage, and I regret to inform you that I have had to 'grease the wheels', as it were. So, I will have to charge you extra. But I have a bit of good news. I was told by one of my contacts that the ship will also make a stop in Veracruz."

"Veracruz? In Mexico?"

"Yes. From there you should be able to get to Uruguay. Especially with the means you have at your disposal."

A deep sigh. "I apologize, *Monsieur* Flaubert. I didn't mean to sound unappreciative. How much extra do you need?"

"An extra five hundred dollars for each of you, plus the price for your passage, which cost four hundred dollars each. I booked you in First Class, which was all that was left. Most people can't afford that. But at least you'll be comfortable.

Now, in order for you to get out of France as quickly as possible, I have also booked you on a flight leaving Orly Airport day after tomorrow. The flights are another six hundred dollars, unless you would rather try going by train. But I can tell you, there is virtually no space on them now."

"No, by air would definitely be better." A quick calculation. "Thirty-three hundred dollars, then?"

"Yes, that is correct."

After a pause.

"Well, thank you, *Monsieur* Flaubert. Would it be convenient for me to pick up the items this afternoon?"

"Yes, or I can have my secretary deliver them. You will see that the names have been changed in your passports."

"Can you tell me what they are?"

"I don't think that would be wise over the phone."

"Of course. I wasn't thinking. But I think I would rather pick them up myself, if that is not inconvenient."

"Certainly. Shall we say about four? Since you know where the entrance is, please come to the same door as before."

"That will be perfect. Thank you."

Arriving at the appointed time, Herbert knocked on the back door of the villa and was let in by the young secretary.

"Good afternoon, *Monsieur* Lenz. Please follow me into the butler's pantry."

After waiting only a few minutes, Herbert was glad to be greeted by his host, as he stepped into the pantry.

"Good afternoon, *Monsieur* Lenz. Here are your passports. Let me show you your new names. You will now be *Louis Faycheux*. Your wife, *Denise*. Your sister-in-law is *Nicole Caron*. I purposely avoided choosing names that use the same initials as your real names. People often do that, and the customs officials look for it, if they are at all suspicious.

The problem, of which you are already aware, is your sister-in-law doesn't speak any French at all. She must avoid speaking to you or your wife in German, at all costs."

"I understand. My wife isn't fluent, but she can answer most simple questions."

"Yes. And besides, you can do most of the talking.'"

Herbert nodded.

"Now, here are your steamship tickets. You are sailing on the SS Quanza on August 9th from Lisbon, as I have told you. It's a Portuguese ship. And of course, you will have to arrange your living quarters in Lisbon until your August departure. Be prepared to find the hotels there booked up, too. All Europe is apparently abandoning the ship, and the main exit seems to be Portugal."

They shook hands. "Good luck to you, *Monsieur* Lenz."

The next evening, they left their apartment and, after considerable walking, managed to hail down a taxi. The streets were becoming ever more deserted, and the normal traffic was diminished. Many taxis had disappeared in the exodus to leave the city. Herbert and the girls had taken the extra precaution to arrive at Orly the night before their flight, because of the risk of being somehow held up.

When they arrived at the terminal building, they were greeted by a mass of people waiting for the next day's flights. After much searching, they managed to find two vacant seats some distance from their boarding area. Herbert insisted that Meira and Edna take them. He lay on the floor at their feet.

The next morning, Herbert awoke to discover a horde of people in the terminal. The line leading to the customs officials had already formed. He roused the girls, who insisted they had to take care of nature's needs, before anything else. Herbert volunteered to watch their three pieces of luggage, while the women took their places outside the restroom. After waiting for the better part of thirty minutes, Meira and Edna reappeared and explained that the restroom was packed. Herbert visited the men's room and returned shortly thereafter.

Meanwhile, the line had grown so long and unruly that the customs officials were beginning to lose control, causing another delay. Finally, Herbert and the girls were able to push their way into line and begin to make their way forward to the passport control. They reached the point that Herbert was facing the customs official.

"*Suivant pour le stand un!*" (Next in line to booth one!), he directed.

"We're all together." Pointing to Meira, he explained, "This is my wife."

"Then you both go there to booth one."

Turning to Edna he commanded, *"Stand deux!"* (Booth two).

In desperation, Edna turned with a pleading look toward Herbert.

Not wanting for them to be separated, Herbert insisted that they were together.

"Vous, avancez ou sortez de la ligne!" (You, move forward or get out of line!), shouted the official.

The three hesitated.

With a brusque grip on Edna's arm, the official pointed, *"Stand deux!"*

Resigned that they could not help Edna, Herbert and Meira approached booth one to be processed.

"Citoyens français?" (French citizens?)

"Oui!"

As he stamped their passports, he dismissed them, directing them through the door to the boarding area.

"Herbert, we can't leave her. We have to wait."

The customs officer gruffly commanded them to move along. Meira was distraught, as she heard an engine start.

A group of people who were cleared through customs, but waiting on standby, watched them with desperation, as they moved toward the steps to the plane's entrance.

As they took their seats, they waited helplessly for Edna to appear on board. Then a standby passenger boarded and took the seat reserved for Edna. The door was closed, the other engines started, and the plane began to taxi away from the terminal. Meira began to scream, *"Wir müssen aussteigen!* (We must get off). We can't leave her here alone!" Herbert gripped her arm and whispered, *"Kein Deutsch!"* (No German!)

The stewardess hurried down the aisle. Herbert explained in French what had happened. "I'm sorry, but we cannot stop the plane to let you off. Your sister-in-law will certainly follow on the next flight."

§§§

"Citoyen français?"
Edna smiled at the customs official and nodded.
"Quelle est votre destination?" (What is your destination?).
She smiled and nodded again.
In dismay, she heard the engines start.
"Madame! Quelle est votre destination?"
She uttered the only French word she knew, *"Oui."*
The official turned to his colleague at the next booth, shrugged and threw up his hands.
"Madame ne parle pas français!" (Madam does not speak French).
She began to sob and tremble as she watched the plane take off through the large window facing the runway.

Chapter Fifty-two

Summer in Portugal

"They told us she'd be on the next flight!"

After landing midmorning in Lisbon, Meira and Herbert enquired how many flights were expected from Paris throughout the day. Three more flights, the last arriving in the evening at 6:20 p.m.

"We should just wait here," declared Meira, as she settled into a corner with their luggage near the Air France ticket counter. With the crush of refugees, there were no seats to be had. Families and groups of desperate looking people milled about. The hubbub of voices, punctuated by the wails and laments of exhausted children, filled the warm, humid air, redolent with the odor of perspiration-drenched clothing.

"Good, but let's get something to eat first. The next flight will arrive at 1:35 pm. We can't do anything until then, anyway."

Meira sighed. "You're right, of course. We have about two hours, but let's stay close to the airport."

They put their two pieces of luggage in a locker at the back of the waiting area and made their way through the crowd to the entrance. Upon stepping out into the glaring sun, the scene was repeated. Lisbon had become a funnel with escapees from all over Europe, and predominantly from the German occupied countries, desperately trying to squeeze through to freedom. In addition, Portugal was hosting the Portuguese National Exhibition at Lisbon that year. Vehicle traffic was reduced to a crawl, impacted by the chaotic throng of pedestrians going in all directions.

Street vendors had seized upon the opportunity to gain access to a multitude of new customers. The fragrances of many varieties of food wafted over the crowd. Typical Portuguese street food included Bifana, a sandwich on light crusty bread filled with sautéed pork seasoned with spices, especially minced garlic, and white wine. Then there was Bola de Berlim, sweet fried dough balls, plain or filled with egg yolk crème or sugar. There were various kinds of fruit, fish, and poultry offerings. Herbert and Meira walked along the street and were undecided which of the tempting choices to make. Finally, Herbert selected a portion of grilled shrimp, served in a fold of paper. Meira decided on a Bifana. They concluded their repast with some fresh fruit, purchasing some extra, which they carried in a cloth bag purchased from the vendor.

"We'd better be getting back," urged Meira.

Shouldering their way back to the airport building and to the Air France counter, they were surprised to see passengers disembarking from an Air France plane and entering the waiting area.

"Did this plane just get in from Paris?" Meira enquired of the ticket agent.

"Yes, madam. The winds were favorable, and they arrived early."

"Oh, Herbert. What if we missed her?"

"If she's here, she won't leave. She doesn't know where we are, and I'm sure she would just wait or ask the ticket agent if anyone left a message for her."

"Good idea!"

He watched her turn back to the counter. Although he couldn't catch the words, he could see the agent shake his head and see disappointment registered on his wife's face.

"No luck, huh?"

"No, she wasn't on the plane."

Herbert and Meira waited anxiously for the arrival of the remaining flights from Paris. The hours slipped by with one flight after another arriving, with no sign of Edna. As they watched the passengers disembark one by one from the final flight of the day, a sense of dread began to overtake Meira.

"What if she isn't on the flight? She will have nowhere to stay!"

Herbert tried to assure his wife, "I'm sure she will step down those stairs any moment."

But it was not to be. When the flight crew had deplaned and were walking towards the terminal, Meira began to panic. She had always been totally unflappable in any situation, and Herbert had never seen her is such an agitated state. This was so out of character for her that he became concerned.

"Edna is every bit as strong as you are, sweetheart. She will be ok. We'll see her first thing in the morning. Let's check again at the ticket counter to see what flight she'll be on."

"I have no listing for Nicole Caron. She was not on any flight today, and she is not listed for tomorrow. I will receive the updated list later tonight, but you will have to come back tomorrow. *Sinto muito.*" (I'm sorry).

Meira shook her head, fighting back tears.

"There's nothing else we can do tonight. Let's go find a hotel, and we'll come back first thing in the morning."

They retrieved their luggage, and headed toward the entrance. Herbert put his arm around her shoulder as they made their way out to the street. Fighting the crowd, they stepped outside.

Meira pulled on Herbert's sleeve and cried, "Look! There's a taxi just letting off some people. Hurry! We'll catch it!"

Just as they neared the curb, a stout middle-aged woman stepped directly in front of them and forcefully opened the passenger door. *"Emil! Komm'. Mach's schnell!"* she shouted in the direction of a small, stooped man struggling with an enormous suitcase to get to the cab. Turning to face Herbert, she showed a thin lipped, grim countenance, as if challenging him to say a word.

Meira's face flushed crimson, and she began to open her mouth, but Herbert pulled her away.

"Let it go," he murmured.

Working their way through the crowd and away from the airport, they walked for a considerable distance. As the mass of people and vehicle traffic thinned out, they finally saw a taxi cruising slowly toward them. Herbert stepped out into the road and hailed him down. They hurriedly got in and closed the door.

"Sprechen Sie Deutsch?" No response.

"*Parlez vous Francais?*" The driver grinned and shrugged his shoulders.

"Do you speak English?"

"Me English no good." Another grin and a shrug.

He looked at Meira in frustration.

She leaned forward and said, "Hotel."

Nodding, the driver grinned. "*Hotel. Si.*" Holding his hand out, he looked with expectation at Herbert. After a pause, Herbert place a U.S. dollar bill in his hand. The driver's eyes and his grin widened together.

Turning his vehicle around, he headed toward the city. After wending his way through a myriad of streets, he finally pulled up before a small establishment.

"You wait in the car," he told Meira. "I'm seeing what's available."

After a few minutes, he returned, his lips set in a tight line.

"No luck?" queried his wife.

"No. They're absolutely filled up."

Turning to the driver, he said "Other hotel!"

Again, holding out his hand, the man grinned.

Herbert's face flushed with anger. He started to speak, when Meira grasped his arm and declared, "Let me try. Give me two dollars."

With a radiant smile, she leaned forward and showed the man the money.

"Good hotel, okay?" and placed one dollar in the outstretched hand. He continued to hold out his hand and grin.

Wagging her finger and shaking her head, Meira said, "No. Good hotel."

With a look of disappointment, the driver frowned, turned, and put the car in gear.

After the better part of half an hour, they reached an outer suburb and stopped before a small house set back from the road behind a wall fronted by a gate.

"This time you wait," directed Meira. Turning to the driver, she pointed toward the house and said, "You come." She stepped out of the car and beckoned to the hesitant man, who stepped out, and they walked together to the gate, where there was a bell cord suspended on pole. Without waiting, Meira pulled the cord, and after a moment, the front door opened. A small woman appeared and called out across the courtyard in Portuguese.

The driver stepped forward and replied. After a brief exchange of words, the woman walked to the gate and opened it. Smiling, she gestured for them to enter. Herbert, watching from the car, saw the three disappear into the house.

After what seemed a considerable amount of time, he saw Meira and the driver reappear and walk toward the car.

"Well, how did that go?"

Smiling, she replied, "You can bring our luggage, and pay the man. You might tip him rather well, because he has brought us to a very nice accommodation. Wait until you see."

As they walked to the door, their hostess waited in the doorway with a welcoming smile. Meira introduced her husband and turning to Herbert said, "Darling, meet *Senhora* Ferreira. She speaks a little French."

Chapter Fifty-three

Lebensmittelvergiftung
(Food poisoning)

She was awakened by the sound of Herbert vomiting in the small sink in their bedroom. She arose, but before her feet touched the floor, he turned and dashed out the bedroom door and down the hall to the toilet.

As she rinsed out the sink, he returned. Bathed in sweat, shaky and pale, he moaned, "God, I feel awful."

"You've picked up food poisoning. I saw lots of this when I was nursing during the war."

"Yes, I'm sure you're right. It's that shrimp I had. I should have known better, but I thought because it was cooked, it'd be alright."

"I thought so, too. But you don't know how long it lay around before they cooked it."

As he got back into bed, he mumbled, "I'm sorry, but I can't leave the house today."

"Of course not. You rest and drink lots of water, but I don't trust the water from the tap without boiling it."

She opened the curtains at the small window and was greeted by early morning sun.

"I'll open this. The fresh air will probably do you good. I'll go down and boil some water. I hear *Senhora* Ferreira stirring around in the kitchen."

"Ask her if she has some garlic. If she does, mince a clove and put it the water after you boil it. Garlic tea will help fight the bacteria."

"Good idea! You rest and I'll be back as soon as I can." She put on her robe and went downstairs.

Herbert pulled the covers up to his chin. In spite of perspiring heavily, he felt chilled.

When Meira returned, she had a small steaming pot and a cup. She poured a cupful of the brew, and the fragrance of garlic filled the room.

As they waited for the tea to cool, Meira declared, "I hate to leave you like this, darling, but I have to go back out to the airport and see if there is any word from Edna. I'll ask *Senhora* Ferreira to look in on you."

"You're right, of course. You should leave a phone number at the Air France ticket counter, have them page Edna with every group of incoming passengers from Paris, and call us when she shows up. Tell *Senhora* Ferreira to come and get one of us when she gets a call from them."

"Very good! I'll go down and try to explain this to her. Drink your tea – if you can get past the smell." A chuckle.

Herbert groaned and with caution put the cup to his lips.

After a few minutes, Meira reappeared.

"How are you?"

He shrugged and muttered, "I've been better. I haven't been this sick since I had that dysentery during the war. I feel like I'm back in France on the Somme."

"I remember that. When I got the word from Eckhardt you were in the hospital, I was terrified until I understood you were just forced to stay near the latrine." She giggled.

He frowned. "What did she say?"

"She doesn't have a telephone, but she suggested she and I go down to the pharmacy in the next block together, and she will explain the situation to the pharmacist. She knows him. I'll leave the pharmacy number at the Air France desk. When he gets a call from the airport, she'll ask him to send his delivery boy here to notify us."

"You've really worked it out. What would I do without you? I knew years ago, that any girl who would go to the front to find her man, like you did, was the girl I wanted to marry. I'd kiss you, but my mouth tastes like the bottom of a birdcage."

She laughed. "I'll kiss you anyway but only on the cheek."

She dressed and went downstairs, had a light breakfast of coffee and rolls with *Senhora* Ferreira, and soon after, they left.

Herbert was roused from his nap by the sound of Meira's footsteps on the stairs. With a shock, he realized he had slept all afternoon and twilight was creeping through the window. Meira appeared at his bedside, pale and distraught, red-eyed from weeping.

"There is no word that Edna appeared on any passenger manifest since we got here. I even had the ticket clerk at the airport telex Air France at Orly airport in Paris to verify this. It's like she never existed." Her shoulders began to shake as tears welled up in her eyes.

Herbert sat up and reached toward her. "Come here, darling." She buried her face in his chest and sobbed uncontrollably.

With a few days' rest, attention from Meira, and good food from *Senhora* Ferreira, Herbert was soon back to his old self.

"I need to call my father and let him know Edna is still in Paris. I don't dare try to write, because in the chaos going on in Germany right now, a letter might not make it, or the censors could direct attention to him. Perhaps the pharmacist will let me use his phone, or direct me to a post office where international calls can be made."

"Oh, thank you for thinking of that. Perhaps you should also contact *Monsieur* Flaubert in Paris. He must have good connections, considering the business he's in."

"Yes, I'll do that. Would you like to come?"

"No, you go ahead. *Senhora* Ferreira has offered to show me how to make Arroz com Marisco. It's a seafood and poultry combination similar to Spanish Paella but more like a stew. I'll try to have it ready for lunch."

"Sounds fantastic! Alright then. I'll be back as soon as I can."

Meira looked out the window. *Where can he be?* she wondered. The savory dish she and the landlady had prepared was partially consumed, but the rest had turned cold and was put in the icebox awaiting her husband's return.

Finally, as the evening dusk was turning to darkness, he came slowly up the stairs, into their room, and flopped down on the bed exhausted.

"Where have you been?"

"You should be glad you stayed home. The pharmacist was apologetic but had no way of connecting his phone to an international exchange. I had to take a taxi into the city to the main post office where that can be done. But with all of these refugees and visitors to the exhibition, the lines there were endless. After what seemed like eternity, actually more like three hours, I managed to get through to my father's phone at home, but he was not there. So, I had to start all over. That meant I had to go back to the main desk, place another call, and take my place in line again. I tried to reach him at the hospital, but he was in surgery. So, I took a chance and left a message with his nurse, who has been with him for years. I had to trust her and hope she hasn't gotten involved with the Nazis.

Then I had to start all over again and put in a call to Flaubert. His secretary picked up, and I explained the whole thing to him. There was no point in leaving a call back number. I'm wiped out. Did you manage to communicate with *Senhora* Ferreira and make that fantastic sounding food?"

She chuckled. "Oh, that went very well. We saved you some. I'll go down and heat you a plate and call you when it's ready."

"Could you bring some up here?"

"Okay, since you've been out battling dragons for my sister, I'll baby you this time," she teased. "But you had room service while you were sick, so don't think it's going to become a regular thing – although, *Senhora* Ferreira would have no problem with that. You bring out her motherly instincts." With a smile, she walked over and patted him on the head.

He studied his wife, as she turned to walk downstairs.

"Thank you, sweetheart."

"Like I said, a treat for today, but it won't become a habit." She waved airily and started down the stairs.

"That was fantastic!" he raved, as he ate the last bite of the *Arros com Marisco*. "I knew I had been blessed with an amazing woman when I found you helping a wounded soldier at the field hospital. But since then, you have been the mainstay of my strength. You're a strong, independent, but loyal and compassionate wife and companion. You continue to amaze me how you can find humor in a crisis. Take today, for instance. I shouldn't have been surprised, but I guess I was a little bit. Some women would have been near hysterics if their husband had been gone for so many hours, but you seemed totally unperturbed."

She listened without comment, and after a pause replied, "I wouldn't say I was totally unperturbed, Herbert. But you were home, you were safe, and knowing you, I expected you to have a thoroughly reasonable explanation – which you did."

Meira leaned forward and looked him straight in the eye. "Listen, darling. I believe in you, and I trust your judgement. You have never really let me down. If I had allowed myself to dissolve in tears every time we had faced a crisis, we would have been done for way back there."

"Well, that's true, and I respect you for that. But look how you've handled your sister being left behind and now missing. Yes, you understandably lost it at the airport in Paris, but you haven't said much about it."

"That doesn't mean she's not on my mind, because of course she is. But letting myself give up hope and sink in despair, would accomplish nothing. It would do us both a lot of damage. And anyway, we're doing all we can, and we must have faith."

"Faith! That's an odd word coming from you. You walked away from your Jewishness years ago during the war when you signed on as an army nurse and defied your father."

"When I say 'faith', I'm not talking about religion. I mean faith in ourselves to endure – whatever may come. I also mean faith in my sister. Edna is quieter than I am, but in many ways, we aren't that different. We come from tough stock. Being Jewish, religious or not, is something that's hard, if not impossible, for a Gentile to understand. We are people who have been on the run for thousands of years. We seem to have a genetic capability to adapt quickly to change and even leave everything behind on a moment's notice, if need be. Remember what I told you about my grandparents. They walked from Russia, with her pregnant. They buried a baby by the side of the road and kept walking. They started in Berlin with nothing, working as rag pickers until my father's time when he and his father established the store and built it up to become a leading establishment in the city.

No, Herbert. I realize that my sister may not be facing a good outcome, but I know her well enough to know that she's not a quitter. She won't give up easily, and that's what I mean when I say 'faith'."

§§§

She had cried herself to sleep. The morning light crept through the high slit window of the cold, dank cell Edna occupied. Curled in a fetal position on her side, she pulled the thin blanket around her shoulders and faced the wall. She turned the recent events over in her mind.

As soon as it had been determined in the immigration office at the airport that her nationality was not represented by the passport she carried, she was turned over to the police, who had transported her to Saint Lazare women's prison. After falling back into a fitful doze, she was awakened by the grating sound of the small window in the door being opened. She sat up and observed in the dim light that a metal plate awaited on the shelf bearing a small loaf of bread. Beside it was a tin cup of water. Edna got up to retrieve the first morsel of food and liquid she had received in the past thirty-six hours. The bread had a sour odor about it, and the water was cloudy, but she consumed both without hesitation.

After using the filthy bucket in the corner, she lay back down and contemplated her situation. Her thoughts turned to her sister, by now no doubt settled in the sanctuary of Portugal. After her ordeal on the St. Louis, she had so hoped she would at last be out of reach of the Gestapo. In the silence and darkness, she realized she was beyond the reach of anyone who would be concerned about her welfare.

Chapter Fifty-four

Les allemands sont là!
(The Germans are here!)

Running feet and shouting . . .

The dim dawn light penetrated Edna's consciousness. She lay in half-sleep on the dirty mattress trying to remember where she was. Then the realization hit her that she was being awakened by an alarming commotion. Why was there so much noise? The groans from her cellmate, a middle-aged prostitute, brought her attention into sharp focus.

"*Les allemands sont là!*"

In the weeks during which she had been confined with the woman, Edna had picked up some rudimentary French, and one word she had learned early on: *allemands* means the Germans! Her heart raced and blood pounded in her ears. *The Germans are here!*

The moment she had been dreading was upon her.

"*Les rats nous quittent!*" (The rats are leaving us), muttered her neighbor, as she made a sweeping gesture with her hands.

Looking at her for a moment in bewilderment, Edna comprehended: the guards and prison personnel were running for their lives. Her shoulders began to tremble. The French woman simply shrugged in resignation.

As the bedlam diminished, the wails of other prisoners echoed up and down the corridors. They banged on the cell doors, shouted and cursed. They were left to be "rescued" by the invaders. But after time passed, that noise, too, subsided. Edna lay back down on her bunk and returned to her usual location, curled in a fetal position facing the wall.

Silence fell over the prison.

Guttural voices roused her and grew louder as the sound of boots on the concrete floor came nearer.

The cell door was flung open, followed by the harsh command, *"Aufstehen! Ihr beide raus!"* (Get up! You two come out), as the speaker stepped back and gestured for them to come.

Edna stood and walked on trembling limbs to the door. The French woman hesitated a moment and then followed. They were met in the corridor by a crowd of bedraggled women shuffling between a row of armed soldiers toward the open entrance to the cell block. After descending two flights of stairs, they were herded to the exit leading to the main courtyard. There they were organized into rows and stood in the morning light awaiting further direction.

Their guards watched impassively. Occasionally, a prisoner would turn to a neighbor and murmur. This was met with a shout from a guard: *"Ruhe!"* (Quiet)

Perspiring under the increasingly hot sun, the malnourished women began to shuffle and some began groan. Then one woman collapsed. She was immediately dragged out by two guards and laid to one side of the formation.

After what seemed an interminable length of time, soldiers brought out four long tables and set them up near the exit. Chairs were placed behind the tables, and two officers and four men in dark suits made their appearance. One officer began speak through a portable bullhorn. In French, he declared that they would be called by name and directed to stand before a table, where an interrogator would be seated. They would be advised to answer questions put to them directly and honestly. Not comprehending the words, Edna soon understood what had been said by the action that followed. The four interrogators dressed in dark suits seated themselves, and the interrogations began. Four by four, names were called. Each of the women stood before the table, as the interrogators looked at passports or other documents when available. The drone of questions and answers filled the courtyard like the sound of bees.

"Caron! Nicole Caron!" Edna stood in a daze, not registering the name. Then a shout: *"Nicole Caron! Avancez immediatement!"* (Nicole Caron! Step forward immediately)

Snapping to attention, she quickly moved toward a table, behind which was seated a red-faced official. A barrage of French, roared past her.

Oh, God! I've annoyed him. Why didn't I pay attention? she chastised herself.

The same scene that had taken place at the airport with the customs officer began to repeat itself. It was quickly determined she didn't speak French. Like a blast of cold water: "*Sie sind, also, keinet Franzosin, wahr?*" (Then you're not French, right?)

What do I do? I can't let them know I'm German, she anguished.

The question was repeated. When this still got no response, the man stood, reached across the table and slapped her across the face.

She broke into hysterical sobs.

The other prisoners were chalk faced, seeing the drama being played out before them.

The man started to walk around the table toward her. Knowing what would follow, she broke down and fell to the ground.

"Get her out of here!" ordered her tormentor. "She needs time to think about it."

Two soldiers picked her up and marched her to the entrance. She was taken up the stairs, through the now empty corridors and returned to her cell. She was shoved in and the door slammed shut.

Part IV

Boomerang

Chapter Fifty-five

Der Krieg schlägt zurück
(The war hits back)

At midnight on the night of June 7, 1940, a French bomber had managed to make its way to the German capital. The French crewmen were astonished to find the city totally illuminated. Because the French plane was not fitted with bomb racks, the flight mechanic and the bombardier just opened the passenger door and began tossing incendiary bombs out the door.

"Eckhardt! Wake up!" Ursula cried, as she shook her husband.

Rousing himself, he was suddenly wide awake as he registered the flash of light in the room, and the rumble of aircraft engines penetrated his consciousness. He sprang from his bed and dashed to the window, which faced north. He gazed at the searchlights in the direction of Tegelersee. Turning to his wife, he exclaimed, "It's an air raid, and it looks like they've hit somewhere in Tegel. They were probably aiming for the Siemens plant!"

Air raid sirens sent up a chorus of screams, and the fingers of searchlights clawed the night sky. Some anti-aircraft guns began firing, but the drone of aircraft faded, apparently uninterrupted.

The bedroom door was flung open. Christina, followed by young Eckhardt and Detlev, stepped into the room.

"What was that?" cried Christina. The boys stood behind her.

Little Detlev was crying. "Mama, I'm scared," as he ran to Ursula.

"It looks like a bomber decided to pay us a visit," cracked Eckhardt.

"A bomber! How dare they!" shouted his eldest son, outraged.

"Yes, a bomber," added his mother. "There's a war going on, in case you hadn't heard."

Red-faced, the boy turned to her. "You sound like you're glad. Why aren't you angry, too."

"Of course, I'm upset. I'm upset that we're in this mess, at all," she countered. "But your *Führer* has all kinds of reasons for going into other peoples' countries, so why should you be surprised if someone out there brings the war back to us?"

Realizing that the discussion was getting out of control, her husband stepped in. "Alright, everyone. This has been a shock for all of us. Let's not lash out at each other."

After several minutes, the searchlights were extinguished, the sirens and guns fell silent, and darkness and quiet returned to the bedroom.

"Okay, that's all for tonight. Everybody back to bed."

Young Eckhardt grumbled and turned away, his younger brother and grandmother following.

"Well, I guess *Herr* Maier has egg on his face now," quipped Eckhardt, as he returned to bed.

"Why would they be targeting Siemens?"

"Well, now with the war going on, we have started to work on military armament contracts for electrical equipment. The Siemens factory and Siemensstadt is the biggest industrial installation near Tegel and is an easy target from the air."

This first bombing raid on Berlin was a huge embarrassment for Hitler, and especially for the air minister, Hermann Göring, who had boasted, "If any bombs fall on the Reich, I will change my name to Maier." "Maier" is a common German name, and in this context, would signify a "nobody".

News of the raid was suppressed, and the Propaganda Ministry announced the next day that an air raid drill had been staged.

Chapter Fifty-six

Arbeit Macht Frei
(Work Will Make You Free)

"*Aufwachen!*"

Edna sat bolt upright. The dim overhead bulb was the only light source in the room. Night had fallen.

She looked into the face of her interrogator, who was seated on the only stool at the small table in the corner.

"*Nun, also. Sie verstehen Deutsch doch. So hab' ich's mir gedacht.*" (Well, then. You do understand German after all. I thought so.)

"When I spoke to you in German, I saw a flash of comprehension cross your face, and your eyes widened. I know the signs. In my work, one learns to read facial expressions and body language very accurately. Let's cut out the charade. Who are you?"

She bit her lip, but did not respond.

"Look. You must be hungry. So am I. I'm having something sent up right now."

Indeed, she was famished. She had been living on sporadic servings of watery soup and stale bread for the last two months and had neither food nor water since the evening before. That had been only a single cup of water and small pieces of potato floating in a greasy broth.

The door opened, and a young soldier carried in a tray of food and a bottle of beer. Edna felt gnawing hunger and was dry mouthed from thirst. As the young man set the tray on the table, the fragrance of roast pork assailed her nostrils. A generous portion of meat in gravy lay next to a bed of noodles. Next to the dinner plate was a paper pastry wrapper containing an éclair. Her stomach rumbled.

"What did you say?" said her tormentor. "Would you like some? There's plenty here," he teased.

Without making a sound, anger at herself surged up as tears started to run down her cheeks. She watched the robust man tuck into the repast before him.

After taking a bite out of the éclair, he leaned forward and in a lowered, but menacing voice growled, "Now, *Fräulein,* let's get down to business. I've had a long day, and my bed is calling me. Don't take up any more of my time, or things will get really unpleasant. So, what's it going to be? Do we do this in a civilized manner, or are you going to force me to be rude?"

After another wordless moment, Edna answered in surrender, *"Ja! Sie haben recht, Ich verstehe Deutsch, und komme aus Berlin,"* (Yes, you're right. I understand German and I come from Berlin.)

Leaning back, with a triumphant smile, he replied, "Now, see that wasn't so hard, was it?"

You have no idea, Edna thought to herself.

"I myself come from *Schwäbisch Gmünd* in the Stuttgart area, and although we don't usually think too highly of you *Saupreussen* (Prussian pigs), you seem like a nice girl.

So, what's your name, girl? *Nicole Caron?* Really? You could have come up with something better than that. Why did you try to change your name, and why were you carrying a French passport? Why were you going to Portugal?"

What's the use? She thought of her unsuccessful attempt to leave on the St. Louis and the heartbreaking return to Europe. Then the escape from Paris and the crushing disappointment of almost making it aboard the flight to Lisbon. Her being brought back to Paris and her imprisonment – and now this! She resigned herself to ending the struggle.

"My name is Edna Friedlander, and I was leaving with my sister and her husband. We were going to South America. But you can't get them! They left on the plane to Lisbon the night I was arrested!" She felt a rush of satisfaction in taunting her adversary.

His face flushed with anger at hearing this.

"So, fleeing Europe! Friedlander! Are you Jewish?"

Straightening her shoulders, she replied, "Yes, I'm Jewish!"

Standing up, he snarled, "Well, we can handle this without further delay. For my part, they could have let you go. If it were up to me, I'd kick every Jew I could lay my hands on out of Europe, and good riddance!"

With that, he turned and knocked on the door. When it was opened, he walked out without another word.

She was held in her cell for another week while the Nazis arrested as many Jews and "undesirables" as they could. These were placed in holding centers in the city's jails and prisons awaiting transport to Germany.

In the chill of predawn darkness, she was taken out of the prison to a waiting truck already filled to near capacity with frightened men, women and children, including a few babes in arms.

They were brought to Châtelet-Les Halles station, the very station where Edna had arrived with Meira and Herbert after leaving Bray sur Somme.

Looking at the familiar location, Edna's thoughts returned to that happy day. *I remember the excitement we felt to arrive in this beautiful city and the bright optimism we felt. I wonder if the little restaurant is still there where we had that excellent lunch. Oh, it was so good to be alive and free.*

They were offloaded and directed to join the throng lining up on the platform and ordered to present themselves at one of several tables. There, they were given name tags and a yellow star of David bearing the imprint *Jude* and a small pin, which they used to attach the symbol to the breast of their clothing. As they shuffled toward the open freight cars, many were dismayed to be forced into such crude conveyances.

When it came to Edna's turn to climb up into the car, she was rudely pushed by a large, stout German soldier.

"Vorwärts, jüdische Sau!" (Move forward, jewish sow)

Once inside the freight car, she had difficulty finding a place to stand in the already assembled crowd. About sixty persons were crammed into the space. One bucket was in a corner for the bodily functions. After more shoving and loading, the door was rolled shut and locked.

Then began the long wait in darkness. The bucket was soon put to use, and the stench began to blend with the odors of perspiring bodies. The heat of the summer day and the press of bodies drove the temperature of the car to almost a suffocating level. A few older people began to faint and fall at the feet of their fellow prisoners.

The train lurched forward, and the long journey to Berlin began where they would be redeployed to their final destinations.

The shifting motion of the train – the heat – the stench – the moaning and wailing of children!

Oh, God! I'm in hell! And I'm so alone! The thought tormented Edna.

Exhausted from stress, lack of sleep and water and food for more than thirty-six hours, many of the elderly, infirm, and children, fell at the feet of others and died.

Through the day and through the night and into the evening of the following day, the train of the abandoned and condemned rolled northward from Paris across the French countryside, passing near the Somme, before crossing the border into Germany, finally reaching the Anhalter Bahnhof near the southeast end of Potsdamer Platz in Berlin. The train was parked on a siding some distance from the terminal building in order to stay out of sight of the civilian population as much as possible. The suffering humanity were left locked in the freight cars, unattended, until into the late nighttime hours. Then, under cover of darkness, the prisoners were offloaded and separated according their assigned destinations – of which they had no knowledge – like the deployment of so-much cargo.

A large group of women, including Edna, were destined for Ravensbrück concentration camp, approximately 50 miles north of Berlin. They were loaded into trucks with covered cargo beds and driven through the darkened streets of the city to the Stettiner Bahnhof, the northernmost rail terminal. There, they were transferred to freight cars. As soon as the cars were full, the train made its way north.

Arriving at the station near Ravensbrück in predawn darkness, they were forced to walk down the mile-long unpaved, muddy road, in a light rain, accompanied by machine gun bearing guards. As they reached the entrance of the camp, they were mocked by the wrought iron slogan over the gate:

ARBEIT MACHT FREI

Edna Friedlander was eventually joined by 26,000 Jewish prisoners from all of German-occupied Europe, including Germany itself, imprisoned in Ravensbrück. In addition, there would be 40,000 Polish women, 18,000 Russian, 8,000 French, and 1,000 Dutch, two of whom were Corrie ten Boom, (author of *The Hiding Place*) and her sister, Betsie. Both were arrested in 1944 for hiding Jews in their home in Haarlem, The Netherlands. (Betsie did not survive).

Approximately 130,000 female prisoners passed through Ravensbrück between 1939 and 1945. Of that number, more than 30,000 died there, with 2,000 killed in the gas chambers. About 15,000 survived until liberation.

Chapter Fifty-seven

Oberleutnant Rudolf Bellon

"There she is, gentlemen. The new Messerschmitt BF 109F," announced *Hauptmann* Dürsteller to the group of pilots of Jagdgeschwader 26 (fighter group) gathered on the second week of August, 1940, at the Luftwaffe base near Saint-Inglevert, Pas-de-Calais. *Oberleutnant* Rudi Bellon was happy to finally be stationed with a group that were heavily involved in the action in the skies over England.

Jagdgeschwader 26 had taken part in the Battle of Britain beginning in May, 1940, but due to poor intelligence, the first forays of the Luftwaffe had not achieved the objectives of destroying the Royal Airforce on the ground, as expected by the leadership – especially by that of Göring. He in turn was not able to keep the promise he had made to Hitler of having the situation well in hand in preparation for the planned invasion of Britain by the Wehrmacht. This meant that as responsibility for the debacle trickled down through the chain of command, and several commanders were dismissed. In order to fix the debacle, Major Adolf Galland was given command of Jagdgeschwader 26 on the 22nd of August, 1940.

The call had come on a warm evening in the previous month. Erika Bellon answered the telephone. "Yes, Bellon residence."

"Adolf Galland here. Is *Oberleutnant* Bellon there?"

"He's at a football match. Can I have him call you back?"

"Yes, of course. Please have him call me as soon as he can. I think he'll want to hear what I have to say. Have him call me at this number."

"Please give me your number. I'm ready to write it down, and I will have him call you, *Herr* Galland, as soon as he can."

"*Sehr gut, Frau Bellon.*"

"*Auf wiederhören.*"

After she hung up the phone, it came to her: *I remember that name! He is the famous Luftwaffe Major Rudi talked about after meeting him at Staaken last summer.*

As she put little Gerhard down for the night, on ominous feeling overtook her. After having suffered two miscarriages, Erika had had a difficult delivery bringing their son into the world in 1937 when Rudi was away in Spain. The three-year old Gerhard, named after Erika's father, was their pride and joy.

When Rudi returned a few hours later, Erika relayed the message from Galland.

Rudi gave the number to the long-distance operator, who informed him she would have to call him back while she put the international call through to France.

After hanging up, he turned to Erika, with a bright-eyed grin.

"France! He's calling me from France! What do you suppose he wants to call me for?"

Slightly biting her lip, Erika was agitated.

After an interminable passage of time, the phone jangled impatiently.

"Hello. Rudolph Bellon here."

"Bellon? How are you? I've thought about you quite a lot lately."

"Yes, sir. I appreciate you saying that."

"Keep this to yourself, but Göring will be giving me command of Jagdgeschwader 26 in the next few weeks. He's guaranteed I'll have a free hand in reorganizing the whole command. He hasn't been happy with the way things have been going around here and has sacked several previous flight commanders. He's passing the whole mess on to me and has charged me with the responsibility of reorganizing the squadron.

Anyway, I have made contact with some capable pilots like yourself that I feel could be assets to the group. Of course, you'd have to get trained on the latest Me BF 109F. She's a beauty. Would you be interested?"

Would he be interested? Is the Pope Catholic? He couldn't contain himself as he babbled, "Of course! Thank you, sir! Thank you for thinking of me. When do I leave?'

"Can you be ready on short notice? My staff will take care of the transfer from Staaken. They will be notified that I requested the transfer, so there's no need for you to explain anything to anyone – except your wife," he chuckled. "Good luck with that one! Then I'll expect to see you as soon as you can get down here. It's great talking to you Bellon. Let me know when and how you're coming."

"Thank you again, sir."

As he hung up the phone, he could see Erika's eyes filling with tears.

"You're leaving, aren't you?"

He studied his shoes and replied, "I'm afraid I'm being transferred to France."

"Why am I not surprised? I know you've felt left out of it here, so I knew this day would come sooner or later."

Embracing her, he stroked her hair. "I'm sorry to leave you and the boy, sweetheart, but there's a war on, and I feel like I'm going to seed just sitting around."

Crying into his shoulder, she whispered, "But it's been wonderful having you nearby and home almost every night. Little Gerhard is going to miss his daddy."

Swallowing the lump in his throat, he murmured, "I know. That's the hard part of this. But there are men out there who've had to leave their wives and families, too, and it's not any easier for them."

"That's no comfort to me. Please, darling, let's make the most of the days we have left. When are you going?"

"As soon as Galland puts through the transfer. Probably within a week."

"A week! God, I miss you already."

Chapter Fifty-eight

Britischer Luftangriff
(British Air Raid)

Eckhardt lay in the dark with his hands behind his head. Ursula was lying on her side close to him, her soft breathing signifying deep sleep.

What is going to happen to us? he asked himself. Any hint of criticism of the *Führer* or the leadership of Germany incited sharp conflict within his family. Young Eckhardt and his younger brother, Detlev, were enthusiastic participants in the Hitler Youth programs. They often joined their comrades in solicitation drives of "donations" for *Winterhilfswerk* (Winter Relief Program), and propaganda campaigns. This involved passing out party leaflets and pamphlets, youth orientation meetings, and any other activities taking up their time outside of school, and keeping them increasingly separated from their families.

Suddenly, his reverie was interrupted by the drone of many aircraft approaching the city from the west. As the drone increased, the air raid sirens began their lament, the searchlights shot their long fingers into the night sky, followed by the pounding of anti-aircraft batteries.

Ursula, by this time awake, cried, "Oh, no. Are they at it again?"

"Yes, and this time they're sending in the big stuff."

Then the bombing began. The blasts could be heard first in the center of the city and then again in the area northward around Tegel and Siemensstadt.

"Let's get everybody downstairs into the cellar," directed Eckhardt. He stepped out of the bedroom and found Christina standing at the kitchen window watching the searchlights weaving to and fro in their frantic search for the bombers.

"Where are the boys?" cried Ursula.

"They went outside to watch," said her mother.

Ursula went to the open back door and shouted to her sons standing in the backyard.

"Eckhardt! Detlev! Get in here!"

Her husband walked to her and placed his hand on her shoulder. "It's alright, dear. The bombers are concentrated over Tegel and aren't a threat to us out here, yet."

Frantic, she turned to him. "I think we should go down to the cellar."

"Let's not panic. Until we see them moving in our direction, we're fine."

Not satisfied, she called to the boys again. "Come inside!"

Muttering, they walked toward her.

§§§

At the outbreak of the war in 1939, the President of the United States (at that time a neutral power), Franklin D. Roosevelt, had requested all major belligerents to restrict bombing to military targets. The French and the British had agreed to honor that request.

The Battle of Britain was an effort by the German Luftwaffe to destroy the Royal Air Force in preparation for the planned invasion of England (Operation Sea Lion). Neither Hitler nor the Wehrmacht High Command believed it was possible to successfully invade England until the RAF had been neutralized.

At the beginning of the Battle of Britain, July 10, 1940, Hitler declared London to be off limits for the Luftwaffe. They were to concentrate on destroying the RAF on the ground, but on the night of August 24, a German bomber dropped bombs on London, ostensibly by accident, in an attempt to drop his bomb load before returning home. Churchill ordered an immediate retaliatory raid on the German capitol. The first raid over Berlin commenced at 12:20 a.m. on August 25, 1940. The targets were Tempelhof Airport in the inner city and Siemensstadt on the eastern border of Spandau. Nearly 200 bombs were dropped in the process.

Although the real damage was slight, with no casualties, except for "Rollo", the lone elephant in the Berlin Zoo, Hitler was outraged.

In retaliation and reassessing how to defend against future air attacks, he responded in two ways: First, the Luftwaffe begin systematically bombing London and targeting British cities in hopes of stretching RAF forces thin. At the same time, he bolstered Berlin's internal defenses.

Hitler ordered the construction of three massive *Flakturm* (flak towers) to defend the city from aerial assault. They were designed to shoot down Allied airplanes and provided both offensive and defensive capabilities. Built around the outskirts of the city, they created a triangle of anti-aircraft fire that covered the center of Berlin. The northwest one was to be in the borough of Humboldthain, with another to the northeast in Friedrichshain. The largest would be built at the Zoo in the Tiergarten.

Hitler was interested in the design of the towers and even made some sketches. Helix staircases at each corner led to the top of the towers with each tower having a radar plotting room, where Luftwaffe staff could follow the progress of Allied bombers over Germany. The radar dish could be retracted behind a thick concrete and steel dome for protection.

With concrete walls up to 11 feet thick, the towers were considered by their designers to be invulnerable to attack by RAF heavy bombers. The multi-level guns could sustain a rate of 8,000 rounds per minute firing in a 360-degree field of fire. The range was nearly 9 miles, although only the 5.0-inch FlaK-40 guns had an effective range to defend against aircraft. Each barrel could fire 10 to 12 rounds a minute; thus, each twin mounted battery was rated to fire a maximum of 24 rounds a minute, and four twin mounts could fire as many as 96 rounds a minute. The guns were loaded electrically, with the ammunition fed into hoppers.

The flak towers were also designed with the idea of using the above-ground bunkers as a civilian shelter, with room for 10,000 civilians and a hospital ward inside. The hospital facility was used to treat wounded soldiers shipped back from the front line.

The Zoo Tower was the most prominent of the three. It was a massive structure. The equivalent of a 13-story building made out of reinforced concrete, the Zoo Tower had anti-aircraft guns on its rooftops and an 85-bed hospital on the third floor. At the top, it featured four 12.8-cm twin FlaK 40-gun mounts, supported by 20 mm and 37 mm guns on lower platforms. Twenty-six feet of concrete protected the tower's sides and 16 feet protected the top. At full capacity, the Zoo Tower could hold up to 350 soldiers and 15,000 people.

Hitler considered the *Flakturm* project to be such a high priority that the German national rail schedule was altered to assist the shipment of concrete, steel, and timber to the construction sites. They were completed in only six months.

Men between the ages of 16 and 70 were forbidden from entering and were instead urged to the front. Younger Hitler Youth, while officially not supposed to be combatants, assisted the military loading the ammunition hoppers.

Chapter Fifty-nine

Intervention

"That Jew lover Lenz had the gall to reprimand me in the dressing room this morning," growled Dr. Helmut Köhler.

"What brought that on?" queried his colleague at Charité, Gerhard Ziegler.

"I was commenting to some of the interns how refreshing it is not to see so many Jews on the streets anymore. Lenz jumped in and told me the hospital is no place for politics, and I should voice my opinions elsewhere."

"Sounds just like him. If you had been talking about anything else but Jews, he wouldn't have said a word."

"Right! And it depends on who's doing the talking. I've heard him lament that Meira Lenz, his Jew daughter-in-law, is no longer here, as she was 'one of the best surgical assistants' he'd ever seen."

"She was good. I'll give her that. I used to watch her in surgery, and she usually had the correct instrument in her hand before the surgeon even asked for it. She got a lot of that experience in the war," commented Ziegler.

"Yeah, maybe. But I also heard one of the other surgeons tell her not to touch an instrument until he asked for it. Typical Jew – liked to show off!"

Ziegler laughed, then continued, "By the way, at my in-law's dinner the other night, I was talking about you and how much you hated Jews and how Lenz gets on your nerves. I think I told you, my father-in-law is pretty high up in the Party. Anyway, when I mentioned that Lenz's son was married to a Jew and they had left the country, he really got interested. As a matter of fact, he said he'd like to talk to you. He gave me his card. Here. Take it and give him a call."

"Very interesting. Why haven't I thought of talking to someone about Lenz before? Yeah! Give me that!"

The long summer twilight merged into evening, as Hans Joachim Lenz and Kurt Wollner sat on the back veranda of the Lenz villa late in August 1940.

"Can I get you another drink, Wollner?"

"Well, I guess so. Thanks. You really have a beautiful garden here, Lenz, and it's so peaceful out here in Dahlem."

"This was my wife's pride and joy, and even though I don't have much time to spend here, I try to maintain it in memory of her. I think she would appreciate the fountain I had installed. But the gardener is a 'trivial expense', as the *Führer* would put it, and I should be donating more to the war effort."

"Right!" was Wollner's droll comment. "And especially since this war was "forced" on Germany."

"Of course. The poor *Führer*! He's had such a struggle trying to deal with our warlike neighbors."

Both men exchanged sardonic glances. Without further comment, they continued to contemplate the gurgle of the fountain.

Dr. Lenz rested his head on his hands and said with a frown, "It's no wonder that Hitler is so paranoid and delusional. His quack physician, Morell, keeps him hyped up on God only knows what kind of junk."

Suddenly their reverie was shattered by the loud crash of the big knocker being hammered on the front door. Startled, they looked at one another.

Again, the impatient hammering of the knocker.

Hans Joachim moved toward the front entrance, opened the door, and was confronted by two men in black suits and hats. He knew at once. *Gestapo!*

Chapter Sixty

Jagdgeschwader 26
(Squadron 26)

As he had guessed, Rudi was transferred to his new post the following week. He was relieved to get aboard the Ju 52 transport on the day of his departure. Initially, his mother, Christina, was tearful, but in good control of her emotions at the farewell dinner at the Meinert home. His sister, Ursula, was also self-controlled, but his wife, wan and listless, only picked at her food. Even little Gerhard, sensing something was not right with Mommy, insisted on sitting close to her, and from time to time grasped her hand. But the evening had ended in strife, which he was only too happy to leave behind.

The two Meinert boys, caught up in patriotic fervor, were loud in their praise of Rudi's opportunity to serve the Fatherland.

"If I ever had the chance to face the enemy like you, Rudi, I would consider it an honor and a privilege to die a glorious death for the *Führer*," boasted Detlev. The tension around the table was palpable, until Erika lunged up and ran into the kitchen sobbing, followed by her son.

"That's enough, Detlev," reprimanded his father.

"What did I do?" questioned the boy.

"How could you say such a thing at a time like this?" rejoined his mother.

"What's wrong with what I said? Every good German feels like I do. These are great days for Germany!"

His brother looked at him with a slight smirk. "You tell 'em, brother."

"Okay, that's it! You can both leave the table," ordered Eckhardt.

Detlev glared at his father as he flung his napkin down, arose, and stalked out. His brother nodded and followed suit.

"What's happened to your boys, Ursula? They used to be such nice kids," Rudi asked his sister.

"They're constantly told they're 'supermen', you know, the 'master race?',," Christina interjected a sardonic answer.

Reminded of his mother's early Communist affiliations, Rudi cautioned, "Careful Mama."

"No, she's right," replied Ursula. "They're getting harder and harder to live with – never mind obedience."

Rudi shook his head and went to the kitchen to soothe his wife.

Eckhardt studied his plate for a moment and then admonished, "Now, Ursula, they're still basically good boys. And you know, at their age, they are under a lot of pressure to fit in."

"Don't lecture me! You're not here all day trying to deal with them," his wife shot back. "And you keep making excuses for what's happening in this country. One of these days, you're going to have to decide just where you stand!"

"That's not fair. But you and Christina are still too reckless with what you say, especially in front of people like Rudi. He's just been promoted by a man close to leaders at the top. He's no doubt grateful for that and would be supportive of them. He wouldn't mean to cause us any harm, but he might inadvertently repeat something he would hear you say."

Both women glared at him, but gave no further response.

§§§

Hauptmann Dürsteller continued his orientation on the new fighter. "BF is the acronym for *Bayrische Flugzeugwerke* (Bavarian Aircraft Factory). The Me 109 prototype was developed under the direction of Willy Messerschmitt and Robert Lusser in March, 1934. You will remember when it made its public debut at the 1936 Berlin Olympics.

Many of you have had experience with the Me BF 109Ds and Es, but let me tell you, this machine is all that and more. Many of our most decorated pilots, such as Major Günther Rall, say this is their favorite airplane. Of course, since you are already familiar with the quirks of the other 109s, you know you must keep the tail wheel locked and set your prop blades to minimum bite on takeoffs and add power steadily.

You won't have enough rudder authority to prevent a swerve to the left, and you'll end up in the grass. We don't want to go there." Chuckles all around.

"But one of the most significant changes is the wing cannons have been done away with, and all your firepower is concentrated on the nose of the airplane, directly in front of your gunsights. With a 20-millimeter gun through the prop hub and two 15 millimeters on the nose cowling, you'll have all the firepower you need.

And as before, the fuel injected engine has proven itself to be a blessing in tight turns and maneuvers. The poor Brits have a great airplane with their Spitfires, but the carburetors have caused them many problems cutting out in turns. Just let 'em hang on to those carburetors." More chuckles.

As Dürsteller continued to enthuse about the new plane, Rudi glanced slowly around the crowd of pilots assembled. Although they blended in, in their grey blue Luftwaffe uniforms, his glance suddenly stopped on a familiar face.

Who is that? he wondered to himself. He studied the face of the tall blond airman with a heavy mustache. He envisioned the face minus the mustache.

Klaus Dieterle!

His mind flashed back to that September day in 1925. He was working as a tram driver on the Lichterfelde line and overheard the conversation between two young men discussing their flying experiences.

What was that other fellow's name? He searched his memory. *Erik – Erik what? Vorbauer. Yes. That's it! Erik Vorbauer! I wonder where he is?*

As Dürsteller concluded his orientation, the group began to disperse and Rudi moved toward his erstwhile comrade.

"Klaus Dieterle!" he shouted.

The man turned. His brow furrowed, as he focused on the source.

His hand extended, Rudi grinned. "Do you remember me?"

Klaus broke into a big smile of recognition. "Bellon! Is that really you?"

"That's my question!" Rudi retorted.

"Wow, Bellon. You're not that scrawny little kid we met on the tram. What have you been up to?"

"Well, I finished up my flight training with Helmut Stock. After that I got on with Luft Hansa. I was with them until 1937. Right after that, I joined the regular Luftwaffe and trained as a fighter pilot at Staaken."

"Back at good old Staaken! You must love that place."

They both chuckled.

"Married?' continued Klaus.

"Yes. I married my stewardess. We have a son almost four. How about you?"

After a sigh, "Well, I finished up at the Technical University in Mechanical Engineering. Then I got a girl pregnant. Married her, but it all went south. I was in Stuttgart at Daimler Benz building cars, but that's not really for me. I've been with the Luftwaffe since '37, and like you, got into fighters."

Rudi looked his companion up and down and after a moment probed, "Where's Vorbauer."

Klaus looked away, then in a subdued voice, "Erik bought it over the Channel about a month ago. We were in a tangle with some Spitfires and he caught a few bullets and was headed home when his plane caught on fire. He jumped out, but he was already in flames. The cords on his chute burned through and he fell straight into the water from about 1,800 meters. I had to watch him go down."

"I'm really sorry he's gone."

"Well, it's great to have you with us, Bellon."

§§§

The Messerschmitt BF 109 is the most produced fighter aircraft in history. A total of 33,984 airframes were built from 1936 to April, 1945.

The BF 109 accounted for 57% of all German fighters produced. After the war, 109 derivatives were built under license in Czechoslovakia until 1948, and in Spain until 1958. More aerial kills were made with BF 109s than any other aircraft in World War II.

From 1937 until Autumn 1944, 31 variants of the Messerschmitt BF 109 were built, beginning with BF 109 A and ending with BF 109K-6. A large portion of production began in concentration camps, including Flossenburg, Mauthausen-Gusen, and Buchenwald.

Chapter Sixty-one

Das Verhör
(The Interrogation)

As the big black Opel sedan pulled up in front of the Gestapo headquarters on Prinz Albrechtstraße, Hans Joachim looked out the rear window at the foreboding structure and reflected how many times he had driven past this building and wondered what it would feel like to be brought here. As he and Kurt Wollner stepped out of the car and were escorted to the entrance, they both carried themselves upright and in a dignified manner. Their escorts reacted accordingly: these were not men easily intimidated.

Once inside, the two men were separated. Kurt Wollner was turned over to two burly jailers and roughly escorted down a hallway and through a solid door. Hans Joachim was brought before a stone-faced female receptionist sitting before a typewriter and after being identified by the accompanying Gestapo men was told to sit on a bench along the wall opposite her desk. As he did, he studied the large lobby and the framed pictures of many familiar and unfamiliar Nazi personages hung on walls flanking a large curving double stairway.

After waiting a short while, Hans Joachim was startled by the shrill clangor of the telephone on the receptionist's desk. Not being able to hear what she was saying, he was unnerved by her glance in his direction, indicating that he was being discussed. With no comment, she hung up the receiver and resumed her typing.

Soon, a young SS man came down the stairway, his high boots resounding with a staccato click on the polished stone stair treads. He stopped before Hans Joachim and tersely announced that *Herr Direktor* Müller expected to see him at once.

Heinrich Müller was a pilot During World War I and was decorated several times for bravery. After the war, during the Bavarian Soviet Republic in Munich, he witnessed the shooting of hostages by the "Red

Army", which brought about his lifelong hatred of Communism. In the Weimar Republic, he became the head of the Munich Political Police Department.

It was at that time he became acquainted with SS leaders Heinrich Himmler and Reinhard Heydrich. Müller had urged the use of force against the Nazis during the *putsch* of 1933, arousing Nazi hostility for his views. Heydrich, nevertheless, admired him for his skill as a policeman and his knowledge of Communist activities.

Müller was a non-political fanatic, driven by an obsession with perfection in his profession and duty to the state. In 1937, a Nazi party deputy reported that, "Criminal Police Chief Inspector Heinrich Müller is not a Party member. He has also never actively worked within the Party or in one of its ancillary organizations."

However, he built a reputation for being adamant about discipline and a determination to serve the German state, regardless of who was in command. He held the belief that it was every German's duty, including his, to obey the government in power without question.

It was Müller, together with Himmler and Heydrich, who developed and orchestrated the pretext for the invasion of Poland, the *Fall Gleiwitz,* which staged an attack on the German radio station.

He was a talented organizer who was utterly ruthless and who lived only for his work. His dedication to his job was so obsessive that Auschwitz Commandant Rudolf Höss characterized Muller as one who could be reached "any time of the day or night, even Sundays and public holidays".

He was appointed Chief of the Gestapo by the age of thirty-nine.

Inadvertently, Hans Joachim felt a chill. He had not expected to be face-to-face with Heinrich Müller, the head of the Gestapo. He followed the SS man up the stairs and down a central hallway and into a large outer office staffed by secretaries and adjutants working at desks arranged in rows on both sides of a central aisle. He was stopped before an adjutant's desk, who upon receipt of Hans Joachim's identity booklet, telephoned the director, who ordered him to enter. His escort opened one of the large oak doors and motioned him in.

Director Müller was seated rigidly with hands clasped on the huge desk before him. On the wall behind him hung the obligatory huge framed portrait of the *Führer*. To the director's left stood a black flag emblazoned with the runic SS symbols, and to his right stood a standard swastika flag.

"*Herr Doktor* Lenz! Please be seated."

Taken by surprise at the courteous, if not cordial, greeting, Hans Joachim seated himself in a deep leather arm chair facing the director.

"I apologize for detaining you so late in the day, *Herr Doktor*. Therefore, I hope we can make this brief. I will come straight to the point.

You have been heard to make unpatriotic remarks about the government and have been accused of being in opposition to the government's policies in dealing with undesirables. More specifically, you have been seen associating with Jews. In fact, your son is married to one, is that not correct?"

Realizing that denial was out of the question and not allowing himself to grovel, Hans Joachim studied the emotionless countenance of his inquisitor with a steady gaze. "Yes, that is correct *Herr Direktor*. My daughter-in-law is from the prominent family of Benjamin Friedlander. But I'm sure you already know all of this, so might we, as you suggested, get to the point?"

A slight smile played on Müller's lips. He replied, "Of course, *Herr Doktor*. You are correct. We have an extensive file on your family, and we have no need to dwell on trivialities."

After a pause, he lowered his voice and with an unblinking stare demanded, "Where are they?"

Somewhat shaken by the abrupt question but determined not to be intimidated, Hans Joachim responded, "To whom are you referring, sir?"

"Your son and daughter-in-law and her sister!"

"The last time I heard from them was in June, immediately after our troops entered France. They were living in Paris."

"We already know that. Our contacts in Paris have determined that they left the city on June 25, three days before our troops entered the city. They have not been seen nor heard from since. But surely they must keep in touch with you?"

Not sure how much he was being tested – *how much did they really know?* But he could tell the truth: he had not heard from Herbert and Meira all summer.

"I'm sorry, *Herr Direktor*. I really wish I knew where they were."

After a long wordless scrutiny under Müller's unwavering, cold blue-eyed gaze, he was again startled with a question from another direction.

"How do you feel about your younger son being a homosexual?"

In spite of himself, Hans Joachim's face blanched.

"How am I supposed to answer that?"

In a softer condescending voice, "It's a simple question. Do you approve of his lover? Do think he's living the kind of life your wife would want?"

Müller leaned back in his chair and raised his eyebrows. "Why have you never remarried? You and Wollner are single men and are together a lot. Are you homosexuals?"

Shock and outrage flashed through him. He broke out in a cold sweat. He didn't how to answer.

Müller let him struggle for a few moments.

Then, "Come on, *Herr Doktor*. Tell me how you feel about your younger son. Karlheinz, is his name, I believe. Do you love him?"

"Of course." His voice quavered. "I do love him, but I wish he had made better choices."

"Oh, were you not proud that he joined the SS?" A sardonic smile crossed Müller's face. "Apparently, *he* is loyal to the *Führer*. He's one of our SS officers, but he's also breaking the law! Paragraph 175 prohibits homosexuality, but we have our eye on him. There are those in our organization who are determined to keep the SS from going the way of those degenerates in Röhm's SA. Remember what happened in '34 to him and his perverts! It could happen again."

His throat was dry, and Hans Joachim could feel his heart racing.

"Now you're involved with this Wollner. I'm so disappointed in him. I've known him for years. He built a fine career in the Berlin Police organization. Now he's become involved in helping Jews, too.

Both of you need to learn that we are not to be trifled with. We're not fools, and we won't tolerate anyone who works against the *Führer*. Not anyone! No matter how high up they think they are. Think about what I have said. If you hear anything from your son and his Jew wife, you come straight to me. If I find you're lying, you will pay for it, do you understand me?" he said through pursed lips.

Hans Joachim just stared at him.

"And, oh, by the way, if you hear of any traitors at Charité, I expect to hear from you. Goodnight. You can go, but I'll be in touch."

Hans Joachim arose and only with maximum effort walked steadily to the door, down the stairs, and outside. The soft air of the summer evening contrasted with the turmoil in his mind. He walked a few meters down the block and away from the most terrifying experience of his life.

What did Müller really want from him? What happened to Wollner?

These questions tormented him!

Chapter Sixty-two

Fliegende Kameraden
(Flying comrades)

Beginning on September 7, 1940, the Luftwaffe carried out intensified day and night bombing raids over London.

As soon as they arrived at Pas de Calais, the reorganized squadron was thrown into combat. As he dressed in the early morning of his first mission, Rudi's thoughts turned to Erika and his little son, Gerhard. He had assured her that he would be able to come through any conflict, given his experience and skill as a pilot. But now, with the reality of combat against a formidable foe, he fought to banish the apprehension nibbling at the edge of his thoughts.

As he entered the mess hall, the smell of fresh coffee, mingled with the tantalizing fragrance of breakfast being cooked, restored his confidence, and he brightened at the sight of Klaus Dieterle beckoning him to his table. Picking up his tray of sausages and eggs and coffee, he seated himself across from his friend.

"Well, Bellon, are you ready to go give the English hell?"

Smiling, Rudi responded, "Absolutely! But don't be surprised if we don't find any, because they know we're coming."

This brought laughter from several young pilots seated within earshot.

After breakfast, they gathered in the briefing room, where *Hauptmann* Dürsteller was placing colored pins in the large map of London. The men found their seats as they continued to crack jokes, assuring one another that success of the coming mission was assured.

Dürsteller turned and commanded, "*Achtung!*"

Silence immediately fell over the room.

"I'm glad to see you're all in good spirits this morning. You're going to need it, where we're going. We'll be covering our bombers as they deliver their loads on the docks in London's East End. Focus on the areas I have marked with pins.

Don't think this will be a walk in the park, you newcomers. The British pilots have shown a lot of progress in the last couple of months. They were pretty green when we started bombing in the Spring, but they learn fast. Plus, they still have their radar and know when we're on the way. So, they're ready for us when we get there."

Then Commander Galland stood up and declared, "You people remember, you need to be on your highest alert. Take your pilot salt. You all know how much more stamina you have when you take your Pervitin! You are expected to take it before your mission. Also, you need to stay within sight of the bombers, but forget about that crap of staying in tight formation with them. If you see *Banditen*, go after them. Don't just cluster around the bombers and wait for them to come to you."

Rudi looked knowingly at Dieterele. They, and many others in the room, understood this directive to be in contradiction to Herrmann Göring's theory that fighters should maintain strict formation around bombers.

As they filed out of the room, they walked to their waiting mechanics, who would help them into their parachute packs. As Rudi and Klaus walked out to the parked planes, they noticed Galland's Messerschmitt with the Mickey Mouse logo on the side of the fuselage.

"I asked Galland about his fascination with Mickey Mouse when he was at Staaken, and he admitted he always liked Mickey Mouse. I got the impression he doesn't really care what anybody else thinks about that."

Klaus laughed and retorted, "At least he doesn't still fly in his bathing suit."

"Oh, you heard about that!"

"Of course. Everybody has. That story has become a legend."

"Maybe he would, if he didn't have to risk ditching in the English Channel."

Rudi laughed and added, "He says he hasn't smoked cigars since the Spanish Civil War."

"Well, that's a big change."

The pilots climbed into the very narrow cockpits, started their engines, closed their hatch covers and taxied out onto the grass runway and became airborne. They immediately began to take their assigned positions near the bombers, and the entire formation headed west. Rudi and Klaus, close to each other as one another's wingman, exchanged salutes.

It was a clear day, with only a light haze to the northwest. As they left the coast of France behind, the fishing boats below decreased in number, and soon they were flying over open ocean. Rudi's thoughts turned to the task ahead and the opposition they faced. He had experience in Spain, but this was his first time in combat, and he had not faced an enemy from a highly-developed industrialized country – a nation of proud people determined to defend their homeland to the very last.

Churchill's words, which he and others had heard over the forbidden airwaves of the BBC on a hidden radio owned by one of Klaus' friends, resounded in his memory:

We shall go on to the end.
We shall fight in France.
We shall fight over the seas and oceans.
We shall fight with growing confidence and great strength in the air.
We shall defend our island, whatever the cost may be.
We shall fight on the beaches, we shall fight on the landing grounds,
We shall fight in the fields and in the streets.
We shall fight on the hills.
We shall never surrender!

Is our hubris leading us into a disaster? he asked himself.

He was roused from his thoughts by the crackle of Galland's voice over the intercom. "There's the coast ahead, boys. We can expect the welcoming committee any minute. On your toes!"

The outline of the Thames estuary became visible.

"Look sharp! There they are at two o'clock. Pick your victims. Keep 'em away from the bombers," Galland commanded.

Within a few minutes, the sky became filled with a melee of swirling fighters, as the bombers droned steadily on toward their targets.

From the outset, Rudi proved to Galland, his commander, that his confidence in Rudi had not been misplaced. He demonstrated that he was a highly skilled pilot who was able to master the Messerschmitt BF 109F as soon as he completed his training. In addition, he and Klaus had prevailed upon Galland to assign them as one another's wingman. As a result, they, together with the other members of III Gruppe, all of whom were seasoned expert pilots, formed a formidable fighting force.

The Luftwaffe saw its best successes at the beginning of the war when losses averaged half those of the RAF. Their adversaries were, for the most part, young boys with little or no flying experience who had been rushed through flight training and thrown directly into combat. As a result, the Germans quickly scored many kills in a short period of time. Adolf Galland himself ran up a victory tally of 37 credited kills.

Chapter Sixty-three

Bomben auf Engelland
(Bombs on England)

"*Kamerad! Kamerad! Die Lösung ist bekannt! Ran an den Feind! Ran an den Feind! Bomben auf Engelland! Hört ihr die Motoren singen...*" (Comrade! Comrade! The solution is well known! Onto the enemy! Onto the enemy! Bombs on England! Hear the motors singing).

"Stop that racket!" Ursula shouted out the front window at her son, Eckhardt and his friend, Jürgen Lauterbacher, as they marched arm in arm up to the front gate.

Startled, they paused and stared at her before continuing up the path to the front door.

"We're sorry, *Frau* Meinert, we just came from the youth rally at the Reichssportfeld, and the band music was fantastic. The youth chorus sang this song, and it's really popular right now."

"Well, this isn't the Reichssportfeld, and you need to keep it down out here."

"Don't try to explain anything to her," interjected young Eckhardt. "She and her mom are pacifists."

Narrowing his eyes, Jürgen queried, "Don't you support our fliers and what they're doing to England? And Eckhardt tells me your brother is a pilot flying with the bombing raids over England. I'm sure he's ready to give his life for the *Führer* and for the Fatherland. Aren't you proud of him?"

Looking away, Ursula muttered, "I love my brother, but I hate this war."

"But the English had it coming," countered young Eckhardt. "The *Führer* has tried to be reasonable with them, but they have spurned his every effort to make peace."

"How do you know all this?" she directed at her son.

"Hitler Youth leader von Schirach was the key speaker at the rally, and he said we'll be in England before the end of Summer."

"Right! Then we'll see just how proud they'll be, stuck up Limeys," added Jürgen.

With sadness in her eyes, she watched her son and his friend go upstairs to the boys' bedroom.

"What's wrong, darling?" whispered Eckhardt to his wife, as he turned to embrace her in their bed that evening.

With muffled sobs, she turned and buried her face in his chest.

"I don't feel like I know Eckhardt anymore. The way he talks to me in front of his friends, and the aggression he shows scares me. I hate the Nazis and what they are doing to our kids"

Wordlessly, he pulled her close.

Wiping her hands on her apron, Ursula hurried to the living room and answered the phone.

"*Ja, Meinert.*"

"*Frau* Meinert, this is Greta Winkler, Detlev's teacher."

"Now what has he done?"

"Nothing exactly, but I need to speak to you in person. Could you come in tomorrow after school?"

Ursula stared into the mirror over the telephone. She was startled to see the pale figure staring wide-eyed back at her.

"Of course. Is Detlev alright. Is he hurt?"

"He's fine, and don't stress over this. I don't mean to alarm you. I just need to clarify a matter with you."

"Could you give me a hint as to what this is about?"

"I'd rather not discuss it over the phone. You know how it is."

Yes, walls have ears – and so do telephones. She began to sense that the woman was not an adversary. Ursula felt the tension drain out of her.

"Oh, and *Frau* Meinert, please don't say anything to Detlev, or let him know I called you."

"Of course. I'll be there shortly after three o'clock, if that's satisfactory. Will Detlev be there?"

"No, he'll be with the other boys in the gym practicing their school sports activities. It would be better if he doesn't know you're here."

"Very well. Until tomorrow then."

"Thank you, *Frau* Meinert."

Perplexed, Ursula replaced the phone on its hook.

The next afternoon, when the school had let out and Detlev had joined his classmates in the gym, Ursula slipped through a door on the opposite side of the building. She was relieved that the hall was devoid of students as she made her way to *Fräulein* Winkler's room.

"Good afternoon, *Frau* Meinert. Please sit down."

She arranged some papers in a neat stack, then turned her gaze to Ursula's anxious face. Biting her lip with apprehension, she waited for the indictment against her son.

"*Frau* Meinert, please don't take offense at what I am about to say. Detlev has brought some attention to a member of your family, which could bring trouble.

In our curriculum, we are required to explain the present political situation to the students. We are covering the new relationship between Germany and Russia. We have to explain that, in spite of past differences between our two countries, we now consider the Soviet Union to be our ally. This, of course, leads to questions from the students. Earlier this week during our discussion, one of the students asked how we can consider a Communist country our friend. This particular student apparently has heard about the clashes between National Socialists and Communists in years past. He informed the class that his father hates Communists and considers them all to be evil criminals. At that point, Detlev declared that his grandmother is a Communist and that she is not an evil person. Was he speaking about your mother, *Frau* Meinert?"

Nodding her head, Ursula explained, "My mother was involved with Communists when she was still living in Wedding in the twenties, which at that time was known as 'Red Wedding'."

"Yes, I remember that," interjected the teacher.

"My mother is not an educated person and was introduced to Communism by some of her neighbors. She was also desperately lonely after my father and two of my siblings died during the Influenza pandemic in 1918. So, I believe she attended their meetings out of a sense of loneliness, as much as anything. She has never had a deep understanding of Communist philosophy, just as she doesn't have a deep understanding of National Socialism. I also believe that millions like her in this country have had their political affiliations influenced the same way."

Nodding her head in agreement, *Fräulein* Winkler replied, "I think you're right. But these are times when our children can inadvertently bring unwanted attention to our families. I'm sorry to alarm you, but as you know, your son will be moving on next term, and I can't vouch for how another teacher might react to such a statement. I'm sure you know what I mean. I haven't discussed this incident with anyone else, but I knew you would want to be informed."

"I completely understand." Rising, Ursula extended her hand. "I want to thank you for bringing this to my attention, *Fräulein* Winkler. I hope this doesn't cause any problems for you for not reporting this."

Smiling, the teacher replied with a twinkle in her eye, "I have no idea what you're talking about, *Frau* Meinert," as she grasped Ursula's hand in a warm handshake.

Chapter Sixty-four

Der Wendepunkt
(The Turning Point)

Rudi saw a Spitfire zeroing in on his assigned bomber. He forced his plane into a sharp dive, so as to hide momentarily under the bomber and come up behind the attacking fighter. He positioned himself behind his unsuspecting adversary and opened fire. He grinned when he saw the fragments tear away from the Spitfire's wing surfaces. *I got another one.* Suddenly, he felt the impact of bullets in the fuselage of his own plane. He hadn't seen the enemy plane, which had come in behind him at a slight angle.

Where the Hell did you come from, you son of a bitch? Breaking off his attack, he whipped the Messerschmitt into a steep climb, up, over, and upside down into an Immelmann maneuver. He righted his ship directly behind his attacker. He set his gunsights on the Spitfire and let his cannons do their work. Smoke appeared from the enemy aircraft, which immediately burst into flame. The pilot inverted his ship and fell out of the flying inferno. Rudi watched as the small pilot chute streamed out of the parachute pack, but the main chute did not appear. In spite of this being his enemy, Rudi's anxious eyes watched as the hapless fellow fell straight down and out of sight.

"Rudi, are you alright?" came his wingman's voice over the intercom.

"Yes. I'm okay. Look out, Klaus. There's a Hurricane trying to take your six o'clock position!"

The dodging and weaving continued, until Galland's voice came through the headphones, "Okay, boys our twenty minutes is up. Time to go home before our fuel runs out."

As they headed east, Rudi looked in vain for the bomber they had accompanied on the outbound leg.

"Klaus, have you seen our guy?" he asked over the intercom.

"No, I guess I lost track of him."

Rudi sank into despair. His mind was clouded. Pervitin had kept him going for four straight days with no sleep. He and Klaus had lost another plane they were supposed to protect. It sank in: *This is the real war!*

Rudi and Klaus Dieterle, as part of Jagdgeschwader 26 – III Gruppe, participated in these attacks during the Battle of Britain and, like all their comrades, were driven to the point of exhaustion. They were permitted only as little as five hours rest between sorties, but with the effects of Pervitin, they rarely slept.

Early in the war, the Luftwaffe had been taking on obsolete and unprepared air forces in enemy countries. The German pilots were fighting for years before the Allied technology caught up and their pilots gained sufficient experience in order to compete.

As the Battle of Britain progressed, the British gained the necessary experience to overcome the imbalance between themselves and their adversaries. They also had the advantage of radar, which the Germans lacked at that time.

German flight crews began to see their comrades missing, and morale was increasingly affected. Thus, the loss of pilots and aircraft began to shift in favor of the British.

German pilots from World War II still top the list of fighter pilots with the most kills. Erich "Bubi" Hartmann flew over 1,400 missions. He was the most successful fighter pilot in the history of aerial warfare, with 352 kills. He was considered to be untouchable as a pilot and has gone down as the greatest fighter pilot of all time.

The top fifteen fighter pilots ever are all German, with over 200 kills apiece. More than 200 of them had more kills than the very top Allied pilot of WWII, with Soviet Ace, Ivan Kozhedub, being credited with 66 kills. Among the top British Aces, James Johnson is credited with 38 kills.

The reason German pilots scored so high is a combination of early superior technology, skill, and time in the air. They were also able to perform a higher number of missions under the influence of the methamphetamine, Pervitin.

"Today gentlemen, we will again accompany over 100 Heinkel 111 and Dornier bombers over the docks in London's East End. Our intelligence service informs us we will encounter only light opposition, as the Brits are down to their last 50 or so fighters."

This information was met with murmured sighs of relief and light applause. Commander Galland was standing near the speaker, *Hauptmann* Dürsteller.

"And another thing, fellows," added Galland, "always remember to keep your wingman in sight. We've lost too many planes lately from them going off on their own."

Rudi and Klaus Dieterle looked at one another, nodded, and exchanged knowing grins.

The group broke up and walked to their waiting aircraft, where their individual mechanics waited to help them put on their parachutes and wish them luck.

Galland and Dürsteller, in the lead aircraft, called for their engines to be started. As their mechanics cranked the starter, the Daimler Benz engines coughed and stuttered into life. They taxied out to the main landing strip, followed by others of JG 26. As soon as they were airborne, they joined the formation of bombers and headed northwest.

Flying at 260 mph, approaching the maximum speed of the bombers, the formation flew the 140 miles from Pas de Calais to London in about 35 minutes. Flying near each other, Rudi and Klaus looked at each other and raised a salute.

They reached altitude, assembled with the other fighter squadrons, and joined the bombers as they left the French coast behind. There was a light overcast over the Channel, and the air was calm. The armada droned toward their target.

The outline of the English shoreline soon appeared on the horizon. Rudi felt the rise of anticipation, enhanced by the effects of Pervitin, as the specks on the ground began to materialize into buildings. Soon he could see the Thames estuary and the river itself leading like a road map to the target.

But just as the formation was making its landfall, Galland's voice shouted over the intercom, "Look sharp, boys. Fighters at twelve o'clock!"

Rudi peered toward the West, and was astonished to see a multitude of specks form into flocks of fighters. *Only 50 fighters, he had said! Where did they all come from?*

Dürsteller's voice came on. "More fighters at two o'clock!"

Rudi looked to the northwest and was shocked to see another huge swarm of Hurricanes and Spitfires bearing down on them.

Within minutes, the Germans found themselves surrounded. Maneuvering and dodging, the Messerschmitts were soon so overwhelmed that in trying to protect themselves they were forced to leave the bombers to fly on unprotected. As a result, the British pilots were able to pick off the bombers in quick succession. One bomber after another was hit and put out of commission. Some were able to turn tail and head towards base, but several crashed into the ocean, with only a few making it back to France. Others, not so fortunate, crashed over the target, or belly-landed in open spaces outside London.

"Rudi!" came Klaus's voice over the intercom. "There are two Spitfires coming after you."

Upon hearing this, Rudi had to give up the chase of a Hurricane, which had just shot down a German comrade from one of the other squadrons.

As Rudi began to barrel roll out of the adversaries' line of fire, he felt his plane give a great shudder. Leveling off again, he was shocked to see his windshield become black. An oil line had been hit and spewed over the canopy – obliterating everything!

Knowing that his ship was mortally wounded, he unlatched the canopy, unfastened his seat belt, and rolled the plane upside down. He dropped clear of the aircraft and began his descent. He popped his parachute, saw the pilot chute stream out from the pack, and was relieved to see this followed with the blossoming of the main chute, which jerked him upward as it filled with air.

He looked down and was relieved to see that he was dropping into a large open area. He was later to learn that he was coming down over Hampstead Heath, in a northern suburb of London. Observers standing on the ground below spotted him and began to rush toward the area where he would land. His feet touched the ground, with knees bent, and he rolled forward as his chute deflated. Before he could regain his footing, he felt strong arms grasp him beneath the armpits and pull him upright.

"Welcome to England, Jerry!"

Somewhat dazed, he focused on the face nearest him and looked into the enraged eyes of an older man wearing an air raid warden helmet.

"Okay, laddie. Hands up!"

The warden and another man roughly searched him and removed his service Luger.

One of the other men, with a wry smile, quipped, "Did you like our welcoming committee?"

"Off you go. March!"

He was taken to a waiting police van, which had been summoned, handcuffed and pushed into the back of the vehicle. For Rudi, the war was over!

Due to faulty intelligence, the Germans had been led to believe that the Royal Air Force was decimated. The British, however, had moved much of their aircraft production west and north, out of Luftwaffe fighter range. Instead of 50 fighters on the 15th of September, the Germans were met with more than 28 squadrons of Spitfires and Hurricanes. The German losses were so great that Hitler postponed the invasion of England indefinitely.

§§§

With trembling hands, Erika read the strange advisory at the top of the postcard.

ZWECKS SCHNELLER BEFÖRDERUNG KURZ UND DEUTLICH SCHREIBEN

KRIEGSGEFANGENER

(For the purpose of faster handling, write briefly and legibly)
(Prisoner of war)

Darling Erika,

I am safe in England. I cannot disclose my location, but I am in a prison camp and am being well treated. Tell Gerhard his daddy misses him and kiss him for me.
With all my love,

Your Rudi

Chapter Sixty-five

Weihnachtsgeschenke aus England
(Christmas Presents from England)

Dr. Hans Joachim Lenz sat in the dark savoring his cognac. He had turned off all the lights at the beginning of the attack, so as not to annoy the air raid warden. But the howl of air raid sirens and the muffled bump of bombs falling in the city center, and in the northern suburbs, no longer disturbed him.

"Frohe Weihacnhten 1940, Hans Joachim," (Merry Christmas 1940, Hans Joachim) he muttered to himself. He smiled at the bitter irony of his thoughts. The British were delivering another of their almost nightly load of bombs on the German capital, and Christmas Eve was no exception.

He was usually so exhausted from the steady stream of injured air raid victims at the Charité, that he often just grabbed a few hours' sleep on the sofa in his office at the hospital. Tonight, however, he had determined he would go home to Dahlem. He would allow himself the luxury of a bath and a few hours in his own bed.

At the beginning of the air raids during the past summer, he would go down to his basement when he was home. But he finally decided he would stay in his library with the lights out during any future raids. In any case, if the house were to receive a direct hit, or if a fire should break out, he wouldn't want to be trapped in the basement under a heap of rubble.

Oh, Frederika, I miss you, but I'm glad you're not here to see what has happened to us. Here's to you, darling. He raised his glass in a silent toast to his dead wife.

His thoughts turned to his boys. *I'm so happy you and Meira are safe in Montivideo, son.* He put his hand in his jacket pocket and withdrew the letter he had received from Herbert in the week previous. He held it in his hand until the all clear sounded. Then he turned on the lights and read it again.

Dear Papa,

We arrived in Veracruz, Mexico, on August 30th. Fortunately, we were among the 35 passengers allowed to disembark. Needless to say, I had to grease some palms. At least I had the means to do it, thanks to your foresight all those years ago during the Depression. Most of the others on board were not so fortunate. I heard that the ship was ordered to return to Europe, but I don't know what happened to them after that.

After spending two weeks in Veracruz, we took a bus to Costa Rica. I would have been glad to stay in Costa Rica. It's beautiful, and the people were very hospitable to us. Understandably, however, Meira was eager to join her parents in Uruguay. We went to Panama and managed to book a cabin on a coastal freighter to Rio de Janeiro. The trip was endless. November is summer below the equator. The air was so hot and humid, Meira and I both slept in separate bunks, and the porthole was open every night. Our sheets were soaked every morning. It seemed we stopped at every little port along the coast of Brazil. We docked in Rio on November 8th. We were so happy to get off that dirty ship. Rio is a beautiful city near the beach, but there are horrific slums on the hillsides called "favelas". Because of our month in Lisbon, we got used to the sound of Portuguese and then hearing it again in Brazil was comforting in an odd way. After a week in Rio, we were able to fly to Montevideo on a Junker trimotor, like Rudi Bellon used to fly.

Mr. and Mrs. Friedlander met us, but that meeting was terrible for Meira. I thought we should have informed them from Lisbon that Edna would not be coming with us, but Meira wouldn't have it, and she had to try to explain it to her mother when we got there.

Mrs. Friedlander hasn't been well for months, her husband said, so when she learned that Edna had been left behind in Paris, she collapsed. She had to be taken by ambulance to a hospital because the shock of the news caused her to have a stroke. She is still under a doctor's care, paralyzed on her left side and can't speak clearly. Fortunately, she still has the use of her right hand and can write on a little slate, but not too legibly.

When Mr. Friedlander mentioned to the doctor that I am a doctor and Meira is a nurse, the man was beside himself with delight. He insisted that when we have our affairs in order, we should contact him. He stated that we would be welcome at any clinic or hospital in the city. We told him we were grateful for his offer and will take him up on it as soon as we are settled.

One last thing, Papa: please don't take any unnecessary risks, but if you have any way of getting information as to where Edna is, Meira and I would be most grateful.

So, there you are, Papa. We are safe. I hear about the air raids over Berlin and hope you are keeping well. Write to us when you can.

Your son,
Herbert

Tears welled up in his eyes, but he was relieved that he could rest easy knowing his son and wife had managed to escape the darkness enshrouding Europe.

Then his thoughts turned to his youngest. *Karlheinz, my boy. What are you doing with your life?*

Chapter Sixty-six

Beschlagnahmt
(Confiscated)

"Where did you manage to get that?" enquired Christina with suspicion, as she scrutinized the ball of Gouda cheese laid out for the evening meal one day in late January of 1941.

"At the market," replied Ursula.

"Just like that?"

"Well, it actually appeared for the first time today. I see more goods and food on the shelves than I saw before the war. They even have silver and Damask table linens for sale!"

"Where's that from?" Detlev piped up.

"It's from Holland," replied his brother.

Ursula gave each person a slice on a square of rye bread.

"That's delicious!" exclaimed Detlev. "Why haven't we had that before?"

"Because the German army was not occupying that country before!" retorted his grandmother, followed by an awkward silence.

"You make it sound like we should be ashamed to enjoy it," accused young Eckhardt.

"Maybe you're right!" declared Christina.

Young Eckhardt turned to glare at his grandmother.

"Look, everyone. I'm sorry I brought it home. I won't make that mistake again."

"But let's just enjoy it, without worrying about its history," said her husband softly.

"Well, I do admit it's good, even if it's confiscated," admitted Christina.

Turning to his father, Detlev asked, "What does 'confiscate' mean, Papa?"

"Steal!" Christina shot back.

"Okay! That's it!" cried Ursula, gathering up the Gouda and taking it to the kitchen. "That's all for tonight," she declared over her shoulder as she left the room.

§§§

During the first years of German occupation, goods of all kinds appeared on the shelves of shops and stores in Germany, as foods, luxury items, industrial products, agricultural products, and on and on were confiscated in all the occupied countries and shipped back to the Reich.

Furniture and household goods were brought to Germany from occupied countries and were given to families displaced in the air raids.

Art from the museums of Europe and from private collections, mostly Jewish, was looted and gifted or sold to the members of the Nazi hierarchy and those who could afford them. In the process, much was lost or destroyed, particularly works designated *"Entartete Kunst"* (Degenerate art).

Chapter Sixty-seven

Vernarrt
(Smitten)

She walks in beauty. She is the image of feminine perfection. Everything about her is beyond description. Her long blonde braids frame a heart-shaped face accentuated by full rose red lips, a petite nose, apple cheeks, eyes like deep blue limpid pools. She has a long-legged figure, and moves with feline grace.

"She's the most beautiful girl I have ever seen," gushed young Eckhardt to his brother.

Detlev, unimpressed, replied bluntly, "She won't have time for you, you ugly jerk!"

A pillow landed on his face.

"What do you know, creep? Get out of here. I have to get ready for a Chemistry exam tomorrow."

Laughing, Detlev left the room.

What if he's right? I'm too skinny, and anyway, what am I gonna' say to her? She's my new lab partner, and she'll see how stupid I am. I've got to pass this test!

He looked in amazement at his exam score. *Eighty-six! Not bad. Not bad, at all.* He looked over at her, and after a moment, as if she felt his gaze, she looked at him. He flashed her a confident smile. Her face registered nothing. After a few seconds of staring at him, she looked away, and resumed writing in her lab journal.

I'm such an idiot! he chastised himself. *Grinning at her like an imbecile! What was I thinking?* He shrank down in his seat and kept his head bowed for the rest of the period.

The bell rang, and he remained seated until she had gathered up her books and left the room. When he walked down the corridor filled with laughing, chattering students, he noticed she walked some distance ahead, alone, not seeming to take notice of anyone around her.

He promised himself to not stare at her again – but to no avail. As he caught up to her at the street crossing, he came alongside and at first looked straight ahead. But then, just as the light changed, he sneaked a sideways glance at her. She took no notice of him.

Her profile is so beautiful. See how the sun makes her hair glow in a golden haze.

He crossed slightly behind her until they came to the end of the block, and she turned at the corner. *I should walk straight home. But where does she live?* He was tempted to follow her. *But no! I mustn't.*

Monika, he whispered to himself. *What a beautiful name! It really fits her.*

She had arrived from Cologne shortly after Easter. When the teacher requested that she stand and introduce herself, she gave her name and stated that her father was an electrical engineer and had begun work at Siemens.

That's perfect! I can tell her my father is at Siemens. We have something in common. That's always a good start, he congratulated himself.

At the end of class, he hurried over to her, as she gathered up her books. He extended his hand. She studied him for a moment, then shook his hand briefly.

"Eckhardt Meinert," he declared.

Without expression, she responded, "Monika König."

He smiled. "My father works at Siemens, too." Getting no comment or response, he forged ahead. "I live on Sandweg here in Spandau. Do you live near there?"

"No, not really."

"If you live in that direction, could I walk with you part way?"

"No, but thank you."

Deflated, he forced himself not to enquire further.

"Perhaps another time, then?"

She looked past him and with a slight shrug, turned to walk away. Stunned, he stood speechless.

Was ist mit ihr denn los? (What's the matter with her?) he wondered.

He lay in the still darkness of his room with his hands behind his head, Detlev breathing softly in the bed next to his. The house was still, except for a soft breeze brushing the window facing the river.

Why does she take no notice of me? Even in lab yesterday, she only spoke when we first got there. When I asked her a direct question about a problem, she answered but offered nothing further. When I tried to talk to her about the fine weather, she didn't comment. School will be out for summer soon, and then I won't see her anymore until school starts.

After a while, sleep slowly enveloped him.

He was walking near the river. Suddenly, he saw her. She was standing at the waters' edge naked. She smiled and held her arms out to him. Then he realized he was naked. He ran to her. They embraced!

With a shock, he awoke. The gray light of predawn filled the room. This was something different. He felt his face flush.

She was already seated at the lab table writing in her lab journal. She had checked out her lab specimens, which lay on the table before her. Placing his books in the bookcase at the end of the room and checking out his specimens, he sat beside her.

"*Guten morgen, Monika.*"

After more than a month since first meeting her, he had finally managed to get on a first name basis with her, after enquiring if he might do so. Surprisingly, she had agreed.

"*Guten morgen, Eckhardt.*"

"Are you going on the joint summer HJ/BDM excursion to Salzkammergut in Austria after school lets out?"

Looking intently at the assignment sheet for the lab experiment, she murmured, "No."

Remembering he had seen members of BDM cluster around her on her first day, but then noticing afterwards he never saw her in the company of other girls, he began to see a pattern.

Struggling with himself whether or not he should put the direct question to her, he finally mustered up the courage instead to ask again if he might walk with her after school.

She turned, and as a smile played about her beautiful lips, replied, "Alright."

His eyes widened and color rose in his face, and with a beaming smile, he declared, "I will meet you after gym class outside the north entrance."

For the rest of the day, as he encountered friends and classmates in classes, they stared at him, and some even enquired why he was beaming and bright-eyed. He bragged, "You'll never guess!"

Being preoccupied with thoughts of the long-awaited rendezvous, he missed much of what was presented and discussed in his classes.

At the end of the day, he waited, breathless, at the agreed location. Tormented with anxiety, he watched students coming through the door. As the crowd diminished, his palms began to sweat, and doubt crept into his mind.

She's not coming. What did you expect, idiot? She really doesn't like you. She finally agreed just to shut you up!

Just then she appeared, walking alone, and he hurried toward her. "Let me carry those," as he moved to take some books from her.

She smiled and declared, "Thank you, but no. I only have these two small volumes. Most of my things are in my knapsack."

He blushed and admonished himself, *don't push so hard. You already know she doesn't like that!"*

Without further comment, they began to walk side by side. After waiting for the light and then crossing the street, they fell into an easy stride.

"What are those books you're carrying?"

"I got them from the library. This one," she said, holding up a small thin blue bound volume, "is a collection of poems from Eichendorff. I love romantic poetry."

Eichendorff? he thought to himself. *I've heard that name, but I'm glad she didn't ask me anything about it.*

"This other one is *Die leiden des jungen Werther* (The Sorrows of the young Werther). Do you like Goethe?"

Caught off guard, he responded hastily, "He's usually too heavy for me, but I do like his poem, *Heideröslein,* when it's set to music.

One of the older boys in our HJ group plays the guitar, and we sing that around the campfire."

A sideways glance to ascertain her reaction – *he saw none!*

They continued to walk. Finally, he enquired, "Why aren't you going with us to Salzkammergut?"

This at first prompted no response. Then, "I don't like crowds of people."

Not knowing what to say to that, he proceeded, "Don't you like the BDM activities?"

"Not especially."

By this time, they had reached the corner where she turned. "Thank you for walking with me, Eckhardt."

"I was happy to. Can I walk with you to school in the morning?"

"My father usually drives me on his way to work."

"Well, then can we walk again tomorrow after school?"

"We'll see. *Auf Wiedersehen*, Eckhardt."

He stood and watched her walk away.

She walks in beauty.

Part V

Arrogance Will Be Punished

Chapter Sixty-eight

Unternehmen Barbarossa
(Operation Barbarossa)

"*Okay, du Faulpeltz* (lazy bones), get up! This is it!" *SS Sturmbannführer* Dieter Lehmann roused Karlheinz in their Warsaw apartment, which had been commandeered from a prominent Polish banker and his family.

Groaning, the groggy young man sat up. "What time is it?"

"It's four-thirty. Hurry up. We can still get a good breakfast at the base if we leave right away."

They, and other members of the German military forces in Poland, had been on standby since the middle of May, when tight security had been enforced after the officers had been informed of the plans to invade the Soviet Union. All had been meticulously organized, and the largest military invasion in history was poised to attack their erstwhile ally. Then everything was put on hold when Italy botched their attack on Greece, and Hitler was forced to rescue them to keep the Allies from gaining a foothold in the Balkans.

But now, the day had finally come. In the early morning hours of June 21, 1941, three division forces of three million German troops crossed into Russian territory along a thousand-mile front.

"I can't wait to see Moscow," Karlheinz declared to his companion driving their Volkswagen *Kübelwagen*. They were part of the SS Division Das Reich with Army Group Center, under the command of Fedor von Bock, headed to Smolensk and on to Moscow.

Grinning, Dieter reached over and squeezed Karlheinz's knee. "Just wait until you get to see Lenin in his glass coffin on Red Square."

Wrinkling his nose, Karlheinz replied, "That isn't what I meant."

Coming to a small village, they were dumbfounded to see women and children standing along both sides of the road tossing flowers at their trucks and military vehicles.

"Do you believe that?" declared Karlheinz.

"Sure, why not? They see us as liberators to free them from the Bolsheviks. But wait until they see what a surprise we have in store for them!" declared Dieter. "Filthy dirty Slavs!"

Karlheinz stared at him.

§§§

"Ekaterina Ivanova?" enquired one of two big men in black suits and fedora hats early on Sunday, June 22, 1941.

"Yes." The young Russian intern had just seated herself in the cafeteria after a night in surgery at the Charité.

"You are under arrest! Come with us!" The men grasped her under her arms and pulled her out of her chair.

As she was marched out of the room, all conversation ceased, and her colleagues sat frozen in their seats or stood motionless wherever they were.

Hans Joachim Lenz almost collided with the hapless woman and her escorts as they met in the doorway.

"What's going on here?" he challenged the dark suit nearest him.

"It's none of your concern. Let us through!"

"She is essential to my surgical team, so if it concerns Ekaterina, it concerns me," Hans Joachim retorted."

"Then you can come with us, too!"

"It's alright, Dr. Lenz" interjected the woman. "I can get in touch with my embassy."

"Except your embassy is now off limits and has been closed. Haven't you heard? Germany is now at war with Russia!" declared one of the Gestapo agents.

Stunned, Hans Joachim was pushed aside, and the two Gestapo men hurried down the corridor, dragging their victim between them.

Finally, he staggered to a chair in a daze. Turning to a nearby table occupied by a group of nurses, he asked, "What did they mean, 'Germany is at war with Russia'?"

"That's right. It was announced early this morning by Dr. Goebbels in a news flash," confirmed the oldest of the nurses. "He says the *Führer* decided it was necessary, because the Russians have been moving toward our ally, Romania."

"I've been in emergency surgery since midnight, tending air raid victims." Shaking his head, he muttered, "Poor Ivanova. She was assisting us, so she doesn't know about it either. She was almost finished with her residency and has the potential of being a brilliant surgeon."

He continued, "Of course, Hitler would be anxious about the Russians moving on Romania. The oil fields at Ploesti would be a major loss.

But what is the man thinking? Surely, he realizes he has now involved us in another two-front war, something for which he has repeatedly accused the generals of causing us to lose the last war. My god, this will be the end for us!"

His listeners offered no comment, but looked at one another with alarm, before standing up and moving away from the agitated doctor.

§§§

"Shoot her!" Dieter Lehmann ordered. "Shoot the bitch, or I'll shoot you!"

Karlheinz looked into the pleading eyes of a young girl, lying on the ground beside her dead mother. The hand holding his service Luger trembled, and the sweat running down his brow seeped into his eyes.

The German offensive had driven deep into Russia, but had encountered fierce resistance at Smolensk. A great battle named after that city ensued in September. The momentum of the German forces was interrupted by Hitler's decision to postpone the attack on Moscow in order to completely conquer the Ukraine first.

During that period, the forces of the SS and the Wehrmacht were utilized in brutalizing the civilian population, with the intent of breaking morale and resistance. When the German forces gained control of towns and villages, men and boys were disposed of immediately. The women and girls were often reserved for the German Army brothels. Some women, however, offered resistance when they were arrested, and especially women who tried to protect daughters being accosted by the Germans. Most of these women and their daughters were then taken into the woods, raped, and shot.

Karlheinz and Dieter were part of a group of SS who were involved in such an action, with Dieter enthusiastically participating. This traumatized Karlheinz, who had never been attracted to any woman. Seeing this new side to his lover, plus a disinclination to extreme brutality, had pushed him near the breaking point.

What would my mother think of me now? tormented him.

"Shoot her!"

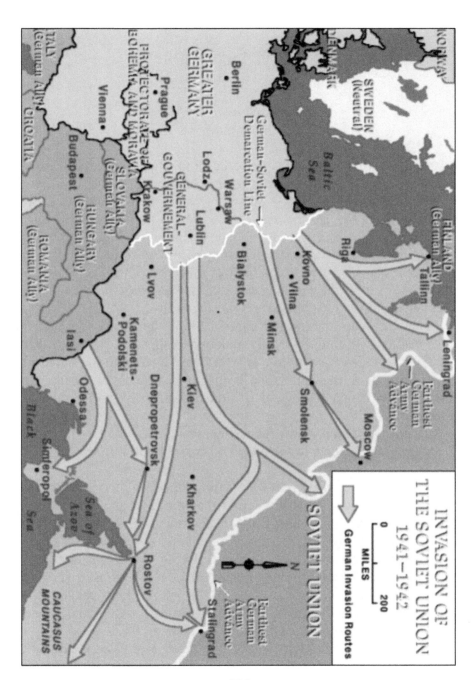

Chapter Sixty-nine

Der Höhepunkt
(The Pinnacle)

"Look at what our troops have accomplished!" enthused young Eckhardt. "Aren't you proud to be German?"

They walked side-by-side on the gray overcast day after school, the October day being punctuated by intervals of drizzling rain.

Monika looked intently at the dead leaves they kicked aside. Waiting for a response, he stopped, turned, and faced her.

"Don't you see? The *Führer* has promised a victory in Russia by Christmas. And at the rate our army is moving, they'll make it with ease. What a Christmas present for Germany!"

She looked up at him and studied him – her brow wrinkled in concentration. "Would that really make you happy?"

"Of course. We won't have to worry anymore about the scheming Communists at our back, and it will open up a whole new territory for German resettlement. Think of it – the Third Reich stretching from Europe to Asia!"

Her face darkened; her frown deepened.

Looking back down at the leaves, she continued walking.

"I don't understand her," he complained to his parents that evening. "We're so close to winning this war, and she doesn't even seem to care. She's so smart, I'm sure she understands that but never comments about anything we're accomplishing in such a short time."

Ursula glanced at her husband, studying the food on his plate, as if trying to decide what to put into his mouth next. She looked across at her mother. Christina stared at her grandson, and then looked at her daughter and opened her mouth to speak, just as Ursula, looking back at her, gave a slight shake of her head to keep still.

"Yeah, I think what our soldiers are doing in Russia is amazing, too," piped up Detlev. "And we've taken care of the 'Froggies'. Maybe after we're done in Russia, the Luftwaffe can go back and finish off the arrogant Limeys, and put a stop to these damned air raids. Nobody'd better give us any shit after that!"

"That will do, Detlev!" The sharpness in his mother's voice silenced him. "We'll have none of that gutter language in this house!"

"Right! You watch your mouth, young man," said his father.

Watching the little drama being played out before him, young Eckhardt said with a smirk, "Detlev is just saying what a lot of people think now. The *Führer* has been saying for years, the German people are the best of the best. What more proof do you need?"

Ursula and her husband exchanged glances.

"What would you like for your birthday dinner next week, son?"

Young Eckhardt, startled by the abrupt change of subject, looked open-mouthed at his mother. "My birthday?" His brow furrowed. "Could we have *Schweinebraten* (roast pork) and *Knödel* (dumplings) with *Rotkohl* (sweet and sour red cabbage)? And can I invite Monika?"

Smiling, Ursula replied, "Of course, you can. But that depends on whether or not I can find a meat market that has some. With the war on, the military has to be supplied first."

"Oh, good!" cried Detlev. "We'll finally get to see Eckhardt's dream girl."

Everyone laughed. Eckhardt ducked his head, red-faced.

"I can see about the food," volunteered Christina. "If I can't find any in the city, I have the time to travel out to Zossen and see what my old contacts from the last war might have."

Ursula laughed. "Oh, Mama! You're amazing. I remember how you kept us alive in those days. You used to spend days at a time on your foraging. We would have starved if you hadn't been so relentless."

Christina smiled. "We had some real adventures, didn't we? Remember when you kids went with me to Zossen, and those two thugs almost made off with our suitcases of food at the train station?"

"Oh, yes! I remember that day! You were like a screaming banshee. Those guys didn't know what hit 'em. You came on like a hurricane and were all over them!"

They were both caught up in their recollections and laughter.

The men watched. Eckhardt and his two sons were astonished at Christina. They hadn't seen her so animated in a long time.

Chapter Seventy

Die Geburtstagsfeier
(The Birthday Party)

The next day, Eckhardt seated himself at the lab bench he shared with Monika, breathless with anticipation.

What if she refuses to come? he fretted.

Then she appeared in the doorway – radiantly beautiful!

After retrieving her lab journal from her knapsack and laying her other books on the bookshelf by the door, she walked toward him

"Guten Tag, Monika."

"Tag, Eckhardt."

After a moment, she became aware he was staring at her.

He fidgeted with his hands and bit his lip.

Frowning, she enquired, "Is something wrong?"

He squared his shoulders and blurted, "Next Saturday is my birthday, and I would like to invite you to come to my house for my birthday dinner. My family would like to meet you. I can come for you and walk you there. Maybe my father can drive us, if he doesn't have to work. Sometimes he has to go in on weekends. Will you come?"

Caught off guard by the rapid-fire invitation, she paused.

"Next Saturday? I usually have to help my mother with shopping and doing laundry on Saturday."

His heart sank.

Seeing his crestfallen face, she quickly replied, "I'll ask my mother if we could shop on Friday and do laundry early on Saturday. What time is your dinner?"

He brightened and then offered, "I can help you and your mother shop on Friday."

She smiled. "That won't be necessary, but thanks. What time?"

"We'll eat at six, but I can come for you at five if we have to walk. If my father is home, we can drive you home afterwards, or I'll walk you."

"Thank you, Eckhardt. I'm sure I can work something out with my mother."

His spirits soared, and he sailed through the rest of day.

Saturday, November 1, 1941, dawned in Berlin, overcast, damp, and cold. But young Eckhardt bounded out of bed, dressed and hurried downstairs, as if he were to be greeted by a bright summer day.

Ursula and Christina were seated at the dining table with their morning cups of tea, having already had breakfast with Eckhardt, who had left for work.

"Good morning, birthday boy!" Ursula greeted her son. He walked to her, bent down and planted a kiss on her cheek.

"Well, maybe we should say every day is your birthday, if I'm going to be greeted like that."

Christina chuckled. "Now, how about one for Grandma?"

He walked around the table and kissed her, too. She beamed.

"That girl must be everything you say she is, if she has that kind of effect on you," Ursula teased.

Throwing his head back, Eckhardt cried, "She's beyond description!"

Laughter all around.

"What's going on here?" asked Detlev from the doorway, who had been awakened.

"Good morning, son. We're just trying to pull your brother back down to earth. He's wound up about Monika."

"All that noise about a girl?" grumbled the younger boy. "I'm hungry."

"Both of you sit down," directed Ursula as she arose from the table. "This morning you get a treat because it's Eckhardt's special day. Pancakes and blackberry jam!"

"I hope you make such a big deal out of my birthday when it comes. Why is turning seventeen so special, anyway?" groused Detlev.

"Why don't you give your brother a kiss, Eckhardt. You gave both of us one, and it really cheered us up," quipped Christina.

Puckering his lips, Eckhardt moved toward his brother.

"Don't you dare! I'll smack you," threatened Detlev, as he moved back a step.

Laughing, Eckhardt retorted. "Not on your life, brother. I wouldn't waste my kisses on the likes of you."

"Right! Save them for the ladies," continued his mother.

"Yeah. Save 'em for your girlfriend," Detlev shot back. "Have you kissed her yet?"

All three looked enquiringly at Eckhardt, who turned beet red.

"Yeah, he has! Look at him!" chortled Detlev.

"Anyway, it's none of your business. Where are those pancakes?" Eckhardt scowled and sat down.

Eckhardt took his cap off, ran a hand across his hair and rang the doorbell, waiting in anticipation. After what seemed like an eternity, she opened the door.

Her long blonde hair was done in a single braid. Her beautiful complexion was highlighted by the sky-blue dress she wore, partially hidden by the plum colored coat. He was riveted by her blue-eyed gaze. Her rose-colored lips were drawn back in a slight smile, showing perfect teeth.

"I'm sorry my father couldn't drive us. He had to go in to work, but I'm sure he'll be home in time to bring us back later. It's only a few blocks to our house."

Closing the heavy door, she replied, "That's fine. It's a nice evening for walking."

He pretended not to notice the package she carried under her right arm. They began to walk toward Sandweg. After a short distance, he took her gloved left hand in his right, and she did not resist. His heart pounded.

They approached his house and entered the front door. His mother met them in the foyer, just as he helped Monika remove her coat.

Extending her hand, Ursula greeted Monika with a wide smile. "I'm Ursula Meinert, and I am so happy to meet you. We hear a lot about you from my son. Welcome."

Eckhardt beamed with pride as he introduced Monika to his grandmother, who also extended her a warm welcome.

Turning to Detlev he announced, "This is my little brother, Detlev, who has been dying to meet you."

Monika smiled and replied, "I hope he won't be disappointed.'

Detlev, blushing, stammered, "N – nice to meet you," then turned and threw a scowl at his brother for being described as 'little'."

Conversation revolved around the circumstances of Monika's family moving to Berlin from Cologne, whereby she explained that her father had taken a position at Siemens. This was met by a response from Ursula, who pointed out that her husband, too, was at Siemens. It was acknowledged that the two men apparently had never met but that Siemens was a huge plant.

Just as they sat down to dinner, which was comprised of the dishes Eckhardt had requested, his father arrived home. After removing his coat, he entered the dining room, where Ursula had set him a place. They began to enjoy the meal, and a spirit of warmth and cordiality surrounded the table.

When the table had been cleared, the birthday cake, a Schwartzwalderkirschtorte (Black Forest cherry cake) was placed before the expectant young man. After he successfully blew out the candles in one puff, and a generous slice was served to each person, *Zum Geburtstag viel Glück* (On Your Birthday Good Luck) was sung. The presents were brought out, for which he expressed appreciation to each giver. The gift that stood out, however, was the beautiful long scarf in patterns of red and blue Monika had knit for him herself.

After much laughter and banter, they adjourned to the living room where conversation continued as they began to get to know Monika better.

Young Detlev, who had been studying her throughout the evening, thought to himself, *Yes, she's everything Eckhardt's been saying about her. Maybe **some** girls aren't so bad after all.*

Chapter Seventy-one

Ravensbrück

The women stood in the chilling November mist, many moving from one foot to the other. Like a gathering of little locomotives, their breath punctuated the air.

Edna surreptitiously scratched under her armpit.

"Du da! Still bleiben!" (You there. Be still.)

Lice! Crawling with them! She didn't mind, though. The little darlings made the guards keep their distance. They almost never came inside the barracks beyond the entrance, leaving the occupants in relative peace. But there were plenty of vermin for everyone. The straw mattresses on which they slept were veritable breeding grounds for the multitudes that plagued the women at Ravensbrück.

She let her thoughts wander back to the days at home with her parents. They had no idea where she was. She knew they were in Montevideo. *It must be beautiful there. All that sunshine. Thank God, Meira and Herbert were probably there, too, by now.*

They stood and waited. And waited! And waited!

A frail, young Polish prostitute, who had until recently serviced German soldiers in an army brothel, collapsed into the muddy puddle at her feet.

Poor thing, thought Edna. *Her syphilis, plus malnutrition, has brought her to this.*

No one dared move to help her up.

The girl had turned up positive in her weekly pap smear and thus had been sent here to work until she collapsed, then to be disposed of in the gas chamber, and finally in the crematorium. These facilities worked around the clock.

At last, the camp commandant, *SS Standartenführer* Günther Tamschke, sauntered across the compound, took his position before the group, and smiled. His smart uniform and well-fed healthy countenance indicated a man content in his place in life and secure in his positon of authority.

Na, schön guten Morgen, meine Damen! Haben wir gut geschlafen? Und was haben wir nun heute vor? Nu, lass uns 'mal sehen. Zeitplan für heute, bitte." (Well, good morning, ladies. Did we sleep well? What do we have on for today? Let's see, now. Today's schedule, please.)

His female assistant, standing nearby, placed a clipboard in his outstretched hand.

"Alright, now. Barrack 5: report to the laundry (used for staff only). Barrack 10: report to the infirmary (again, mainly for staff). Barrack 12: report to the morgue (a holding tank for inmates waiting to be shipped to the crematorium). Barrack 8: report to the main gate. You'll be assigned to work at Siemens in Berlin (on military projects)."

"Jetzt zum Frühstück! Na, los! Nicht trödeln! (Now, to breakfast! Well, move it! No dilly dallying!) shouted Irma Griese, one of the stoutly-built guards.

As the gang organized themselves alphabetically into their assigned positions, one emaciated elderly woman shuffled a little too slowly and received the sharp sting of a whip across her back. She whimpered.

"Na, kitzelt's Oma?" (Well, does that tickle, grandma?) *"Beeil dich doch!"* (Hurry up then) shouted Elfriede Müller, the wielder of the whip, whose treatment of prisoners was so harsh, she became known as *Die Hyäne von Ravensbrück* (The hyena of Ravensbrück).

"Breakfast" was a stale hard roll and weak tea.

Chapter Seventy-two

Ein Gewissenskonflikt
(A conflict of conscience)

The early November morning light penetrated the blanket of fog as Eckhardt drove along Siemensdamm. He wondered why he had been notified so late the previous day to report to his department head an hour earlier than usual. As he turned into the parking area adjacent to his building, he saw others of the department leadership walking toward the entrance. When he stepped out of his car, he was greeted by his colleague, Horst Müller, who had made it clear early on that he was less than enthusiastic about the current regime.

"Well, Meinert, are we ready to go hear about the next brilliant strategy to win this war? *Herr* 'GröFhaZ' is on the job!"

This was an acronym meaning *"Größter Feldherr aller Zeiten"* (Greatest field commander of all time) referring to Hitler, who saw himself as a brilliant military strategist. This hubris led him to override his generals and take charge of more campaigns as the war went on. The results contributed largely to the disastrous outcome of the war for Germany – the Battle of Stalingrad being a prime example.

Two engineers walking past turned and stared at the commentator. One smirked. The other frowned.

"Keep it down, Müller, for chrissake," muttered Eckhardt, as he approached the speaker.

At this, Müller laughed and put his arm around Eckhardt's shoulder. "Why? Aren't you proud that you're an important part of the success our soldiers are having for the glory of the Fatherland?"

Scowling, Eckhardt eased away from the arm around his shoulder.

"Really, Eckhardt, you need to come up out of it and take a look around more. Fence-sitting days are just about over!"

His face flushed with the sting of the accusation. Eckhardt hastened his steps, briskly walked away and entered the building without a backward glance.

"This is the situation, gentlemen. We have been awarded the contract to build the searchlights to be installed in the flak towers and anti-aircraft installations all over the country.

With the increasing demand of the military for more troops, our workers and assemblers are being drafted faster than we can replace them. Therefore, they will be replaced by guest workers.

These people are being recruited from those who sit idle in our correction facilities and consume resources but do not produce. This program is to put an end to that and at the same time, reduce the shortfall in our labor force.

Any of you who speak other languages must make your supervisors aware of this, as many of these people are from the new territories of the Reich. It will be your responsibility to make sure they understand their assignments.

I have here the lists of new workers assigned to each team under your individual responsibility.

As I call your name, come forward and pick up your packet. Are there any questions?"

Except for soft muttering, there was no response.

"Guest workers! Did you ever hear such bullshit?" sputtered Müller are they closed the door of the two-desk office they now shared.

"When Lipschke asked if there were any questions, of course no one dared ask the obvious one of why these 'guest workers' from 'new territories' are even here!" he continued. "And did you hear 'correction facilities', as he euphemistically puts it? He means 'concentration camps' and probably even 'prisoner of war camps'."

"Right! No one dared ask! Not even you, Müller!" Eckhardt shot back.

Müller grinned. "Yeah. You got me there. Look, Meinert, I know you think I'm a fool for not keeping my mouth shut when I should. But what's being done in the name of Germany is criminal, and I don't believe I'm alone in thinking that. We're all going to pay for it, mark my words!"

And that Lipschke! What a snake! Where did he come from? He hasn't been with the company all that long. How did he, and a few others around here, move up in the ranks so fast? Yeah, he works for Siemens! I bet his real employer is the Gestapo."

"All the more reason for you to keep your opinions to yourself, Müller!"

"I don't know what to do, Ursula, except do my job and stay away from people like Müller. I admit that a lot of what he says really gets to me. But he's gonna' put a noose around his neck sooner or later, and I just don't want to be pulled into it."

Ursula lay her head upon his chest. The silence of the house was only broken by their soft breathing in the dark.

"Of course, darling, you mustn't put yourself – and all of us – at risk. But you're hard to read. Sometimes it's almost as if you approve of things going on now, and I know you're not really that kind of a person.

But just think about those poor people! 'Guest workers'! 'Forced labor'! That's what they really are! Müller's right! We should be ashamed of what this government is doing to our country – and to other countries!"

Eckhardt stared into the darkness, one arm behind his head. Turning to embrace his wife, he whispered, "You're right. But I can only take it one day at a time." He kissed her.

The head of Siemens from 1933 to 1941, was Carl Friedrich von Siemens, youngest son of the founder of the firm, Werner von Siemens. He was an avowed believer in democracy and detested the Nazi regime.

During the war years, Siemens was primarily responsible for the manufacture of electrical goods, and limited its involvement in the manufacture of armaments.

§§§

"I'm gonna be a pilot like my uncle Rudi after I finish school and get my *Abitur,*" boasted young Eckhardt to Monika.

"Does that mean you'll be bombing women and children?"

He stopped in his tracks. His mouth hung open at a loss for words.

"I don't know. What makes you ask that?"

"Just wondered how you feel about that."

They walked on in silence.

"I'm glad you came to my birthday dinner last week. And thanks again for the scarf. It's beautiful. I wore it to church last Sunday."

"I'm glad you like it. Has your family heard anymore from your uncle Rudi?"

"Not for a while. Sometimes I see Grandma reading his last letter again, and she starts to cry."

"I'm sorry. My sister lost her fiancé in Poland before we moved here from Cologne. She was devastated, and now she won't go out with any other fellows. I hate this war!" she cried vehemently.

"Sshhh!" admonished Eckhardt, looking around. He felt indignation rising in his breast triggered by the indoctrination he had heard for years in the HJ. "You don't want anyone to think you're a defeatist. Think about what the *Führer* has done for us!"

"Well, you certainly do the *deutscher Blick* (German glance around) to perfection!" she said, with a sardonic look. "Can't you express a thought of your own, or do you rely on everything you've learned from the Hitler Youth?"

Red-faced, he muttered, "Are you making fun of me?"

She touched his sleeve. "Don't be so sensitive, Eckhardt. I'm only teasing you."

She was moved by the hurt she saw in his eyes and reached out and took his hand. He looked at her and was encouraged by her warm smile.

"Have you told you family about your plans to join the Luftwaffe?"

"Yes, and it didn't go over too well. My Grandma is absolutely opposed to the idea. She says one pilot getting shot down in the family is enough. Mama isn't delighted with the idea either, but she understands that the alternative is to join the Wehrmacht or the Navy. Either way, I have to do military service."

"You see why I hate this war?"

Chapter Seventy-three

Ein Neuer Gegner
(A New Adversary)

JAPANISCHER ANGRIFF AUF PEARL HARBOR HAWAII!

(Japanese Attack on Pearl Harbor Hawaii)

"Unbelieveable!"

"What's that, Dr. Lenz?"

"I can't believe the hubris, the arrogance and stupidity of some people nowadays!" declared Hans Joachim to his nurse, as he laid aside his copy of *Berliner Morgenpost,* on Monday morning, December 8, 1941.

She stared at him with a blank expression.

"I'm sorry. Did you hear that the Japanese attacked the Americans at their naval base in Hawaii yesterday?"

She shook her head.

"Can you see what this might mean for us?"

She frowned, uncomprehending.

"We are part of the Tripartite Pact, which was signed last September together with Italy and Japan. President Roosevelt has now declared war on Japan. Therefore, Germany is obliged to support Japan."

"Did the Americans declare war on us?"

"No, but I don't see how we can stay out of it."

After a moment, she replied, "My father was in the last war, and he has said for years, Germany lost all hope of winning it after the Americans got involved."

"Of course. He's right. And I hope Hitler remembers that before he starts anything foolish with them this time. But we'll have to wait and see.

We're already in over our heads in Russia, and it's not going well – in spite of what we hear from Goebbels. Please don't quote me on that, *Fräulein*."

She smiled. "Of course not, Doctor."

§§§

On December 11, 1941, Hitler declared war on the United States.

Chapter Seventy-four

Ausserhalb Moskow stehengeblieben
(Bogged down outside Moscow)

"I'm glad I didn't shoot her!" declared Karlheinz. "I've killed soldiers and partisans who would have killed me, but I'm glad I didn't kill that girl and others like her."

"You're still a pussy! I should have shot you myself that day! I've had to finish jobs for you over and over, starting with the Poles at your estate and then Russian pigs across this country," mocked Dieter. "You're useless, and I'm sick of you!"

Karlheinz looked at him unwavering. *What's the matter with me? What did I ever see in him? A killing machine with no heart!*

As the months passed and they moved through towns and villages, Karlheinz watched his companion's ruthlessness and bestiality increase, which oddly made him more and more aware of his own empathy and humanity. He watched Dieter kill without hesitation – and apparently with relish.

The two had followed the campaign with their SS division and Army Group Center throughout the summer, autumn and winter of 1941. Their Blitzkrieg thrust had propelled them at lightning speed across Russia throughout the dry months, until the autumn rains began to turn the unpaved roads into troughs of bottomless mud.

Then the temperature dropped, eventually as cold as minus 30 degrees Fahrenheit. The morass thickened and froze into concrete-like expanses, swallowing them and their vehicles. Finally, it brought the parade of fools to less than 10 miles from their goal – the center of Moscow!

Trucks were frozen in mud up to their axles; tanks paralyzed by their frozen treads; the fields and roadways littered with dismembered vehicles – and dismembered human corpses. Snow and snow and more snow! The broken remnants of SS Division Das Reich huddled in holes and ditches, their breath turning to instant ice crystals. They died one by one, of wounds untreated, malnutrition, dysentery and exposure. They looked at one another with the same unspoken question in their eyes: *Why are we here?* Then the light in those eyes flickered and died.

Karlheinz was numbed by the horror all around him. *Corpses! Naked mothers, sisters, grandmothers! Pits filled with tens of thousands of naked human beings! Burning barns and villages! Dogs snarling and snapping at each other as they fought over human remains! Wild eyes and cheering as the SS machine guns rattled into the endless piles of bodies.*

Mama, forgive me! Papa, I will come back to you! Karlheinz swore to himself.

God help us if we are captured by the Russians for what we have done!

The exuberance and confidence of the previous summer was forgotten. Their contempt for the people whose homes they had destroyed, and whose families they had brutally murdered, had turned to fear. The Russian people and the Russian landscape had devoured them, just as they had devoured another conqueror in 1812.

Chapter Seventy-five

Gerettet
(Saved)

"We're being sent back home and then on to France!" The news flashed through the remnants of SS Division Das Reich like wildfire. Karlheinz had awakened each day throughout the winter of 1941 – 42 amazed that he was still alive. After the overwhelming Soviet Winter Counteroffensive had taken place in February 1942, Das Reich had lost 10,690 men, or 60 percent of its combat strength. They had then been designated to have a one week leave at home on their way to their new deployment in France.

In the weeks since Karlheinz had caught Dieter Lehmann raping and then immediately killing a young Russian soldier, Karlheinz had avoided contact with his erstwhile friend as much as possible. He moved away from the shelter they had taken in the back of a wrecked truck and had joined a small group of others in the ruin of a farmhouse. Dieter, unaccustomed to being rejected, had become ever more vicious in his bullying.

But now Karlheinz could rejoice in being sent away from the hell of Russian winter and the defeat before Moscow – and also away from his antagonist. They were transported to the rear in trucks and vehicles that were still operational to a railhead still in German hands. There they were loaded onto freight cars to begin the long arduous journey back to the German border, where they were transferred from the Russian wide gauge train to the German gauge train. After days of suffering in unheated freight cars, the luxury of enclosed passenger coaches was indescribable. But the normal overnight journey to Berlin of peacetime, now stretched into a stop and go of three days, due to damaged tracks which necessitated rerouting and pausing during air raids as they neared the capital. As the train finally arrived at Berlin's easternmost rail terminal, Stettiner Bahnhof late in the evening, the men were appalled to see that the building was now roofless and battered from air attacks.

After the experience of being mauled in Russia by those supposed to be *Untermenschen*, and now proof of the Allies' ability to bring the war to Germany, Karlheinz had his faith in the invincibility and superiority of the German military severely shaken.

But the cream-colored busses, streetcars and subways of *Berliner Verkehrs-Aktiengesellschaft* (Berlin Transport Corporation) were for the most part still running on schedule. At first, Karlheinz thought of telephoning his father, but after seeing the long queues at the public telephone booths, he decided to abandon that idea.

He started across the city on a bus, which had to make several detours around rubble of ruined buildings and streets. As the city center at Alexanderplatz was reached, Karlheinz opted to go to the nearest U-bahn entrance and take the subway to Steglitz - Zehlendorf and get off in Dahlem. Unsure what reaction his SS uniform might have caused, he was glad he had chosen to wear his army greatcoat and a nondescript stocking cap taken off a dead Russian.

Had word of the atrocities committed in Russia by his division reached the civilian population in Germany?

It was well past midnight when he walked from the U-bahn stop to his father's street. As he neared the house, he was relieved to see that it had been spared in raids. His gentle knock on the door at first elicited no response. After waiting a few moments, he knocked again with more force. Light appeared through the stained-glass transom over the door. After hearing the bolt of the security lock unfasten, the door was opened by his father, who peered at the gaunt, dirty unshaven person on his doorstep, at first without recognition.

"What do you want?"

Then he realized he was facing Karlheinz. Tears streaming from his eyes, he wordlessly stepped forth and embraced his boy.

Chapter Seventy-six

Abgelehnt
(Rejected)

"Why aren't you eating, dear?" said Ursula to her son, Eckhardt. He shook his head, and continued to pick at his breakfast roll with his fingers.

"Not hungry."

"Are you sick?"

No answer.

"When you're ready to talk, I'm ready to listen," she said, as she stood up and began to clear away the dishes.

He sat and stared through the dining room window.

Monika studied his face. The sparkle and exuberance she had come to expect and appreciate in Eckhardt was not there. He seemed oblivious to the movement of people and murmur of voices in the warm atmosphere of Kranzler's, where they had met for coffee.

The early months of 1942 had brought an increase of air raids, now that the American 8th Airforce had joined the British in the attacks on Berlin. But the real damage to the city was slight. The psychological effect on the citizens, however, was increasingly unnerving. And although this had begun to take its toll on everyone, she felt something else was bothering him.

"Your coffee is getting cold."

He looked up, as if seeing her for the first time.

"Eckhardt, have I done something to offend you? You've hardly said anything to me since we sat down. Did you ask me here for any particular reason?"

"I'm sorry, Monika. I'm being rude."

A long pause. She looked at him, waiting.

"I got turned down by the Luftwaffe."

"What do you mean, 'turned down'?"

"They said my grades on my Abitur were just marginal, but mainly I couldn't pass the eye exam for a pilot. They suggested that I could qualify for an administrative position, but that's not being part of the real Luftwaffe. I don't want to be a paper shuffler or an errand boy."

She reached across the table and grasped his hand.

He shook his head. "Why can't I measure up? There were a few tall blond Aryan types, and I bet they had no trouble getting in!

It's just like when I was a kid in school. People would fall all over my little brother, Detlev, because he's blond and blue-eyed, and I'm not. People like me are just second class in this country now. Maybe I really am inferior."

She gripped his hand. "Do you really believe that?"

"Don't you?"

"No!"

His eyes narrowed and a frown crossed his brow.

"Why not? It's what the Party says."

She smiled. "That's ridiculous."

He leaned forward. "What do you really believe, Monika?"

She looked away. "This is not the time nor place to discuss this."

They finished their coffee with little else to say.

"You mean you actually help soldiers of the Wehrmacht desert and hide? That's treason!" blurted Monika as they walked along Charlottenburger Chaussee bordering the Tiergarten.

Her brother, Rolf König, smiled at her surprise.

"What's treason? Either you believe Hitler is a legitimate leader of Germany, or you don't. I don't!"

"Yes, but to help German soldie…"

"Or sailors, or airmen, or even SS," he interrupted.

"Okay, then any member of the military. You help them desert? If you're caught, you'll be shot right along with them," as they turned into the Tiergarten.

He shrugged. "So, what's the difference? We could be shot or sent to a concentration camp for passing out leaflets – which we do. You did it yourself when you still lived in Cologne. And when we can collect the propaganda leaflets dropped by the Allies, we stick them in mailboxes or under doors, too!

Come on, Monika. It's time to get proactive. These boys who want to desert are demonstrating they finally realize our country is being run by a gangster government, and they don't want to fight for them anymore. The Nazis are thugs! And if we stand by and let them represent us to the world as Germans, we deserve to be judged right along with them.

The time for talk is over. We need to convince every German we can reach to take up our cause and overthrow these criminals and perverts and take our place again in the community of nations. Otherwise, we will become the pariahs of the world, and history will remember us as a nation of indifferent sheep who were willing to endorse the inhumanity of this regime by our silence."

Rolf had always demonstrated his passion for his beliefs, but she had never heard him go on like this.

"Too many of our people now hide behind slogans such as *'Politik ohne mich'* (Politics without me). That won't work! You support political movements by your involvement – or noninvolvement.

Let's sit down here."

They had come to a park bench in the Tiergarten, which by now had been largely devastated. The pathways that had formerly provided a cool retreat from the bustle and noise of the great city, were now littered with the shattered remains of trees and shrubbery. But the deforested landscape still offered a sanctuary from the madness and destruction going on around them, and a place where Berliners could air their true feelings to one another – safe from the prying eyes and ears of neighbors, and others in the pay of – or under the pressure of the Gestapo!

"Didn't you tell me your boyfriend is in the Hitler Youth?"

Wide-eyed, she raised her head abruptly. "Why do you ask me that? Never mind. We have to get back."

She stood up and started to walk away. He caught up with her and they continued walking without another word.

Chapter Seventy-seven

Land of Enchantment

"*Was hat er gesagt?*" (What did he say?) asked Willi Bauerdick, Rudi's closest companion in the barrack they shared with twenty other men, all German prisoners of war.

"We're being shipped out," responded Rudi.

"Shipped out? Where to?"

"He didn't say. Just that we're to be ready to leave at 0600 hours tomorrow."

The formation was dismissed. They walked across the compound of Eden Camp near Malton in the Yorkshire Dales, where they had spent the previous winter and spring.

Their captors had fed and treated them well, but nevertheless they had suffered considerably from methamphetamine withdrawal due to the Pervitin the Luftwaffe had issued them. Now recovered, the remoteness and peacefulness had seemed far removed from the agony and chaos that engulfed their homeland and other parts of the world.

"I wonder what that's all about and where we're going, Rudi."

"I'd like to know myself. Hopefully in time we'll find out."

As soon as they had had supper, most were engaged in writing to their families on the long tables in the dining hall. Most kept their heads down to hide the tears that welled up in their eyes. Rudi stared at the blank paper before him, trying to marshal his thoughts.

My Darling,

We have just been informed we are being shipped out tomorrow. I have no idea where, but as soon as I know more and am allowed to write to you, I'll let you know.

I have to keep this short. Give that boy a hug and kiss for me. Take care of yourself.

Ich liebe Dich!

Rudi

The British POW camps had by this time been filled to maximum capacity, and the government prevailed upon the United States to take the overflow.

The train carrying the Germans arrived at the station in Southampton after the all-day journey from Malton. The trucks carrying them to dockside were covered, shielding them from the curious, and even hostile, eyes of the public.

As they were assembled on the quay, the outline of a large ocean liner captured their attention.

"That's the '*Queen Mary*'," murmured a soldier standing near Rudi and his companion.

The great ship had been painted grey, hiding its traditional livery of black hull, white superstructure and three orange funnels.

The Germans' faces registered surprise and excitement when they were informed they would be boarding the ship and taken across the Atlantic to America.

The large public rooms had been stripped of their prewar furnishings and converted into dormitories. Two thousand men were bunked and fed on the four-day crossing from Southampton to New York. They were allowed to shower and receive a fresh change of clothing. They traveled at full speed on a zig zag course to dodge the lurking wolf packs of German submarines.

"Wouldn't it be ironic if we were sunk by a U Boat?" commented a prisoner one evening at dinner. "After all we've been through, killed by our own people!"

"It happens. Probably more often than you'd think," responded another.

"There she is!" cried out Willi, as they passed the Statue of Liberty.
"Wow!"
"Have you ever seen anything like that?"

"Look at the size of those buildings!"

They were allowed on deck and lined the railings as they entered New York harbor. They were speechless! The magnificent skyline of the city far surpassed anything many of them had ever seen in pictures. The skyscrapers! And towering above them all, the magnificent Empire State Building, which had been completed ten years earlier.

After leaving the ship, they were escorted by Military Police to busses, which transported them to the railway stations. They craned their necks to take in the sights, as the busses drove through the streets. The evidence of a great nation of well-fed, prosperous people, although at war, overwhelmed them.

"Look at those cars! Look how they're dressed! Look at those women!" The excited comments went back and forth among them. Those bound south were taken to Penn Station; those bound west, to Grand Central.

Rudi and Willi looked at the name tags fastened to their lapels, with their names and destinations.

"Roswell, New Mexico!" exclaimed Willi. "I thought we were going to be in the United States!"

"We are. New Mexico is a state in the far southwest of the United States, but it's on the border with Mexico. So, you'd better behave yourself, or they'll push you over the border," Rudi teased.

Frowning, Willi grumbled, "You don't have to make me feel stupid, smartass!"

They were fed sandwiches and coffee on the platform before they were directed to board the Pullmans designated for them. Once on board, they were surprised to be assigned berths with clean sheets. The big change which had been made were the bars on the windows.

As night fell, the train left Grand Central Station and began the long journey westward.

The men settled into their comfortable berths. Lights were extinguished, except for small night lights at the ends of the corridors, and the soft clickety-clack of the wheels lulled them to sleep.

"Breakfast! Everybody up!" The MPs strode up and down the aisles rousing the prisoners.

Rudi raised the window shade in his berth and stared out at endless manicured rows of cornfields. In the distance, he could see a white farmhouse and large red barn. The bright morning sun illuminated the brilliant green of the fields, and an aura of peace and prosperity lay over the scene. He pulled aside the heavy privacy drapery and swung his legs out into the aisle and stood up.

"Watch it, bud! Don't shove!" growled another disheveled prisoner. Then he realized he had stepped into a line of men in their underwear lined up to use the washroom and toilet facilities at the end of the Pullman car.

"Where are we, comrade?" he asked. "Someone said we are in a place called Ohio. We're headed to Chicago."

Ohio! Chicago! Places he vaguely remembered hearing about. But in America! He felt a rising excitement to actually be in the *"Land der fliegenden Brathändl"* (land of flying roast chickens), as he had heard the wry reference made to the United States.

After washing and dressing, the men were directed to the dining car. There, they were served breakfast cafeteria style and directed to tables, each occupied by four men.

Breakfast! Orange juice, scrambled eggs, sausage and pancakes! The men were fascinated with the strange sweet brown syrup in small pitchers on each table. The word passed around that it was made from tree sap! Strange people, these Americans. But nevertheless, they poured it onto their pancakes and ate with relish.

As they ate, they discussed the scenery rushing past the windows: the clean farms and towns they passed; the automobiles and the houses; evidence of a peaceful, abundant land. And so vast!

After they had passed through Chicago, which also prompted much comment, as had New York, they traveled southwest through Illinois, until they met the Mississippi. After crossing the river, the tracks turned south to parallel to the mighty Mississippi River, continuing through Iowa and into Missouri, past the town of Hannibal.

"That's where Tom Sawyer lived!" declared Rudi's seatmate. He, like many of the young men, had heard of and read about the legendary boy who grew up and played on the mighty river.

Then the scenery gradually changed from the verdant landscape of the Mississippi Valley to the flat open plains and wheat fields of Kansas.

And the land seemed to go on and on and on.

By the middle of the third day, they entered the mountainous country of Colorado, reaching the summit of the Raton Pass on the Colorado-New Mexico border, as the sun descended in the West.

During the night, they passed through Albuquerque. The next morning, they awoke to peer out their windows at a dry semi-desert, framed by distant mountains. As the hours passed, the land again became flat and open in the desert stretches of southern New Mexico. Finally, their destination: Roswell!

They disembarked from the train and formed up to march to a line of waiting busses, which would take them to the prisoner of war camp outside of town. Some dusty civilian cars and pickups were parked near the station, and Rudi noticed the bright yellow license plates with lettering. He read the curious inscriptions above and below the numbers: "Land of Enchantment – New Mexico."

Chapter Seventy-eight

Monika bringt sich zum Vorschein
(Monika reveals herself)

"Can I trust you, Eckhardt?"

He looked at her and knew that no matter what, he could never bring himself to do anything to harm her.

They had gone to the Gloria Palast on Kurfürstendamm to see the popular film, *Die große Liebe,* starring the Swedish singer, Zarah Leander. After the movie, they walked toward the U-Bahn entrance nearby. *What a kind man he is,* she thought. *He is not judgmental, and he assumes the best of people. He is so thoughtful. And such puppy dog eyes!*

Eckhardt stood alongside her and could hardly control his pride. As they waited for the U7 to Spandau, Eckhardt turned her question over in his mind: *Can I trust you?* But what did she mean?

Monika had always been quiet and reserved. Only in the past few weeks had he begun to feel he was being allowed to get a glimpse of her inner self.

On the ride out of the city, they sat close holding hands but exchanged no more words. As they came up the steps from the subway, he turned to her and asked, "Why did you ask me if you could trust me?"

As if not hearing him, she walked with her head down. When they emerged into the open, he grasped her hand.

"Monika?"

"Let me ask you a question," she countered. "When you said all those things about yourself not being a 'true Aryan' and so on, do you really believe that?"

Frowning, he looked at his feet as they continued walking.

"Sometimes, Monika, I get a strange feeling that you don't really believe in the Nazis, but it does seem that people like my blond brother do get pushed to the head of the line, and everyone makes a fuss over them. Look at all the posters of Hitler Youth and SS men. Most of them are blond and tall."

"Why do you think that is?"

He struggled to come up with an answer.

"The *Führer* says the true Aryan is a superior man."

"Does he?"

"Well, that's what we hear from our HJ leaders."

After a moment, she continued, "Look at Hitler! Look at Goebbels! Look at Franck! Why aren't they tall and blond?"

He felt himself becoming uncomfortable and agitated. He returned to her original question.

"Why do you think you can't trust me?"

She stopped, turned to him, and looked him directly in the eyes.

"I don't believe any of that stuff about Aryan supremacy!"

"Are you contradicting our leaders?"

She continued to look at him unblinking. "If you want to put it that way, yes!"

He began walking quickly away.

"Are you going to leave me?" she called after him.

He stopped, turned around and walked back to her.

"I'm sorry. I didn't mean to. But do you realize what you're saying? You're saying the leaders are liars. Monika! That could get you arrested!"

"You've told me about your father's best friend and his wife. They served their country with honor. Are they traitors to the German people?"

"No, Monika," he whispered. "They were good people, and they loved Germany very much. There are some things about being a Nazi that I have not made peace with. I do not like having to spy on my parents because of some of their friendships in the past. My Grandma is old and harmless. Sometimes I even feel guilty because I really liked mothers' Jewish friend, Meira."

The sound of his own confession annoyed him. He straightened up and quickly added, "But we must accept the fact that there are unpleasant duties to be performed. We must obey without question!"

Obey without question...Obey without question...Obey without question...

She smiled. "Can I trust you?"

Chapter Seventy-nine

Bei der Kriegsmarine
(With the Navy)

Could she trust him?
Young Eckhardt lay in his bunk in the darkness lulled by the low thrum of diesel engines of a Type VIIC U-boat running on the surface.

He had turned the question over in his mind in the intervening weeks since he had completed his training for submarine service.

So now, Eckhardt found himself on board one of Germany's most advanced submarines patrolling the waters off the western coasts of Ireland and England. Its mission was to target and sink vessels transporting men and armaments from Britain's newest ally, the United States.

This had come about from the urging of his schoolmate, Alex Deschke, when he was voicing his frustration over being rejected as a Luftwaffe pilot one evening over a beer with his friend.

Alex had begun to relate the experiences of his older brother on the Eastern Front, who had just been returned to Berlin on medical discharge, suffering from severe frostbite and subsequent amputation of all his toes. He listened to his friend continue to expound on the virtues of being in the navy, with the certainty of being clean, sleeping on sheets, and fed hot food. No sir! No lying in freezing mud and being shot at for him!

"No, I want no part of the Wehrmacht and the possibility of being sent to Russia," he declared.

"I'm going to Hamburg and volunteer for submarine service. You should come with me, Eckhardt."

"But why submarine service?"

Alex claimed to have researched the question thoroughly with a cousin serving on a U-boat, who had pointed out that a big draw was the extra pay, better food, and a close, more relaxed atmosphere than that on surface vessels.

In the end, Eckhardt had been convinced, and he broke the news to his family the next day. His father had supported him, using his own experience as a foot soldier suffering in the hell of the trenches in the previous war to help persuade Ursula and Christina.

Young Detlev, of course, was enthusiastic. *Wait until he could tell his friends!*

But Eckhardt's mind kept returning to the question that had nagged at him since leaving home: *should Monika trust him to keep her secret loathing for the Nazi regime? Was she a traitor? Was he a traitor condemned by his silence?*

§§§

Eckhardt, his son Detlev, and his mother-in-law, Christina listened with rapt attention to Ursula, as she read her son's letter to the family.

Dear family,

I'm sorry I can't write more often, but I only have two days at our base in Saint-Nazaire while our U-boat is here for maintenance, which doesn't allow time to travel home to Spandau. We have been well fed and taken care of, and I am well. We have been on patrol constantly, with no time for writing. We have heard that we will probably be given a longer leave next time we come into port, because our engines will be due for an overhaul. I will probably have time to come home.

Please take care of yourselves, and don't worry about me.

Love,

Eckhardt

Ursula looked up with tear brimmed eyes.

"Not worry about him! What does he think?" sputtered Christina. "He's out there in that tin can underwater. We all know if they're hit, they'll go straight to the bottom. At least on a ship, they have lifeboats."

"Mama, please!" pleaded Ursula. "I didn't want him to go on a U-boat. But I don't need you to paint a picture for me!"

Eckhardt reached across the table and grasped his wife's hand. "It's a war, sweetheart. But at least he's dry and clean and has a bed to sleep in. He's not standing hours on end in freezing muddy water with bullets flying over his head. And he doesn't have to worry about his lungs being rotted with gas and slowly strangling to death, like we did."

She dried her eyes with her apron. "Thank you, dear. I wish I could take more comfort in what you say. But thanks."

Young Detlev piped up, "I think that would be exciting! He's doing a great thing for the Fatherland. With men like my brother out there, we'll win this war and show the damned Americans they're no match for us. Besides, they're a mongrel race and all soft from their fat way of living."

The adults looked at him. He was repeating what was being pounded into him by teachers and youth leaders on a daily basis. How could adults poison children's minds with such evil lies?

Eckhardt thought about the "guest workers" who now were seen at Siemens and other industries across Germany. He tried not to look at their faces, with downcast eyes and looks of despair and total resignation registered there. He had warned his colleague, Müller, over and over to mind his tongue, but in his heart, he knew the man was right. Germany was indeed being led by the Pied Piper and would surely be called to account.

Christina reflected on the time when she had seen her husband, Detlev, go off to war and the effort she had put forth to feed her children, only to lose two of them, and her husband, at the very end of the conflict to the terrible Spanish Influenza.

Here we are going through it all over again, she thought. *What will be the end of us?*

§§§

Dear Monika,

 Life on a U-boat is very hard. Most of the time is dull and spent checking and maintaining the boat and weapons systems. Discipline is very strict, but I can see it is necessary. We don't have much space to move around or sleep in. Some guys have to sleep with the torpedoes, and the mechanics have to sleep in the engine room with all that noise, heat, and stinking air. The rest of us work in eight-hour shifts and have to "hot-bunk" with other guys. This means we share the same bunk taking turns sleeping. There is one lavatory on board and no shower, because we only have a water supply for drinking. If we are under attack and submerged, we can't flush the toilet because the discharge would be spotted on the surface by the enemy.
 We cannot carry fresh food on board because it will be contaminated by the diesel vapor, so we're left with only canned goods. Sometimes we go for weeks without seeing the sun. We will have to wear the same clothes for six months, so don't run when you see me, because I will need a haircut and a shave.
 It's different than I expected, but I'd still rather be here than lying in the mud.
 Please extend my greetings to your parents,

Eckhardt

§§§

 The backbone of the German U-boat fleet was the Type VII C of which 568 were built between 1940 and 1945. Its length was 220 ft. 2 in. and width was 20 ft. 4 in. amidships. On the surface, it was propelled by two Germaniawerft 6-cylinder diesels – and submerged by two Siemens Schuckert GU electric motors. Its surface speed was max 18 knots and submerged speed max 8 knots. The range was 9,800 miles at 10 knots surfaced and 92 miles at 8 knots submerged.

It could carry up to 14 torpedoes and had four torpedo tubes forward and one rearward. Deck armament consisted of an 8.8-centimeter rapid fire gun with a capacity of 220 rounds. The crew numbered between 44 and 52 members living in close quarters. The maximum operating depth was 750 ft.

The oxygen volume would sustain life for 44 men for about 5 hours before the carbon dioxide level would rise to the point where cognitive disorders would manifest themselves. Alkaline cartridges would then be utilized for air purification. Ten oxygen cylinders were used as a last resort before it became necessary to surface.

The men would go for weeks on end, seldom seeing the sun or sky, because they often ran submerged in the daytime and on the surface at night to avoid detection by the enemy. They wore the same unwashed clothes sometimes for as long as six months and would return to port with shaggy hair and long beards.

Chapter Eighty

Selbsterkenntnis
(Self-Recognition)

The insistent but faint jingle seemed to echo as if in a large chamber. Karlheinz turned in half sleep and buried his face in the pillow. The sound stopped. The shock of silence brought him fully awake. He lay in the darkness trying to remember where he was. *At home in Dahlem!* He drew the satin comforter up around his shoulders and reveled in the luxury of the large bed.

The jingle started again. It was the telephone in his father's room down the hall. *Why didn't he answer it?*

He switched on the bedside lamp and picked up his watch from the nightstand. Five o'clock!

Hans Joachim must have already left for the hospital. The phone's shrill ring persisted.

Karlheinz threw back the comforter and walked naked to his father's room, flung open the door, and strode across the room to the irritating noise and picked up the receiver.

"Guten Morgen. Lenz hier."

"Sturmbannführer Lenz?"

"Yes, speaking."

"Oberleutnant Kessler hier. I'm calling from Stettiner Bahnhof. You are needed here immediately."

Baffled, Karheinz stammered, "But I'm on leave."

"Never mind that. You are needed here right away. We have a larger consignment of prisoners than we expected, and you are to help with loading them on the train. You're in Dahlem, so we will expect you within the hour! Orders from the *Kommendantura*."

The phone went dead with a click.

Karlheinz looked at the receiver before replacing it in its cradle.

Muttering to himself, he returned to his room and began to dress without shaving. He then returned to the telephone and called the taxi central number and ordered a pickup as soon as possible.

He went down to the dark kitchen and took out a large bratwurst left from the previous evening's meal. He wrapped it in a slice of rye bread and munched on it as he walked to the front entrance. He finished his hurried repast just as the lights of the taxi turned into the driveway.

Closing the door and locking it with his key, he walked to the waiting car, entered, and directed the driver to his destination.

As they drove through the unlit streets, lighting having been eliminated since the beginning of the air raids two years previously, he watched a few pedestrians making their way in the chill of predawn darkness.

Nearing the station, they were stopped in the street before the building by barricades manned by SS guards. The authorities kept the general public away when prisoners were being processed for transport to the camps.

Karlheinz paid the driver and stepped out of the warm car into the icy winter air. He showed his identity card to a guard and made his way into the shell of the terminal. He was directed to one of the platforms where there was a mass of miserable looking men, women, and children being jostled and pushed into lines forming up before open freight cars. Large Doberman and German Shepherd dogs on chain leashes held by SS men barked and nipped at the people who were pushed out of line by the pressure of those behind them.

Karlheinz went to a table manned by clerks stamping passports and documents and handing out name tags.

"*Sturmbannführer* Lenz?"

"Yes, sir," he replied to the man behind the table.

"Go down there to section eight," he said as he handed Karlheinz a clipboard with passenger manifests attached. He pointed to a group of SS officers standing before a makeshift sign displaying the indicated number.

Taking the clipboard, he turned and made his way through the melee toward his assigned post. As he walked parallel to the lines of people, the children stared, but the adults either kept eyes averted or looked at the ground.

Trying not to look at the faces of the condemned, Karlheinz looked straight ahead.

He reported to section eight and received his assignment assisting with registration of people as they were brought in. It was the beginning of what would become a grueling day. He had convinced himself he could cope with the stress and danger of foreign frontline battle. But such inhumane treatment of German civilians – especially children – was beyond his capabilities. And now this!

A young mother with three small children stood before him wearing a coat with a yellow Star of David on the left lapel. She answered his questions in a voice so soft he had to ask her to repeat some answers. She was carrying the smallest child, a little girl sleeping on her mother's shoulder. Karlheinz noted the small face reflected the delicate beauty of the mother. A superior officer approached to oversee the process.

"You need to speed it up here!" he barked at Karlheinz, who was struggling to hear the woman's response to a question above the chaos around them.

"Speak up, stupid sow!" shouted the officer.

The child awoke and raised her head. Her large blue eyes looking straight at Karlheinz registered sudden fear. Then she began to cry.

"Shut that brat up, or I'll give her something to wail about!" threatened the officer.

Two children clung to their mother's skirt, their small faces pale in abject terror.

Karlheinz brusquely concluded the interview and passed the woman on to a female colleague handing out name tags. He was disturbed by the encounter, and he had similar experiences throughout the morning. The stress of this, together with the push to get the people loaded into the freight cars before the general public could be allowed on the platform left him shaken and exhausted.

Toward the end of his duty, he had the feeling that he was being stared at, and he inadvertently looked into the face of a young man in the line passing before him. Their eyes met.

The face was gaunt and pale. The clothes were dirty and disheveled. But the layer of years between them fell away. It was Egon Wolf!

The pleading eyes of his long-ago friend looked at him, as if expecting to be acknowledged.

Karlheinz stopped short and almost said his name. *Maybe I should report to my superior that Egon has been taken by mistake.*

"You, Lenz! Come over here!"

The sudden command of one of the other officers cut through his brain. Jerking himself up, he hurried away. Egon looked after him with tears of desperation and lost hope falling from his eyes.

After the ordeal of the day, Karlheinz was tortured by the image of Egon's pleading eyes.

He was my first friend! He took me in! How could I turn my back on him? What is wrong with me? I betrayed the first love of my life!

He was shaken with sobs of guilt. The taxi driver studied him in the rear-view mirror.

That evening, he related his ordeal to his father as they sat at the small kitchen table sharing a simple *Abendbrot* (light supper).

"I've been in battle and seen men killed around me, as well as women and children! But Papa, that was the worst experience of my life!

And seeing Egon! I just left him there!" He lost control and began to sob again.

Hans Joachim's tired sadness left him unable to offer a word of comfort.

"Tell me, son, why have you been so drawn to such people?"

Karlheinz studied his fingernails before answering. Looking up at his father seated in his leather chair by the library fireplace, he replied with muted voice, "I have asked myself that same question over and over.

In the beginning, I was mesmerized by the show of pride Hitler inspired in people. We had been told Germany was entirely to blame for the last war, which didn't seem fair! We were told to bear the financial burden for damage caused by the war! That would continue to be extracted from us, even during the Depression, when our economy was reduced to nothing! In other words, we were made to feel that God had turned His back on us and that being born German was a curse. The only country which showed us any leniency was America, until the Depression made it impossible for them to help us.

Then along came Hitler, who reinforced our feelings of resentment and told us that we should not only lift our heads but even be proud to be German! We were the land of culture, the land of Goethe, Beethoven and Brahms! We were the land of science and technology! German doctors, like you, Papa, were the best in the world! Even the German people were the best in a world populated by inferior races – especially Jews! They were responsible for all the world's misery, and they had led us into war and betrayed us!"

Hans Joachim interrupted him. "Yes, we know all that. But you grew up in a house with enlightened people. Didn't you ever make comparisons between the Nazis and your own family? We're not that kind of people."

"Yes, Papa. You are absolutely right. But it seemed to me growing up, that everyone always admired Herbert more. Herbert was smarter; Herbert was more clever and talented; Herbert was liked by the girls; and so on and so forth.

I was sent to the estate with Rudi Bellon, a street kid from Wedding. But Grandmama insisted he was a guest and should sit at our table, even though he didn't know how to hold a knife and fork properly. So he was as good as I was, and nobody looked up to me!"

After a few moments, Hans Joachim commented, "It seems to me, son, you have been nurturing a lot of self-pity for a long time. Didn't you feel you were loved, especially by your mother?"

With a wistful expression, Karlheinz looked up.

"Mama was the only person I felt I could talk to. And suddenly she was gone! Then I met Egon Wolf. He was the first person who made me feel special."

Hans Joachim resisted the temptation to point out that the relationship had been founded on sex.

"When SA men began to appear on the streets, they were so virile, and strong, and confident. Unless I had Mama to back me up, I never felt confident. Finally, after joining their group, I felt like I belonged to an organization that I could be proud of. At least that's what I thought then."

"What you're really saying, son, was that being around these men, you began to benefit from their supposed virility, strength, and confidence," interjected Hans Joachim.

Karlheinz nodded. After a pause, dropping his gaze, he admitted softly, "That's true. I really felt that way when I was with them."

"But they were thugs!" interjected Hans Joachim

Karlheinz's face flushed crimson. "But afterward, the SS began to appear, and they were even more spectacular and powerful! When I met Dieter, he looked so fantastic in his uniform – the epitome of German manhood! I wanted to be just like him.

But I knew that the SA had been brutal. The people they beat up had deserved it – or at least I told myself that.

But nothing prepared me for what I saw the SS do in Poland and in Russia! I realized then I could never do some of the things they did and which they expected me to do, too.

And then this morning! Egon! What have I become?

I think of you and mother. What would she think of me? What do you think of me?" He looked at his father through tear-filled eyes.

"So, here I am! I know now the things that are happening in the name of Germany are not the characteristics of a civilized nation. We have lost our way! I want out. I wish I had left, like Herbert did! What can I do now, Papa?"

"My dear boy, I failed to see how unhappy you were, and I am sorry for that. I can't go back and undo the past, but be assured, I will do anything to help you from this time forward. God, how I wish we had talked like this a long time ago."

Father and son perceived one another for the first time and gazed at each other in a light of new appreciation and understanding.

Chapter Eighty-one

Torpedo los!
(Fire torpedo!)

Monika was interrupted from making breakfast when she heard a knock at the door. She didn't expect to see her brother, Rolf.
"What are you doing here?"
"I was called here on short notice to help with our organization."
"Who's that, Monika?"
"It's Rolf, Mama!"
Mrs. König raced out and embraced her son, followed by her husband, who shook Rolf's hand. "Have you had breakfast, son?"
"No, I'm starved."

Monika and Rolf lingered over their coffee. They were alone in the apartment after their parents had left.
Rolf stirred his coffee and asked, "Why did you flare at me that day when I asked you about Eckhardt being in the Hitler Youth?"
Monika didn't answer right away, but after a moment she said, "Because you implied he was a fanatical Nazi, and that's not fair. You just don't know him."
"I'm sorry. I didn't mean to imply anything. What's he doing now?"
"He's in the Navy. He's a submariner."
"A U-boat sailor! Oh, that's just great. He's out there sinking ships, drowning thousands of men."
"How dare you!" she bristled. "He would have been drafted, like every other young man, if he hadn't joined the Navy. *You* should be grateful for the Rheumatic fever you had as a kid and for the heart murmur you got from it. Otherwise, you would be out there somewhere instead of having the freedom to go around starting trouble."
His hurt expression stabbed her heart. She reached out and grasped his arm.

"I'm sorry, Rolf. I didn't mean that."

"Well, I believe I'm serving my country better than if I were in the Army."

"Yes, you are. And if you knew Eckhardt, you'd see he would agree with you. But he's trapped."

"Yes, like millions of other young Germans. And that's why if we can help them get out of their traps, we'll do it."

Monika studied her hands. "Is that why you're here? To start something in Berlin? You didn't come to visit us, your family?"

"Of course, I came to see you and Mama and Papa! But we also want to organize branches of the *Edelweißpiraten* all over Germany – and we especially want to find people right here under Hitler's nose who are sick of the Nazis!"

Turning to her brother, she asked, "What can I do to help?"

Smiling, he patted her hand. "I was hoping you'd say that. We know through our contacts, that the HJ and the BDM are stepping up their drives to raise money for the so-called 'winter relief program'. We also believe a lot of that money is being siphoned off to the Nazis. Some friends of ours here in Berlin have agreed to join us next Saturday during the HJ rally at the Friedrichstrasse station. We want to throw a scare into the little punks. And if we can get hold of their collection cans, we'll use the money for our expenses in this work. Will you join us?"

She bit her lip and then declared, "Yes!"

§§§

In the late 1930s in western Germany, many young people between ages 14 and 18 were attracted to a movement that called themselves the *Edelweißpiraten* (Edelweiss Pirates). This attraction was based on a rejection of authoritarianism in the Nazi youth organizations, the *Hitler Jugend* for boys, and the *Bund Deutscher Mädel* for girls who were restricted to their respective gender groups. In contrast, the casual meetings of the Edelweiss Pirates offered German adolescents the freedom of intermingling between the sexes – and even opportunities for sexual experimentation.

Among subgroups of the Edelweiss Pirates were the "Navajos" in and around Cologne, the "Kittelbach Pirates" in Oberhausen and Düsseldorf, and the "Roving Dudes" of Essen.

At first, in their rejection of Nazi authoritarianism, the Edelweiss Pirates' behavior tended to be restricted to petty provocations. Eventually, though, their activities moved beyond hiking and camping and defying restriction on free movement, and they became highly antagonistic to the Hitler Youth – even ambushing their patrols and taking great pride in beating them up. One of their slogans came to be *Eternal war on the Hitler Youth!*

The Edelweiss Pirates represented a group of youth who rebelled against government regimentation, and therefore attracted unwanted Nazi attention. One Nazi official stated in 1941, "Every child knows who the Kittelbach Pirates are. They are everywhere; there are more of them than there are Hitler Youth. They beat up the patrols. They never take no for an answer."

As the war progressed, many Edelweiss Pirates collected propaganda leaflets dropped by Allied aircraft and distributed them in public places and pushed them through mail slots. Finally, they went so far as to support the Allies and encourage and assist deserters from the German military.

§§§

Young Eckhardt's eyes burned with sweat dripping from his eyebrows. The diesels idling made the only sound to be heard in the U-boat as the crew waited with taut nerves for the command from the bridge. The captain, with his officer's cap turned backward on his head, stared intently at the profile of a freighter moving into the crosshairs of the periscope.

"Fire one! Fire two!"

The parallel wakes of the torpedoes pointed straight amidships of the doomed vessel.

Complete silence in the submarine!

The crew waited to hear the muffled explosions from torpedoes exploding in the bowels of their victim. When they came, cheers resounded throughout the boat, and the order was given to surface and survey the damage.

The hatch was opened. Eckhardt and some of the crew emerged from the conning tower and assembled on deck. As expected, the freighter was aflame from bow to stern and began to break up. Like a huge animal in the throes of death, with a sigh of escaping air, she slowly rolled over, the desperate crew scrambling over the hull to escape the encroaching water. As the bow began to point downward, the men clustered near the stern and the exposed rudder and propellers. Little by little, the figures crowded closer together, until there was no more room. Then men were seen to surrender themselves to the waves. The ship finally let forth a huge belch of air and disappeared beneath the surface, leaving heads bobbing in life jackets in the icy water.

"Maybe we could pick some of them up," whispered a young seaman standing next to Eckhardt.

Shaking his head in sad resignation, Eckhardt replied, "We can't. There is room on this submarine for 45 men, and we are already a full crew. Poor devils!"

Another voice murmured, "It would be more humane to shoot them. They were cruising with no escort, and a man can't last more than a few minutes in that water. I've heard some U-boat commanders have done that. But of course, that's unofficial."

"That's terrible, but you're right," responded Eckhardt. "My God! This is February in the North Atlantic!"

As if to underscore his words, light sleet began to issue from the leaden sky.

After waiting on the surface to receive the next radio transmission from *Befehlshaber der Unterseeboote* (BdU) (Submarine Command Center) in Kerneval, occupied France, they were given the codes with instructions for their next intercept. The *Oogah* of the klaxon horn was heard, signaling all on deck to return below for the hatch to be closed before the dive.

Throughout the month, Eckhardt and his German wolf pack had had great success stalking large convoys of ships on their crossings of the Atlantic. They relied on the supposedly unbreakable Enigma code to transmit and receive orders and co-ordinate movements. U-boats usually patrolled separately, in a strung-out coordinated line across likely convoy routes and engage individual merchants and small vulnerable destroyers when possible.

However, when a convoy was located, an alert would go out to BdU, and the individual submarines would congregate into a pack, which consisted of as many U-boats as could reach the scene. The U-boat commanders were given a probable number of U-boats that might show up and when in contact with the convoy, would give call signs to count the number that had arrived. If their numbers were high enough, compared to the threat from military escorts, they attacked. U-boat commanders could attack as they saw fit. Although the wolf packs proved a serious threat to Allied shipping, the Allies developed countermeasures against it.

After sinking a freighter one evening, just as the submarine disappeared beneath the surface, a British heavy cruiser sped upon the scene, having narrowed in on their position using the SOS signal immediately sent out by the radio man aboard the freighter. Their High Frequency Direction Finder allowed Allied naval forces to determine the exact location of the enemy radio transmission.

The sonar on the cruiser had already been activated, and it picked up the ping bouncing off the hull of the U-boat. The cruiser captain, although he was eager to hunt for the perpetrator of the disaster, nevertheless took the time to lower lifeboats manned by his own crewmembers with the task of collecting survivors. But in the meantime, his radioman had been busy transmitting to other ships in the convoy from which he had come. Two destroyers were detached from the main group and sped at full speed to the area and began a crisscross pattern in a sonar search. Once a grid had been established, depth charges were launched from the fantails of each destroyer.

Down below, the U-boat commander, realizing he was being hunted, issued a crash dive order to the maximum depth for which his ship had been designed. For a Type VII such as his, this was 250 meters, or 820 feet.

As the depth gauge redlined at 250 meters, the explosions of depth charges closed in. All lights except the dim red emergency lights were extinguished to save the batteries, and the men stood mute in their sweat drenched dungarees and tank tops, staring into the hot stinking darkness.

"Down another 20 meters!" ordered the captain.

As they descended slowly, pressure began to exert itself on the hull. Leaks popped, the glass on instrument faces began to shatter, and the air thickened. Men began to gasp. The depth charges continued to search for their target.

After an eternity, the sound of depth charges receded, and they could hear the engines of their pursuers fade.

"Five knots ahead, bearing 124!" came the command. The U-boat crept away, running on its electric motors. When they could no longer hear the depth charges, they surfaced in the falling dusk and sped away at full speed toward their home base at St. Nazaire to have the ship gone over for damages and repair.

They had survived to fight another day.

Chapter Eighty-two

Karlheinz – Panzergrenadier
(Karlheinz – Tank Grenadier)

"There she is, gentlemen. The Panzerkampfwagen VI H, commonly known as the Tiger I. This is classified as a 'Heavy Tank' and is manufactured by Henschel & Sohn in Kassel. It is 8.5 meters long to the tip of the forward gun, 3.6 meters wide, 3 meters high, with a ground clearance of .5 meters. It weighs 57,155 kilos. You must know these numbers, because you will be traveling across rough terrain, fording rivers, charging through heavy forests and driving over or under bridges. The main armament is the very reliable and time tested 8.8 cm cannon. You are protected by armor between 2.5 cm and 12 cm thick. The foolish Americans are challenging us with their ridiculous little Sherman, which is a joke in comparison to a Tiger. The Sherman shells literally bounce off our thick armor.

Our Tiger carries a crew of five: a commander, a gunner, a loader, a driver, and a radio operator. It is powered by a 700 horsepower Maybach V-12 with a fuel capacity of 2,051 liters and has an operational range of 195 road kilometers and 109 kilometers cross country. The top speed is 40 kilometers per hour and between 19-26 kilometers per hour cross country. That's 63 tons of mobile firepower!

You will be trained to know her well. Learn to use her, and she will take care of you. Be proud of her. She is an example of superior German engineering. There is nothing like her in the whole world. You should appreciate the honor you have been given to be a part of this elite organization, and the opportunity you have to demonstrate to our inferior foes what it means to confront the German fighting man. Conduct yourselves as true Aryan men, and bring home honor to the Fatherland and to your *Führer. Heil Hitler!*" The training commander raised his right arm in the Nazi salute, turned on his heel, and walked away.

Karlheinz and his comrades looked with awe at the menacing, yet beautiful, monsters being turned over to them at their training station near Toulouse, France in January, 1943. They were part of the division now designated as SS-Panzer-Grenadier-Division "Das Reich".

Karlheinz had not known what his assignment would be when he was ordered back from Russia in the previous November. But after his week of leave in Berlin, which had proven to be a time of reconciliation and better understanding with his father, he felt confident he could deal with any task he might be given. Therefore, when he received his training order as radio operator in Tiger I Fo5, under the command of *SS Gruppenführer* Gerd Ziegler, a hardened veteran of service in the invasion of France in 1940, and later on the Eastern Front in 1941 – 42, he felt he had at last been given the recognition he had always sought.

After receiving their individual assignments, Ziegler gathered his crew in their barrack to introduce himself. He was a tall, muscular, man in his early thirties. His steady blue-eyed gaze was intimidating to those who would challenge him, but reassuring to those who depended upon his leadership. His voice was like the low growl of a powerful motor idling but ready to unleash a blast of power in the blink of an eye.

"My name is Klaus Mannfried Ziegler. I come from Grossweil, near Garmisch-Partenkirchen in Bavaria. I have fought for the *Führer* starting with the war in Spain in 1936, and in the campaigns up to the outbreak of the war, and thereafter in France and Russia.

I cannot add more to the words you have just heard, and I thoroughly endorse them, as you should, too. As he pointed out, we are being given the responsibility of a technological marvel, an example of German design and workmanship. I expect you to support me in the maximum application of its capabilities. When we face the enemy, I expect you to follow my leadership and execute my commands without question. Anyone who shows himself less than a German soldier will be dealt with by me. Anyone who shows cowardice under fire will be shot. Are there any questions? Good. Dismissed!"

After he left, the remaining crew members, the driver, the gunner, the ammunition loader, and Karlheinz, looked at each other. The driver, a former fisherman from Helgoland, grinned and said, "Did he need to tell us he was from Bavaria? That Bavarian accent you could slice with a knife. The only thing he didn't say was, *'I bin a Bayer, host mi?'* (I'm a Bavarian, understand me?')"

A wave of laughter went around the group.

The loader quipped, "You should talk, with your *Plattdeutsch* (dialect typical for northern Germany)."

"I only speak *Platt* at home," protested the driver, red-faced.

"Just messin' with ya," reassured the loader, giving him a slap on the back.

"You must be from somewhere around Magdeburg," volunteered Karlheinz.

"Guilty! I'm from Lostau. You hear my Saxon nasal twang, don't you? And you're a Berliner, but are you as cocky as your accent declares?"

Karheinz grinned. *"Ja, selbstverständlich. Ick bin doch Berliner, klar?"* (Obviously, I'm certainly a Berliner. Is that clear?"

Then turning to the gunner, who hadn't been heard from, "What about you?"

"I'm from Hanover."

"Oh, that's where they speak *real* German," interjected the driver. "You'll have to teach the rest of us."

Chuckles.

"Well, most importantly, let's make a good team and do our country proud," he continued.

"No, most importantly, let's not get on Ziegler's bad side," said Karlheinz.

More laughter.

§§§

The Tiger I has been called an outstanding design for its time, but it has also been criticized for being over-engineered. Tiger production ran from 1942 to 1944 using expensive materials and labor-intensive production methods. It was prone to track failures and breakdowns and due to its high fuel consumption, was limited in range. It was difficult to transport. In mud, ice, and snow it was vulnerable to immobilization. Frozen mud and ice would become clogged in the complex road wheel pattern and jam them solid. This became evident on the eastern front in the muddy season and in periods of extreme cold.

Chapter Eighty-three

Wiederkehr nach Rußland
(Return to Russia)

"I knew it. We knew we wouldn't stay here forever, but to have to go back to Russia!" grumbled Karlheinz to his fellow crew members, as Ziegler, the tank commander, walked away. He had just informed them that they would take part in the campaign to commence at Kharkov, 400 miles south of Moscow, on February 19, 1943. In response to the question raised about leave time, the answer was blunt: no leaves.

Karlheinz and his comrades were not the only ones stunned by the announcement. After the disastrous surrender of General Friedrich Paulus and the German 6th Army at Stalingrad on February 2nd, and the loss of 800,000 troops killed, wounded or captured, Hitler's generals were aghast at his determination to send men into Russia once more.

"I thought we had been blessed to get out of that wretched country alive after Moscow, and now he expects us to throw ourselves into that frozen hell again!" ranted the driver.

"Let's keep it down, comrades," pleaded the loader. "The officers are under a lot of pressure and won't tolerate any defeatist talk. There are ears everywhere, and they won't hesitate a second to put any one of us up against a wall to be shot."

Heads nodded. They returned to their barrack with no further comment.

A week was spent loading the tanks and equipment on flatcars for the trip to Kharkov. Passenger coaches were connected to the same train, and the long journey began.

As they traveled across Germany and passed through Berlin, Karlheinz was appalled at the damage the city had suffered since his last time there. He gazed out the window as they passed familiar landmarks, and he was heavy-hearted not to be able to see his father again. Hans Joachim had sent a few short letters to his son in France, but Karlheinz, not allowed to reveal information about his new assignment to Russia, had responded with noncommittal comments about his general welfare, assuring his father that he was well and proud to be part of the newly formed SS Panzer division.

Leaving the capital behind, the arduous journey continued into Pomerania, passing through Deutschkrone and Bromberg, only a few miles from his family's former estate at Schloß Hoehenberg. As they passed the station at Bromberg, he reflected on that long-ago summer day almost a quarter of a century before, when he and Rudi Bellon were met by the old estate manager, Mr. Lewandowski in the old barouche pulled by the matched Trakehner horses. He recalled how annoyed he was to have to be seen with the "street urchin" from Wedding.

He chuckled to himself. *What an arrogant ass I was! Rudi Bellon! He went on to have a great career as a flight captain with Luft Hansa, distinguished himself as a fighter pilot in the Battle of Britain, survived being shot down and captured, and now, father informed me he is a prisoner in New Mexico. I wish I could trade places with him!*

At the Russian border, the train trucks (wheel assembly) had to be changed to accommodate the wider gauge tracks. Then they continued across the wide, frozen landscape of Russia. The men around him became silent, as they gazed through ice-coated windows at the desolation which seemed to engulf them. Their spirits dropped with the falling temperature.

§§§

"Karlheinz, Du alte Pflaume!" (You old thing).

The hand clapped on his shoulder caused him to jump, startling him from a groggy nap. He turned to face Dieter Lehmann.

Since arriving in France, he had managed to avoid contact with his erstwhile "friend". The incident with the young Russian soldier had extinguished any feeling he had for Dieter. In France, he had formed a close friendship with the members of his tank crew. Because their billets were on opposite sides of the camp, and both had been tied up with their training schedules, it had been easy to avoid him. He had caught Dieter staring at him across the dining hall from time to time, where he was involved with his crew. But Karlheinz turned away and pretended not to notice.

"How've you been?" enquired Dieter with a smile.

"Fine."

"Let's go somewhere and talk."

Hesitating, trying to think of an excuse to not respond, he stared dumbly at Dieter, who grasped his arm with a firm grip. He half-pulled Karlheinz from his seat. Allowing himself to be escorted out of the compartment and into the aisle, they made their way to the end of the car and out into the vestibule between the coaches.

Dieter extracted a cigarette from his inside coat pocket and lit it, not offering one to Karlheinz, who smoked only sporadically.

"What's up with you? I've noticed how you've been avoiding me. Don't you miss me?"

"I've just been busy with training."

"We've all been busy with training, but you seem to have time to sit with those other fellows in the dining hall or in the canteen."

At a loss for an answer, he shrugged.

"I need us to be friends like before." Dieter leaned in close as he half-whispered the words.

Feeling trapped, and afraid they might be seen by someone going back and forth, he pushed back. "Be careful. Not here."

Leaning back to take a long drag on his cigarette, Dieter chuckled as he exhaled a cloud of smoke. Then he leaned close and whispered in Karlheinz's ear, "Well, just remember, you belong to me."

He chuckled again, patted Karlheinz on the cheek and returned to the coach.

Karlheinz stood in the biting cold of the vestibule for a long time as the words sunk in.

Chapter Eighty-four

Endlich, Freiheit!
(Finally, Freedom!)

After the surrender of the German Sixth Army at Stalingrad on February 2, 1943, the Soviet forces were free to mount a huge attack on both the German Army Group South and Army Group Center leading to Soviet recapture of Kharkov, Belgorod and Kursk. On February 19, Field Marshal Erich von Manstein launched a counterstrike at Kharkov, which involved the 2nd SS Panzerkorps, Das Reich, newly arrived from France.

Karlheinz and his comrades, though still exhausted from the long rail journey, had only two days to refit and organize before being thrown into battle. After more than two weeks of heavy fighting, they finally encircled and defeated the Soviet armored units south of Kharkov. Von Manstein then began his offensive against the city on March 7. The Panzerkorps had been ordered to encircle Kharkov from the north, but their leaders decided instead to hit the city directly on March 11. This led to four days of fierce house-to-house fighting.

Klaus Ziegler was a man driven by an obsession to be at the forefront of every battle. He drove his men relentlessly and as a result, found himself alone as his tank emerged from a side street onto the town square in the center of the city. Directly across from him on the opposite side of the square, he saw two Soviet T-34 tanks facing him, separated from them by a large badly damaged fountain. A firefight immediately began between the opponents.

Enclosed in the hot darkness, Karlheinz heard the deafening roar of the cannon, which rocked their tank with its recoil.

Then the ear-splitting sound of enemy shells hitting the Tiger's frontal armor was terrifying, but fortunately they could not penetrate the thick steel plate.

Suddenly Ziegler, peering through the periscope, shouted, "We got one! Let's move in closer!"

Again, "We hit one of the tracks, and they can't move. Let's go around this and hit him 'em up close."

The driver pushed the throttle forward and turned the vehicle to go around the fountain. As he did so, he exposed his vulnerable left side to the enemy. The Russian reacted immediately and fired. The blast destroyed the track and the wheel assembly. Another shell hit just under the turret near the engine compartment, which burst into flame. The heat was mounting, and the interior was filling with smoke as flames broke through the rear partition.

"*Scheiße!* Evacuate!" commanded Ziegler.

Desperate for air and escape from the flames, the driver opened the front hatch and pulled himself out. As he prepared to jump to the ground, a blast of machine gun fire cut him down. The commander opened the top hatch of the turret and was also immediately shot as he attempted to extricate himself. He fell back into the interior, blocking access to the hatch. The loader pulled him to one side, and he too, in full panic, managed to get outside. But then receiving a blast from the Russian machine gun, he, too, fell to the ground dead. Karlheinz, whose jacket had caught fire, pulled himself through the driver's hatch as bullets buzzed over his head. Crawling on his belly, he wriggled to the side of the tank opposite the Russians and rolled to the ground. The Tiger was by now engulfed in flames, and Karlheinz began rolling to put out the fire on the upper left sleeve of his jacket.

He knew the Soviets would eventually abandon their crippled tank and probably come to check.

I must get away!

Crouching low, he ran towards the ruin of a burned-out house, keeping the burning tank between himself and his enemy. Hiding behind a still-standing wall of an interior room, and bathed in the sweat of fear, he lay totally still for the rest of the day.

Karlheinz carefully peeled the charred fabric from his arm, exposing burned flesh. Full feeling had returned, and he felt tears of pain on his cheeks. He shivered from the biting cold, but discovered it numbed his pain and was grateful for the relief.

Fortunately, the remaining Russian tank had departed, taking all of the crewmembers of both tanks with it, leaving Karlheinz the only living being.

He raised himself on feet gone numb from lack of movement and cold and made his way back into the warren of narrow streets leading to the position where he guessed his unit to be. After what seemed like an interminable trek, he saw the glow of a cigarette in the dark.

Was the smoker German or Russian?

"*Halt! Stehenbleiben!*" (Halt! Freeze!)

"*Bitte, nicht schiessen, Kamerad!*" (Please, don't shoot, comrade) Karlheinz replied to the welcome sound of a German voice. He stumbled forward and collapsed into the sentry's arms.

"Help over here!" cried the man, as he staggered under the weight of the now unconscious Karlheinz.

Flickering firelight roused him, and he realized he was being tended by a medic in the light of a campfire surrounded by men of his unit. Many he did not recognize, but one face stood out in the crowd.

"*Nah, Junge!*" (Well, boy). Dieter's voice brought him to full consciousness. "What kind of trouble did you get yourself into this time? You see! I can't take my eyes off you for a minute."

Wondering how he should reply to that, he just stared.

"I'm sorry we're too far from a hospital out here," interjected the medic. "I've dressed the wound and put Prontosil (sulfa drug) on it to fight off infection. As soon as possible, we'll have you sent home to recover."

The last words washed over Karlheinz in a wave of relief.

Home! Will I ever see it?

"But for now, I'll put you in the care of your friend here. He's been very concerned about you. How did you get separated from us?"

Karlheinz began to explain how their commander had aggressively pushed forward until they encountered the Russians on the square and the battle that followed.

"I'm sorry, but there were no survivors except me."

"You were in Ziegler's Tiger, right?"

"That Ziegler was always a glory hog!" commented someone in the group. "And you're the only survivor? You're damned lucky, man."

At the mention of Ziegler's name, heads nodded.

Dieter stepped forward. "Come on kiddo. I arranged for you to bunk in with me tonight."

Relief and apprehension fought for control in Karlheinz's brain.

"Come on, kid. We've got to move out."

Karlheinz was roused from a fitful sleep by Dieter.

"You'll be riding in our tank. There's no place else to put you, and of course I won't leave you behind. It'll be cramped, but as soon as we can make contact with a transport unit, you'll be taken out of here."

Other crew members helped Karlheinz climb aboard, and he found a place behind the radioman. The convoy began to move forward and soon found themselves in the square. They saw the burned-out Tiger. The bodies of Karlheinz's crew still lay where they had fallen. Without stopping, they continued around the fountain and passed the abandoned Russian T-34. Moving through the other side of the city, now mostly in ruins, they encountered no resistance. At the outskirts, sporadic artillery fire began to intensify. Moving into the open countryside, they spotted a group of T-34s lined up along the fringe of a distant stand of trees. The adversaries moved toward each other, and an exchange of cannon fire commenced. Tanks on both sides were hit, and some began to burn and explode. Men trying to escape were caught in machine gun fire and mowed down like rows of wheat.

Then the battle stopped, and Russians, running out of ammunition and out of fuel, began to leave their tanks and walk forward with arms raised in surrender.

"Look at them, the scum!" growled Dieter. "Why don't we just shoot them here and now and save ourselves the trouble!"

However, the prisoners were organized into columns and escorted by guards to the rear to be transported to camps in occupied territory.

"Well, that's a good day's work! What did you think about that, kiddo?" exulted Dieter as they formed up. They returned to the outskirts of the city and parked the Tigers in a semicircle for the night.

After they had eaten from their rations, they began to gather in groups for relaxation. Some had decks of cards and began to organize games of *Skat*.

"Come on, kid! Let's go for a walk. It will do you good."

At first, Karlheinz protested that he didn't feel up to it, but as he had done since they first met, he gave in to Dieter's insistence. They walked into a deserted street and soon were out of sight. After a few minutes, Dieter grasped Karlheinz's right arm and urged, "Let's step in here," walking toward the entrance of a partially destroyed house. They entered a bedroom and found the room surprisingly intact. The bed was still covered by pillows and blankets.

"This is where we'll sleep tonight," said Dieter with a grin.

Suddenly, a whimper was heard from beneath the bed.

Dieter knelt and peered underneath and exclaimed, "Well, what do we have here?" He reached forth and dragged out two small children – a boy and a girl of about 6 or 8 years old.

"Well, we can't have this," he said. "Nits make lice!"

He then began to unfasten his holster. Karlheinz knew in an instant what Dieter had in mind. Like a flash he unfasted his own holster and drew out his Luger. Seeing what was happening out of the corner of his eye, Dieter turned and with a smile said, "So, you've finally got some balls! Good! I'll let you do the honors." But his eyes widened as he saw Karlheinz point the weapon at him.

"What . . .?" he started to say, just as Karlheinz pulled the trigger. A small red spot appeared between Dieter's astonished eyes. He fell forward without a sound.

Not quite believing what he had just done, Karlheinz stared at his Luger as if he didn't know where it had come from.

The ashen-faced, wide-eyed children clung to each other, hunched over and trembling.

Coming to his senses, Karlheinz turned to them and motioned with his arm still clutching the gun and said, *"Geh!"*

Like frightened rabbits, the two waifs sprang to their feet and dashed out the door.

Karlheinz collapsed on the bed, sat, and stared at the corpse before him.
God! What have I done? What do I do now?

Chapter Eighty-five

Monika gibt zu
(Monika admits)

"So now you know," declared Monika.

It was early Spring of 1943. Eckhardt and Monika walked along the bank of the Havel in Spandau, not far from his home on Sandweg. He was home on a two week leave while his U-boat was being overhauled at St. Nazaire.

"But how could you and those others turn against your country?"

She had admitted she and her brother were part of the anti-Nazi youth group in Cologne who identified themselves as the "Edelweiss Pirates".

"We are not against Germany. We are against the gangster government under Hitler leading our country down the path to destruction. And don't think we are alone. My brother has a friend at the University in Munich who was acquainted with Hans and Sophie Scholl."

"Who's that?"

"At the Ludwig Maximilian University in Munich, there was an anti-Nazi student organization called *Weiße Rose*, led by Hans and Sophie Scholl and Christoph Probst. They organized underground meetings and distributed these leaflets telling the truth about the war and what the Nazis are doing. They distributed leaflets denouncing the Nazi government and the murder of the Jews.

Last February, they began contacting other resistance groups like the *Kreisau Circle* and the *Schulze-Boysen/Hamack Gruppe*. They got caught tossing leaflets from the upper level of the university assembly hall and were arrested. The Gestapo guillotined them four days later."

Eckhardt, his face pale, took a step back. Her face was flushed with passion; her mouth set in a thin line of determination; her eyes awash with tears.

"And you are involved in such a group, after what you just told me happened to them?" he asked in a shaky voice.

"Yes! And I'm not sorry!"

"Aren't you afraid?"

"Of course, I'm afraid! I think about it all the time. I lose sleep. When I hear the telephone ring or someone knocks on our door, my hands sweat and feel like ice. But I'm more afraid of what is going to happen to us when Germany loses this war. After what our troops are doing across Europe – especially in the East, I shudder to think of what the Russians will do when they come – and you can believe they are coming!"

"Why are you so sure we'll lose the war?"

A sardonic laugh.

"How can we not lose the war? Look at the facts! We're fighting the biggest countries in the world. Germany against America and Russia? Not to mention the British Empire! Wake up! You, and too many other people in this country, hang on every word that Goebbels sends out! Remember when Goering said if a bomb falls on Berlin, his name would be Meier? Well, look around! The Allies are sending over bombers day and night now. We have allowed Hitler and his thugs to do everything Hitler said he would do in *Mein Kampf*. Have you even read it?"

Eckhardt, looking at his slow stepping feet, shook his head. "We were given copies when we joined the Hitler Youth, but my mother took it away and said she didn't want it in the house."

"Well, anyway, he laid out his intentions for the whole world to see, and most Germans haven't even bothered to look."

"Maybe they're afraid to look."

"Now you're starting to think," she threw back at him. "But can I trust you now?"

Her words hung in the air.

"Monika. I love you. I love you with all my heart, and I trust *you* more than anyone else in this world! Yes, you *can* trust me!"

"Those poor men." commented Ursula.

Eckhardt had told her in a low voice about the sinking of the last freighter, while he helped her dry dishes. His father was working late to make up time lost in the air raids. Christina and little Detlev had gone to bed, so all was quiet in the house.

"And to think, if you were hit, would the enemy pick you up?"

"Probably, but everybody understands there is no room on a submarine for extra people. If *we* were hit, it would be from a surface vessel, and they pick up survivors all the time."

He had given her the answer he knew she would want to hear. In his mind, he, like others serving on submarines, knew if they were hit, it would almost certainly be with depth charges. They would be immediately flooded and sent to the bottom.

"Mama, if I tell you something, can you promise not to tell anyone else – not even Papa?"

She rinsed another plate and set it aside for him to dry.

"If you think you should."

He repeated the essence of his conversation with Monika. He searched her face for a reaction. She didn't seem alarmed by what he had said.

As she dried her hands on her apron, she turned to him and said, "Sit down, Son," indicating a chair at the small breakfast table against the kitchen wall.

"I'm not stupid, Eckhardt, and neither is your father. Of course, we all know how my mother feels about these people. But I don't want you to mention this to anyone else.

Monika is a fine beautiful girl, and I can understand why you're attracted to her. But those things she told you – I want you to forget them. And don't let her talk you into getting involved with those friends of hers. She's playing with fire, and it's only a matter of time before she brings the Gestapo down on herself and her family. You need to detach yourself from her. People know you've been seeing her. You have also been seen walking together. But it needs to stop."

"I'm surprised at you, Mama. I would have expected you to be on her side. I know you don't like the Nazis. That came across a long time ago. Now, you want me to abandon the girl I love?"

"It has nothing to do with how I feel about the Nazis, but your father and I are trying to hold our family together and get through this war alive."

He retorted, "That's what wrong with everyone in this country. Many people knew what Hitler planned. But they went along with him, because they fooled themselves into thinking that things would get back to normal – and then he would be dealt with."

She shook her head with a weary smile.

"Things weren't 'normal' before Hitler became Chancellor. We were desperate. We never really recovered from the last war, and then the Depression hit and we were starving – again! I say 'again', because we starved during the war and for years afterward. We were just beginning to recover – with very little help from anyone except the Americans. Hitler came along and promised to get us back to work. And he did!

Now, I admire young people like Monika, but I shudder to think what will probably happen to them. She told you what has already happened to some. So, I don't want you to get caught up in it." She reached across the table and grasped his hands in hers and continued, "Please, promise me you won't! So, break it off with her, and find somebody else!"

The kitchen clock ticking was the only sound in the room.

Chapter Eighty-six

Ein Flüchtiger
(A Fugitive)

"I haven't heard from my son since he was here last winter," Hans Joachim declared. He had been summoned again to Gestapo headquarters on Prinz Albrechtstraße.

His interrogator, Müller, tapped his desk with a pencil and looked at him with an icy unblinking stare. After a long pause, he responded, "Your son was last seen in Kharkov in February. You do understand what happens to deserters?"

"Perhaps he was taken prisoner," Hans Joachim suggested.

This elicited a derisive laugh.

"An SS man taken prisoner by the Russians in the midst of a deadly battle? Really, Dr. Lenz! Don't insult my intelligence. The Russians are *not* inclined to treat Germans amicably and most certainly not the SS!"

Hans Joachim studied his sweaty hands in his lap. *What the man said was true. Stories had trickled back to Germany of how the Germans treated Russians during the invasion of their country and how the SS had been especially brutal.* No, to expect that his son could have survived capture? He knew that was an exercise of self-delusion.

"Now, to another matter. Have you heard from your other son married to the daughter of the Jew Friedlander?"

"No."

"There you go again. Why do you persist in insulting me? Our people in Montevideo also inform us that old Benjamin Friedlander lives with your son, since his wife died. We know, because that's what Herbert's last letter said."

Trapped!

The only sound in the room was again from the pencil being tapped on the desk.

341

"Well, that's it for now, Doctor Lenz. But if you hear anything from Karlheinz, you will let us be the first to know, won't you, Doctor?" The gray eyes penetrated his soul.

Hans Joachim rose to leave.

"By the way, I'm happy that you have finally reconciled yourself to the fact that Dr. Köhler is now in charge of your surgical unit at Charité. It was time to relieve you of the responsibility. You can see, he's really a very capable surgeon, and it's too bad you and he had differences in the past. I'm sure you understand now. He can be helpful, and you need to follow his example.

Heil Hitler!"

Köhler! That bastard! Of course, he's behind all this, Hans Joachim groused to himself, as he unlocked his car and got behind the wheel. *I knew he had it in for me since he came to Charité. He's a Nazi snake and obviously has connections in the Gestapo!*

His mind jumped to the interrogator's question about Karlheinz. *Where was he?* Then Herbert's name popped into his head.

Oh, my boys! Will I ever see either one of you again?

He stifled a sob and concentrated on the rain-washed darkened street as he peered through his tears.

§§§

Karlheinz shoved Dieter's corpse under the bed. He was shaking with terror. He knew he didn't dare return to his unit and try to explain why he was alone.

He made his way back to the street and hurried in the opposite direction from where he and Dieter had come. In his uniform, he knew he was a walking target – either for the enemy or for his own people. A change of clothing became his top priority.

As he walked past ruined buildings, he saw corpses lying among the rubble and decided he would have to look for one approximately his size and build.

After looking to no avail for several blocks, and with darkness coming on, in a narrow side street he was relieved to find a group of men who had been massacred – either by Germans or Russians. Half buried by other corpses, he discerned the body of a young man who had been shot in the side of the head but was otherwise not damaged.

Moving quickly, he pushed the other bodies away and set about undressing the selected corpse. He was satisfied that the man had been dressed in working overalls, shirt and a heavy coat. The boots were scuffed but in good shape. The pain in his burned arm was intensified as he removed his own clothing down to his underwear. But he was grateful for the pain, because the burn had obliterated the blood type tattoo on his upper left arm that marked him as a member of the SS. Shivering in the cold, he dressed as quickly as his shaking hands would permit. He covered the near naked corpse with others, and moved away from the ghastly spectacle.

Then the question of how to dispose of his uniform? He debated whether or not he should dispose of everything but decided he would keep his Luger with its seven remaining cartridges in the clip and a spare clip, fully loaded with eight rounds. He was grateful he had a small container of wax covered matches with a small compass mounted on the cap. That, and his watch, a pocket flashlight, and a knife he had carried since he joined the SS were all the survival tools he kept.

He was sorry to part with his heavily lined greatcoat, but knew he didn't dare be seen in it. He rolled it and his uniform around his regulation boots in a bundle and clambered over the rubble of a nearby building, making his way through the interior to one of the back rooms. Using the gloves he had taken off the dead man, he clawed away bricks and dirt until he had dug a hole big enough in which to bury the bundle. After depositing it in the hole and covering it with rubble, he returned to the street, which he was glad to see was empty. Without further delay, he made his way out of the city and into the countryside.

As darkness enveloped him, and the bone-chilling cold increased, he knew he had to find shelter for the night. Using his compass, he headed away from main roads and walked in a northwesterly direction. After trudging for a few hours across frozen fields, he came to a deserted farmstead. The house had been burned to the ground, with only roofless walls standing, but an outbuilding remained largely intact. As he entered the dusty darkness, he determined this had been a storage building for tools, most of which were gone. In one corner, he discovered a tarpaulin covering the disassembled four-cylinder motor and drive train of a tractor. He burrowed beneath it and lay between the motor and the back wall before falling into an exhausted sleep.

"Ist 'was drin?" (Is there anything in there?)
"Nee, nur alter Krempel." (No, only old junk.)
The German voices startled Karlheinz into immediate wakefulness. Dim light fell on the wall he was facing, as the German soldier partially lifted the tarpaulin, and determining it covered the derelict motor, let it fall back.

Karlheinz lay bathed in the sweat of terror in the darkness, deathly still and barely breathing.

The two soldiers grumbled to one another, kicking broken tools and pieces of scrap lumber before departing. Outside, they joined their comrades, who had been searching for plunder or partisans. The rumble of vehicle engines accelerated as the group drove away.

Not daring to move for fear of stragglers entering the shed to investigate, Karlheinz waited until he heard nothing.

He slowly raised the covering and stood up. Standing with his ear cocked, he paused before walking to the door and peering out. His eye caught movement emerging from the ruins of the house. A chicken cautiously walked into the yard, softly clucking as it went.

His stomach grumbled. After a few moments, he made a soft clucking sound. It attracted the chicken and it came toward the shed to investigate. Karlheinz knelt and continued to entice the animal, which walked trustingly toward him. The bird stopped, just beyond arms reach. The two eyed one another. The man sprang forward and grabbed his prey, which began to squawk. Without hesitation, Karlheinz twisted the head and snapped the neck.

He looked at the dead creature, trying to decide what to do next.

When spending summers at *Schloß Hohenberg* as a boy, he had watched the gamekeeper dress birds for the kitchen. He knew he had to find water to complete the task. Carrying the chicken by its feet, he began to search for a water source.

Searching the whole area, he found no streams nearby. *Perhaps they had transported their water from somewhere else. But I see no trace of water barrels or water storage facility. Where did they get it from?* He decided to look inside the ruins of the house. He looked into the rubble of what had been the kitchen with no success and returned outside.

In despair, he sat on the debris of a collapsed outside wall and began to sob.

Then he saw a partially buried corner of a trapdoor. He lay his chicken to one side and began to clear away the stones and mortar.

Finally, after struggling for what seemed like eternity, he cleared the trapdoor which he lifted. Using his flashlight, he walked down a narrow stairway leading to a cellar under the house.

Eureka!

As he played his light around the small room, he saw row upon row of glass jars and bottles containing preserved meats and produce, and in a corner, a pump, which gave out clear water. Shaking with delight, he began to open jars and sample the contents, and using an empty jar, he quenched his thirst. *Preserved meat! Pickled fruits and vegetables! Canned garden vegetable of many varieties!*

He ate and drank his fill!

But how to find a way to take these treasures with me?

He emerged from the cellar, and saw the dead chicken. *Sorry, old girl. You died for nothing, but I would have to build a fire and I can't risk giving away my position.*

He hurried back to the storage shed, removed the tarpaulin, and using his knife began to cut out a meter square of fabric and some narrow strips. Returning to the cellar, he selected items that he deemed most vital and carefully laid them in the makeshift knapsack. After he had folded the corners together with the strips, he filled several jars with water and put them in the large pockets of his coat.

The sun cast a bleak wintry light on the still landscape, and although he was tempted to linger in the relative comfort of the cellar and its trove. *But I must continue on my way and make the best use of the short winter daylight.*

As he began to walk away from the farm, he paused once more to get his bearings. Looking around the still countryside, he resumed his trek across the frozen fields.

Chapter Eighty-seven

Briefwechsel
(Letters exchanged)

Roswell, New Mexico
Thanksgiving 1942

My sweet Erika,

Hopefully, this reaches you by Christmas. I have just returned to our camp outside Roswell. Some of us were allowed to join American families we work for to celebrate their national holiday they call Thanksgiving. We would call it "Ernte Dankfest".

Allen and Claire Rogers, the family I work for, own a ranch near Roswell, where they raise cattle, and they have been very kind to me. They have three kids from 8 to 17: two girls and a 17-year old son. He'll be finishing high school next Spring and says he'll join the army and hopes he won't have to kill any Germans. He's a shy fellow, and we get on well. They raise a lot of their own food, and we had turkey, which is an American bird. It's like a huge chicken. I didn't like some of their food – For example, they eat corn. We call that "Mais", which we only feed our livestock in Germany. And then pumpkin pie! I ate it, but I didn't like it – too sweet and too spicy.

I must close because I don't have any more space. Please write me soon. My heartfelt love to you and to Gerhard. Tell him his daddy misses him.

Ever yours,

Rudi

§§§

Berlin-Tempelhof
February 8, 1943

My darling Rudi,

I got your fascinating letter yesterday, and wanted to answer you right away. Last week on January 30, the British bombed us twice that day – the day to commemorate when the Führer was made Chancellor in 1933. My father says the British did it to interrupt Goering's and Goebbels' speeches they made over the radio. He also said you are lucky to be away from all of this, and I agree.

Gerhard and I met your sister, Ursula and her family, at the Weihnachtsmarkt in Spandau, but it was not like it used to be. We had Christmas with my parents, and our dinner was not as interesting as your Thanksgiving. My mother managed to buy two squirrels that someone caught in the Tiergarten. Imagine! There are still squirrels in the Tiergarten! My mother had saved back some seed potatoes in the air raid shelter and that was the mainstay of our meal.

I am so happy you are being taken care of, and don't worry about us. We are a lot of the time with my parents, and my father's air raid shelter in his backyard is stocked with water, flour, and potatoes. In addition, we supplement that with what can be obtained from our ration cards. We are allowed 245 grams of meat per week per person when available.

Tell me more about New Mexico. I hope you can get pictures from someone. Little Gerhard asks about you all the time. I must close.

With all our love,

Your Gerhard and Erika

§§§

Santa Fe, New Mexico
March 20, 1943

My dearest Erika,

I am sorry to be so slow answering your letter, but some of us have been moved to another camp near Santa Fe in northern New Mexico, and I have been busy with the move. New Mexico is a strange place, and here is so different from Roswell. I wish you could see it. We are near the mountains. They are not like our mountains in Germany, but beautiful. I am working with a Mexican American sheep rancher near here. Many of the people here speak Spanish, and I am learning a little from him and his family.

Tranquelino Baca and his wife Soledad have five children. One son is away in the Navy in San Diego, California. They showed me his picture and are very proud of him. I have learned to like chili. It's very spicy, but has a wonderful flavor. Soledad makes a fried bread on her stove top, called "tortillas". They are used for many kinds of Mexican food.

I like these people. They are humble and generous. They live simple lives, but they work hard and raise their children to do the same. I will send you some postcards, when I get a chance. They pay us 80 cents a day, and we are free to use the money as we like.

Must close. I wish I could hold you.

Yours Ever,

Rudi

§§§

Spandau
May 5, 1943

Dearest Son,

Erika and Gerhard were here last evening, and she shared your letter with us. I am so happy you are safe and living in such a beautiful place. After you wrote about Santa Fe, I went to the Staatsbibliothek (library) *and found some interesting information about New Mexico. You must send us some postcards and pictures.*

You mention food in your letters. It's wonderful that you can experience so many different types. We know so little about America. Most of us think Americans eat only hot dogs and drink Coca Cola. We are so ignorant about them.

Tell Mr. and Mrs. Baca I am grateful to them for being so kind to you. When Erika read the part about you being friends with Mexican Americans, little Detlev was angry and said I must tell you not to forget you are German.

Ursula and Eckhardt send their love and are happy you are safe. They worry about young Eckhardt somewhere in a U-boat.

I am proud of you for being a fine man. Your father would be proud of you, too.

Love,

Mother

§§§

Spandau
June 28, 1943

My dear Son,

It is with heavy heart I write this letter.

There was an air raid a week ago in the area around Tempelhof when Erika and Gerhard were staying with her parents. The street where they lived was devastated by fire caused by the bombs, and their house and several houses on that block were obliterated.

The firemen searched in the wreckage for two days for bodies, and finally found Erika and Gerhard. They were not burned, but were under bricks and rubble. She was holding Gerhard close to her breast, and they probably were killed instantly. Her parents were also found, and were badly burned. It is strange they were all in the house and not in the backyard shelter.

Eckhardt and Ursula made all the arrangements for the funerals and they were buried yesterday in the Heidefriedhof in Berlin-Mariendorf.

All our hearts go out to you, son. Try to be strong and know we love you.

Mother

Chapter Eighty-eight

Ende eines Traums
(End of a Dream)

He was awakened by the sound of muffled singing. Karlheinz crept to the window of the small sexton's cottage in the cemetery he had occupied for several days outside a village in Poland.

He had made a thousand-mile trek from Kharkov to Bromberg in Pomerania in eight-months, toward his ultimate goal of Schloß Hohenberg. Living like the fugitive he was, he had traveled mostly under cover of darkness making his way through forests and across fields, finding shelter in abandoned houses and outbuildings, often in ruins. He had foraged and stolen, even from the dead. When he chanced upon battlefields, he joined others, peasants and refugees, who unashamedly went through the pockets and clothing of fallen soldiers. The quest was not for money, but for food.

Now, he saw a small funeral procession making its way up the hill, the deceased in a plain wooden box transported on a farm cart. Two men carried shovels over their shoulders, there no longer being a sexton to dig the grave beforehand.

He gathered up his meager possessions and scurried out the door which faced away from the road. Bending over, he dodged among the tombstones to a small copse at the rear of the cemetery, crouching behind some fallen trees and shrubbery.

He watched as the mourners made their way to a location some distance away from the cottage. The men slung their shovels to the ground and began to dig. In the damp soft earth, the grave was dug to a shallow depth. After a surprisingly short time, the grave was ready, the box was lowered, and the priest began to read from his missal. Upon completion of his incantations, a dreary hymn was offered by the group, primarily two women dressed in shabby black clothing and a small boy. The departed one was laid to rest, and each member of the party filed past the open grave and dropped a handful of soil on the box. Then with no further delay, the two men began to shovel the earth back into the grave.

Karlheinz watched with relief as the party walked back the way they had come, and the stillness was only broken by the wind in the trees.

I must get away from this place of death!

The soft wetness of snowflakes on his face woke him in the roofless ruin of a small farmhouse. Winter had returned. It was October of 1943, and he knew he was nearing his destination.

Rousing himself, he sat with his back against a wall. Taking a lump of sour bread wrapped in a filthy rag from his pocket, he used a knife found in the sexton's cottage to carve a chunk from the nearly frozen bread. He opened his canteen, which he had kept inside his coat, and poured a trickle of water on the morsel to soften it. He chewed slowly and washed it down with more water. After the meager breakfast, he packed away his commodities, and surveying the bleak winter landscape, cautiously continued his journey.

All through the day as he trudged on, he buoyed himself up with the thought of reaching the estate, and the security and comfort that awaited him there.

Finally, as night had almost completely enveloped the landscape, he stood before the gateway of the estate. Mustering all of the energy he had left, he began to trot up the long driveway, which in former times had been covered with smooth gravel, but now was marred by muddy ruts and choked with weeds.

The outline of the big mansion was silhouetted against a darkening sky illuminated by an autumn moon. He looked to the right, expecting to see the lighted windows of the estate manager's cottage.

I'll get him to let me in.

But the small house was dark, nor was there any light to be seen in any of the outbuildings.

As he reached the circular driveway leading directly to the front door of the mansion, he suddenly realized the doorway was an open maw. He walked to the entrance and peered inside. Moonlight shone upon snow on the floor of the interior. Broken timbers had been left from a fire. The house was roofless! There was nothing left!

In a daze, he leaned against the stone stile of the doorway, sank to his knees and buried his face in his hands.

Part VI

The River of Fire

Chapter Eighty-nine

Phlegethon

At the beginning of World War II, RAF bomber command had focused on military targets. However, after studying which parts of the German Blitz on Britain had had the most effect, the strategy changed. Two considerations were how targeting the civilian population would destroy German morale and reduce the labor force, which would limit industrial production.

Hamburg, as the nerve center of the German navy, was one of the primary targets of the Allied bombing campaign. Prior to July 24, 1943, Hamburg had been spared from large air raids, but shortly after midnight on Sunday, July 25, it all changed. The coordinated efforts of the Royal Air Force and the American Army Air Force were to drop a combined total of 10,000 tons of bombs delivered by as many as 792 planes on Germany's second largest city of 1.75 million people. The British led off that night to be followed the next day by the Americans, which would be the pattern for the duration of the bombing campaign, a total of eight days and seven nights.

The raids resulted in the destruction of more that 133 miles of street frontage and cause fires to link up and create a firestorm climbing three miles into the sky and generating heat as high as 1,400 degrees Fahrenheit. The fire would suck air out of the city and create its own wind with velocities as high as 150 miles per hour.

The heat was so intense that steel structures melted, wood exploded, stonework and masonry glowed red hot, and human beings burst into flame. The asphalt melted and trapped people in the sticky mass as they died screaming in flames. Those seeking refuge in bomb shelters would be asphyxiated as the oxygen would be sucked out by the fire and replaced with carbon dioxide, or they would be cremated alive as they were ignited from the intense heat. The bomber crews leaving and returning to England reported the glow of burning Hamburg could be seen from the coast of England, a distance of less than 500 miles. 40,000 people were estimated killed.

It is reported that when Hitler was informed of the suffering and damage in Hamburg, he was advised to go there as a gesture of support to the citizens. However, he refused and sent *Reichsmarshall* Herrman Göring instead.

Göring's well known boast prior to the onset of British bombing attacks on Berlin in 1940, was that if any enemy bomber should reach the German capital, his name would be "Meier". When he made public appearances in Hamburg, some hecklers called out, "Well now, *Herr* Meier, what do you have to say now?"

§§§

August 21, 1943
Baca Ranch
Lamy, New Mexico

Dearest Mama,

Thank for your letter from June 28. My heart is broken. I can't believe they're gone. I have dreams Erika is lying beside me and we're talking. Then I wake up and no one is there. And my boy! I can't even talk about that. You are going through such terrible times there, and I'm living in this sunny, peaceful land with no danger. I feel guilty.

As an officer, I'm not required to work under the Geneva Convention, but I have volunteered to help the Baca family with their little ranch. It reminds me of working on the Hohenberg estate years ago. Tranquelino is teaching me how to handle sheep. His sheep need to be sheared twice a year –

once in the early Spring, and now again in late Summer and Fall. That gives the sheep time to grow a winter coat. Shearing is a hot sweaty job, but I enjoy it because it keeps my mind off Erika and Gerhard. I'm not very good at it yet, because I still nick their skin once in a while, and that makes me feel bad. Tranquelino is very patient with me. My hands are getting as soft as a girl's from the lanolin in the wool. After work, we look forward to Soledad's good cooking. I think you would like her Mexican food.

I must close. All my heartiest love to you and to Ursula and her family.

Rudi

"August 21st! And now it's the end of October!" Ursula exclaimed. "That's more than two months. The mail delivery is getting worse and worse!"

Christina nodded sadly, folded the letter, and looked around the table at her family, who were lost in thought about what they had just heard.

"I'm so glad he's safe and out of all of this," ventured Ursula. "I wish I could say the same for my son." Eckhardt took her hand and gave it a firm squeeze.

"I envy Rudi the experiences he's having," he continued. "He'll come back a different man."

"Right!" little Detlev burst forth. "He's being surrounded by all those dirty Mexicans, eating their dirty food, living like them, – maybe sleeping with them. He's forgotten who he is and isn't any good to his country and his people."

"That's enough!" cried his father. "You're talking about a man who is far away on another continent because he was serving his country, and then learned his wife and son were gone. Now he's lucky to be with people who care for him."

"That's right!" added his mother. "You just keep your mouth shut! Why would you say such a thing about Uncle Rudi?"

Rising from the table, Detlev shot back, "After all the *Führer* has done to teach us to keep ourselves pure from those other degenerate races, you talk about people caring for him! They are polluting him! You make me sick!"

He stormed out of the room and went up the stairs two at a time. The room was still as the three adults looked at one another.

"My God! To think, youngsters like him are the future of this country!" concluded his father.

§§§

Phlegethon is the river of boiling blood and fire where murderers, war-makers, plunderers, and tyrants are immersed.

> *"As they wallowed in blood during their lives, so they are immersed in the boiling blood forever, each according to the degree of his guilt."*

Dante Alighieri
– The Divine Comedy

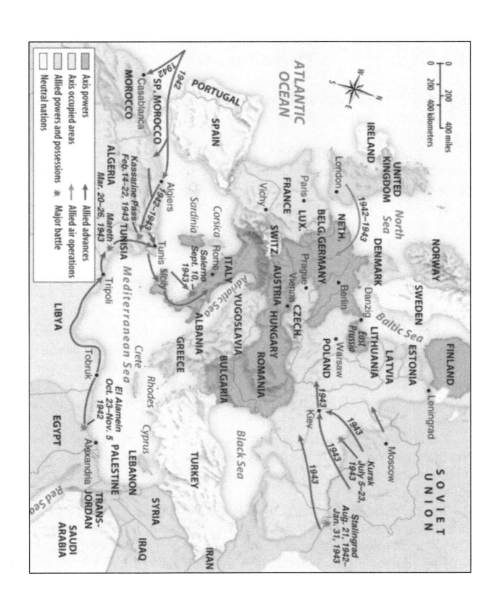

Chapter Ninety

Gebet beantwortet
(Prayer Answered)

"Well," began Eckhardt as he and Ursula sat on the crowded gently swaying subway car. "Do you think that was worth all the effort?"

They had gone into the city on the evening of November 18, to the Gloria Palast on Kufürstendamm to see Zarah Leander's latest film, *"Damals"* (Back Then).

"Oh, absolutely! Any film with Zarah Leander is worth every effort. But this one is her best."

With a slightly amused smile, he looked at her.

"I'm glad you think so."

"And it was good to get away from the house and forget the war for a while."

"I can't disagree with you on that," he replied.

They had decided to travel into the city on the U-Bahn rather than drive. The streets were either bomb damaged or blocked with debris of ruined buildings. In addition, gasoline rationing had become severe. But the inducement of the newest film featuring the very popular Swedish actress had been too much for Ursula, an avid Leander fan, to resist.

Eckhardt, on the other hand, had never been very impressed by her. Her deep voice, which many described as "smoky", was too near masculine for his taste. But he was happy to support his wife in her enthusiasm.

As they finally reached the Ruhleben station, the westward terminal for the U2 line, located next to Spandau, he took her hand. They started toward the stairs leading to the surface, emerging into the chill November night. Walking toward their parked car, the air raid sirens sounded over the city, followed by the distant rumble of bombers heading their way.

They paused.

Eckhardt cocked his head. "That sounds like a lot more planes than usual. I think we'd better go back downstairs."

"But Mama and Detlev are alone in the house!" cried Ursula.

"We can't get home in time from here before the bombs start falling. They're coming from the West and will hit this area first. We can't help them at home if we get ourselves killed. Let's go back." He firmly took her arm, returning to the shelter of the subway station.

At first, she resisted.

"Ursula, come on!"

Then she relented and with bowed head let him lead her.

They, and many of their former fellow travelers, were joined by others from the vicinity desperately seeking shelter from the bombs that were now beginning to fall. The pushing, shoving throng was being swallowed into the mouth of the U-Bahn entrance.

She grasped Eckhardt's arm, and he tightened his grip to keep them from being separated.

Halfway down the stairs, the crowd suddenly stopped moving. An elderly woman had stumbled and was sprawled across the steps.

"What the hell?"

"Come on! Move it!"

"For god's sake, go!"

Shouts and curses burst forth, as panic swept over the mob.

As the unfortunate perpetrator of the delay was helped to her feet, they resumed their descent. Finally, the crowd dispersed as they reached the subway platform.

"Let's move away from the entrance," declared Eckhardt.

They found a corner at the far end of the platform and seated themselves on the floor, as muffled thumps of bombs falling overhead penetrated the gloom.

She curled herself next to her husband and laid her head on his chest as he kissed the top of her head.

Oh, Mama! Oh, Son! Please, God protect them! coursed through her mind.

"Wake up, sweetheart. Let's go home."

In a half-daze, Ursula raised her head.

Where am I? flashed across her brain.

Just then the rush of air being forced from the subway tube by an oncoming train gave her the answer.

"Is it over?"

"For now," answered her husband, squeezing her shoulder.

As they joined the throng making its exhausted way to the stairway, no words were spoken. The only human utterances heard, were mothers comforting small children and infants fussing and crying for their beds.

They found their car covered with dust from explosions but otherwise undamaged. Eckhardt and Ursula flicked off the windshield with their handkerchiefs, opened the doors, and wearily sank into the softness of their seats. As he started the engine, he placed his hand on her knee.

Giving him a tired smile, they understood the unspoken words between them – *We made it!*

As they made their way homeward, they drove around burning buildings and wrecked vehicles impeding their progress.

At last, they arrived at their own front door. The house stood, and a welcoming light beckoned them through a front window.

The door burst open, and young Detlev ran to the front gate as they got out of the car, with Christina following close behind.

Ursula, with tears of relief washing her cheeks, embraced her son. Eckhardt walked up from behind and embraced them both, then reached out his arm to include Christina. They stood wordless for a long moment, savoring their mutual relief and gratitude.

Ursula turned to her mother.

"Where did you go during the raid?"

"We were carrying some blankets to the toolshed with a flashlight, when *Frau* Lortz next door saw us. She and her daughter and two grandchildren were walking to their fruit cellar at the back of the yard. She called over and told us to join them. We were so grateful. She has been a good neighbor once again."

Laughing, Ursula enquired, "Did she pump you for the latest doings of our family?"

"Be nice, Ursula," retorted Christina. "We know she likes to pry, but she's good hearted. We should take something to her next time we're baking."

"God knows when that will be. Rationing has gotten so bad this year. You can be willing to sell your soul for a few grams of sugar and get no takers."

"I'm so glad you're home Mama," interjected little Detlev. "You, too, Papa."

They walked with their arms around each other to the open front door.

"You know, sitting in *Frau* Lortz's fruit cellar got me thinking," declared Christina, as she helped Ursula prepare dinner on Saturday following the big air raid. "We should think about getting ourselves better prepared with our food situation."

"You're right, Mama," responded her daughter. "Food rationing has become worse since last Summer. And in spite of what Goebbels, and those other liars tell us, this war is not going well."

Christina, who had never been an admirer of the Nazis, nodded in agreement. "I can't get the memories of what we went through in the last war out of my mind. God forbid we should have to go through that again. I had a full-time job just to keep us from starving." She finished peeling potatoes and begun to cut them up.

Ursula chuckled. "I remember. You chased all over this city for a few potatoes or a head of cabbage."

Christina turned to Ursula. "Who was that classmate of yours whose uncle had a farm out by Zossen?"

Ursula's brow furrowed in concentration. She recalled, "You mean Gudrun Stegmeier? I haven't seen her in years. We meant to keep in touch, but you know how people lose contact. I wonder if her uncle still lives on that farm. I don't know how I could contact her. She's probably long-since married and goes under a different name."

"You could try to trace her if you know her last address."

"I don't think I should do that, especially in these times. You don't want to bring attention to yourself or anybody else by asking too many questions. Next thing you know, the Gestapo takes an interest and starts asking *you* questions. No, I think I'd better not go there."

Christina suggested, "Let's just go out there. We can take some suitcases like we did before to carry food home."

Ursula brightened. "That's a good idea. We'll take Detlev, like you took us kids to help carry. I'll call the school on Monday and say he's sick. He'll be glad to get out of a day at school. We'll make an outing of it. It'll do us all good to get out of the city for a few hours."

After supper, Ursula laid out their plan to Eckhardt and Detlev. As predicted, Detlev was delighted. A holiday spirit filled the house all the next day in anticipation of the upcoming excursion.

Chapter Ninety-one

Rückkehr nach Wünsdorf
(Return to Wünsdorf)

Monday, November 22nd dawned with a light overcast, but was otherwise not unpleasant.

As soon as breakfast was over, and Eckhardt was off to work, Ursula called Detlev's school and explained he had an upset stomach and needed to stay home. The two women and the boy, with three suitcases among them, made their way by bus to the Lehrter Bahnhof, where they hoped to board the electric railway to Zossen, about 25 miles south of the city. However, upon arriving at the station, they were informed that service to Zossen would be delayed due the transport of troops. They could expect to wait at least two, or even three hours before being allowed to board a train.

"Let's just go home," complained Detlev.

"We can't do that because you're checked out of school. You want to show up there late and explain that to your teacher?"

He muttered something incomprehensible and sulked at the end of the bench away from his mother.

"Kids! Why do we put up with them?"

Christina smiled. "For the same reason I had to put up with you and your siblings."

The three of them settled in for a long wait, and Christina soon nodded off.

The loudspeaker barked the announcement that boarding for Zossen was underway on platform two. They gathered up their luggage and made their way to the train. Almost four hours had passed. They found a compartment occupied by two other disgruntled passengers, an elderly man and his wife. Taking their seats, the elderly woman looked them up and down.

Traveling through the suburbs of Tempelhof, Mareindorf, Lichtenrade, and Schönefeld, they remarked to one another how the destruction of the air raids lessened further from the center of the city. It was refreshing to see the fields, lakes and woodland of the countryside. Finally, after a little more than an hour, they arrived at the station in Zossen. It was now early afternoon.

Stepping outside, Ursula turned to Christina, "Do you still remember how to get to the farm, Mama?"

Christina smiled. "Oh, yes. I have pictured this place in my mind. But I'm amazed at the changes. Zossen used to be just a little town, but look at all the uniforms. Now that the military have moved their headquarters out here, it has an entirely different feel. Oh, well. Let's start walking to Wünsdorf. As I recall, it's only about a half hour walk south of here."

With that, they picked up their suitcases and began walking along the road, which now was busy with military vehicles moving back and forth. Eventually, they reached the private road leading to the farm. After twenty minutes, they stood before the front door of the house.

"Well, here goes," said Ursula, as she knocked three times.

Seconds ticked by. No response.

She tried again, more resolutely.

After what seemed an interminable wait, the door was opened a crack, and a wizened face appeared.

She explained that she was an old friend of his niece, Gudrun Stegmeier. remember?

After a long pause, he enquired suspiciously, "Have you talked to Gudrun?"

"I must confess I have not. It's been so many years, and I'm afraid we've lost contact."

"I should think you have. Gudrun and her two children were killed in an air raid last year."

Shocked at this news, Ursula offered her condolences.

"What do you want?"

Stepping forward, Christina interjected, "During the last war, I came here with my children. We were starving, and you saved our lives. We were hoping you might still have commodities to sell, as you used to. We're prepared to pay well."

He looked at her with an appraising stare. A flash of recognition registered in his eyes as he remembered this same woman from all those years ago. Then, "I do remember you. I can't farm like I used to, due to the shortages of fertilizers, but I can let you have a few things. Wait a moment."

With that, the door was closed.

Ursula turned to face her mother and shrugged.

"We've come out here for nothing," grumbled Detlev.

"Patience, young man," admonished his grandmother.

The door opened and the old farmer appeared, wearing a rough cap with earmuffs and a heavy mackinaw.

Wordlessly he led them to the same barn as years before. The odor of the barn triggered memories for Christina and Ursula. Young Detlev wrinkled his nose disapprovingly. Going to the same empty horse stall, he began to remove a layer of hay, grasped the large iron ring on the floor and lifted the trapdoor. Making his way carefully down the steps leading to the cellar, he called them to follow. As they reached the floor, he switched on an electric light. Last time, he had used a kerosene lantern to illuminate the gloomy cellar.

As before, there were crates and barrels filled with sand containing root vegetables and apples. There were cabbages wrapped in newspaper and a few hams suspended on wires across the ceiling. Without comment, the three visitors began to pack their suitcases as their host laid out the items before them on a table.

The suitcases, being stuffed to capacity and closed, Ursula began to count out the required amount in *Reichsmarks*.

Unexpectedly, the old man enquired, "Would you like to stay for lunch for a modest price – a good home-cooked meal? Nothing elaborate, but prepared with fresh food off the farm." The city dwellers accepted without hesitation.

As they walked back to the house, he explained, "My wife died soon after our son was killed in Poland. My daughter and her two little girls live with me now, as their apartment building in Wilmersdorf was bombed out. Her husband is in the army in Libya with Rommel and the *Afrika Korps*. She's a very good cook. I'll tell her to set three more places. You can come in and wait by the stove in our parlor."

His daughter was a cheerful, chubby young woman, who nodded and greeted them by shaking each of their hands.

After a short wait, she called them to the small dining room adjacent to the kitchen. "How are things in Berlin?" she asked, as she fetched the roast pork and potatoes from the kitchen and placed them on the table.

"Terrible," replied Christina, who then related the experience regarding the raid of the previous week.

"Yes," added Ursula. "My husband and I were terrified we had lost Mama and my son." She turned and smiled at Detlev, who was busy enjoying the delicious food set before him.

"I'm so glad to be out of all of that," replied the young woman. "My girls can finally sleep here without having nightmares."

Ursula nodded with understanding. They continued to discuss the increasing hardships brought about by the war.

Then young Detlev blurted, "Faith in the *Führer*! We must have faith in the *Führer*. He has promised we will come out of this and be better Germans! I can't believe what I'm hearing!"

The adults looked at him without comment. Ursula frowned, and Christina pursed her lips in a tight line.

Finally, with the threat of oncoming darkness, Christina spoke up. "Ursula, we had better go. We don't want to walk back to the station in the dark. Besides, it's getting colder, and we could get caught in snow."

"Why don't you stay overnight and start back in the morning?" suggested the cheerful young woman. "We have an empty bed in my brother's room, and your son can sleep on the living room sofa."

"Oh, thank you very much, but my husband is expecting us back tonight, and Detlev has school in the morning."

"You can call him," continued the old farmer.

"You have a telephone?" Ursula was somewhat surprised.

"Yes, in the pantry behind the kitchen."

"I don't know. What do you think, Mama?"

"Well, that's for you to decide," Christina replied.

"Oh, let's stay here, Mama," Detlev piped up.

"You're not in any hurry to walk in the dark, are you, young fellow?" teased the old man.

"No, or pass up another day off from school," added Ursula with a frown.

Finally, though, she relented. She called Eckhardt, who agreed they should not undertake a return trip to the city at night. She and Christina helped clear away the lunch things, while Detlev grudgingly agreed to play the board game, *Mensch, ärgere Dich nicht* on the dining table with the little girls, aged 7 and 9. After such a long, exhausting day though, his eyes began to droop, and soon he dozed off in the middle of an argument between the girls as to whose turn it was.

Ursula walked over and gently nudged him. "Come on, sweetheart. You need to get to bed."

He allowed himself to be raised and guided toward the sofa in the parlor, not responding to being called by the endearment, which normally would have evoked a protest. *A real Aryan man shouldn't be called such things.*

The young mother directed, "Put that the game away, and go to your room and read a while. We will have *Abendbrot* (light supper) before going to bed."

Christina, feeling every one of her sixty-six years, stated that she, too, was very tired and begged to be excused to go to bed. She was shown the bed she would share with Ursula.

When Ursula and her hosts finally were able to relax at the dining table, they sipped tea and continued their discussion.

"We all had such high hopes for Germany after the last war," lamented the old farmer. "Then, we allowed ourselves to become so desperate we were ready to listen to anyone who held out any hope. Now, look where we are! We should have recognized the signals soon after *he* became Chancellor. The signs were there, but we refused to see them."

"My husband says the same thing," replied Ursula. "He says we are going to pay a big price for what is being done now in the name of Germany."

"I was in *Bund deutscher Mädel* when I was a girl," declared the young woman. "We were bombarded constantly with propaganda, and my husband, who was in *Hitler Jugend,* says they were too. Most of us were in it for the activities and outings, but even though we didn't realize it, much of the propaganda seeped into our minds until we couldn't tell what was true and what was a lie."

"Detlev is going through the same thing now," said Ursula in a sad, soft voice.

Their discouragement and frustration continued to be voiced until early evening. Ursula arose and said, "I'm sorry, but I feel like following my mother's example. Would you forgive me if I don't join you for supper?"

"Of course. You know where the room is, so feel free to do whatever you like."

Chapter Ninety-two

Wüstenlandschaft
(Wastelands)

The house was vibrating. A rumble like nothing heard before penetrated her sleep. Ursula's eyes focused in the darkness on the faint outline of the north facing window. She threw off the down comforter and sprang from her bed, unaware of the cold floor as she hurried to the small window. She unlatched it and swung the inner sash into the room, and then opened the exterior window. Cold air blasted into the room. She couldn't see the aircraft above the cloud layer, but the vibrations of a thousand engines could be felt by her bare feet through the floor. Just as her brain registered they were heading toward Berlin, she heard the muffled explosions of the first bombs.

"Get away from the window, Ursula!"

"It's a huge air raid, Mama. This sounds bigger than anything we've seen."

"Be glad we're here," responded Christina.

"Yes, but Eckhardt is *there*! We have to call him!"

Closing the window, Ursula hurried through the door and downstairs. She found the phone in the pantry and tried to contact the operator. It was not a dial telephone, but a simple country party line, which required all calls to go through the operator at the central exchange. At first, there was no response.

They're probably swamped with calls now, she told herself.

She waited in the dark a few minutes and tried again.

Finally, after another try, the operator came on the line.

"Number, please."

"Spandau 72 44 861"

She could hear the ring at the other end of the line but no answer. After several rings, the operator returned.

"There is no answer. I'm going to disconnect."

"No, please. Let it ring a little more."

She heard an exasperated sigh.

After several more rings with no response, the operator stated, "I'm sorry. I can't stay on this line any longer. I have other callers waiting."

The line went dead.

Frustrated and terrified, she returned to the bedroom where she found Christina sitting up in bed.

"Eckhardt didn't answer the phone. We need to get home as soon as possible."

"We'll have to wait until daylight," Christina replied.

"I don't want to wait until then. I want to go now!" With that, she went downstairs to awaken Detlev, but when she went into to the parlor, he was already sitting up.

"Detlev, get dressed! We're going home!"

As she turned to go back upstairs, she was startled by the light in the kitchen. She was confronted by her host.

"What are you doing, *Frau* Meinert?"

"We're leaving." She then explained that she had been unable to reach her husband.

"You can't leave now. You and your mother and a boy walking back to *Zossen* in the dark? It's out of the question. And besides, there is a curfew in effect because it's now a military center. Civilians are not allowed on the streets until after 6 a.m."

Ursula buried her face in her hands and was racked with sobs.

The young woman appeared and embraced her. "Come sit down. I'll make some tea."

Hearing the voices downstairs, Christina appeared and sat beside her daughter and held her against her breast.

Detlev came and sat across from them, trying hard to control his own emotions.

Soon, tea was served, along with bread and blackberry jam, with which they all tried to calm themselves. The muffled explosions in the distance continued relentlessly, and no one dared give voice to the foreboding they shared.

As the train neared the western outskirts, it became increasingly evident they had not been spared. Detlev, whose nose was pressed to the window for the entire journey, cursed the Americans and British under his breath for the outrage they had perpetrated on his city. The Lehrter Bahnhof itself, had suffered extensive damage. Ever mindful of a constant Germanic belief in punctuality, the bus schedule had always been taken for granted as being reliable and punctual. Bus schedules were now marred by intermittent delays and interruptions. Detours became necessary to avoid streets blocked with rubble. Many buildings were totally gone, while others were left with portions sheared off exposing furnished apartments open to view. Stone walls several stories high teetered on collapse, endangering passersby on the streets below.

When the bus reached the end of their street, Sandweg, the driver announced the bus could proceed no further. Christina, Ursula and Detlev, carrying their heavily loaded suitcases, stepped from the vehicle and commenced to walk up the street, now rendered unfamiliar.

As they neared their home, two gaping lots in the place of familiar houses greeted them.

Then – their own house – gone!

"Bastards! Filthy Allies! How dare they? We'll get even!" raged Detlev. Christina and Ursula stood frozen with shock.

Setting down her suitcase, Ursula ran toward the still standing front gate, only to be greeted by a pile of rubble. She fell to her knees, convulsed in sobs, howling like a dying animal.

"Eckhardt! Eckhardt! Eckhardt!" she screamed. Christina rushed to her and knelt beside her, holding her and placed her own tear flooded face on her daughter's shoulder. Detlev, sobbing and shaking with rage, stood still, unable to bring himself closer.

Then – Eckhardt bolted out of *Frau* Lortz's front door.

"Darling! I'm here!"

Their good neighbor, *Frau* Lortz, hearing the commotion in the street, followed Eckhardt out her front door. The now homeless family were clustered in a group hug, with Eckhardt stroking his wife's hair and murmuring comforting words.

"All of you come into my house," directed *Frau* Lortz in a warm but firm voice. "We all need to strengthen each other now. Come on." Eckhardt smiled at her with gratitude and relief.

As they entered the foyer, *Frau* Lortz turned to Christina. "Will you help me? You can cut some bread while I put the kettle on for some tea."

Christina wavered, wanting to stay and comfort her daughter. But then she smiled and nodded. "Yes, of course. The three of them need some time to themselves. Thank you, *Frau* Lortz."

"Oh, darling. What do we do now?" Ursula asked her husband.

"I don't have a quick answer to that. Right now, I'm just grateful we are all here together and safe. Last night when the raid started, I was beside myself because you three were out there somewhere, and I didn't know if you were safe."

"I'm sorry. I tried to call you, but you didn't answer. And with the raid going on, I imagined the worst." She reached for Eckhardt and encircled him and Detlev in her arms. The boy, who was beginning to compose himself, drew back.

"I don't understand you two," he admonished his parents. "You talk about gratitude, but you don't seem a bit angry with the bastards who did this to us!"

"That's enough, boy!" flashed his father. "Of course I'm angry. But not just with the British. I'm angry at everybody who started this war. I'm angry at myself and many others like me for going along with them. Deep inside, I knew we were being led into disaster and fed lies about it. Grow up, son! Take a hard look around you! Look at yourself and what you have become!"

"What's that supposed to mean?" Detlev retorted. "What are you going to do about it? Are you just gonna' hide in a corner somewhere until they bomb us to pieces? Not me! I'm a man! I'm gonna' fight 'em!" he finished, shaking his fists as rage surged in his flushed face.

Young Detlev turned on his heel and left the house, slamming the door behind him.

Eckhardt, in despair, and Ursula, blinded by tears, surveyed a son who was now a stranger.

"Come into the dining room," came the call from Christina, as she appeared smiling in the doorway. As they assembled around the dining room table, Christina opened the suitcases and began to lay out the precious commodities on the table. *Frau* Lortz' eyes widened.

§§§

> ***Luftangriff vom 22 November. Viele feindliche Flugzeuge stürzten ab! Minimaler Schaden für die Stadt!***
>
> (Air raid from November 22nd. Many enemy aircraft brought down! Minimal damage to the city!)

Hans Joachim, shaking his head, laid his newspaper on the canteen table at the hospital. "Unbelievable! Those idiots!" he murmured.

"What did you say, Dr. Lenz?" came from a nurse seated at the next table.

"Nothing."

He got up and left the room.

The most effective air raid executed by the RAF during the war over Berlin occurred on the night of November 22, 1943, when 440 Avro Lancaster bombers caused severe damage to the residential areas west of the city center of *Tiergarten, Charlottenburg, Schöneberg and Spandau*. Amazingly, the phone systems remained operational throughout the war, as the phone lines in metropolitan areas were buried underground and suffered no damage from the bombings.

.

Chapter Ninety-three

La Boda
(The Wedding)

Christina gasped. Ursula, hearing her mother, looked up from mending clothes as they sat at the dining room table with *Frau Lortz*. Few clothing stores were still open among the bombed buildings, forcing many, like these women, to mend and repair their families' clothing.

Dear Mama,

I am so glad you and the family have a home with your good neighbor, Frau Lortz. Please give her my best wishes and thanks for taking you in. But it must be hard for you to look next door every day and see only the foundation of your own house. I wish I could be there to help you through this hard time.

New Mexico is a strange land, but I have come to love it and its people. The climate is amazing. Blue sky and sunshine almost every day. It was cold during the winter, but a dry cold. It snowed a few times, but usually not much, and always melted in a day or two. Now, the warm weather is here again. The altitude is about 1,800 meters, which keeps the temperature down and provides a cool breeze.

The Baca family have really taken me in and made me part of their family. They have a beautiful daughter, Graciela, which means "Grace". Her name suits her perfectly. We have grown very close over the last several months. I would not have survived the last year without her support.

Since we have worked for Americans, and the authorities believe they can trust us not to try to escape, we have some freedom of movement. Last Christmas, I was allowed to go into

Santa Fe with the Baca family, and the air was filled with the scent from the fireplaces burning the local cedar and pine. The Mexican people have some interesting Christmas traditions, but my favorite is the Luminaria. A Luminaria is a brown paper bag with sand in the bottom for weight and a candle placed in the sand. Then the people place many luminarias around their houses on outside walls or along the sidewalks and driveways – even on the roofs. When they are lit, they are a sight to behold!

I was thinking about all of you on Christmas. I went to midnight Mass with the Bacas on Christmas Eve and remembered you in my prayers.

Everyone is very friendly – even to me! My English is getting better, but of course I have a strong German accent. I am also learning Spanish from Graciela. She laughs at me, because she says she has never heard a "gringo" speak Spanish with a German accent. A gringo is a non-hispanic white person.

Graciela and I and are considering marriage, but marriage between Prisoners of War and American citizens is not allowed. Graciela and her family are devout Catholics, and in order to get married I have decided to get baptized. I wish you could be here for that. I have almost completed my Cathechism, or Rite of Christian Initiation

I must close, but Give my love to Ursula and her family.

Rudi

"Rudi is marrying a Mexican girl!"

"What?" blurted Ursula incredulous.

"Yes. He has taken up with one of Mr. Baca's daughters. He goes on and on about how beautiful she is and how she loves him. Her name is Graciela. That means 'grace', and he says it fits her perfectly. He is going to become a Catholic."

Nobody said anything.

Finally, *Frau* Lortz ventured, "In a way it's understandable. He's a young man alone in a far-off country having lost his wife and baby. And who knows if he'll ever return home."

"Well, Mama? What do you think about that?"

Christina frowned, perplexed.

Addressing *Frau* Lortz, she replied, "I guess I see your point. But such a different culture. And become a Catholic!" She snorted. "Religion! What's that got to do with anything?"

"Does he say anything more about that, Mama?"

"The Baca family are Catholic, and apparently very religious. It's probably what the girl's mother wants, so I wonder how devout Rudi really is."

Ursula smiled. "Weren't you a Catholic, Mama? Papa's family were French Huguenots and of course Protestant. You left the Church to marry him, didn't you?"

"That's true. I haven't thought of that. But now I don't care about religion in general, and I'm surprised Rudi does."

Ursula, realizing her mother held that view because of the atheistic influence of Communism, nevertheless kept silent, but concluded, "So, you see? Some People change religion for love."

Later, at the dinner table, Christina announced the news to Eckhardt and Detlev.

Detlev, upon hearing this, reacted as expected. "Marry a Mexican? A German marry a Mexican? Mixing his Aryan blood with a Mexican!"

Eckhardt slammed his fist on the table. "That's enough!"

"Why are you mad at me?" blurted the boy. "The *Führer* doesn't want us to mix with inferior races."

"Your uncle is in another place and may never come back to Germany," retorted Eckhardt. "You need to think about what you say, instead of just repeating what you've heard."

Ursula interjected, "Calm down, Eckhardt. He's just surprised. Mama and I were, too, at first. But we finally decided that from what Rudi has told us, the Baca family are simple hardworking people who have taken him in. We should be grateful for that. And Rudi says they and the girl helped him through a terrible time after Erika and Gerhard were killed. They're devout Catholics, and Rudi apparently has found solace in the Church, too. He may never come back, and if he has found peace there, I, for one, am happy for him."

Christina nodded in agreement.

Detlev, his head down, muttered, "I hope none of my friends hear about this."

"What was that?" challenged Eckhardt.

"Nothing!"

Father and son glared at each other.

"You should write to him right away," declared Ursula. "Let him know his family supports him in whatever he decides to do with his life

Frau Lortz, taking this all in, only smiled.

§§§

Dear Son,

I was so happy to get your letter and learn that you are well. As you know, I don't put much stock in religion, but if that makes you happy, it doesn't change anything between us.

The family was surprised that you are hoping to marry the Baca girl, and again, I just want you to be truly happy. I understand that learning about your wife's and son's death was terrible for you, especially being so far away in a strange land with people so different from us. I hope you're not making this decision just because you are lonely. But if you truly love this girl, you know I will support you in your decision.

Ursula sends her love and apologizes for not writing more often, but the war is making life for all of us so difficult. She is exhausted just trying to take care of her family – and even more so in another woman's house. I'm sorry you are so far away, but I am grateful you are safely away from all of this.

Love,

Mother

Chapter Ninety-four

Die Navajos
(The Navajos)

The young voices lusty singing filled the morning air, as the Hitler Youth battalion marched along Friedrichstraße enroute to the big railway station.

*Es zittern die morschen Knochen
der Welt vor dem roten Krieg.
Wir haben den Schrecken gebrochen,
für uns war's ein großer Sieg*

*Wir werden weiter marschieren
wenn alles in Scherben fällt,
denn heute da hört uns Deutschland,
und morgen die ganze Welt.*

(The rotten bones
of the world before the red war tremble.
We broke the horror, it
was a great victory for us.

We'll keep marching
when everything falls apart.
Because today Germany hears us
and tomorrow the whole world.)

As they neared the building, a large group of young men and women forming a barricade came into view. Suddenly the air was rent with the sound of American Indian war cries, drowning out the Hitler Youth. Perplexed, their battalion faltered and shuffled to a halt. The boys looked at each other, baffled.

"We're the Navajos!" shouted a husky youth in lead position of the opposing group. "You kids need to go home to your mamas." The HJ leaders were thrown into confusion.

Detlev Meinert, in the second row of the HJ, looked around the shoulder of the boy in front of him. Searched the faces of the opposition, he wondered what kind of Germans they were. He was startled to see Monika König. She was standing next to a tall young man talking to her. Then her eyes widened as she locked stares with Detlev. Her face flushed, and she looked away.

"Who are these people?" Detlev asked the boy standing next to him.

"I think they're part of a group of traitors who call themselves the 'Edelweiss Pirates', but I never heard of 'The Navajos'. Anyway, here's our chance to bash some heads and show this scum what they get for challenging us."

As if he had spoken the thoughts of the others, the leaders took up the cry, *"Los Jungs!* Let's get 'em."

They rushed the human barricade and were met with fists and clubs. The chaos spread like wildfire through the two groups, and soon bloody faces appeared on both sides. Detlev found himself in the middle of a stampede as those behind him rushed forward. Losing his balance, he fell to the ground. He curled himself into the fetal position to cover his face and keep from being trampled. Shouts, screams of pain, and curses resounded all around. Just as he was about to resign himself to being stomped to death, two arms reached down and pulled him to his feet. He found himself looking into Monika's face. She held on to him with both arms as they made their way to the edge of the crowd. She pushed him in front of her into a doorway.

"What are you doing here, Monika?"

"Never mind that. Get out of here!"

Detlev gave her a shove. "Leave me alone!" He tried to push his way past her and rejoin his friends.

Shaking her head, Monika tried to lift him in her arms. Failing that, she began to forcefully walk down the street, dragging the kicking and screaming child.

The melee, in the meantime, had moved away from them, providing a break for her to take Detlev in the opposite direction. As she did so, she passed Sepp Klein, another HJ youth, who shouted Detlev's name. Monika started to run. Just as she reached the corner of Unter den Linden, she saw police vans racing toward the battle.

She put Detlev down and gave him a nudge towards home. "Go on! Go!"

He turned the corner and ran up the boulevard.

"Why do you put yourself in such situations?" questioned Ursula crossly, as she washed his face and bandaged a cut on his forehead in *Frau* Lortz's bathroom

"Somebody has to stop those traitors." He was ashamed his words had not matched his actions. He didn't mention that he had been terrified. *I'll never be a coward again!*

After a long pause, "I saw Monika there."

"Monika, Eckhardt's girlfriend? Isn't she too old to be in BDM? Were those girls there, too?"

"Not BDM! She was with the others. She's a traitor, too!"

Ursula stopped and leaned forward to look him straight in the face.

"Monika König was with the protestors? I'm sure Eckhardt knows nothing about that!"

"I don't know. Maybe he does. He's been different since he's been with her. He doesn't talk about the *Führer* like he used to. He even met the *Führer* and shook his hand!"

"Now you put those ideas out of your head, young man. Right now, he's in the Navy serving his country doing one of the most dangerous jobs there is."

Detlev muttered to himself, as he stood up and went out to the toolshed, where he and his father were now sleeping.

"Why were you letting that girl drag you away? Who was that?" Sepp Klein put to him bluntly the next day at school.

Caught by surprise, Eckhardt blurted, "She's my brother's girlfriend."

"Oh, that girl you went on about when she came to your house for dinner? I remember! What's her name? Marta? No, wait Monika! Monika from Cologne!

I remember how you went on and on about how beautiful she was. She is that – I could tell, even in that oversized parka she was wearing.

Does your brother know she's involved with those *Edelweißpiraten?"*

Thoroughly shaken up, Detlev turned and walked away without answering.

Sepp watched him. "Well, well, well!" he said to himself.

§§§

Although the first groups of *Edelweißpiraten* were formed in the late 1930s among young people between 14 and 18, unfortunately, these young people had neither the necessary central leadership, nor means of coordination available to them needed to spark a nationwide youth uprising. The groups were identifiable by their Edelweiss badges, common style of dress and opposition to the paramilitary nature of the Hitler Youth.

Other anti-Nazi youth groups appeared in various parts of the country. In Hamburg, a group known as the *Swing Kids* imitated American teen hairstyles and dress of the period they saw in American movies, which were circulated underground. The *Swing Kids,* being fans of American swing music, danced the jitterbug and other popular dances of the time to records of the big band era, such as Benny Goodman (a Jew), Artie Shaw, Glenn Miller, Tommy Dorsey, Count Basie (a black musician), and others.

Of course, information surreptitiously communicated around Germany concerning the *Weiße Rose* (White Rose) student movement in Munich formed by the brother-sister team of Hans and Sophie Scholl (who were beheaded) had a big influence on these youth groups as well.

The Nazi response to the *Edelweißpiraten* at first was mild in the prewar years. But as the war continued, and the Pirate's activities became more extreme, so did the punishments. Individuals arrested by the Gestapo were sent to prison or to concentration camps.

But the government repression did not break the spirit of the groups, and their rejection of the Nazi order continued. In November 1944, Himmler ordered a group of teens publicly hanged in Cologne. The anti-Nazi youth continued to assist German military deserters and others hiding from the Nazi regime until the end of the war.

Chapter Ninety-five

Fremdarbeiter
(Foreign Workers)

"I've gotten to where I hate going to work," murmured Eckhardt to Ursula in their darkened bedroom.

"About half my team is comprised of non-Germans. I try to treat them as fairly as I can, but the Nazi stooges keep a close eye on our operations. I can't be caught dealing with the foreign workers in a way that looks like I'm going easy on them or fraternizing with them."

"Fraternizing?" questioned Ursula.

"Yes, there are penalties for fraternizing, and a person can be sent to prison – even to a concentration camp for it – depending on which Nazi is making the charge."

He listened to her soft breathing and could sense her indignation.

She replied, "Not to bring up the past, darling, but remember how you were impressed by what Hitler promised to do for Germany and even by what he did do in the beginning?"

"Yes, you're right, and I'm amazed that I didn't take his threats seriously about what he meant to do with Jews and other *Untermenschen* (sub-humans). But I think a lot of Germans made the same mistakes I did."

"How do you think others at Siemens feel about using forced labor in their operations?"

"It depends on their level of belief in the government. My officemate, Müller, as usual, thinks we have sunk to a new level of degeneracy. He tells me the term 'foreign workers' is a shameless euphemism. He calls them 'slave laborers! I've come to agree with him.

Before the war, we had foreign workers who came voluntarily and were paid the same as Germans and had the same benefits. In the early days of the war, they came from the neutral countries. But now, they come from the German occupied countries and are paid a fraction of what a German receives – if indeed paid at all!

We see women and teenage kids, who are barely fed and who work until they're exhausted. They disappear and are replaced immediately by some other poor soul, who works until she or he drops. Then that person is replaced and so on and so on."

"How dreadful," whispered Ursula.

"You have no idea! I'm so glad you don't have to see that day after day."

She turned and embraced him.

"My poor darling. My poor, gentle darling."

"Our world is coming to an end, Ursula. They've destroyed those peoples' lives, and are destroying ours, too.

Look at our boys! One risking his life in a submarine and the other turning into one of *them*. He's becoming the kind of person I would never have had anything to do with in normal times."

"Oh, don't say that! He's still our child. We can't give up on him. One day this will all end, and he will become our little boy again."

"I can't imagine what it will be like when this is over. It might be worse!" He gave a bitter chuckle.

§§§

Nazi Germany used forced labor as never before seen in world history. The economic exploitation of conquered countries became a substantial part of the German economy, and at its peak comprised twenty percent of the German labor force. Approximately 12 million people from almost twenty nations – about two thirds from Central and Eastern Europe – were transported to Germany during World War II.

There, many died a result of their treatment – savage brutality and extreme malnutrition were the main causes of death. Many others were civilian casualties of Allied bombing.

Even before the war, slave labor was utilized by the Nazis. In the early days of the Third Reich, labor camps were established for the so-called "unreliable elements" of German society. Criminals, homosexuals, political dissidents, Communists, Jews, and anyone else the regime wanted disposed of were targeted. There they were worked until they were unable to work, and many died as a result of their treatment in these camps.

A class system was established for foreign workers brought to Germany based on decreasing levels of workers from well paid workers from Germany's allies (Romania, Bulgaria and Hungary) and neutral countries (Spain, Sweden and Switzerland) down to forced labor from the conquered countries.

The German corporations that used slave labor included, Thyssen, Krupp, IG Farben, Bosch, Daimler-Benz, Demag, Henschel, Junkers, Messerschmitt, Siemens and Volkswgen, as well as subsidiaries of foreign companies, such as Ford Motor Company and General Motors.

Chapter Ninety-six

D-Day

"Your mission is to resist the initial landing and fire on any force that happens to land in front of you," came the words of Field Marshall Gerd von Rundstedt, *Oberbefehlshaber-West*, High Commander of the German Western Army under General Erwin Rommel. He was speaking to the soldiers manning the batteries that lined the Normandy coast. "We are part of the *Festung Europa* (fortress Europe). We have poured 17 million cubic yards of concrete, enough to build 270 of the American's Empire State Building and laid 1.3 million short tons of steel, enough to build the Eiffel tower 160 times over. We have placed almost six million mines in Northern France, and don't forget our little *Rommelspargel* (Rommel's Asparagus - slanted poles with sharpened tops) on all the beaches.

We have spent years preparing to repel this invasion, doing everything that human ingenuity and German military engineering can achieve. We have one million German soldiers like you to defend this coast. What the *Führer* has built is an impenetrable defensive fortress of concrete and steel that stretches from the cape of Norway to the Spanish border and can repel any Allied landing. When they come, we will drive the swine back into the sea!"

§§§

On that night of 6 June, none of us expected the invasion anymore. There was a strong wind, thick cloud cover, and the enemy aircraft had not bothered us more that day than usual. But then – in the night – the air was full of innumerable planes. We thought "What are they demolishing tonight?"

But then it started. I was at the wireless set myself. One message followed another. "Parachutists landing here –

gliders landing there," and finally, "Landing craft approaching."

Some of our guns fired as best they could. In the morning, a huge naval force was sighted. That was the last report our advanced observation posts could send us, before they were overwhelmed. And it was the last report we received about the situation. It was no longer possible to get an idea of what was happening. Wireless communications were jammed, the cables cut and our officers had lost control of the situation. Infantrymen who were streaming back told us that their new positions on the coast had been overrun or that the few bunkers in our sector had either been shot up or blown to pieces.

When we tried to get through to our lines in the evening, British paratroopers caught us. At first, I was rather depressed, of course. I, an old soldier, a prisoner of war after a few hours of the invasion. But when I saw the material behind the enemy front, I could only say, "Old man, how lucky you have been!"

And when the sun rose the next morning, I saw the invasion fleet lying off the shore. Ship beside ship. And without a break, troops, weapons, tanks, munitions and vehicles were being unloaded in a steady stream.

Anonymous German Private's View

The D-Day invasion on June 6, 1944, was an overwhelming success for the Allies – but it was an unmitigated disaster for the Germans!

The foundations of the Wehrmacht's defensive strategy in the West, the so-called Atlantic Wall and the placement of panzer divisions, were utter failures. The invasion force penetrated through the wall within the opening minutes of the landing. Only a single panzer division managed to head toward the beach. The Germans had no ability to maneuver, no counterattacking force, no tanks, no aircraft, and were basically immobilized in their bunkers. There was nothing that could have driven the landing force back into the sea. The Germans had an abundance of bunkers and batteries, but what they needed were more soldiers and equipment in the area. Their million-man army was spread over 2,000 miles of coastline.

While many factors fueled the catastrophe, the failure of the Wehrmacht was due to the shear overwhelming power of its adversaries. The wealth of the Allies and their industrial might was simply unstoppable. The thousands of ships, aircraft, and the nine divisions on the Allied side were backed by millions of reserves waiting as a follow up force. The Wehrmacht had only three divisions to deploy in the area – and no navy or air force.

Although Hitler had slept in with orders not to be disturbed, and General Rommel was back home celebrating his wife's birthday, nothing was going to change the outcome of D-day.

§§§

Hans Joachim hunched over his small short-wave radio in the basement of his home on the evening of June 6, 1944, which he had managed to hide from the authorities. He had the volume turned as low as possible in order to hear the news from the BBC German language broadcast, which was forbidden.

Like all German citizens, he had had to surrender his large Telefunken console radio, with its shortwave capabilities, after the outbreak of the war. The only radios then offered the public were the small limited range radios known as *"Volksempfängers"*. These could only receive broadcasts from German and Austrian stations. Therefore, the only news broadcasts available were authorized by Goebbels Propaganda Ministry.

"The Allies have landed in France on the beaches of Normandy and are pushing inland!"

Leaning back in his chair, a slight smile playing on his lips, he heaved a sigh. "Finally!" he whispered in the silent gloom.

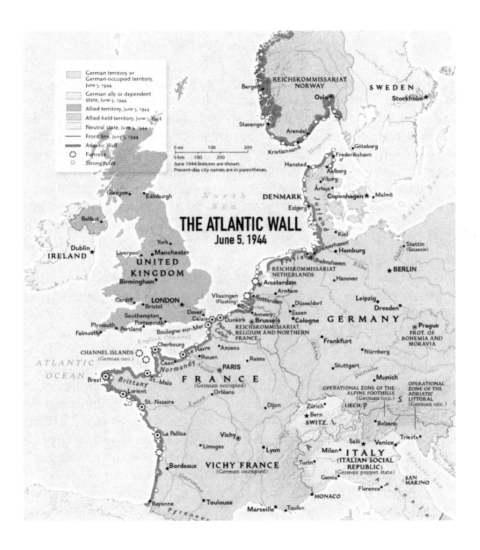

Chapter Ninety-seven

Einsamer Wolf
(A Lone Wolf)

Eckhardt stood on the conning tower with the commander and two other crew members. They peered intently in all directions to no avail. The dense fog that enveloped the U-boat restricted their vision to only a few meters. They had been tracking the progress of a large convoy of troop-carrying ships bringing reinforcements to France along the coast of Cornwall in southwest England.

After the D-Day invasion in July, the Allies had been relentless in pursuing U-boats which had terrorized shipping in the North Atlantic since the outbreak of the war. By winter of 1944, over 600 U-boats had been sunk out of a fleet of over 900. The feared "wolfpacks" were decimated and scattered.

The diesels were near idling as the submarine crept through the fog, when suddenly it cleared and they emerged into the early morning light. But they were terrified to see a British destroyer dead ahead coming at them full speed and firing with its forward deck guns.

"Dive!" shouted the commander into the intercom. The klaxon blared as he swung himself into the hatch of the conning tower, followed by the others. By the time the last man had scrambled down the ladder and barely closed the hatch, the deck was submerged. By then the conning tower was awash, the diesels were switched off, and crewmembers braced themselves by grasping overhead pipes, bulkheads, bunks, and anything fastened to the walls and ceiling as the submarine dove at a steep angle toward the ocean floor.

Eckhardt, hanging onto an overhead pipe, lost his grip and was thrown against the corner of a cabinet. His head took the full impact, which resulted in a deep gash on his forehead. He braced himself as the warm trickle of blood ran into his right eye.

"Damn!" he muttered under his breath.

Before they even had reached the bottom, the boom of depth charges reached their ears and their stress levels escalated. The boat began to shake and throw some men off balance from the reverberation of explosions. They settled on the bottom in near darkness with only the dim red emergency lights on.

Then began the ordeal! The destroyer circled above, dropping depth charges in a closing spiral pattern. The ping of sonar came closer and closer. Suddenly, they heard the sound of a depth charge bouncing off their hull. They braced themselves for the end. Some men were shaking and weeping and muttering prayers. But it failed to detonate! When it dawned on them that they had been spared, some began to sob. But immediately afterward, another charge exploded so near it rocked the ship violently. Leaks began to shower seawater down on the heads of the hapless men. A large leak near the periscope tube began to flood the floor. But they could not move or make a sound, lest they give away their position to the probing radar from the destroyer. They stood as water crept up their legs.

The circle of explosions gradually moved further away and the sonar became fainter. *Had the British commander lost his bearing?*

Finally, after what seemed an eternity and with water up to their ankles, the commander ordered, "Repair Team!"

Once the flood had slowed to a trickle, the pumps were engaged, and the electric motors activated at reduced speed. They turned in a northwesterly direction and crept away.

They circled around Ireland and Scotland in the North Sea, on the surface – and ever watchful, especially in the daytime. The original plan had been to sail directly from England back to their base at *St. Navaire*, but with the increase of patrols by Allied surface vessels and aircraft, the decision was reached to make directly for a German port.

They ran on the surface as soon as they left the waters off Scotland behind them. The commander and crew members kept a constant watch for enemy aircraft with their binoculars. They knew the enemy had developed long-range radar with the ability to spot them before they themselves could be seen. But with the urgency of getting to port with their damaged vessel, which prevented them from being submerged for long periods of time, the commander decided he had no choice but to make for home.

They were all unwashed and filthy, but Eckhardt was worse. Because of undernourishment, he was gaunt and pale. His Navy greatcoat now sagged around his bony shoulders. The makeshift-bandage the radio operator, acting as the medical officer, had wound around his head, was stiff with blood. In the two days since the damaging attack, he had developed a fever. The radio operator had informed the commander, who ordered Eckhardt to see a doctor as soon as they docked, and gave him a written authorization to that effect.

When the U-boat limped into the harbor of Hamburg, it had to thread its way through the wreckage of sunken ships to the submarine pens. Eckhardt and his shipmates standing on deck stared at the gutted ruin of the city. Where walls still stood, the dead eyes of window spaces looked back at them. The blackened ruins presented a graphic reminder of the great Allied air raid of July 1943, which had lasted eight days and nights, and had taken an estimated 40,000 lives.

"God!" declared a shipmate standing next him. "If this is what's left of Hamburg, what will Berlin look like?"

"What indeed?" responded Eckhardt. "My family lives there. My girlfriend too!"

"You, poor bugger!"

After the boat was docked in its pen near *Vulkenhafen* on the southern bank of the Elbe, the men, with their duffel bags slung over their shoulders, trudged down the gangplank. The radio operator, waiting on the pier with a group of officers from other U-boats, called, "Meinert! Over here!

I wanted to send you to the nearest hospital, but I've learned it's only partly still intact and is filled beyond capacity. There is an emergency medical facility on the Binnenalster (inner Alster basin) near the center of the city. A truck to transport you and your crew into town is waiting outside and will drop you there. With your authorization from the commander you will be seen right away. Good luck!" he stated as he shook Eckhardt's hand.

"Thank you, sir."

"That's a nasty gash. You should have had stitches right away, and now it's badly infected," grumbled the nurse, as she cleaned the wound of pus and matter.

"There are no available doctors at the moment, so I'll take care of it myself. We're short on supplies, but I can put some sulfa on it as a disinfectant. Hopefully, by the time I've finished, a doctor can see you and decide what you should do."

"Thank you, sister."

Eckhardt had fallen into an exhausted sleep and was held upright, squeezed between an elderly woman and a soldier on the rear seat. The rumble of the bus engine was the only sound to be heard as the vehicle proceeded with caution along the Hamburg to Berlin autobahn in the darkness, penetrated only by a small aperture of light produced by the blackened headlights.

When Eckhardt had been informed that he would receive a pass by the examining doctor allowing him to go home, he was overcome with relief. He had thought he would make the journey by train, but when he learned that the rail lines between Hamburg and Berlin were so heavily bomb-damaged and would necessitate several delays and detours, he opted for the bus.

The trip in peacetime took less than four hours, including stops to take on and let off passengers. But they had been underway now more than five hours. Once, they had pulled over to extinguish all lights to avoid being spotted by enemy bombers. Everyone on board sat in tense darkness as the menacing motors thrummed overhead.

The light of early morning penetrated his consciousness as they reached Falkensee, just before Spandau on the northwest edge of the city. The Ruhleben bus station was reduced to a pile of rubble. Eckhardt, in his dazed condition, had a difficult time getting his bearings. Familiar landmarks were sparse, and he had to focus intently to not get lost. But he plodded on in the icy morning gray light toward the Sandweg and home.

Chapter Ninety-eight

Eckhardts Verwirrung
(Eckhardt's Confusion)

As he turned into Sandweg, Eckhardt felt a sense of relief wash over him. The way from the bus terminal had required his maximum effort. Weak and exhausted, bathed in feverish sweat in spite of the cold, and experiencing waves of nausea to the point of having to stop and retch once, left him only able to proceed with an agonizing shuffle.

But relief turned to confusion, as he looked up the once familiar street. Several houses were roofless, burned out blackened shells, and some were totally gone – including his own!

What has happened here? he asked himself. *Why didn't Mama tell me about this in her letters?*

Then he recalled the conversation he had had with the shipmate on the U-boat as they entered the harbor at Hamburg. Now, he had his answer!

As he neared the pile of rubble that had once been his home, he noticed that their neighbor, *Frau* Lortz, had been spared the fate that had befallen his family. His strength spent, he staggered to her front door and knocked. The door was opened by his father!

"Papa!" he cried, as he fell into the man's arms.

Hearing the familiar voice, his mother rushed to the entrance and helped her husband bring their son into the house. Christina came out of the kitchen, and seeing her grandson and the condition he was in, cried out, "Oh, my God! Bring him to the sofa!"

"What have they done to him?" cried Ursula.

Frau Lortz came out of her room, saw the spectacle, and immediately went to her linen closet and brought out a pillow and a blanket.

"Cover him! He's shaking from the cold," she declared, as his parents laid him out on the sofa. He immediately fell into an exhausted sleep.

Dim light penetrated the darkness of the small bedroom. Ursula sat beside him and took his hand as he drowsily opened his eyes.

"Mama?"

"Yes, son. How are you feeling?"

With a weak grin, he muttered, "Fit as a fiddle!"

Ursula chuckled.

His father appeared in the doorway. "How's my boy?"

Then Christina peered around the door frame.

"At least you're clean. We can be in the same room with you now. It took both your mom and dad to wash you. I insisted, before I let you have my bed."

"And that beard!" interjected his mother. "Papa had to cut it as short as he could with the scissors. You'll have to shave the rest off yourself."

This brought laughter all around.

"I don't want to take your room, Grandma," he protested.

"It's alright. Your papa is sleeping on the couch, and I'm sleeping with your mama. We're quite comfortable. Remember the old days in Wedding, Ursula?"

"I sure do. My brothers and sisters and I slept on the floor."

"This is way ahead of my bunk on the U-boat. Thank you, Grandma."

Hearing the levity, *Frau* Lortz called from the kitchen, "I have some soup ready for him."

§§§

Why haven't I heard from her? The thought had tormented him before he returned home, and convalescing with time on his hands, Eckhardt pondered the question over and over. In between air raids, Berliners had moved forward in their lives as best they could, and now during such a lull, Eckhardt had determined to get an answer.

"You're still too weak, and besides, it's cold outside," protested Ursula when he revealed his plan to walk to the girl's house.

He smiled. "Don't fuss, Mama. Remember what I told you about my life on the U-boat? Anyway, look out the window. The sun is out and Spring is coming. Fresh air will do me good."

Another air raid had destroyed the U-boat pens at Elbe II, and Eckhart's U-boat had been severely damaged at its pier shortly after he left Hamburg. This, in addition to his slow recovery from the blood poisoning that had set in from his head wound, prompted his attending physician in Spandau to recommend his medical leave be extended, which was accepted. It was now the middle of March, and the days were getting longer. In spite of chilly weather, there was a hint of Spring in the air.

"Be sure to take your *Soldbuch* (military identification booklet) and your leave authorization with you," admonished Ursula as he put on his greatcoat, which she had brushed and cleaned as well as she could. "The Gestapo and the SS are stopping and checking identification. They're looking for deserters. Anyone they suspect can be executed on the spot. In some parts of the country they're hanging them on lamp posts. Make sure to be home before dark, and don't forget the curfew."

He walked the few blocks to Monika's house without stopping. When he came to her street, he was met with a similar scene as that on Sandweg. Some houses were vacant, roofless, and windowless shells. Some had been reduced to piles of rubble, and some were intact. He was relieved to see that Monika's was one of these.

He came to the front gate, which was hanging askew on one hinge and open. As he approached the front door, he could see that on closer examination, the house had sustained some damage. The stucco was chipped from shrapnel from bombs that had destroyed neighbor's homes. One upstairs window facing the street had been shattered and replaced by a sheet of plywood. But the building still stood.

He rang the doorbell, and after a long pause, the door was opened as far as the inside chain lock would allow. The sallow face of *Frau* König appeared, and she looked at him suspiciously, until she finally recognized him.

"Ah, it's you *Herr* Meinert."

"Good day, *Frau* König. Is Monika at home?"

The woman stared at him. Her face crumbled, and tears coursed down her cheeks.

They looked at one another wordlessly, until Eckhardt repeated the question.

"Monika is gone."

"Gone where?"

"They took her away."

"Who did?"

"*They* did!"

Then he comprehended.

"Why?"

"She and her brother were both arrested," she said in a near whisper.

His heart sank. *The Edelweiss Pirates!* He recalled the sense of danger he had felt when Monika had revealed her involvement with that resistance group. Now, his worst fear had been realized!

"Your brother did it!"

"My brother?"

"Monika was afraid of that. She told me about seeing him with the Hitler Youth at the demonstration rally at Friederichstraße station. She hoped he wouldn't betray her, but I'm sure he did.

Monika is dead. She and her brother were both beheaded at Spandau Prison. The Gestapo informed us, and I shouldn't even be talking to you. My husband has been inducted into the *Volkssturm* and is on the Eastern Front somewhere in Poland. I haven't heard from him for six months. He might be dead, too. Please go away!"

Stricken and at a loss for words, Eckhardt could only stammer. She closed the door before he could reply.

Blinded by tears, he turned and staggered away from the house. He made his way home with agonizing effort. His head was spinning, and he was perspiring heavily by the time he reached *Frau* Lortz's front door.

Ursula held him close to her breast as he poured out his anguish.

"And she thinks Detlev reported Monika!"

"I can't allow myself to believe that. He told me about how Monika had dragged him away and made him to leave that day. He was grateful to her."

"Well, *Frau* König thinks he did. I'll never forgive him!" cried her son.

Christina interjected, "They're making killers out of those kids."

Shaking her head, Ursula's eyes misted.

Chapter Ninety-nine

Brüder Konflikt
Brothers' Conflict

Raised voices came from the boys' room. "Damn you, Detlev!" A crash resounded.

Ursula froze. She looked at her mother, who turned, white-faced with open mouth. Both women ceased preparing dinner. Ursula wiped her hands on her apron and hurried to the foot of the stairs.

"What is going on up there?" she demanded.

The door flung open and smashed into the wall. Young Eckhardt, flushed with rage, raced down the stairs, pushed past his mother without a word, and charged out the front entrance, slamming the door behind him.

The stunned woman went up the stairs and peered through the open door.

"Detlev?"

Wiping blood from the corner of his mouth, Detlev turned and went back to his bed. He lay down with his face to the wall.

"Go away!" was the response. "Leave me alone."

She waited.

"What has happened up here?"

No response.

"Detlev, answer me!"

"I don't want to talk to you."

"What have I done?"

"I just don't want to talk now."

Christina entered the room and enquired in a soft voice, "What's happened?"

Turning to face them, Detlev blurted, "I don't want to talk to you, either, you old Commie!"

Furious, Ursula stepped forward, her hand raised to slap the boy's face, when her mother grasped the upraised arm and admonished, "No, Ursula. Let it go."

At a loss, hesitant about what to do next, both women studied the distraught youth.

Finally, "I want to talk to Papa. *Please* leave me alone!"

After a pause, Ursula and Christina closed the door and went downstairs.

"I don't know what came over them," lamented Ursula to her husband that evening. "When young Eckhardt left, he slammed the front door so hard, your mother's picture fell off the wall. He hasn't come home since."

His brow furrowed, Eckhardt studied his plate.

"I tried to get Detlev to come down for dinner, but he refused. He's been upstairs in his room all afternoon and won't talk to us. He also insulted Mama again – calling her an 'old Communist'. He says he wants to talk to you but didn't come down when you came home. Can you go up and talk to him?" she pleaded.

With a sigh and wearily laying his napkin beside his plate, Eckhardt arose and went upstairs. He tapped on the closed bedroom door. "Detlev, it's Papa. Can I come in?"

Eckhardt waited in the hall until he heard the soft response, "Come in."

As he opened the door, he saw Detlev lying on his bed facing the wall. Sitting on the edge of the bed, the father laid his hand gently on the boy's shoulder. "What's wrong son?"

"Eckhardt hates me."

"You don't believe that, and neither do I."

"No, this time he *really* does."

Turning to bury his face in his father's chest, Detlev sobbed, "He thinks I betrayed Monika to the Gestapo."

"Betrayed Monika to the Gestapo? What are you talking about?"

"He went to her house and saw Monika's mother. She told him Monika and her brother had been arrested and were executed at Spandau prison."

Stunned, "Executed? My God! When?"

"I don't know."

"Why does he think you had anything to do with that?"

"Her mother told him I had been the one to report seeing her at the Navajos demonstration at Friedrichstrasse."

"Did you?"

"No."

Eckhardt took a deep breath and slowly exhaled.

"Sepp Klein saw me talking to Monika that day and asked who she was. I told him she was Eckhardt's girlfriend, and he knew right away that was Monika. I didn't mean to tell him. He must have reported it to our HJ leader."

He began to shake with sobs again and then buried his face in his pillow.

"I'm so sorry! Eckhardt really hates me! He said so! He even said he wanted to kill me!"

Chapter One hundred

Detlev zur Pflicht gerufen
(Detlev Called to Duty)

"You're being assigned to do what?" cried Ursula in astonishment.

"We're supposed to report to the Zoo flak tower tomorrow. They're going to train us to be ammunition loaders for the anti-aircraft batteries."

"They're putting kids in a situation like that? Wait until I tell your father about this. He'll have something to say about that!"

"What either one of you has to say about it, doesn't matter. We're at war, and if we're needed, then we have to go."

"Well, we'll see about that!"

Detlev shrugged and went upstairs.

"He's probably right, Ursula. As crazy as things are right now, I wouldn't be surprised at anything they tell us to do."

Ursula, numb with anguish and outrage, looked at her husband in disbelief, as they sat in the kitchen after Detlev and *Frau* Lortz had gone to bed.

"But we're his parents. He's a child. How can they do this without at least consulting us?"

He looked at Christina, who, up to this point, had witnessed the drama without comment. Then she nodded and spoke up.

"They're beasts! I've hated them since we first heard of them. I agree with you, Eckhardt. Nothing they do surprises me.

But I hear what you say, Ursula. He's a child, and you should not have to hear about this from him. You have rights as a parent. If you want to protest, I'll support you."

"I think you both had better think about whom you're dealing with. You women are here at home most of the time. You're not out there dealing with these people every day like I am. Trust me. They're dangerous! *Really* dangerous! And the way things are going with the war, they're starting to feel desperate. Why do you think they're resorting to putting kids in flak towers? If they're feeling cornered, you shouldn't push them."

"So, what are you going to do as his father? Nothing?" retorted Christina.

He looked at her, saddened by her tone. He could sense a lack of respect. Conversation ceased.

The next evening, as they were finishing dinner, a firm knock came at the front entrance. Eckhardt opened the door and found himself facing a young man, who stepped into the vestibule without being invited, causing Eckhardt to step back. Closing the door behind himself, the stranger began, "Is your wife here, *Herr* Meinert? I need to speak to you both."

As they went to the dining room, the young man took a seat at the table before being asked. Taking off his gloves and laying them on the table, he looked appraisingly at each person. *Frau* Lortz rose, excused herself, and went to her room. Christina, firm lipped, returned his stare unblinking. Ursula, red-faced with indignation at the intrusion into her family, glared at him. Detlev looked at his plate. Eckhardt, with clenched fists held rigidly at his sides, stood aghast in the doorway.

"I understand you have a problem with Detlev being asked to serve his country in this hour of need," the intruder began without preamble. Detlev squirmed in his seat.

"As his Hitler Youth leader, I am here to inform you that your attitude has been noted. Yes, it has been noted! You need to understand he is not yours! He belongs to the Reich! He is on loan to you, providing you agree that the rights of the State preclude yours. That's the situation, whether you agree or not."

Ursula opened her mouth to speak.

"Save it, *Frau* Meinert! Nothing you have to say makes any difference. If I hear about anymore dissent from you on this, next time, you can discuss it with the Gestapo!"

He rose and put on his gloves. Raising his arm in salute, he cried, "Heil Hitler!" Turning on his heel, he walked to the front door, went out and slammed it behind him.

The family, frozen into speechlessness, looked at one another.
"I told you so," said Detlev.

Determined not to show fear, Detlev handed ammunition brought from the cellar by elevator to another HJ youth, who then placed it in the hopper, which in turn automatically fed it into the breech of the gun. The deafening explosions of the batteries, together with the detonation of bombs falling all over the city, penetrated the ear protectors worn by the Flak crew. It left them with ringing in their ears, which would continue for hours after the firing had ceased. The bombers, some of which were spotted by the searchlights and often hit, came in wave after wave for hours, day and night in the early months of 1945. The enormous amount of ordinance flung at the enemy did not seem to make a dent in their swarms. The combined capacity of the Allies to rain death and destruction on the dying city was endless and unstoppable.

Detlev, like thousands of other German boys, had been part of the Nazi youth movement since he was ten years old. They were indoctrinated with Nazi ideology which emphasized loyalty to Hitler and the State above all else – even parents and family. By the time he was assigned to serve as a flak helper in the Zoo tower, he was convinced that his goal in life should be to do whatever was required of him.

If I should die in the effort, so much the better! There can be no greater honor than to be remembered as one who spilled his blood for the Führer and the Fatherland!

§§§

Hitler had formulated the propaganda used to gain the minds of Germany's people – including its children – in chapter VI of his *Mein Kampf* as follows:

All propaganda must be presented in a popular form and must fix its intellectual level so as not to be above the heads of the least intellectual of those to whom it is directed.

Alfons Heck, a former member of the HJ, and author of his two books, "A Child of Hitler: Germany in the Days When God Wore a Swastika" and "The Burden of Hitler's Legacy" put it this way:

We five and six-year olds received a daily dose of Nazi instruction, which we swallowed as naturally as our mother's milk. The very young became defenseless receptacles for whatever was creamed in to us. To us innocents in the Hitler Youth, the Jews were proclaimed as devious and cunning overachievers. Especially in their aim of polluting our pure Aryan race, whatever that meant."

Another former member of the HJ stated:

My defense of the Hitler Jugend is that even at sixteen, few of my comrades had any inkling that they were pawns of an evil empire. Bombarded by incessant indoctrination from kindergarten on, and surrounded by adults who were either captivated themselves, or lacked the suicidal courage to tell the truth, they never had the luxury of any choice. To expect a child to be that discerning was ridiculous.

Consequently, Detlev gave no thought to the little family in Spandau. He was encouraged to rebel against his parents in order to belong to the state. Indeed, he was totally given over to the task at hand: destroy the enemy!

§§§

Young Eckhardt stumbled into the home after 3 days of heavy drinking. "Where is the little shit?"
"He's been taken from us. They took him to work in the flak tower!"

§§§

"I have to report back to my unit in Hamburg," announced young Eckhardt to his family a week later after returning from a medical exam.

"My doctor informed me that even though he thinks I should have more time to convalesce. They are being ordered to cut medical leaves short for anyone who is ambulatory."

"In other words, if you're not crawling, you have to 'fight for the Fatherland'," was Christina's sardonic comment.

"That's enough, Mama. Don't make us feel any worse," reprimanded Ursula.

"Hmmph!" snorted the other.

"That's okay, *oma*. I expected to be called back before now."

"Well, son," replied his father. "I remember the last days of the war in '18. We knew the end was near, and everyone just tried to keep their heads down and not volunteer for anything. It's all about survival now. And it can't last much longer."

The young man smiled. "Right, Papa. After being on a submarine, you can bet I understand that thinking perfectly."

The father patted his son on the back.

Chapter One hundred-one

Suche nach einem Zuhause
(Search for a home)

"Eckhardt, I need to speak with you," declared Ursula, as her husband removed his coat one evening in March 1945.

Wondering why she couldn't tell him what she had to say, he followed her through the house. As they passed the kitchen, he greeted *Frau* Lortz standing at the sink washing potatoes.

"*Guten Abend, Frau Lortz.*"

She nodded but did not reply.

Curious! She has always been cordial. Have I done something to offend her?

They continued to the door leading to the backyard. They stepped outside, and he asked, puzzled, "What is it?"

"We have to find someplace else to live."

"Have I said or done something wrong? *Frau* Lortz didn't speak to me just now."

"It has nothing to do with you or any of us, personally. She didn't speak because she feels badly. You know she admires you, tremendously.

She received a letter this afternoon from a sister in Stettin. She, her daughter and two small children had to evacuate their home and move west. They were in Königsberg with thousands of refugees. The Russians moved into East Prussia and were close to Königsberg, when the two women and children tried to leave by train, but the last train to Berlin left on January 22nd. So, they are walking to Berlin now with a mass of refugees. It's a miracle that the letter got through, but *Frau* Lortz expects them to arrive here anytime. She will, of course, take them in. But that means we have to find someplace else."

As Eckhardt took in the dreadful news, his frown deepened. He replied, "Of course. We're grateful to her for letting us stay here this long, but we can't expect her to put them and us up at the same time. There's clearly no room for us all."

He paced, his head bowed in concentration. Ursula looked at him. Then his face brightened.

"I have an idea, but I don't want to raise any false hopes."

"Dr. Lenz said we are more than welcome to stay at his house," Eckhardt told the three women the following evening as he entered the front door. "I called him at Charité from my office this morning. He also said he was sorry to hear that we lost our house. If he had known, he would have had us move in with him sooner."

"Oh, *Herr* Meinert, I'm so relieved you have a decent place to stay now," declared *Frau* Lortz. "It takes a load off my mind. I hate to put you to so much trouble."

"No, *Frau* Lortz. It is we who should apologize for putting *you* to so much trouble," admonished Ursula. "But we are so grateful."

"Exactly right," affirmed Eckhardt.

"In any case, I'm glad we have gotten to know each other better," added Christina, as she clasped her neighbor's hands in hers.

"One more request," said Eckhardt. "May I leave my car with you? Driving is next to impossible now. In any case, I don't have any gasoline coupons – even if I could find a place to buy any. Just in case, I can't come back to get it after this is all over, I'll leave a letter with you stating that I have signed it over to you."

"That's out of the question," she retorted. "Of course, you can leave it with me as long as you need to, but we won't have any talk about you signing it over. Anyway, I can't drive. We never had a car and I never learned."

"Well, I don't want to impose on you anymore. Someday we'll make it up to you."

She smiled. "Don't give it another thought, *Herr* Meinert. I just hope you come back to Sandweg."

"Oh, we'll be back. The property next door still belongs to us, and Ursula and I already have plans to rebuild."

"Absolutely!" confirmed Ursula.

"I'll look forward to that," beamed *Frau* Lortz.

Like many in the city at that time, they tried to keep their spirits up, knowing in the back of their minds, the Russians were drawing near Frankfurt an der Oder, about 50 miles east of Berlin.

Then Christina added her bit of Berliner dark humor: "Well, enjoy the war, everybody. The peace will be terrible!"

Chapter One hundred-two

Wieder ein Soldat
(Again a Soldier)

By the following Saturday, the three had almost finished packing everything they owned in five suitcases. *Frau* Lortz had collected the mail from the post office, home delivery having been eliminated at the beginning of the year. Wordlessly, she handed two letters to Eckhardt, one with a Hamburg postmark, obviously from young Eckhardt, and the other a grey envelope which had been rubber stamped with an ominous eagle and swastika. Eckhardt looked at it for a moment before taking it from her. He held it and studied the emblem. Ursula and Christina watched him open it, carefully read it, and then announce, "Well, it's finally come. I thought I'd hear from them before now, but here it is. I'm to report to the local *Gauleiter* (Nazi district commander) here in Spandau two days from now."

Ursula, with tears already running down her cheeks, embraced him.

"Oh, darling, I thought you had a military deferment from the lung damage you have from the gas attack in the last war. And besides, you are doing important work for the war at Siemens, and you're 52!"

"I thought so, too. But now they are calling up anyone who can carry a rifle between the ages of 16 and 60, regardless of medical conditions."

She buried her face in his shoulder, and he held her close.

"Well, at least I can get you and your mother settled in at Dr. Lenz's house."

After a cursory physical examination, Eckhardt received his "uniform", which consisted of a black armband displaying the words *Deutscher Volkssturm Wehrmacht*. He then faced his *Kompanieführer* (Company leader), a staunch Nazi, who was an auto mechanic in civilian life.

"Well, Meinert, I see you are a manager at Siemens and served in the trenches in the last war. We need men of your expertise as instructors. You are hereby promoted to the rank of *Zugführer* (Platoon leader). Most of the older men, like yourself, also have military experience and will become competent very quickly with a refresher course in handling firearms. Your real challenge will be dealing with these kids of the Hitler Youth, most of whom have never held a gun in their hands. But they have been well trained to understand discipline by their youth leaders, so you don't have to coddle them. Make men out of them!"

The thought passed through his mind, *just like they made "men" out of my sons – especially Detlev. What they really mean is to make killers out of them.*

"Thank you, sir," he responded. "May I ask which weapon I will be using in my instruction?"

The officer did not look up, but replied, "We will expect you to be versatile. Heil Hitler!"

That sounded ominous, but Eckhardt did not press further. "Heil Hitler," he muttered, turned, and walked out.

"My god, what do they expect us to do with this junk?"

Startled, Eckhardt looked up from inspecting the *Gewehr 71* rifle in his hands. The same thought had occurred to him, but the man standing next to him had voiced it.

They were at a shooting range in Spandau and had been given these rifles to be used in training new recruits – adults and young boys. The *Gewehr 71* dated to the previous century and had already been considered obsolete in 1914 when Eckhardt's generation served in the last war.

"Did they get these things out of a museum?" continued his neighbor.

In spite of himself, Eckhardt grinned and replied, "Yes. I saw some of these in the *Zeughaus* (Armory museum). Makes you wonder, doesn't it?"

"What's all this jabber over here?" shouted an officer, as he walked toward them.

"Where are the *Volkssturmgewehr* 1-5 rifles I heard were made just for us?" countered the complainer.

"Look fella, we're doing the best we can. We didn't expect things to go this far, and unfortunately the demand has become so great that the suppliers can't keep up. So just shut up, and stop spreading discontent, or I'll have you up for insubordination."

Eckhardt felt a chill as he watched the drama being played out before him.

"Do you have anything else to say, before I write you up?"

"No, sir. Sorry, sir."

The officer turned and strode away.

"Man, you shouldn't have attracted attention like that," reprimanded Eckhardt. "Don't you know they're hanging people from lampposts for practically nothing?"

"You're right. But I think we can see the handwriting on the wall. They're scraping the bottom of the barrel when they have to depend on guys like us. Half of us are in no shape to be out here, and then they expect us to face a mechanized army intent on destroying us, with weapons like these?"

Eckhardt turned away without comment. *I need to stay away from this guy,* he thought to himself. *But he's right, of course.*

By the time Eckhardt had been conscripted into the *Volkssturm*, the supply of weaponry had become so desperate, that a wide variety of weapons had been implemented. Not only obsolete ordinance of German manufacture, but also captured Soviet, Belgian, French, Italian, and weapons from other sources were distributed to the *Volkssturm*. In the final months of the war, shotguns, and items taken from museums, such as muskets, and even crossbows were used.

Volksturm literally translated means "folk assault", but in real terms was a national militia and had existed as a plan since about 1925. On Hitler's orders, it was activated on October 18, 1944, when he directed Martin Bormann to recruit six million men between 16 and 60 as part of a German Home Guard, and to be placed under *Wehrmacht* command when in action. Heinrich Himmler was responsible for armament and training. As the Nazi party was directly in charge of organizing it, each *Gauleiter* was to oversee leadership, enrollment, and organization of each unit in his district.

Goebbels' propaganda portrayed it as a movement stemming from fervid patriotism, and indeed, Hitler counted on fanaticism to be the driving force among its members. But morale was undermined by the lack of uniforms and weaponry, and many realized that, in fact, this was a desperate attempt to turn the tide of the war, or at least to stem the rapidly approaching Soviet forces.

A bitter joke which made the rounds asked the question, "Why is the *Volkssturm* Germany's most precious resource?"

The answer: "Because its members have silver in their hair, gold in their mouths, and lead in their limbs." The goal of conscripting six million was never reached.

§§§

The Soviet offensive against Berlin on April 16, 1945, involved three Soviet fronts. Two attacked the city on the east and south, and a third on the north. On April 20, which was Hitler's birthday, the 1st Belorussian Front under the command of Marshal Georgy Zhukov advanced from the east and north and began shelling the city center, and the 1st Ukrainian Front under Marshal Ivan Konev attacked the southern suburbs.

The Berlin garrison, which was reduced to several exhausted divisions of the *Wehrmacht* and *Waffen SS*, and poorly trained members of the *Volkssturm* and the Hitler Youth, all under the command of General Helmuth Weidling, was all that stood in the way of the Soviet onslaught. By the end of the following week, the Red Army had taken the city.

In the Zoo flak tower, terror reigned. Tens of thousands of civilians who had taken shelter there, and over 300 wounded soldiers and civilians in the hospital on the third floor, were reduced to panic as the Russian artillery pounded the building. Detlev, and other boys of the Hitler Youth, labored furiously to keep the hoppers filled with ammunition for the anti-aircraft guns, which had been pointed at the ground to ward off the attackers. When he returned to the elevator to pick up another load of ammunition, he saw two boys huddled against the outside wall weeping and shaking.

"You there!" he shouted. "Cowards! What do you think you're doing there? Get out of there, before I report you to one of the sergeants. Move your asses!"

Even though the two boys were older than Detlev, he being 13, they didn't challenge his command.

"I want to go home," wailed the younger of the two.

"If we don't stop the Russkie pigs here, we won't have a home to go to!" he countered.

He delivered a swift kick to the complainer. "Move it!"

Hitler and his bride of one day committed suicide in the *Führerbunker* in the center of Berlin on April 30. The defenders of the Zoo flak tower fought so fiercely, that the Soviet commanders decided to go around it, rather than try to take it.

On May 2, surrender negotiations with the tower commander, Colonel Haller, brought the fighting to an end, and the civilians were allowed to leave. The adult personnel of the tower defenders were taken prisoner, and the young Hitler Youth released.

Most of the boys were glad to be able to go home, but a few thoroughly indoctrinated youths were determined to carry on the fight against the hated invaders – young Detlev Meinert being one.

He had found some hand grenades in the arsenal, and he hid one inside the oversized army greatcoat he had found.

As the boys walked out of the building, they went their separate ways. Detlev began to walk along Kantstrasse which connected with Kurfürstendamm. Not having any particular destination in mind, he wandered aimlessly along the ruined boulevard.

Maybe this is a bad idea he thought. *Maybe I'll just get rid of this thing.*

But then he saw a group of Russian soldiers walking arm in arm toward him, and his rage and hatred were reignited.

They saw the wretched looking urchin coming toward them, and began to call out to him, *"Privet malysh! Podoydi syuda!"* (Hey, kid. Come here.)

He set his mouth in a grim line of determination and walked to them. They continued to laugh and joke among themselves, a few not being much older than he was.

Smiling, he walked into their midst. One slapped him on the back. He reached under his coat and pulled the pin. As he waited for the blast, he gave a Nazi salute and shouted, "Heil Hitler!"

Chapter One hundred-three

Götterdämmerung
(Twilight of the Gods)

What was that? Ursula asked herself.

She and Christina had settled into Dr. Lenz's home, and he had expressed appreciation for them being there. He was happy to have the house occupied full-time, as he was now on almost round-the-clock duty at Charité with the Tsunami of civilian and military casualties.

She roused herself and walked to the room next to hers, where Christina had also arisen. They met, as Christina opened her door. Before either could speak, a resounding crash was heard downstairs in the kitchen. They looked at one another in wide-eyed fright. Loud laughter was heard accompanied by raucous voices speaking Russian!

"What can we do?" whispered Ursula.

With no reply, Christina pulled her back into her room and closed the door. The two women clung to one another in the dark, shaking with terror. The laughter and voices moved from the kitchen into the dining room and then into the main hall, and from there they were heard ascending the stairs.

"Oh god, mama! What can we do?"

"Shh! Be quiet."

They heard the men enter Ursula's bedroom next door.

"Frau, komm!" The women heard closet doors being opened, drawers being pulled, and objects being thrown on the floor as the invaders searched the room for money or valuables.

Footsteps came to Christina's door, which was flung open and the lights were switched on. Four disheveled young Russian soldiers stood grinning in the doorway.

"Frau, komm!" cried one, as he moved toward them. He reached for Ursula, who backed away from him. He grasped her and pulled her toward him as she struggled to free herself.

"Don't fight him!" cried her mother, who in the meantime had been caught by two of the others. They were ripping her night gown as they threw her on the bed.

Detlev forgive me, rushed through Christina's mind, in a mental appeal to her long-dead husband. Then the Russian was upon her.

Ursula was dragged back to her room and similarly assaulted by the other two Russians.

Christina lay dazed on the bed. She had been used and abandoned. As her awareness returned, she heard angry Russian voices downstairs. Someone was shouting in a commanding voice. There was a babble of muted responses, and she heard the front door being opened and closed.

She arose and walked on unsteady feet to her daughter's room, where she found Ursula lying naked, curled and trembling in a fetal position on the bed. The sheets were disheveled with a smear of blood on one.

"Ursula, dear," she murmured as she folded her in an embrace.

"Oh, mama. How can I ever face Eckhardt? He'll never touch me again."

"Don't think about that now."

They walked with their arms around each other to the adjoining bathroom. After helping one another wash and dress in bathrobes, they returned to the bedroom and were confronted with a new stranger. Frozen with renewed terror, they faced a Russian officer.

"Who are you?" he barked in German. This was responded to by another voice in Russian. Two other officers entered the room. They immediately began a rapid-fire conversation in Russian.

The two women clung to one another, as the Russians discussed their fate.

The first officer turned to them and commanded, "You, get out! We are taking this house for the Soviet military."

Christina opened her mouth to explain their situation but was cut short.

"You, get out now!" as he unfastened his holster.

"Let us dress, please," pleaded Christina.

"Alright, but you do it now!" He turned and with the other officers left the room.

The women hurriedly put on clothes and then began to pack two of their suitcases. Before they could finish, the officer returned, and seeing what was taking place, strode to the bed and flung the suitcases on the floor. He turned red-faced and shouted, "Get out now!"

Sobbing, they stumbled down the stairs, the officer right behind them. They left through the front entrance and paused, not knowing where to go. The officer, who had followed them out of doors, shouted again, "Get out!"

§§§

Der Führer ist an seinem Kommandoposten in der Reichskanzlei gefallen und hat bis zum letzten Atemzug gegen den Bolshevismus und für Deutschland gekämpft. (The *Führer* has fallen at his command post in the Reich Chancery, fighting to the last breath against Bolshevism and for Germany).

Eckhardt and a few exhausted members of his *Volkssturm* unit hunched over the *Volksempfänger* radio they had found in the basement of a bombed-out warehouse in the Weißensee district of Berlin which still had electric power. The announcement had come from Hamburg radio on May 1, 1945.

"Well gentlemen, I guess that's it!" he declared. "We're out of ammunition, out of food, and the Russkies are all around us. I wish we could have held out until the Americans and British got here, but I can't ask any of you to sacrifice yourselves any longer. We have already lost so many comrades – and I believe, in vain. You have proven yourselves to be valiant soldiers for Germany, but now it's time for you to think of yourselves.

I will tie my handkerchief to my rifle and go up and try to find a Russian officer, who I hope will allow us to make an honorable surrender. Does anyone object?"

He looked into their dirt-encrusted, gaunt faces. A few nodded in agreement, but the rest just looked at him expressionless.

"Good. You all stay here, and when I find an officer, I'll direct him back here."

He stood up, took his battered rifle, tied the handkerchief to it, and made his way up the steps and across the rubble strewn floor to the entrance. After having spent hours underground, he blinked in the daylight. He began to walk toward Hansastraße, where the rumble of vehicles told him he would find someone to whom he could surrender.

Crack! The shot came from the ruined facade of a tobacco shop across the street. He ducked into a doorway. He held his rifle out into plain sight, hoping the white handkerchief would be acknowledged. After a few moments, two Russian soldiers emerged and, crouching low, crossed the street.

"Ty, nemets, vykhodi!" (You, German, come out!) shouted one, his rifle pointed toward the handkerchief. Understanding the intent of the command, Eckhardt waved his signal and cautiously emerged from the shelter of the doorway.

The two Russians looked at their captive with scowls of mistrust. One stepped forward and snatched the rifle from Eckhardt's hands and gave him a violent shove with his own weapon, accompanied by a torrent of Russian. Sensing a great hatred, Eckhardt, with his hands raised high above his head, allowed himself to be pushed and prodded forward. As they reached the intersection with Hansastraße, he was pushed toward a staff car in which two officers sat, their heads bent over a large city map.

As the soldier called their attention, the officers looked up, and seeing the prisoner, one turned and called a young soldier standing with a group of others. After receiving instructions, the young man approached Eckhardt, and in fluent German asked if he wished to surrender. Eckhardt replied in the affirmative. He proceeded to explain that he was the representative for his unit, who were waiting to also surrender. This was relayed to the officers, who then directed Eckhardt should lead them back to the warehouse.

Eckhardt, the interpreter, and six armed guards walked back to the warehouse, where he was sent down to bring out the others. As he led his men out into the daylight, the captors began to react. Some spat at them, other pushed and shoved them. One walked up to an elderly man, who had miraculously survived the bitter fighting of the previous days and slapped him across the face.

Eckhardt stepped forward to protest, when one of the soldiers kicked him and sent him sprawling to the ground.

The interpreter said something to the soldier, who spat on Eckhardt and stepped back. The interpreter stood over him, as he stood up. "If you wonder why these men hate you so much, you need to know they have been fighting Germans for five years. Your people invaded my country and did the most horrible things you can imagine. In my town, the families of some partisans who had been fighting you, were herded into a church, locked in, and burned alive, women, children, and old people. My brother's wife was raped and then thrown out of a truck and left to die. She recovered, but told us how she was passed from man to man in a group of twenty Germans. Each of these men can tell you stories as bad, or worse.

So, if they let you live to surrender to the officers, count yourselves lucky."

The tragic group made their way to the waiting officers, who ordered that they be taken to a nearby compound, where thousands of prisoners awaited transport. There, they were processed, interred, and left to stand in the crowded enclosure with others, some of whom had collapsed from hunger, untended wounds and exposure. Some had managed to keep their heavy greatcoats, but many were in uniforms, coatless, and some even shirtless.

Fortunately, it was the beginning of Spring, but there were no guarantees the sun would always shine, and rain is a frequent visitor in Berlin's northern climate. At night, many slept crouched together for warmth.

After several days of meager portions of stale bread or rotten meat being distributed, if indeed they were lucky enough to receive anything, some succumbed to the conditions and were found dead in daylight. Then groups were moved out for transport to Russia.

Eckhardt was by now separated from his comrades of the Spandau unit. A few days after their surrender, they were finally roused in the early dawn hours and began the march in a long line of men to the

Stettiner Bahnhof. There, they were herded into freight cars for the long ride to Russia and ultimately on to the Gulags of Siberia.

§§§

By the beginning of May 1945, Berlin had been captured by the Soviets. After Hitler's suicide on April 30, Grand Admiral Karl Dönitz, per Hitler's order, had been appointed Head of State and Supreme Commander of the Armed Forces. He immediately implemented *Regenbogen-Befehl* (Rainbow Order), which was the code name for the plan to scuttle Germany's U-Boat fleet to prevent them falling into Allied hands. At the same time, he wanted to remove Germany from the war. Therefore, he commenced negotiations the with western Allies through the commander of Allied 21 Army Group in North Germany, Field Marshal Bernard Montgomery.

On May 3, young Eckhardt and his fellow crew members scuttled seven U-boats in their pens at Hamburg. Their own vessel had been buried under tons of concrete during a heavy air raid the day after their arrival. But now, they watched with heavy hearts as each U-boat sank beneath the surface, after they had opened the sea cocks. Upon completion of their demolition at Hamburg, they were ordered to continue the work at other German U-boat bases, including Flensburg, Wilhelmshaven, Cuxhaven, and the Kiel Canal.

In the early hours of May 5, the order was given to continue scuttling, until it was countermanded eight minutes later. This had come about as a result of the surrender negotiations being conducted with the Allies, who stipulated destruction was to cease, and the remaining boats were to be handed over intact and undamaged.

On May 8th, Germany surrendered unconditionally, and all naval units, submarines as well as surface craft, in ports and at sea, were surrendered. Their crews, after being interrogated and debriefed, were for the most part released.

"Well, Meinert, what are your plans now?" queried Lothar Gensch, one of Eckhardt's shipmates, with whom he had formed a friendship as they worked together since his return to Hamburg. They had chided one another about their respective accents, Eckhardt with his racy

Berlin argot, and Lothar speaking in the softer tones of his native Mosel Valley.

"Plans? What plans?" he retorted. "I haven't heard from my mother since my father was drafted into the *Volkssturm,* and she and Grannie were moving to Dahlem to Dr. Lenz's house. His son, Herbert, and my father fought in the last war together and are close friends."

They walked together to the battered shell of the main railway station, where they hoped to be able to purchase space on trains, each to his destination. After standing in line for more than an hour, they were told that rail traffic to Berlin was suspended, but the main line southward through Cologne was still operating.

"Now what do I do?" cried Eckhardt in exasperation.

"You should just come with me," suggested Lothar. "My family has a small vineyard near Cochem. I can't wait to get out of these cities, and it would do you a world of good, too. You can stay with us as long as you like, and in the meantime, perhaps things will stabilize in Berlin."

Eckhardt was relieved and touched by the generosity of his friend. "Thanks, comrade. Are you sure it won't be too much of a burden on your family, especially now?"

"Don't worry about it. We have a garden and some chickens. We also know farmers in the area. Even with the war going on, people in places like that have resources that don't exist in the cities. Besides, I had two brothers and one was killed in North Africa. The other is missing. So, there's plenty of room."

Eckhardt threw his arm around his friend's shoulder. "I can't thank you enough. I owe you one, brother!"

They bought tickets to Koblenz, where they would change to a local to Cochem. They were cautioned that due to delays, the trip could take several days.

"What do we care!" laughed Lothar. "We're tourists now."

"Right!" retorted Eckhart. "We've got time, if nothing else."

Of the approximately 40,000 men who served on U-boats between 1939 and 1945, fewer than 10,000 survived.

§§§

Crack! Crack! Crack!

Hans Joachim was startled out of sleep. He had collapsed on the small couch in his office at Charité after almost twenty hours performing surgery.

Those were gunshots here inside the hospital, flashed through his mind.

Without even slipping on his shoes, he dashed out into the corridor, where he was confronted with patients and medical staff running in panic from the ward at the end of building.

Grabbing the sleeve of a young nurse, he demanded, "What's going on?"

"It's the Russians. They're in the building shooting people in their beds and throwing them on the floor!" She pulled away from him and continued to run.

The thought never occurred to him to join the mad throng. Instead he turned and began to run in the opposite direction. As he drew near the entrance to the ward, he nearly collided with Helmut Köhler, the hardcore Nazi surgeon who had caused him so much trouble over the years.

"Out of my way!" shouted Köhler, as he tried to push past Hans Joachim.

"Where do you think you're going, you bastard!" he cried as he grabbed the man by both arms. "No, you're not! You come with me!" He turned him around and shoved him back into the room.

"Let me go! They'll kill me!"

"They might, especially if you don't take off that Nazi party pin, you idiot!"

Köhler looked down at his lapel. "Oh, god! I forgot about that," as he ripped the small round emblem off and threw it on the floor.

Hans Joachim kicked it under a cabinet as they walked past. Then they saw a Russian officer and two soldiers hauling murdered patients out of bed and placing them against a wall.

"*Privet, tovarisch!*" (Hey, comrade!) Hans Joachim shouted at the officer.

Startled, the man turned, *"Ty govorish' po-russki?"* (You speak Russian?)

"Nemnogo." (A little bit.)

Then commenced a verbal back-and-forth, whereby the Russian began to show grudging respect for the man who challenged him. Köhler stood mute and also began to see the measure of the man he had scorned.

Finally, Hans Joachim turned to him and explained, "He says we have to remove our patients, because the beds are needed for their wounded. He's giving us one hour to clear out the beds."

"But where are we going to put all these patients?"

"I've asked him if we could use the basement area, the storage areas, the canteen, and any other available spaces. In return, I've promised him you and I will assist his doctors tending their patients. You go round-up those cowards who almost knocked me over, and bring them back here to help. And you'd better not take off. Or I can just tell him who you are, and that you're an ardent Nazi and save us all a lot of trouble right now. What's it going to be?"

Red-faced with stifled hatred, the other muttered, "Okay."

"Move it!"

As Köhler walked away, Hans Joachim reflected, *Well, I guess it all comes down to this.*

Götterdämmerung!

Epilogue
Auferstehung
(Resurrection)

"Okay, boys! Prepare yourselves," Captain Vasily Zakharov warned his troops – young replacements that had been recently sent up. They were part of a column driving on the muddy road leading to the entrance of *Ravensbrück* concentration camp on May 30, about 55 miles north of Berlin.

"I know that some of you think what you saw these devils do in Russia was the worst thing anyone could do to other people, but I helped liberate *Auschwitz* in Poland last January, and I couldn't believe what I saw there."

They looked at him, some apprehensively.

The SS guards had tried in March to evacuate the camp by transporting 5,000 prisoners to two other camps, *Mauthausen* and *Bergen-Belsen*. Then in April, a forced march had begun of 20,000 more prisoners to *Mecklenburg* in western Pomerania. But this was thwarted when the marching columns were stopped by advancing Russian troops, who liberated them. *Ravensbrück* was then abandoned, as the remaining SS guards fled for their lives.

As Captain Zakharov and his company approached the entrance, with the mocking wrought iron slogan, *Arbeit macht frei* (Work will make you free) above the gate, a ghostly silence was perceived, which stifled conversation. An odious stench assailed their nostrils.

Inside the compound emaciated figures stood and watched them, and piles of corpses were strewn about, or heaped in huge piles. The smell of decomposition was heavy in the air. Some of the men began to retch, and others covered their faces with handkerchiefs or the sleeves of their coats.

Their trucks pulled up in the large square near what had been the administration building. Captain Zakharov ordered his men to form groups to search the rows of barracks for survivors and carry them out to be identified as much as possible. Yiddish and German were the prevailing languages spoken, but most of the languages of Europe were also represented.

As the captain and several assistants went from barrack to barrack, they found still breathing humans, most of whom were unable to sit up or speak. But at the entrance of one building, an emaciated woman stood holding a baby.

Zakaharov walked toward her and in his halting German asked as he pointed at the small creature, *"Dein Baby?"* (Your baby?)

The woman looked down at the small face looking up at her. *"Das ist er jetzt."* (He is now.)

"Dein Name?"

"Edna Friedlander."

ABOUT THE AUTHOR

James Cloud is a retired educator with more than 40 years of experience teaching History, Government, German, and English as a Second Language. In  addition, he taught U.S. Citizenship prep classes to new immigrants. Among his awards are The Adult Educator of the Year in Utah. The author attended the Institute of Arts in West Berlin and worked as an interpreter for the British Military Mission during the Cold War years. While living in Germany, he developed an intimate knowledge of both East and West Berlin. Cloud later completed a Master's Degree in German Linguistics and Literature at California State University at Fullerton.

Cloud was born and brought up in New Mexico shortly before the outbreak of World War II. His first-grade teacher in 1943 was Jewish. Minerva Kohn was a loved and respected woman in Las Vegas, New Mexico. His memories of her led to an interest in Jewish culture and traditions. At the same time, his circle of friends and acquaintances included many people from the German-American community. The effects of World War II had a profound influence on him, leading to a lifelong fascination with these two cultures. He also developed friendships with many Jewish people during his years in Boston, where he worked at the Gillette Company.

His years of teaching brought him in contact with people of many nationalities and cultures. Cloud has attempted to bring together in this novel his impressions gained from interactions with these groups - most especially with German and Jewish people - and how they in turn have related to each other.

Printed in France by Amazon
Brétigny-sur-Orge, FR